When all the birds Leap

David G Stokes

Copyright © 2024 Orpheus Press

All rights reserved.

To my wife.

CHAPTER ONE
Shot Down

November 1943
Northern France

Part one.

The walk down into the valley took about forty-minutes at a cautious pace and he crossed the bridge that led into the village at around two o'clock and passed a sign that said *Lealvillers*. The sign was bent and peppered with bullet holes and the first house he came to had almost completely collapsed. Three walls were gone; but miraculously the roof was still hanging on. As he walked past he looked at the staircase leading to a second floor that was no longer there. It seemed strange. Wallpaper, even a window had survived, while the rest of the house, its beds and curtains and cupboards and chairs lay dead beneath pink rubble.

The house next door was undamaged. An old woman sat on the doorstep washing cutlery in a bowl of water. She looked up at Wellum as he approached. She rubbed a spoon with her thumb and watched him.

'Bonjour madame.'

She nodded back without smiling.

'Bonjour.'

'Er, ca va?' Wellum tried to sound casual.

The old woman nodded and rinsed the spoon.

'Bien. Merci.'

Wellum pointed at the destroyed house and the holes in the road-sign.

'Des Soldat Allemands?'

She shrugged.

He pointed towards the centre of the village. 'Soldat?'

She looked in the direction he was pointing and fished another spoon from the water.

'Des soldat Allemands? Dans le village?' Wellum pointed at the floor. 'Ici?'

She shook her head.

'Non.'

He looked back along the road that led out of the village, expecting to see a German patrol rolling towards him at any moment, then he looked towards the church. The woman carried on at her washing bowl.

'Er, excusez-moi, mais avez-vous un verre d'eau…sil vous plait?'

She looked at his injured hand.

'Etes-vous Américain?'

'Anglais.'

She nodded again and stood up and dried her hands and opened her front door and went inside. Wellum looked around the deserted street and watched the curtains in the destroyed house, flapping softly in the breeze.

She came back and handed him a glass of water.

'Merci madame, merci beaucoup.'

As Wellum drank, she reached into her apron and produced an apple, green and round.

Wellum handed her the glass and took the apple and smiled.

'Merci.'

The woman picked up the bowl and tipped the water into the gutter and turned as if to go back into her house.

Wellum reached out a hand.

'Excusez-moi, attendez un instant, sil vous plait.'

She turned to face him from the doorstep.

'Er, l'eglise, un pretre?' He pointed at the church spire.

The woman nodded. 'Oui, le Pere Marcelin. Dans le gite a cote de l'église.'

The churchyard was small with only a single bench for mourners and neatly trimmed borders and a handful of crooked gravestones scattered here and there. Wellum pushed open the gate and walked along the path. He looked at the pale blue sky and then at the graves. He ached everywhere.

He banged on the church door and waited, his head down, listening. He flexed the fingers on his hastily bandaged hand and winced as he felt the new scabs opening and the dried blood cracking on his palm.

He knocked again.

He went back along the path and out of the gate and wandered down the road to the cottage next door. It was a squat, comfortable looking building with a low roof and there were lights on inside and a line of soft grey smoke floating from the chimney.

Wellum walked to the door and gave what he hoped was a polite knock and after a moment it opened and the smell of beef stew rolled out. The vicar looked at him. He was a small, slightly built man and Wellum put his age at around seventy. He was stooped at the shoulders and had a full head of thin white hair that blew softly in the breeze as he stood on the doorstep and regarded Wellum with sharp, glittering eyes. He looked at the pilot's face and then at his flying jacket and boots and then at his hand.

'Pere Marcelin?'

'Oui.'

'Parles-tu Anglais?'

'Yes,' said the priest. 'Can I help you?'

Wellum raised his injured hand.

'I wondered if you might be able to help me sort this out, or point me in the direction of a doctor.'

'You are British…Are you lost?'

'Not exactly no. I'm a pilot, with the Royal Air Force. I got shot down.'

'Where?'

Wellum leaned towards the priest and spoke in a hushed voice.

'Father Marcelin, are there Germans here?'

The old man took a step back.

'Where?'

Wellum lifted his chin.

'Here, in the village. Is it occupied?'

Marcelin shook his head.

'No my child, there are no Germans here. There have been none for some months now.'

Wellum relaxed and gestured towards the distant hills.

'About three miles to the north. I bailed out.'

The two of them stood.

'You have no supplies....nothing?'

Wellum shook his head.

'No.'

The priest glanced over Wellum's shoulder and looked each way along the street.

'Has anybody seen you come here?'

'Only one woman I think. On the way into the village, next to a bombed house. She gave me some water.'

'Alright, that's fine,' said the priest. He opened the door and gestured for the pilot to come inside.

Wellum sat at the kitchen table with his back to the fire while Father Marcelin closed the shutters at the window and put a kettle on to boil.

He came and sat down. Neither man spoke. Eventually Wellum broke the silence.

'I apologise for just turning up like this, but I'm afraid I'm lost.'

The priest studied him. 'Are you armed?'

Wellum nodded. 'Yes. I have my service revolver.' He patted the left side of his chest.

The priest shook his head. 'What is it that you want my son?'

'Mainly some help with this.' He raised his bandaged hand an inch.

The old man studied the hand over his glasses.

'How did this happen?"

'As I bailed out I assume.' He flexed his fingers slowly. 'I must have caught it on the canopy as I jumped - or something like that.'

The priest nodded thoughtfully and looked at Wellum.

'Are you hungry, thirsty?'

Wellum nodded.

'Yes I am. Both…'

The old man turned and went into the kitchen and opened a cupboard and took out a bowl. He went to the stove and lifted the lid on a pan and took the bowl and ladled stew into it. He put the bowl and a glass of water on the table, then took a loaf and broke it in two and passed half to Wellum, then he came and sat down and dropped a spoon next to the bowl.

'Please, eat.'

Wellum picked up the spoon and smiled in thanks and ate the stew, breaking off chunks of the new white loaf and dipping them into the bowl. The priest watched him.

'What is your name?'

Wellum wiped his mouth on a napkin. He tore off a corner of bread and sat back in the chair.

'My name's Harry, Harry Wellum.'

The priest looked into his eyes.

'And I am Father Nicolas Marcelin.'

Wellum dipped his spoon and continued eating.

'Good to meet you Father,' he said through a mouthful of beef and carrots.

The fire crackled and Wellum could feel his strength returning.

'When you have eaten I will have a look at your injury.'

Wellum placed his blood-stained hand palm down on the table and the two men looked at it. Wellum nodded. 'Yes, I'd be grateful for that Father.'

'Is it painful?'

'Wellum gave a grim smile and nodded. 'Yes, it's throbbing like Christ knows what.' He looked at the priest apologetically. 'Sorry. Er yes, yes it is quite sore.'

'What is your rank in the airforce?'

Wellum finished the stew and put the spoon in the bowl and pushed the bowl forward an inch. He ate the last of the bread.

'Squadron Leader.'

'Are you a bomber pilot?'

Wellum shook his head.

'No. Spitfires.'

'A fighter pilot then?'

'I was, yes.'

'And now?'

'Reconnaissance.'

'In a Spitfire?'

Wellum nodded and began taking off his flying jacket. He winced in pain as he pulled his arms free of the bulky, leather coat. The priest looked at Wellum's pistol, exposed in its shoulder holster, almost nestling in his armpit. Marcelin slid his spectacles to the end of his nose and studied the gun. Wellum ignored his look and went on.

'Yes. I flew a fighter early in the war and during the Battle of Britain. Now I fly what's called a Mark 11.' He dropped his jacket on the floor next to his chair and patted his breast pocket and pulled out his cigarettes. 'I suppose you could best describe me as more of an observer these days; taking photographs and gathering intelligence.' He looked at the scarf wrapped around his injured hand. 'Leave the combat to the younger chaps, eh? Lucky sods.'

He gave another weak smile at his clumsy use of language, but he was too tired to apologise again. He wobbled the cigarettes at the priest. 'Would you mind awfully if I smoked Father?'

The priest took his eyes off the holster and stood up and went back into the kitchen. He took the kettle from the stove and poured water into a teapot.

'Not at all, please, carry on.'

He put the teapot on the table and took away Wellum's empty bowl. He returned with two cups and then an ashtray. He poured tea and added milk. Wellum took a sip and closed his eyes and sighed.

'Thank you Father Marcelin.'

The priest smiled.

'So, you were shot down today while you were taking photographs?'

Wellum nodded and lit a cigarette. 'Yes.' He blew out smoke and took another sip of tea.

'What were you taking pictures of?' Persisted Marcelin.

Wellum gave a nonchalant shrug.

'Mostly of German positions.'

'Mostly?'

Wellum nodded. He tapped his cigarette at the ashtray. 'I flew in over Calais and took some photographs of the German defences there, then as I came south I spotted what looked like an artillery convoy heading west from

Doullens, so I came down lower and took some pictures of that too. I was climbing out and getting ready to head back home when I got ambushed by two 109's. They might have been flying protection for the artillery convoy, who knows? but I spotted them late so...' he raised his shoulders in a slight shrug. 'Here I am. Bloody silly mistake to make really.' He sucked on the cigarette and lifted up his hand.

'Would you mind?'

'Of course,' said Marcelin. 'One moment.' He stood up and left the room. Wellum crushed out the cigarette and gritted his teeth and started to gingerly unpick the knot holding the scarf in place around his wound. After a few minutes the priest came back in and placed a first-aid box on the table.

'Ah, non, non, non,' he chided as he saw the pilot struggling to remove the makeshift bandage. 'Ici laissez-moi, sil vous-plait.'

He sat down and held the pilot's hand in his and took a pair of scissors from the box and began carefully cutting away the bloodstained scarf. He looked over his spectacles at the pilot.

'So, where will you go now?'

Wellum ignored the question in favour of watching the priest work. 'You've done this before.'

Marcelin smiled.

'Oui,' he nodded. 'I was a battlefield medic in the Great War.' He cleaned the cut with iodine, the smell of it and the cold pain in his hand made Wellum sweat.

'I was at Ypres and Thiepval. I lost many friends, but also by God's grace, I helped save lives too.'

He took fresh gauze from the box and a cream coloured roll of bandage that was cool and clean.

'So…? Where next?' he asked again.

Wellum sighed and contemplated the question. He didn't want to think about moving at all. The fire was warm at his back and Marcelin's cooking was good and the cottage felt safe.

'Well, I suppose I ought to find somewhere to stay for a while, a few days maybe.' He looked at the priest, listening and working quietly and he felt he could trust the man.

'Then I should try and complete my mission.'

Marcelin looked at him. 'But how is this possible?'

'Earlier, when I was walking here, to the village, I think I spotted some hills where my aircraft went down. If I can get to it, there's a chance I could salvage the cameras and the images I took.'

The priest paused with the new bandage in his hand. 'And then?'

'And then I'd need to contact London somehow and find a way of getting back to England.'

Marcelin placed a thin layer of gauze over Wellum's knuckles and began to wrap his hand with the clean bandage.

The fire crackled and spat. When he had finished Marcelin put the scissors and the iodine and the leftover gauze and bandage back in the box and took out a bottle of pills. He unscrewed the lid from the bottle and shook two small white tablets onto his palm and then dropped them onto the table next to wellum's teacup. He put the bottle back in the box and carried the box to the sideboard.

'Just aspirin.'

Wellum picked up the tablets and swallowed them with what was left of his tea.

The priest looked at him.

'There have been no Germans here in the village for a few months now, but there are many soldiers still in the area. More pass through each day. Some going east, or retreating north. Hitler has taken many and sent them to Russia. Others, we have seen going back west towards the cities and coastal towns, new recruits, mostly Waffen SS, to fight some more, people say against the Resistance and incase the Allies ever arrive to help us. I'm not sure it is safe for you to stay here.'

Wellum nodded.

'I understand. But in the church, maybe I could hide? Stay hidden I mean, just for a day or two? and then I'll be gone I promise. I doubt the German soldiers would come to the church even if they do return.'

Marcelin sighed and raised a finger. 'You do not know the SS.' He shook his head. 'You can stay here tonight. I have a spare room. Tomorrow, if I can I will get help and hopefully spare clothes too. God will show me the way. And then you can perhaps find your plane and your cameras. Though I think, maybe you should really just go. Forget the work, the mission and leave - go home.'

Wellum thought about it and nodded.

'I'm sure you're right Father, but at least if I try to salvage something from this sodding mess, I won't get such a massive bollocking when I *do* get back to London.'

The priest gave a slight shrug and nodded.

'Of course, of course.' He looked at a clock, ticking quietly on the mantlepiece.

'I need to go out now. I must visit one of my parishioners. Old widow Chervalier. She is close to death and takes her only comfort in prayer. I must go to her.' He came and stood by the fire and took a poker from a stand on the grate and shoved it deep into the dog basket, breaking up the burnt and blackened bits of wood. He put the poker back on its hook and picked up a log and dropped it into the middle of the flames. The fire caught it immediately and roared at the taste of fresh fuel, throwing out a barrel of heat that rolled into the room.

He straightened up and rubbed an aching hip then turned to Wellum. He pointed at the ceiling, 'I will show you the spare room and the bathroom. I will put on some water before I go out so you can wash yourself. If you want to sleep, sleep. I will be back around nine o'clock, if you are resting I won't disturb you.'

'Thank you Father. I really am very grateful.'

'Bless you.' Said Marcelin. 'You are most welcome my son.'

Wellum sat up in the bed and checked his watch.

It was three in the morning.

He reached under the pillow and took out the pistol and thumbed back the hammer and stepped quietly onto the floor and listened. A flash of distant light at the window then a muffled crump and thud. He walked over and moved the curtains an inch with the barrel of the gun and looked out towards the sound. On the horizon, almost hidden by rooftops and trees, another muted flash illuminated the night for a moment, followed by a dull thump. Wellum put a fingertip to the window. On the next explosion he felt a small vibration of the glass. The air raid was at least ten miles away. On the ground it must be devastating.

He released the hammer on the pistol and let his hand drop to his side and watched the explosions and the anti-aircraft fire and listened to the thudding sound of men killing men. His mind played over the encounter with the Messerschmitt 109's. He shook his head in disappointment.

'You're a bloody fool.' He whispered to the curtains as more flashes illuminated the sky.

He came down the stairs and into the kitchen at nine. Father Marcelin was nowhere to be seen but there was a note on the table and the fire was lit.

Monsieur Wellum
I am in the church. I have left you some food. I will be back by ten and will re-dress your hand.
M.

Wellum dropped the note on the table. The priest had left half a loaf of bread, a plate of butter, some cheese and ham. There was also a bottle of milk and a glass.

After he had eaten, Wellum took his compass and notebook and sat at the table. He held the compass between his finger and thumb and watched the small red needle wobble left and then right before steadying itself on north. He looked at the wall the compass was pointing to, then got up and crossed the kitchen to the nearest window and checked the compass again and looked out of the window to try and get a bearing on where he was. He looked at his notes and turned and pointed at another wall and went and looked out of a different window. He had come back to the table and was scribbling in his notebook when the door opened and father Marcelin came in.

'Ah, bonjour. Avez -vous bien dormi?' He placed a brown parcel on the kitchen sideboard and tutted at himself.

'I apologise, I am sorry. Did you sleep well?'

'Yes, thank you. I was very comfortable.'

'I heard you get up at around three. Did the bombing wake you?'

'Yes. Bit jumpy I suppose.'

Marcelin noted the pistol in Wellum's shoulder holster once more. 'Of course, that is to be expected, you are far from home and getting shot from the sky, I'm sure, would make most people a little shaken up.'

Wellum nodded.

'Would you like some coffee?' Asked the priest.

'Yes, please.' Wellum paused. 'I'm guessing the bombing was over Amiens?'

Marcelin nodded gravely. 'I'm afraid so. The allies must damage the German war machine, I understand this, but they are destroying many beautiful cities as they do it. The Germans do it too, without care, they use their artillery carelessly and too often.'

'Who would the Germans be fighting with artillery?'

'There are large Resistance groups fighting hard. If the Wehrmacht find out where they have stores or weapons hidden in towns and villages they will often use artillery to flush them out or destroy their supplies.'

The priest ran the tap and filled the kettle and set it to boil on the stove. He pointed at the brown parcel.

'I have managed to find you some better clothing. A family in the village, they lost their son early in the war. They have given some of his clothes. I think they will fit.'

He passed the parcel to Wellum who weighed it in his hands.

'Thank you Father, please tell them thank you, from me. Very much.'

Marcelin smiled and collected two cups and took a coffee can from the cupboard. 'I will.'

He spooned ground coffee into a pot and poured on the boiling water. It smelled good.

As he carried the pot and the cups over to the table Wellum asked,

'Do you have a map Father? Of this area?'

The priest nodded. 'Of course, yes. Do you need it now?'

'Now would be good,' replied Wellum. 'I'd like to get a better idea of where my aeroplane might be.'

'How is your hand?'

Wellum flexed his fingers.

'It still smarts but it's much better than yesterday.'

'Excellent,' said the priest. 'Let me get that map and then we can drink our coffee and take a look for your machine. I'll clean your hand after that.'

Father Marcelin gestured with his chin for Wellum to move the coffee pot and the cups to one side and he spread the map out on the table. Wellum peered at it. It covered an area of about five-hundred-square-miles from

Louvencourt in the north down to Harponville in the south. Lealvillers was roughly in the middle, surrounded by fields and woods. The next nearest town was Acheux-en Amienois just a half-mile away to the north-east. Wellum had his notebook out and was looking at elevation lines and roads marked out on the page before him. He tapped the map.

'Here. I think this is where I landed on my parachute. He ran his finger up an inch. 'And I think this is the hill I climbed. He traced a diagonal line to what appeared to be a wooded area. 'So I think this is the forest where my Spitfire went down.'

Marcelin held his spectacles on the end of his nose and read the map. The forest lay between two towns; Varennes and Harponville and was only five miles from Lealvillers.

'Alright, this is good. We can go through Varennes. The priest at the church there, Father Rieu, he is a good friend and will help us if we need.'

'We?'

'You do not wish me to come with you?'

Wellum considered the question.

'It might be useful, but I didn't want to assume.'

The priest nodded. 'I have spoken to one of the farmers here in the village; Jean Grillot. He has agreed to take us out this afternoon.'

'You told him about me?'

The priest nodded.

'Do not fear Monsieur Wellum, I delivered Jean into the world and his good wife and all five of his daughters and buried both his grandparents and his mother. He will not betray you - especially to the Germans.'

Wellum looked at his watch. 'What time this afternoon?'

'Grillot will come here at one o'clock and take us wherever we want to go.'

'On his tractor?'

Marcelin laughed.

'He has a small truck, for transporting animal feed and equipment.' He pointed at the parcel.

'Go and change. See if these clothes fit.'

'We might need tools; spanners and screwdrivers, mechanics tools, to get the cameras out.'

'I shall go and see Grillot now and tell him that we will be heading to Varennes and then to the forest. I will ask him to bring his toolbox.'

'Regardless of what we find, I ought really to be contacting England soon, even if it's just to let them know I'm alive. If I can salvage the cameras from my aeroplane that'll be a bonus. Do you know of anyone locally that might have a radio.'

Marcelin shook his head. 'I have already been considering this and there is no one, not in Lealvillers. Perhaps when we arrive in Varennes, Father Rieu might know of someone.'

CHAPTER TWO
The Hanged Man

The road to Varennes was uncomfortable, but thankfully the journey was short.

Wellum had opted to sit in the back of the open truck between hay bales and a few sacks of animal feed. He had a good view all around and could watch the road behind them, just in case they were followed. Father Marcelin sat in the passenger seat alongside the comically large farmer Grillot, a sullen, quietly spoken man with gigantic hands and broad shoulders. Despite his obvious introvert nature, Wellum was glad to have him acting as chauffeur. He seemed solid and reliable.

As the truck bounced through the puddles and potholes, Wellum habitually scanned the horizon. It was a clear day, but cold. He looked at the pale blue sky, mottled here and there with towering clouds, hard and white and as he looked, high up he caught site of remote black specks, barely visible, beating eastwards. He guessed they were at around thirty-thousand-feet; 'Lancaster's' he thought, heading home from bombing German cities by the look of their formations. More than likely based at Alconbury or Binbrook. He tried to count them but couldn't.

They passed ploughed fields of dark wet soil. Cold ruts of earth turned over like open wounds unsown and empty, while cows grazing lazily on what was left of the early winter grass watched them from countless pastures as they went. Wellum looked back at them and thought about the thousands of similar beasts grazing on the farmlands outside Brussels and Warsaw, London, Amsterdam and Berlin, unaware of this *other* world raging chaotically so close to theirs. The world of politics and of Blitzkrieg, counter-attacks, espionage and death. He wondered who was the smarter, them or us?

As they got close to Varennes they passed a mauled German Tiger tank lying abandoned by the side of the road. Its left track had broken and had been shirked off the wheels, gathering in untidy coils near the kerb. Its turret was twisted a quarter turn clockwise and its gun pointed up at forty-five degrees, the end of the muzzle peeled back like a banana. It had clearly suffered a misfire and there was a gaping hole in its right flank that could only have been caused by an anti-tank-missile. Clearly the Resistance in Varennes were brave and well equipped. The whole mess was black with soot and it had obviously burnt red hot for some time. Wellum could see that the paint was burned away to grey nothingness and the metal body had buckled grotesquely due to the heat. No one inside could have survived. It was a hideous sight, but like something from a dream, people came and went, walking or driving past it, none of them paying it the slightest attention. Wellum wondered why it had been left there.

Twenty yards further on he saw the reason. A man, hanging by his neck from a lamp post, his dark suit looking too big for his shrivelled corpse. The Germans had tied what was left of an old anti-tank weapon to him. Wellum noticed that someone had taken his shoes and around his shoulders the Germans had hung a sign.

Cet homme tue des soldats Allemands

As they passed by Marcelin crossed himself, but Jean Grillot kept his eyes on the road. Wellum looked at the dead man, turning slowly on the rope, as the people walked by on the street below, and he wondered what sort of place he had landed in.

Varennes was a busy town. Much larger than Lealvillers, but even though there were people on the streets going about their business, somehow the atmosphere felt brooding and unsafe. As they drove along in Grillot's truck some of the locals watched them through slant, sleepless eyes, while others looked only at their own feet. There were damaged buildings everywhere, broken and bullet riddled and many of the roads in the town were impassable; blocked as they were with rubble and abandoned German vehicles and artillery pieces.

The truck took a series of side streets and detours, threading a route expertly amongst the destruction, until after a while, they pulled to a stop beside a row of low houses, the last of which butted up against the grey stone wall of a church.

Grillot turned off the engine and got out and came to the back of the truck and lowered the tailgate and gestured for Wellum to climb down. Once the pilot was out Grillot closed the tail and locked it and got back in the truck and started it up. Father Marcelin was stood on the pavement.

'We go here Monsieur Wellum, ici.' He pointed towards the end house.

Wellum touched the priest's elbow. 'Where is Grillot going?'

'There is a blocked road, down that way, behind the church. I asked him to leave the truck there. He will join us here. Come on we should get inside.'

He turned and walked towards the end house asWellum cast another look around. The street was empty of people. He instinctively touched his left armpit, checking the pistol was in its holster and followed the priest.

Marcelin knocked on the door. After a moment someone opened it an inch and looked out. The priest leaned towards the doorway and Wellum heard him whispering. The door closed for a moment and then opened once more and Marcelin slid quickly inside gesturing eagerly that wellum follow him.

The hallway was dark.

'Avez-vous été suivi,' said a voice from behind them.

'Non,' replied Marcelin. 'Grillot est avec le camion. Il sera ici dans un instant.'

A soft knock at the door followed.

'Ah,' said Marcelin. 'Il est la.'

The door was opened and Grillot shuffled into the cramped hall as someone squeezed between them and ushered them towards another door that led into the rest of the house.

'Venez, attendez ici. Je dirai au Pere Rieu que vous souhaitez le voir.'

They were in what appeared to be a drawing room that was modestly, but comfortably furnished. A leather sofa faced an unlit hearth in the centre of the room and there were rows of shelves lining the walls that groaned and bowed beneath many books.

After a few minutes the door opened and an old priest walked in, leaning on a stick. He looked older then Marcelin and he was helped into the room by a young woman, no older than twenty-six or twenty-seven thought Wellum. She was dark and serious and her hair was unfashionably short and she wore trousers and black boots and a khaki shirt made of rough material. She smiled briefly at Father Marcelin and nodded at Grillot and then looked curiously at Wellum. She watched him as she guided the old priest towards a chair.

'Merci, Brielle,' Rieu said, patting her hand. 'Merci, je vous appellerai dans quelques instants.' He nodded and smiled at her reassuringly. 'Ne vous inquiétez passa va.'

The woman stroked his shoulder and smiled and nodded towards Marcelin and looked again at Wellum.

'Per Marcelin.'

Marcelin smiled back at her. 'Nous ne le garderons pas longtemps, Brielle.'

'D'accord.'

When she had left Father Rieu sighed and looked at Marcelin.

'So, here we are. It is good to see you Nicolas. You are well I trust?'

Marcelin took the older priests hand and kissed it.

'Father Rieu yes, I am well.' He touched his forehead, 'praise be to God.'

Rieu crossed himself. 'Amen, father Marcelin, amen.' He looked at Grillot.

'Bonjour Jean. I hope your0 family are well also.' Grillot kissed the priest's hand and nodded silently. Rieu turned to Wellum.

'And who are you my son? I do not believe we have met.'

Wellum stepped forward and held out his hand.

'Hello Father Rieu.' He glanced at Marcelin. 'My name is Harry Wellum.'

'Ah, you are English?'

'Yes Father, I am.'

The old priest studied him for a minute, nodding slowly. He looked at Marcelin and pursed his lips and turned his palms face up.

'So Gentlemen.' He looked back at Wellum. 'How can I help you?'

'Monsieur Wellum is an English pilot,' Marcelin explained.

Rieu studied Wellum once more.

'He came to my church yesterday, asking for help. He was shot down. He came to the church.'

'What were you doing when you were shot down Monsieur Wellum?'

'I was taking photographs.'

'He thinks perhaps he knows where his aeroplane crashed,' Continued Marcelin. He gestured with his hand. 'We are taking him to the forest, near Harponville. On the west side.'

'I need to try and get the cameras off the aeroplane, if they're still there,' said Wellum.

Rieu nodded. 'But why have you come here?'

'I need to contact London, or my airfield, and tell them where I am.'

'I said you might know of someone with a radio.' Said Marcelin. 'I was going to telephone you first but since we were passing I thought it would be safer to come in person.'

Rieu nodded again.

'Oui. I think Brielle might know of someone in the town with a radio that could help you.'

'Thank you Father,' said Wellum.

The priest peered towards a grandfather clock that was ticking at the other end of the room.

'If you are going on a quest to find your aeroplane today you ought to go soon. Officially there is still a curfew, even though there are only a handful of Germans left in the town. If you are out on the streets after ten o'clock, it can only bring trouble.' He turned to Marcelin.

'You do not intend to go Nicolas?'

'I *was* going to go, yes.'

Rieu shook his head. 'No, you should stay here. We will wait for them here.'

'But I thought it would go easier if we are stopped.'

Rieu held up his finger. 'No Marcelin, you will be killed.'

'You think there's a chance we'll be stopped?' said Wellum.

'Maybe. There are German troops moving day and night. They come and they go. If they are leaving they will probably ignore you. But if they are new troops coming back this way to fight, SS even, they will of course stop you and ask for your identification. This thing you do, it is not without risk Monsieur. You are behind enemy lines, remember that.' He paused in thought and rubbed his high forehead with his thumb. 'I will talk to Brielle. Maybe she can be persuaded to go with you.'

Wellum frowned. 'Are you sure that's a good idea Father?'

Rieu nodded. 'Oui Monsieur. Do not worry, she knows this area just as well as Jean Grillot here and believe me, if you do get into any difficult situations with the Wehrmacht, she will fight, of that you can be assured.'

Wellum relaxed, though he did rather hope that any fighting could be avoided.

In Father Rieu's kitchen below a framed painting of the last supper, Wellum showed the map to Brielle and explained to her and Jean Grillot where he expected they might find his plane. They had studied it carefully, occasionally muttering to each other in French. At one point Brielle lent on the table with her elbows and bending over the map traced her finger along a road. Wellum looked at her hand. She had tanned skin and slender, fragile looking fingers, but her nails were cut short and were stained with gun-oil and dirt. She stood up and looked at him.

'Are you armed monsieur?'

Wellum nodded. 'Just a pistol.'

She turned and looked up at Grillot.

'Jean?'

The farmer shook his head.

'Non, but I have a hammer in the back of the truck.'
Brielle shook her head.

'It's fine, I will find something for you.'

She faced Wellum once more. 'How big are the cameras on your plane and how many are there?'

Wellum described the shape and size, miming with his hands as if he was holding an imaginary box. 'About this big and there are three of them.'

'Can we carry them out, perhaps, one each?'

Wellum scratched his cheek. They're not exactly light.' He looked at Grillot and then back at Brielle. He nodded, 'yes we'll be able to manage, I'm sure.'

She checked her watch.

'Jean go and bring the truck as close to the house as you can. Reverse up to the door, we will be out in five minutes. Monsieur Wellum, stay here please.'

Grillot nodded and went out one door and Brielle went out another. Wellum collected the map from the table and folded it and put it in his jacket pocket. He put a cigarette in his mouth but didn't light it, then he took out his revolver and checked again that it was loaded. He put the gun back in its holster and zipped up the jacket and sat down in one of the mismatched wooden dining chairs and waited.

Outside in a small cobbled courtyard next to the house, Grillot was sat in the truck with the engine running when Brielle and Wellum went out the front door. As she dropped the tailgate Brielle turned to Wellum. 'Give me the map monsieur.'

Wellum opened his pocket and fished out the folded map. As he handed it to her, Brielle passed him a black holdall.

'Here, you keep this in the back.'

Wellum weighed the bag in his hand.

'What's in here?'

'Some weapons. A torch, two pistols and a Sten machine gun with three magazines. Four grenades and some water.'

Wellum nodded and heaved the bag onto the back of the truck and jumped in after it. Brielle lifted the tailgate and locked it in place.

'Are you leaving me with all these guns?' He asked.

Brielle opened her overcoat. She had a MAS-38 sub machine gun hanging from a shoulder sling that had been perfectly hidden by her coat. Wellum wasn't sure if the sight of it made him feel better or worse.

'The Sten is loaded but leave it hidden unless you need it. Put the bag under the seat next to Jean's toolbox. Leave it unzipped.'

She climbed into the cab beside Grillot who now looked larger still with the short, slender woman next to him. Wellum unzipped the bag and peered inside. He picked up a grenade and inspected it, flicking the pin to check it was firmly in place. He checked the other three and lifted out the sten. He checked the breach and clicked the safety catch off then back on again and put it back in the bag then he dropped the magazines out of each pistol and checked them before finally lifting out the torch. He turned it on then off and put it back and slid the bag under the bench seat and sat down. As the truck pulled slowly away and joined the empty roads of Varennes he lit his cigarette and he looked at the people walking by, their heads down, their faces all haunted with the same gaunt, hollow emptiness.

They approached Harponville from the west and took a left turn at a crossroads heading north towards the forest. After two miles, Grillot pulled the truck off the road and parked it behind a small group of larch trees, and turned off the engine. It was a little before four o'clock.

'We will need to move quickly,' said Brielle as she opened the back of the truck and took the bag from Wellum. 'This is as close as we can get.'

'How far are we from the crash site?' Asked Wellum handing the toolbox down to Jean Grillot.

'Not far, if we head north from here and if the plane is where you think it is, then I guess no more than fifteen minutes.'

Brielle handed one of the pistols to Grillot who shoved it into his pocket, and she passed the Sten to Wellum and zipped the bag closed and threw it over her shoulder.

'Come,' she said. 'It is this way.'

They walked a few yards along a fire break that led away from the truck. It was overgrown with ferns and filled with rocks but after a few minutes they turned north and found a path that weaved its way deep into the forest.

The trees were a mix of evergreen conifers - mostly Spruce and Pine and the ground was covered in a deep layer of rust coloured needles and pine cones. The air was dry and a still calm enveloped them as they walked making each footstep seem louder in the quiet shade that hung beneath the green canopy. The forest felt enclosed and safe, and they made their way in silence along a narrow path that was strewn here and there with fallen logs and the exposed roots of trees all covered with emerald moss that was thick and wet and fragrant.

After a while Brielle stepped off the path and crouched beside a large fern. She gestured for Wellum and Grillot to join her as she dug in her pocket and opened up the map and spread it on the ground.

'I think we are close,' she said quietly. 'See, here is the fire break where we came in.' She ran her finger a little way along a crease in the paper. 'And I think this is where we are now. If you are right, the plane won't be far from here.' She folded the map and put it away and lifted her face and smelled the air. 'Can either of you smell smoke?'

Wellum stood up and sniffed.

'Yes I can smell it. Burnt wood and aviation fuel.'

Grillot pointed over Wellum's shoulder. A few hundred yards west of them a group of trees stood on a small rise. One was lying on its side, splintered and torn with the tail of an aeroplane clearly visible sticking up out of the bracken close by.

'La, regardez.'

They hurried from the path and waded through the knee-high bracken. As they approached the broken trees Wellum held up his hand and slowed the group to a more cautious pace. He got a few feet further forward and stopped.

The Spitfire lay crumpled and burnt to an almost unrecognisable tangle of framework and engine parts. The cockpit was a mess. The leather cover of the pilot's seat had all burned away and its skeleton sat nakedly gawping at what was once the aeroplane's control panel. Everything was melted or burnt to nothing and covered in an oily black residue. A faint trail of smoke drifted from beneath where the engine once sat. The only pieces of the aeroplane left in any sort of recognisable state were the tail, snapped off and sitting upside down amongst the undergrowth and part of the propeller which was folded and buckled as if it had been fashioned from nothing stronger than wet clay.

Wellum approached the wreckage and touched his hand to the metal frame.

'It's still warm but it's not hot.'

'Where are the cameras situated?' Asked Brielle.

'There's one in that case on the port side and two in that case there.' Wellum pointed through the carnage at two grey boxes, bolted inside the broken airframe.

'Won't they have been damaged by the fire or the crash?'

'It's very likely yes, but those cases are fire proof and if the cameras have survived, hopefully the film inside will still be alright.'

Brielle looked at her watch.

'How long will it take to get them out?'

'If the three of us can manage to roll this frame over, getting to the access hatches won't take long.'

Brielle dropped the bag next to a broken tree stump.

'Right come on. Let us try together now, it's getting late and we are more likely to encounter the Germans after dark.'

They each carried one of the cameras back down the path.

It was almost six o'clock when they arrived once more at the truck, and the darkness of the forest gave way to the grey dusk and the sight of a pale moon already sitting low over the hills towards Varennes. It had turned cold. They put the cameras into the back of the truck and covered them with a large dirt-coloured tarpaulin. Wellum began climbing in after them when Brielle stopped him. She shook her head.

'No, not after dark. You'll have to sit in the cab with me and Jean. It will look less suspicious.'

Wellum jumped down.

'Bring the guns, we will keep them with us - just in case.'

The three of them squeezed into the front of the truck and Wellum dropped the bag of guns at their feet. Brielle unclipped her MAS-38 and laid it on top of the bag. As they pulled away Wellum reached for his cigarettes and offered one to her. She shook her head.

'Non, merci.'

He proffered the crumpled packet to Jean Grillot who nodded with a silent frown of thanks and took a cigarette and slid it behind his ear. Wellum sat back and looked at Brielle. She was smiling. Wellum lit his cigarette and shook out the match and wound the window open an inch and dropped the match out. He glanced at Brielle and smiled too.

After a while Wellum said, 'Are you Father Rieu's daughter?'

Brielle looked at him and shook her head.

'Non.'

He tried again. 'A niece, perhaps?'

'Non.'

She gave a slight sigh.

'Pere Rieu is my guardian. He is all the family I have, but we are not blood related.'

'So…?' Said Wellum, flicking his cigarette at the window.

'So…my family were all killed; my mother and father and sister. When the Germans first came, during the Blitzkrieg. We were living in Arras. My Mother's family had lived there for many generations. When the Germans came and overran us in May of nineteen-forty, some families refused to give up their houses when ordered to. A detachment of Wehrmacht were stationed with tanks in the town and the soldiers moved into peoples houses and threw them out on the street. My father refused to leave and when they found out he was a jew, they arrested him. I was at the local shops fetching groceries when they came back for my mother and sister, I knew nothing of what had happened. A friend found me and told me they had been taken, then a colleague of my father hid me. I heard that the German soldiers took some people to the edge of the town, my family along with them, and they shot them.'

Wellum grimaced.

'What, they just took them out there and killed them?'

Brielle nodded.

'Oui. It has been happening all over France, and in Poland, and Holland and everywhere in Europe that the Germans have invaded. They kill easily, everywhere, all of the time. But where there are Jews, there they have been especially busy.'

Wellum looked out of the window. Everywhere outside seemed suddenly black and a lightning fear ran through him. The thought of race killings, of mass murder. He imagined the horror, the fear.

After a while he said,

'How did you arrive in Varennes?'

'I ran.'

'You ran?'

'Oui, yes. I stayed hidden for almost a month after my parents disappeared and I thought I would lose my mind I was so afraid. But I was also angry. I begged my father's friend to let me leave and asked him to help me get to another city somewhere but he refused. He became frightened also and one night I overheard him talking to his family about handing me over to the SS. That night while they slept I took some bread and apples and I left.'

'How old are you?'

'I'm twenty-five.'

'What happened after you ran?'

'I walked all night and slept the next day in the back of a truck, very similar to this one. It was burned and broken by the side of the road, near a town called Moyennville. There were cars everywhere, all broken and burnt like the truck. Shelled by tanks, shot to bits by the Wehrmacht. And bodies too, dozens of them lying where they fell. There was a dead man at the wheel of the truck. Burnt. I stayed there all day. When it went dark I moved again and got as far south as Miraumont. I knew there would be Germans there so I stayed on the outskirts of the town. There is a village, slightly to the northeast called Iries. I went there and in the morning I went to the church. I asked for sanctuary and the priest, Le Per Boivin, he took me in.'

'Like Father Marcelin helped me.'

She nodded.

'He sheltered me and looked after me and introduced me to a group who were fighting back against the occupation.'

'The Resistance?'

'Oui. I stayed with them until Christmas and then I went to Varennes to help start a group there.'

'You went to Varranes alone?'

She shook her head.

'No, I was not alone.'

When they arrived back in Varranes the streets were deserted. They took the cameras from the truck and hid them in Father Rieu's cellar.

'Do you know anyone in town that develops camera film, someone you trust?' Asked Wellum.' The negatives would be easier to transport than the undeveloped film.'

'I think so, yes,' said Brielle. 'I will ask for you tomorrow. I will also take you to a safe place, somewhere with a radio so you can make contact with your people in London.'

'Thank you, said Wellum. 'I really do appreciate your help.'

'We are fighting the same fight. You do not need to thank me.'

It was decided that Wellum should stay in Rieu's house that night and go with Brielle in the morning to contact London. Father Marcelin and Grillot would come back the day after for an update and to see if they were needed.

Wellum stood in the hallway which was lit with a single candle that flickered and danced in the breeze of the open door. He shook them both by the hand.

'Good luck my son,' said Marcelin, kissing Wellum on both cheeks, his eyes reflecting orange sparks in the candle light. 'May the Lord deliver us all. God Bless you.'

'Thank you Father,' said Wellum, holding the old priest's hand. 'I shall see you the day after tomorrow.'

A woman from the town called Madame Blanchet had cooked food and they sat in the kitchen and ate potatoes and beans in a thin gravy with bread and cheese. As they ate, Father Rieu asked many questions about The war, and how the battles were going in Italy and in the east.

'I think Hitler has bitten off more than he can chew in Russia.' Rieu shook his head sadly.

'But at least his campaign against the Red Army has weakened his hold here in France. A fact I hope that the leaders of your country and of America will soon make an advantage of, eh?'

Wellum looked at him and then at Brielle. She was watching him, as if waiting for an answer.

'I hope so too,' he replied.

When they had finished their meal Brielle showed Wellum to the spare bedroom. Madame Blanchet had heated some water and left soap and a clean towel. The bed was a low military cot.

'The bed we stole from the Wehrmacht,' Said Brielle. 'The blankets are our own.' As she turned to leave she stopped and said. 'Was Pere Rieu right monsieur? Will the British and Americans come soon? We hear rumours, here and there, and we live in hope and do what we can, but the people of France are tired. The Germans are rounding up many Jews and Gypsies and people who are disabled or blind or crippled. They take them away, on trains, into Poland and beyond. We know this, but we cannot stop it. There are too many. We resist where we can, but we need help. I am afraid that they will erase us all and burn all of Europe if the war goes on much longer. The Nazi's are fuelled only by hate and despite the courage of my people we are all afraid…everyday.'

Wellum looked at her. So young, but already old. Her eyes were deep wells of sadness, and in their depth, he recognised a desperate need, far more urgent than any of her words could express. Like a fleeting moment - here, then gone again, he saw her pain and her hope. A person buried inside a husk, looking out, waiting for a time when it was safe to begin her life again. He had no words to comfort her. Nothing he could say that would erase the leaden burden of surviving in the hell that had been spun all around her, day after day, with only hope as her balefire.

His reply sounded flat.

'Soon Brielle. Things are moving quickly…I can promise you that. Like you said, we are fighting the same fight.'

She looked at him and somewhere deep in her dark eyes a flicker of light shone for an instant and then went out.

Obergefreiter Konnig poured hot coffee into his mug. He lifted the cigarette from the ashtray and sucked hard on it and blew out smoke and placed it back in the ashtray. He looked out of the sentry-box window. Headlights were on the road, coming towards the camp. He checked his watch and blew on his coffee and sipped it and looked at the lights. They were definitely coming this way. Konnig doused the cigarette and cursed under his breath. *Who the fuck visits a German Panzer division all the way out here at midnight?*

He shouldered his rifle and had another sip of coffee and trudged outside into the cold. He turned on the searchlight positioned next to the barrier that barred the way into the camp and shone it towards the approaching vehicle. A black Mercedes rolled almost silently to a halt, its engine ticking in the darkness. Konnig approached the driver's window and was directed towards the passenger sitting in the back seat with an almost imperceptible flick of the driver's eyes.

Haupsturmfuhrer Ansel Wolff wound the window down and looked at the sentry. The SS lightening bolts flashed on his collar and the skull and crossed bones of his cap badge glittered as he turned to address the young corporal.

'Who is the commander here Obergerfreiter?'

The corporal gave a smart salute, clicking his heels together. He stared straight ahead, his chin high in the air.

'Hauptmann Stein, Herr Haupsturmfuhrer.'

'A captain?' Wolff looked past the sentry post towards the camp. 'Where is the major?'

'Herr Haupsturmfuhrer, I must regretfully report that Major Beloff was killed, three days ago now sir. Hauptmann Stein is the camp commander now.'

'Where can I find Captain Stein, corporal?

The young soldier pointed past the barrier at some wooden huts clustered together in the gloom.

'The Captain's hut is the last one on the left Herr Haupsturmfuhrer.'

'Does he have a radio in his hut?'

'Yes Sir.'

'Very good Corporal. Please raise the barrier and then radio the captain and tell him to get up and make coffee. Tell him to collect me from my car when he is dressed.'

Konnig clicked his heels again and gave a salute as the window went back up. He trotted to the barrier and lifted it and stood to attention as the SS officer passed him without another look.

Captain Max Stein swung his legs out of his cot and rubbed his eyes. He picked up the watch sitting on the table and squinted at it then he got up and lifted the handset from the radio that was buzzing in the darkness of his cabin, a red light blinking on the top.

'Yes what is it? He demanded.

A voice jabbered at him.

Stein took a step to his right and looked out of the window at a car rolling through the camp towards his hut.

He pressed a switch on the radio and spoke into the handset.

'Right, did he say why he was here?'

'No Herr Captain, just that you should make coffee.'

Stein replaced the handset and looked at the car again and then dragged his trousers from a hanger. He threw on a shirt and heaved on his boots then he hastily filled a coffee pot with water and spooned in some coffee from a can. He lit a small gas stove and put the coffee on it to boil and he used the same match to light a log burner and he threw the match inside once the kindling took flame. He neatened the blankets on his cot and put a few personal items in the desk draw, straightened his hair and went and opened the door.

'Captain Stein?' Said the SS officer as he got out of the car and approached him.

Stein gave a `Nazi salute.

'Yes Haupsturmfuhrer. How can I help you?'

'I am Captain Ansel Wolff.' He gestured towards Stein's hut. 'Can we talk in here?'

'Yes, yes of course, said Stein. 'Please, come in.'

Stein turned two seats round by his desk and lit an oil lamp. He poured the coffee and handed a steaming cup to Wolff.

'Thank you,' smiled the SS.

'Have you come far?' Asked Stein.

Wolff placed the cup on the table and took off his gloves.

'From Saint-Quinten. I've been stationed there for the last month, but now...he spread his arms and looked around the hut. 'I am here.' He smiled.

Stein lit a cigarette and offered one to Wolff. The SS refused.

'No, thank you.' He said holding up a hand.

Stein blew out smoke and drank his coffee.

'When you say you are here. What exactly do you mean? Why are you here?'

'Captain Stein, can you tell me what you have been doing here in northern France for the last six-months?'

'Am I under some sort of investigation?'

Wolff gave a less than reassuring grin.

'No Captain, you aren't under investigation. I am merely trying to ascertain how busy you and you're panzer division have been recently.'

Well, since more than half of my men were taken and sent to Russia in February we haven't been doing very much at all.'

'And before February?'

Stein shook his head.

'Local patrols, a few skirmishes with pockets of resistance.'

'And before that?'

Stein looked at him. His pristine, dark grey uniform and his fresh haircut and clean face. He was even wearing cologne. A herbal musk that sat at odds with the stove smell and the coffee and the damp mould of the wooden hut. Stein touched the stubble on his own chin and wondered if he looked as shit as he felt.

'Many of us were at Westerplatte in thirty-nine, in Norway from April nineteen-forty then with Field Marshal Rommel at Arras.'

The SS officer nodded.

'Have you seen Paris?'

'No, not yet.'

'Ah, but you are missing out my good captain, really. It is very beautiful.' He smiled again.

'I believe so.'

'How many men do you have here?'

'Forty-three.'

'And tanks. How many?'

'Six.'

Wolff drank his coffee and unbuttoned his overcoat.

'What happened to your commanding officer?...er, Major Beloff I believe.'

'Yes, he was killed in an accident, last week. Crushed by a reversing tank I'm afraid. Is that what this is about?'

'No, do not worry. Are you the only captain here now?'

'No, there is also Hauptmann Jeutter. I got the command because of my service seniority, that's all.'

'Can captain Jeutter cope on his own?'

'What do you mean?'

'Well, can he run your division until a replacement for the unfortunate Beloff can be found.'

Stein nodded. 'Unless the Allies invade France before then, yes he can cope.'

'Good. That is good.' He took an envelope from his inside pocket. 'Captain Stein. I have orders with me that I am to commandeer your good self and ten of your finest men to accompany me on a little field trip.'

Stein threw his cigarette into the log burner. It had been a while since he'd done anything more diverting than chase a few local militia around the nearby woods.

'What kind of trip?'

Wolff opened the envelope and took out several pieces of paper and a map, folded in four. He put the papers on Stein's desk and unfolded the map.

'We are here.' He pointed at the north edge of a town called Peronne. It was riding a curve on the Somme where the river Cologne and Somme met. He traced his finger diagonally north-west to where there was a red mark drawn on the map. He held his finger there.

'A little under two days ago the Luftwaffe shot down an RAF reconnaissance aircraft in this area.' He tapped the map with his finger. The 109 pilots reported that the pilot of the stricken plane bailed out and that his aircraft crashed in a forest nearby.'

Stein looked at the map.

'Harponville, Varrenes...I know these towns, they are only around forty-kilometres away. What type of aeroplane was it? Why were there not more crew?'

'The Luftwaffe said it looked like a Mark Eleven Spitfire. If the pilot survived he is probably still hiding in this area. The RAF only use their best pilots to fly the Mark Eleven - usually ex fighter pilots with lots of experience. The British will want him back.'

'I'm sure,' said Stein. 'What was he looking for, do we know?'

Wolff eyed the tank captain.

'We're not certain yet, but obviously we need to find out.' He paused. 'So, that brings me to you and your men, Hauptmann Stein.' He refolded the map. 'You and I are going to find this pilot and his aeroplane, before he can escape from northern France.'

Stein pointed at the papers on the desk.

'Are these my formal orders?'

Wolff picked up the papers and unfolded them and handed them to Stein. He checked his watch.

'Why us?' Asked Stein as he read. 'There are infantry soldiers in Perrone. Almost a Garrisons worth. Why not go there?'

Maybe somebody in Berlin likes you? Who knows. Now, can you get a driver and ten of your men awake and have them ready to leave within the hour?'

Stein looked at the SS and nodded.

'We will need a truck too obviously. We won't be using tanks.'

'That's a relief,' said Stein handing back the orders. 'Three of them have broken down.'

Wolff shook his head but looked unsympathetic.

'Which cabin was Major Beloff's? I assume it is now unoccupied?'

'Yes, it's hut five. I'll get one of the men to put in fresh bedding.'

'Excellent.' said Wolff standing up. He poured himself the last of the coffee. 'I shall wait in my car. Send someone to fetch me when my hut is ready. He checked his watch again. I will see the men in the briefing room at exactly one-fifteen. We will start our search immediately after that. '

'Mess hut,' said Stein.

'Excuse me?'

'We don't have a briefing room. We use the mess hut.'

Wolf tutted.

'Tut tut tut, my good captain, you really have been slumming it out here in the middle of fuck knows where haven't you. Broken machinery, half your men sent to Russia, an accident prone major and a mess hall...sorry, hut, that has to double as a briefing room.' He grinned. 'Very well. I will brief the men in the mess hut at one-fifteen. After that, you will all be under my command.' He finished the coffee and handed the empty cup to Stein. 'Carry on Hauptmann Stein. Please, rouse the men from their beds and make ready to leave.'

CHAPTER THREE
Samphire

The next morning Wellum stood by the window and smoked. He looked down into the street below. An old woman, stooping and hobbled, dug around in a row of dustbins pulling out scraps and inspecting them as one might hold up a pear or an apple in a greengrocers shop. As she shuffled between the bins she dragged a cart behind her laden with what looked like her life's possessions. There had been a frost in the night and in the road, all the puddles were frozen. Wellum checked his watch and tamped out his cigarette and the next time he looked, the old woman was gone.

They crossed a small bridge at Rue de Provence and passed many building destroyed by artillery or bombs. There looked at have been many battles in Varranes and bullet holes peppered almost every wall, chewing holes in the timber and blowing chunks from the masonry. There were piles of rubble everywhere.
'Is it far?' Asked Wellum.

'No,' said Brielle. 'Just a few minutes more and we are there. The next street along and we are there.'

A rough, barking wind was blowing, making their coats flap as they went and as the clock in the town square struck eight, the sun crested the highest building in the city and poured the weak autumn light of morning upon them. Brielle led the way, moving swiftly along the empty pavements but never seeming to rush. She had a purposeful, determined way about her and as she walked, ever she checked behind her, looking in the reflections of shop windows quickly and skilfully in the well practiced manner of those that live constantly as prey. Wellum had to stride to keep up with her. Eventually they arrived at a bookshop and Brielle stepped close to the door and tapped rhythmically in code. Wellum turned and surveyed the street one last time before the door opened and the pair were ushered hastily inside.

A short, slightly ruffled looking man bobbed his head and looked at each of them before settling his eyes on Wellum. He was balding and wore round spectacles with thin frames that seemed to blend so seamlessly with his features that he might well have been born wearing them. He nodded fleetingly at Brielle and made a grunting sound aimed towards Wellum.

'Pierre, Cet homme, il a besoin d'utiliser la radio.'

'Pourquoi?'

'C'est un pilote Britannique, il doit contacter sa base.'

The man gave a sort of noncommittal shrug.

'Il a des codes, frequences?'

Brielle looked at Wellum.

'You have the frequencies to use?'

Wellum took out his notebook and held it up.

'Yes.'

'Oui.'

The man eyed Wellum uncertainly for a moment more before Brielle broke the silence.

'Pierre, sil vous plait. Vous devez nous laisser entrer. Faites-lui confiance. Il est avec moi…It's ok Pierre, really.'

The man looked at her and she reached out and touched his elbow. He smiled thinly and looked at Wellum.

'Follow me monsieur.'

He led them through a door and up a staircase, past boxes of books and stacked up volumes and tomes of indeterminate age. The whole place smelled of old paper and wood polish and it reminded Wellum of libraries past where he would spend hours immersed in the same musty dryness, pouring tirelessly over page after page.

They came to a landing, similarly bestrewn with books and magazines and newspapers, and the man approached a door. He turned a key and went inside, followed by Brielle. The room beyond was no bigger than a large stationary cupboard and apart from even more books, there was a desk and chair sitting against the far wall. The man approached the desk and slid out the chair and sat down. He put a pair of headphones over his ears and pushed a button on a black radio that was sat on the table in front of him. The radio illuminated into life and a dial on one of the meters swung to the right and bounced back and stopped. The man slid off the headphones and handed them to Wellum.

'Here, please take these, sit.'

The two men swapped places and Wellum put on the headphones.

'Do you have a morse key?'

'Of course,' said the man. He reached down the side of the radio and unravelled some wires. He placed the key on the desk in front of Wellum and plugged in the wire. Wellum adjusted two screws on the sides of the switch and tested the spring tension by tapping it up and down a half dozen times. He rolled the side screw another quarter turn and adjusted the headphones and opened his notebook and put it on the desk in front of him. He read, then he held one of the radio dials and turned it. He read some more and took another dial and turned that too.

Small adjustments.

Wellum traced his finger down the page and reached forward and clicked a switch and took a third dial and moved it a quarter turn to the left. He touched his finger to his left ear as if listening and then holding the morse key lightly, starting tapping out a message. After a series of taps he stopped as if waiting for a reply then tapped out another short burst of code.

Lotus this is Samphire
Lotus this is Samphire
Do you read me?

He waited.

Lotus this is samphire
Javelin is down
Repeat javelin is down
Over

Suddenly a series of high pitched notes emitted from the headphones. Brielle heard them and she put her hand on Wellum's shoulder.

Samphire this is Lotus we read you
Javelin is down
Understood
Feared Samphire was lost
What is your your current location and status

Wellum finished writing down the reply and tapped out his response

Am in Varennes, north of Amiens south of Arras.
Unhurt
Managed to retrieve cargo from Javelin
Will endeavour to deliver to mother
Can safe passage be arranged?

Samphire wait out

The room went quite, with the barely audible hiss of the radio filling the silence. All ears waited for the beeps to recommence. After two minutes, they came back.

Samphire Lotus
Are you able to recontact at zero-nine-thirty on this frequency?

Wellum looked at his watch.

Roger

When All The Birds Leap

Roger Samphire Lotus out

Wellum took off the headphones and re-read the notes he'd made.

'What did they say?" Asked Brielle.

'They want me to make contact again in an hour.' Brielle checked her watch. Then turned to Pierre.

'Can we stay here until then?'

The man nodded. 'Oui Brielle, of course.' He turned to Wellum. 'Would you like some coffee?'

By the time Stein had selected ten men and Wolff had briefed everyone in the mess hall, it was after two a.m. They had got onto a truck with Wolff following in his Mercedes, and had driven along deserted roads through the darkness for an hour. At a crossroads, Wolff and Stein had scoured a map spread out on the bonnet of the staff car, illuminated by torchlight. They decided to begin searching the woods outside Varennes, starting on the border of a village called Cresse and working around in an arc that led roughly east to west.

The men went into the trees at four o'clock and while the soldiers searched for the fallen Spitfire, Wolff sat in the Mercedes reading while Stein lingered in the back of the truck and smoked.

At sunrise they were moving again. Heading in the direction of the Luftwaffe pilot's last known sighting of Wellum on his parachute. After three more hours of searching they found it, and Wolff had demanded to be taken to see the wreckage of the plane when news had been delivered that the burnt and broken aircraft was found, but that the cameras had gone. He had slashed his way impatiently through the undergrowth with his cane and stood and looked at the charred tangle of metal. He had stood there staring at it for a long time.

They drove into a wide valley a few miles from the forest and dropped the men in pairs at various points along a road. They were instructed to search every hedgerow and drainage ditch between there and a group of hills some two miles to the north which was where the truck would meet them. For the journey up onto the high ground, Wolff had insisted that Stein join him in the back of the car so they could talk.

'It is warmer too,' Wolff said with a smile, holding open the door and ushering the tank captain inside.

Once they got onto the hills the two officers fell into a moody silence, each of them looking out of separate windows at the view. Eventually Wolff turned to face his colleague.

'You seem a little underwhelmed by our mission Captain Stein.'

'I'm just tired.'

'You have found your recent promotion taxing?'

'No, I think its more a case of finding this whole fucking war taxing.'

The SS looked at him.

'You are not enjoying the war?'

'Are you?'

'Well of course,' replied Wolff enthusiastically. 'The promotion of National Socialism and the deliverance of a thousand year Reich? Who couldn't enjoy that?'

Stein looked at him again. Despite being awake for God knows how long, Wolff still appeared fresh and clean and ebullient. He was polished from his boyish blonde hair, right down to his finger nails.

'Have you done much fighting Haupsturmfhurer?' Stein asked.

Wolff grinned back at him.

'Captain Stein, I have been in the SS since I was eighteen years old. I was there the night Rohm was arrested for his treason against the Fuhrer. I was a member of the hummingbird squad that executed seven members of the SA in Stadelheim prison and I was one of Kommandant Eicke's bodyguards on the night he himself executed Rohm in his cell. I have met the Fuhrer on five separate occasions. Have you? I helped organise the liquidation of jews in Blonie in Poland as well as in Torzeniec. I was in Kornic in thirty-nine helping to organise the purge there. In May of nineteen-forty I was here, like you, in France, but fighting in a different way. The SS way. Tell me, *Hauptmann Stein*, how many enemy soldiers have you personally been responsible for eliminating?'

Stein shrugged, 'I don't know, I'm not keeping count.'

'Well you should,' insisted Wolff. 'You should. How else will you know how much of a difference you made in the final analysis? How will you know? Go on, please, how many, roughly, if you had to guess?'

Stein stared into Wolff's pale blue eyes, then turned away.

'Forty maybe. Perhaps fifty.'

The SS officer laughed.

'Max, listen to me…just so that we are clear.' He leaned in closer to Stein. 'I was one of the officers at Lestrem, and took part in ordering the execution of ninety-seven British prisoners after they were captured near Dunkirk. So you see in just *one* of my many actions in the struggle so far, I have made an impact *twice* greater on my battlefield than you have in the entire campaign, on yours. So don't question me about battles and fighting. When this war ends, and we stand in Berlin before the monuments to our victory, I will have made certain that I have the blood of a thousand enemies on my hands. And each one will count. Each one will be a joy. A necessary joy.' He turned and looked out of the car window as a young corporal approached them carrying a collapsed parachute under his arm. He turned back to Stein. '…And this British pilot, trust me. He will be one of them.'

The corporal dropped the parachute by the car and saluted. His colleague dropped Wellum's flying helmet and did the same.

'Excellent work Corporal,' said Wolff as he climbed out of the Mercedes. He took the map from his pocket and unfolded it. 'Show me where you found these things.' The corporal pointed at the map. Wolff looked past him down into the valley below. 'About a half mile in that direction Sir,' said the corporal, gesturing back the way he'd come up onto the high ground. 'The parachute and flying helmet were hidden in a bush bordering some cattle fields. Just past that tree line.'

Wolff reached back into the car and came out with binoculars. He put them to his eyes and surveyed the distant fields.

When All The Birds Leap

'He won't have stayed in this valley, he said removing the binoculars and looking around. He lifted them again and glassed some hills to the north. 'And if he didn't come this way, I'm betting he made for those hills over there.' He passed the binoculars to Stein as the remaining soldiers began arriving wearily onto the hill.

'Very good gentlemen. We are close. Come, we'll go and see if there are any signs of our prey up on those hills.'

'Don't you think we should let the men rest? They've been awake since one o'clock this morning,' said Stein.

Wolff turned to face him

'Hauptmann Stein, get these men on the truck. You can ride with them. While they are under my command they are acting Waffen SS, no longer simple *panzer grenadiers*.' He spat the words as if it were an insult. 'And that means they can go on for longer, they can work harder, fight harder, and that includes you Captain. They can rest soon enough.'

It took a while for them to find a road up onto the northern hills, but when they got there Wolff got his reward. It was almost nine-thirty and the sun was creeping higher in the sky and a fresh morning breeze blew up to meet them from a stream running quickly along in the valley below.

'There, you see,' said Wolff, once more passing the binoculars to Stein.

'A worthy place for any lost pilot to find rest and shelter, wouldn't you say?'

Stein looked down onto Lealvillers. It's village folk going about their morning business as cockerels called and hens scratched in their dirt pens and cows lowed softly in the fields.

He handed the glasses back to the SS, a sick feeling settling in as Wolff looked through them and grinned.

'Come on,' he said quietly. 'Let us get down there and see what we find.'

At exactly nine-thirty, Wellum, Brielle and Pierre were back in the storage cupboard preparing the radio for Wellum's next call to London.

He made sure the radio was still tuned to the correct frequency and began tapping on the morse key. After a moment, Brielle could hear muffled beeps coming from the headphones as someone on the other end punched out a reply.

Wellum turned to Pierre.

'They want to talk to me on the wireless, Pierre can you set up a microphone?'

The Frenchman did as he was asked, unraveling a line of flex and placing the microphone down on the desk in front of the pilot. Once the set was rigged Wellum turned to them both.

'Would you mind waiting for me downstairs. If London get's a sniff that there's anyone in the room with me I'll be for the chop when I get home. You understand?'

'Of course,' said Brielle. She turned to Pierre. 'Pierre, alley, nous pouvons attendre en bas des escalier. Donnons au pilote un peu d'intimité.'

'Thank you,' said Wellum. 'I'll be as quick as I can.'

When he was alone he turned back and hovered his mouth by the microphone.

'Lotus, this is Samphire. Are you reading me? Over.'
The frequency hissed.
'Lotus this is Samphire, come in.'
'Samphire this is Lotus, reading you loud and clear.'
Wellum was surprised at how relieved he felt.
'Harry, it's Peter.'
Wellum grinned at the microphone.
'Peter, good morning old chap.' He glanced at his watch.
'I'm surprised you're out of bed.'
'Well, a little bird told me that some silly sod had got himself shot down over France and needed rescuing.'
'Your little bird was right I'm afraid.'
'What happened?'
'Got into a tangle with a couple of 109's. I had one of them pinged, but the other one snuck up on me from behind and shot me down.'
'Are you alright?'
'Yes, I'm fine.' He looked at his injured hand and flexed his fingers as if testing them out. 'I found my way to a village and the local priest took me in.'
'Where are you now?'
'I'm in a town called Varennes, with someone connected to the Resistance.'
'You trust them?'
'Yes, they helped me find my plane and got me in contact with you so…'
A pause.
'I got the cameras from Javelin and I'm trying to get the films developed before I head home.'

'Ok, good. You think you might have anything interesting?'

'Mmm not really. Some defended German positions near Dieppe and a convoy of artillery heading west just north of Amiens. That's about it.'

'Alright, well, if you can get the films developed before noon today, at least you'll have something to show Cartwright at your debriefing.'

'Before noon? why what's the plan?'

'The heads here have been chatting it over and it seems they've come up with something. Do you have a pen and some way of making notes?'

'Yes, I've still got my notebook.'

'Very well, listen in... Cartwright has a contact at the SOE and apparently he's managed to pull in a favour. You said you were in Varennes, is that correct?'

'Yes.'

'Alright, you are to proceed south to Rouen as soon as possible today. When you arrive there you are to make contact with an SOE agent who's codename is *Armada*. He is being given orders as we speak to rendezvous with you tonight after eighteen-hundred-hours at a Brasserie called *La Petit Savoie* on Rue du Montparnasse, it's in the old city, close to the cathedral. He will take you to a safe house where you will await further instructions. You have until twenty-one-hundred to meet him otherwise he's gone. We are working on a route to get you home as soon as possible, so get to Rouen and meet Armada and sit tight.'

Wellum finished writing and keyed the microphone.

'Are there Germans in Rouen?'

'I'm afraid so, yes, a few infantry platoons are garrisoned just outside of the city but it's mostly naval personnel. The Kriegsmarine have some warships and we suspect some U-boats in dry dock being maintained and repaired. But there is also a strong Resistance. You ought to be safe until we can bring you back in. Unless of course you do anything stupid Harry.'

Wellum smiled again.

'I won't.'

'Scout's honour?'

The pilot held up three fingers.

'Scout's honour.'

'How will I know Armada when I see him?'

'He'll be reading *Proust*. When you approach him he will be sitting by the bar. You are to order a vodka martini with two olives. If he puts his book face down on the table you are safe to approach and make contact. Your codename is *Firefly*. When you first make contact you are to ask 'are you waiting for someone?' Armada will reply, 'I am waiting for a colleague from the library.' Can you ask him that in French?'

Wellum scribbled more notes.

'Yes, I think I can stretch to that.'

'Very good. Now, remember Harry, memorise what I've said and then burn your notes, ok?'

'Alright I will.'

'Do you have any way of getting to Rouen?'

'So far I've had the use of a small truck, but that's left the area and won't be back until tomorrow. I suppose I could make a telephone call and ask if the chap could come back today.'

'Yes, whatever you do you need to move quickly. It's important you make that rendezvous tonight. Cartwright has pulled out all the stops to get you in with this SOE chap, and I doubt Armada could be persuaded to come back out if you don't show up as planned.'

'No problem, I'll get moving.'

'Fine. When you get to Rouen you are to make contact with Lotus to confirm you are with Armada. We'll get on with the planning at our end. Got all that?'

'Yes.'

'Don't forget, destroy your notes and make contact tonight. Good luck.'

'Thanks. Out'

Wellum took off the headphones and re-read his notes, then he tore the pages from his notebook, scanned them once more and lit them in one corner with his cigarette lighter. He held the burning pages in his fingers then dropped them into an ashtray on the table. He watched them burn to black ash then poked them into a fine powder with his finger and stirred the contents of the ashtray together until it was once more just a heap of cigarette butts and ash and used matches. He turned the wireless to standby and left the room.

Brielle was sat in the back of the shop drinking coffee and speaking quietly with Pierre as Wellum came into the room.

'Ok?' Asked Brielle.

Wellum nodded.

'Yes, but I need to get back to Father Rieu's house.' He looked at Pierre.

'Thank you Monsieur.' He held out his hand and the Frenchman shook it. 'De rien, monsieur pilot, good luck.'

Brielle kissed Pierre on the cheek.

'Merci Pierre, restez en sécurité. Au revoir.'

They left the bookshop into a flat grey morning. The streets were getting busier. Brielle stepped off the pavement and crossed the road, leading the way once more. She changed her route from earlier in the day and headed for Rieu's house with a sudden sense of urgency she did not quite understand. The pair walked on in haste and silence and as they walked, each of them would occasionally catch the eye of the other and then quickly look away. As they got back into the priest's house, Wellum spoke first. 'Does Father Rieu have a telephone?'

'Oui,' said Brielle.

'I need to contact Father Marcelin and ask if Grillot can come back here today with his truck.'

'Why, what is happening?'

'I need to get to Rouen.'

'Today? Is this the plan?'

'Yes. My contact in London has arranged for me to meet someone there who is going to shelter me and then help get me back to England.'

'Who is the person you must meet.'

Wellum looked at her but didn't answer.

'Monsieur Wellum, you can trust me…surely by now you know that?'

'Harry.'

'What?'

'My name, it's Harry.'

'Harry, ok. Who are you meeting in Rouen?' She paused, waiting for Wellum to answer. 'A French person? English? Who?'

'Please, right now, I just need you to help me contact Father Marcelin.'

'No Harry, you also need me to help you get to Rouen, and if I do, then I also need to know who you are going to meet.'

'I was hoping Grillot could take me. Come with me I mean.'

'And do what? Jean is a kind and helpful man, but he is a farmer Harry, not a fighter. I can help you. I want to come with you.'

Wellum saw the same dark light flicker across her face that he'd seen the night before.

'Alright,' he conceded with a relieved sigh. 'Thank you.' He paused then went on. 'We'll need weapons. Can you organise those quickly?'

'Of course, yes, and food and water and medicine.' She nodded towards a door. The telephone is in the hall. I'll find Pere Rieu and get Marcelin's number.'

Wellum sat in the dimly lit hall and waited, thinking over what the coming days would bring. He thought about meeting Armada and then he thought about contending with German soldiers. He took the last cigarette from its packet and looked at it. His last English cigarette. The thought of smoking the rough French brands made him almost contemplate keeping it for a special occasion. 'No one will ever fully understand the sacrifices I have made for King and country, will they old boy?' He put the cigarette in his mouth and lit it as the door opened.

'Here,' said Brielle, handing him a slip of paper with seven digits written on it in a wavering hand. 'This is Pere Marcelin's telephone number but I think I should make the call, the Germans have listening devices on all of the telephone lines in France. They are always monitoring our conversations.' Wellum took the paper and read the number.

'Alright,' he agreed handing it back to Brielle. 'Tell Marcelin we are going on a day trip to visit your aunt in Rouen and we need to bring her some cattle feed from the farmer so we need the farm truck.'

'Do you think it's wise that I say we are going to Rouen?'

'It's only fair that we tell Grillot how far we need to go, he'll have to inform his family.'

While Brielle spoke to Father Marcelin, Wellum went to the widow and moved the curtain to one side with his finger and looked out onto the street. Since coming off the radio to London he had begun to feel hunted for the first time since he'd landed in France, and rather than an optimism for getting on the move back home, he felt an anxious uncertainty plucking upon him deep within. He opened the window an inch and dropped the cigarette out as Brielle put down the phone.

'What did he say?' Asked Wellum.

'He said that he would go to Jean's farm and ask him and then contact us here in thirty minutes.'

Wellum checked his watch and headed for the door.

'Right well, we'd better get things ready.'

'Harry wait,' said Brielle with an urgency in her voice.

'What's wrong?'

'I'm not certain, but Father Marcelin, just now, as we were ending our conversation, he seemed distracted somehow, and I think that I heard shouting.'

'Shouting? In the house?'
'No, outside, in the street.'
'But you're not certain?'
'I think I heard it, like men shouting.'
'Alright well, we have thirty minutes to wait for Marcelin's call. If it doesn't come, in thirty-five minutes we're leaving anyway.'
'D'accord.'
'Can you get everything we need and have a think about the best way to get to Rouen if Grillot can't take us.'
'Of course.'
She headed for the door.
'You wait here Harry. I'll speak to Rieu as well.'
'It may be best not to tell him where we're going. I mean, it might be safer for him if he doesn't know.'
'I agree. What about your cameras, and the film?'
'There's not time for that I'm afraid. Can you destroy them, or use them maybe, after I've gone?'
'Oui, they may come in useful.'

After twenty minutes they were stood in Father Rieu's kitchen once more as Brielle ran through an array of items gathered hastily upon the rough, wooden dining table.

'This everything I think we'll need, and probably as much as we can carry.' She pointed her way around the inventory. 'The Sten gun we took out yesterday and my MAS-38. I can hide that under my jacket all the way to Rouen. Two grenades each and some spare magazines for both automatic weapons. I don't have any spare rounds for your pistol though, I'm sorry. A water canteen each and some dry rations we stole from a German patrol, we can use those if we get forced to hide or go anywhere cross country on foot. There's enough food to last us three days, which will be plenty. I can't imagine we'll ever be that far from a village or town, but better to have them than not. A torch and some basic first aid supplies.'

Wellum nodded.

'Excellent, thank you Brielle.'

She reached into her back pocket and brought out an envelope.

'You had better take this too. We are likely to get stopped.'

Wellum took the envelope and opened it as Brielle began collecting their supplies and packing them into two small rucksacks. Inside the envelope was a folded and slightly battered sheet of paper. Wellum put the envelope on the table and opened the paper. It had 'Carte D'identite' Printed across the top and a faded photograph stapled into a box on the right hand side. A young man stared at him. His eyes penetrating like Wellum's. He had the same tousled hair as the pilot but slightly darker, and he wore a short, dark beard.

'Cedric Allard,' Wellum read aloud. 'From Miraumont? Is this who came to Varennes with you?'

'Oui.' Said Brielle as she knelt down buckling the bags. She held one up for Wellum to take.

'Who was he?'

Brielle shook her head. 'It doesn't matter who he was. We don't have time to get you any forged papers before we leave.'

Wellum looked at the photograph.

'But, he doesn't really look *that* much like me. I don't have a beard, and our hair's too dissimilar.'

'The Wehrmacht don't really study the photographs that well, not like they did at the beginning of the occupation. If we do get stopped it will probably be a routine check. Here.' She handed him a soft grey cap with a peak. 'Wear this, then I think you're likeness will be enough.'

'The beard?'

She rolled her eyes.

'You shaved it off, alright?' She dropped his bag at his feet and headed for the door.

'I'll tell Rieu we are leaving now.'

Wellum looked again at Cedric's photograph, the identity card ripped and charred along one edge. He looked at the young man's eyes, watching him from another time, then he folded the paper and put it back in its envelope and put the envelope in his shirt pocket.

A few minutes later Brielle came back into the kitchen.

'I do not think Pere Marcelin will contact us now, do you?'

Wellum checked his watch, the call was almost fifteen minutes overdue.

'It looks like you were right about the shouting. Something must have happened.' He shouldered his bag.

'Do you know anyone with a vehicle? A car, or even a motorcycle perhaps?'

'Not in Varranes no, some people on the outskirts of town maybe, but no one I can call right now. Not someone that might travel immediately.'

'What about buses or trains?'

Brielle considered both.

'There are no longer any buses to Rouen, but possibly a train. We would struggle to conceal our weapons though and there would definitely be guards at the station, both here and at Rouen.'

'What about neighbours? Do you know anyone with a car or truck?'

'There are only one or two.' She paused, then went on. 'Wait, there *is* a car, an *Avent* parked just two streets away. It has been there since the day before you came to Varennes. Pierre said it had been abandoned by two German officers that stole it from another town and were making their way back to their camp on the outskirts of Harponville. He said that that there was a rumour they had taken another car from here and continued on in that.'

Wellum nodded. 'That sounds like our best bet.'

'Can you make it start?' Asked Brielle.

'If it's got fuel in the tank, I'll get it started don't you worry.'

CHAPTER FOUR
Wolff in Lealvillers

Wolff arrived in Lealvillers that morning like a plague blown in on some riven wind dragged up from the underworld, who's only purpose was to inflict misery and pain.

The Germans drove into the village square close to the church and stopped. The soldiers climbed down from the truck and began shouting at the few locals that had stood watching the vehicles pull up. It was loud, unorganised shouting, moving people roughly away or ordering them to stand still and not move.

Marcelin, still holding the phone to Brielle watched them arrive and heard the shouting. When he hung up the phone he went to the window and looked out.

Stein jumped down from the cab of the truck and looked around the quiet, early morning streets. He waved towards his men and they stood in a line facing the Mercedes as Wolff got out.

'Where should we start?' said Stein. Wolff looked around the square; Squat buildings on either side and a small tavern nestled in one corner with the churchyard and church in another.

'How many houses do you think there are?'

'No more than forty in the whole village I doubt, and maybe half a dozen farms.'

'Send the men out in two's, have all the people they can find brought here into the square, including the church. And tell them not to forget to check any outbuildings or vehicles while they're looking. We'll do a more thorough search once we have everyone here.' He pointed at the tavern. 'I'm going to wait in there.'

Stein set the men about their tasks, telling each of them that once they had rounded up all of the people in the village they could rest and eat, then he joined Wolff in the tavern.

The SS was sitting at a table by a window that overlooked the village square. He was watching the church. As Stein walked in Wolff turned and addressed a middle-aged man and a young woman that were stood behind the bar.

'Come here,' he gestured with his hand. 'No not you, you.' The man took a step back as Wolff pointed at the woman who looked to be around nineteen. 'Come,' he said again waving her towards him with a smile. Stein came and sat on the opposite side of the table, while the SS chauffeur stood guard by the door.

The young woman came slowly towards the two German officers. She was blonde, but not German blonde and she wore a simple skirt and a blouse covered with an apron.

'Please,' said Wolff, dragging out a third chair. 'Sit down.' The woman sat cautiously and placed her hands on the table in front of her. Stein lit a cigarette and turned to the landlord. 'Make coffee, enough for thirteen.' Wolff glanced at him and then looked back at the girl as the sound of people being rounded up in the square outside began filtering in through the window. The landlord began making coffee in two pots.

'What is your name fraulein?'
'Madeline.'
'How old are you?'
'Eighteen'
'Do you work here, in the tavern?'
'Oui, sometimes.'
'Is that your father?'
'Yes.'
'What is his name?'
'Gaston.'
'Gaston what?'
'Picare. Gaston Picare.'

The landlord put the coffee pots on the bar and took mugs from a shelf and arranged them on a nearby table.

'Monsieur Picare,' Wolff called to the landlord. The man stopped what he was doing and looked at the German.

'Please, bring me and Hauptmann Stein our coffee.'

The landlord poured two cups, strong and black and brought them over and put them down, one in front of each of the soldiers. Wolff smiled at him.

'Thank you. Now, do you have bacon?'
'We have a little yes.'
'And cheese and bread?'
'Yes.'

'Very good. Please bring out what you have, my men have been awake all night and need a good breakfast.'

The Landlord looked distractedly out of the window as more people filled the square. The soldiers corralling them into groups of men and women, shouting and pushing.

'Herr Picare?' Said Wolff. The landlord looked back at him. 'Our breakfast, if you please.'

The Frenchman nodded and trotted back towards the bar and the kitchens beyond.

Stein drank his coffee and smoked. He looked out of the window at the growing scene and wondered if he should go out and keep an eye on things. He looked at Wolff who was sat impassively, drinking his coffee and watching the girl. The atmosphere had grown leaden and thick. Stein didn't like it. He'd seen his men change as soon as they had put on their SS armbands and were told by Wolff that they were now Waffen troops under his command. An electricity had gone around the mess hut while they were being briefed, and some of the men seemed to grow excited - their youthfully exuberant dreams being fulfilled. He'd noticed one or two of them glancing at each other, grinning, and he was surprised now how many of them seemed to be relishing the task of rounding up the villagers - something that none of them had ever done before. He looked out of the window and watched them. He saw one young corporal, no more than a boy in his early twenties, Egon Goethe, pushing an old woman roughly along the pavement with the butt of his rifle. He was shouting at her, his head bent forward on a stretched neck, bellowing almost directly into her ear to move and stand against the wall. He remembered how only last week, Goethe had been teased by some of the other troops after receiving a letter from his mother that had reduced him to homesick tears. *Now look at him* thought Stein, *frightening old women and farm boys because he is wearing lightening bolts on a black armband.*

The landlord started putting out plates and cutlery for the soldiers. He had brought half a ham up from the cellar and two blocks of local cheese. He broke bread into pieces and put it in a bowl and brewed more coffee and filled a pitcher with water.

'Have you eaten breakfast yet Madeline?' Wolff asked as he stood up and removed his leather overcoat. She shook her head.

'Would you care to join us?'

'Non, mercy, I am not hungry, thank you.'

'Very well,' announced Wolff heading towards the buffet. 'Captain Stein, please bring in five of the men from outside to have breakfast, you and the other five come back inside in thirty-minutes and you can eat. After that we will speak to the prisoners.'

Stein made towards the door, taking his pistol from its holster as he crossed the room. He stopped and turned.

'Prisoners?'

Wolff picked up a plate and began loading it with ham and cheese.

'Villagers, Hauptmann Stein. I meant villagers.'

The square had been divided in two. On the west side stood men of varying ages. They looked grim and stared bitterly at the soldiers standing in front of them with their machine guns aimed at the group. On the other side, the women and children huddled together, guarded in similar fashion.

'You five, go inside and eat.' Stein pointed at two of the five men left guarding the women. 'Baur, and Vogel come over here and watch the men.' Stein looked on as the soldiers rearranged themselves and he gave Goethe a black look as he doubled past him towards the tavern. He looked at the people. Many of them stared back at him defiantly, some with anger, some with fear. The air seemed eerily quiet like only they existed in the world and all else around them in the fields and the forests had fallen from the earth. A raven cawed in the pale light, standing on a gravestone in the churchyard it watched the villagers shivering in the cold. Stein went to the truck and climbed into the back and found an overcoat. He put it on and lit another cigarette and with his pistol still drawn he jumped down and smoked and stamped his feet and stood alongside his men.

After thirty minutes the first five soldiers came out of the tavern, shouldering their weapons and wiping their mouths as they came. Stein placed them on guard and sent the others in to eat. He didn't follow them inside.

He observed again the faces of the village men, some watching him, some looking across the square waving reassuringly to their families. One man looked back at him. A priest. He was old and short, with a calm, kind look gathered at the corners of his eyes. He looked at Stein and smiled softly and nodded. A recognition of some sort. Stein winced out a smile and nodded back.

When the remaining troops had eaten, they came back out once more and took up their positions pointing their weapons at the crowd. Stein glanced at his watch and headed back inside the tavern. Wolff was sitting in the same chair, the young woman still sat in front of him, unmoved and staring down at the floor. Her father was stacking the dirty plates and cups.

'I think it's time we got on with things,' said Stein, pouring the last of the coffee and warming his hands on the cup. 'It's cold out there and these people have been stood outside for over an hour.'

Wolff checked his own watch and nodded in agreement. He stood up and put on his overcoat and fastened the buttons and then the belt.

'Monsieur Picare, on behalf of myself and my men I would like to thank you and your lovely daughter for your kind hospitality and for the wonderful breakfast that you have provided us with today.'

The landlord stopped wiping down the table and tucked the cloth into his apron. He nodded at the German.

'You're welcome.'

'And now, if you don't mind, would you and Madeline please join us outside in the square.' He gestured towards the door. The Landlord came from behind the counter and removed his apron and dropped it on a table. He held out his hand and Madeline took it and together they walked out, followed by Wolff and his chauffeur. Stein cast a last look around the tavern and went out after them.

In the square, the people stopped talking.

The raven watched the gathering from the cemetery, its head tilted to one side. It cawed loudly and hopped from grave to grave as Wolff appeared and the sound echoed around the small square. One or two people turned and look towards the church.

Wolff pointed to the ground and the girl and her father stopped and stood.

'Villagers of Lealvillers, good morning to you all. I am Haupsturmfuhrer Wolff of the SS and I have come here today with my men on a very important mission. We have been informed that a British spy parachuted into this area two days ago. His aircraft was shot down a few kilometres away but he bailed out. And he survived.' He paused and looked at the men. 'We *know* that he survived. Now, we have tracked this man's movements and we strongly believe that he probably came here, into your village at some point on the day he fell from the sky. As you are all no doubt aware, harbouring enemies of the Reich is *illegal*. It is a crime.' He turned and spoke towards the women. 'We are here to find this man. That is all. We are here to find him and to arrest him. If you help us, we will leave this place as we found it. If you help us, this will be your reward.' Wolff walked back towards the tavern and stood by the landlord and his daughter. 'So, does anybody here know anything about this pilot?' He looked along the lines at each of them. Stein looked at them too. The soldiers shuffled and held their weapons tighter and the atmosphere grew thick and oppressive once more. A baby began crying and it's mother held it close to her and soothed it through trembling lips. Wolff waited.

'No one knows anything?'

The baby cried into it's mothers blouse as she held it and rocked it. Many of the women felt a wave of fear go through the group, the vulnerability of the infant and its mother triggering some primal urge to protect, or run.

They huddled closer together and they reached for each other instinctively as another woman began a low, moaning wail as the fear grew. A man shouted from across the street and a guttural rumble went through the men, it too driven by the growing threat of danger. The young soldiers looked from one to the next and shuffled anxiously from foot to foot. Stein took out his pistol and cocked it. Wolff took out his own pistol and held up his hand like a king. He waited for the crowd to settle, then he spoke again.

'Please tell us what you know and we will leave.' He waited in the heavy air. He waited for a long time. Eventually he spoke again.

'Nothing?' He paused for the last time. 'Very well.'

He turned and put his pistol against the side of Madeline's head and shot her. An act so sudden, there appeared to be no sound, but the raven jumped from the gravestone and flew cawing up into the sky. For a moment no one moved as the young woman collapsed lifelessly at her fathers feet. A pink mist hung in the air and as her head hit the cobbles it pumped a thick river of dark blood into the gutter. The landlord fell to his knees and wailed and clutched at his daughter's shoulders, lifting her soft corpse towards him. Wolff took a step forward and put the pistol against the back of his head and shot him. This time the sound was deafening, caroming off the buildings and ricocheting all around the square. Several people ducked and someone began screaming.

'Get back,' warned Wolff, turning his pistol on the crowded pavements. 'Get back in line.'

A man stepped from the curb, into the road and a young obergerfreiter hammered several rounds into him with his machine gun. The man fell dead, holding his stomach. More shouting rose up from every side and Wolff raised his pistol and shot a woman standing next to the mother with the crying baby.

'Enough.' He shouted over the voices. 'Quiet.' He pointed his pistol in the air and sent two more rounds smoking towards the sky. 'Quiet!'

Stein walked to the dead girl and her father and crouched down and rolled the man onto his back. He turned and looked at Wolff and shook his head questioningly.

'What the fuck are you doing?'

'Not now Captain Stein,' said Wolff, eyeing the crowd. 'Not now.'

Stein stood up and berated the young corporal who had panicked and shot the man.

'Vogel! Du idiot, was zum teufel hast du dir dabei gedacht?'

The soldier stood shaking and sweating in the cold air.

'Now, listen carefully,' said Wolff, continuing to address the villagers. 'I want the men to go into the tavern and sit on the floor. If anyone moves or talks we will shoot three of the women. Understand?' He reloaded his pistol as he turned to the women. 'I want all of you to go into the church and sit on the floor. If any of you move or talk we will shoot a child, do I make myself clear?' He pointed at Father Marcelin. 'You, priest. You go with the women. Explain to them that if they know anything about this pilot they should say so immediately. Time is running out, and soon we will begin killing more people. Tell them that, be clear. ' He turned to the soldiers. 'You two take the women to the church, you and you take the men into the tavern.' He looked at his chauffeur standing on the edge of the scene with his pistol drawn. 'Schubert you go with them.' The rest of the men he sent to search the houses. 'Captain Stein, wait here and make sure everyone goes where they should. Meet me in the church when you're done.'

Once Stein had ensured the men had all gone about their correct duties, he ordered Goethe and another man to drag the dead bodies into a house next to the tavern and to get a pail of water and wash the blood off the cobbles. By the time he headed towards the church it was almost midday, but the sun remained low on the horizon and it was cold.

Inside the church, the women sat huddled together in the knave. One or two were crying softly but no one spoke. The baby had settled, but the smell of fear hung thickly in the air, constricting and soaked with adrenaline.

Marcelin sat close by the group, holding the hand of a frail looking woman who appeared to be asleep. He watched Stein walk in and approach one of the soldiers standing guard.

'Where is Captain Wolff?'

'He went next door to the priest's house.'

Stein looked over at Marcelin, then back at the soldier.

'Why has he gone there?'

'I'm not entirely sure Hauptmann.'

'You, priest, come over here.'

Stein walked towards the back of the church. Marcelin watched him and then got slowly to his feet and kissed the woman's hand and placed it gently on her chest. He followed to where the German stood waiting for him. Stein gestured to a pew.

'Please Father, sit down.'

The old man sat and looked calmly back at the soldier. Stein felt judged.

'I wanted to apologise,' he began.

'What for?"

Stein gestured, 'for what happened outside, in the square.'

'It was not you fault.'

'Well, I still feel I need to apologise.'

'You are not SS?'

Stein shook his head. 'No.'

'What regiment are you from?'

'I'm a captain with the tenth Panzer Division.'

'Ah, from Stuttgart?'

'How do you know that?'

'In the last war, I pulled a German boy from a burning tank, after the battle of Ypres.

He told me he had been stationed at Stuttgart.'

'Did he live?'

Marcelin shook his head. 'No.'

Stein looked at him.

'You are different to the SS captain. That is clear. You do not want to fight.'

'I'm not sure anymore.'

'I understand. War can do this. Once, where there was conviction, now maybe, there is doubt?'

'I'm not in a confessional am I?'

Marcelin smiled.

'No, of course not. But I see it. I saw it earlier, in the square. You do your duty of course, but I think you also understand the pointlessness of all this.'

'I question the need for all of the killing, yes.'

'You have a family? Waiting for you at home?'

'No.'

'Those people, shot in the square today. They all had families.'

'What is your name?'

'Marcelin.'

'Father Marcelin, where is God? Why does he allow this?'

'You mean why does he allow war? A good question my son.'

'My wife was killed, and my child, my daughter, by British bombs.'

'When?'

'Last summer. I have not been back to Germany since.'

'Do you blame God for their deaths?'

'Father, I doubt now if God even exists.'

'In the past, in the Great War, I often wondered the same thing. I questioned my faith many times sitting among the puddles as men jabbered with fear from the constant shelling. The madness, the filth and the death were everywhere in the trenches. Inescapable, day after day.'

'But you remained faithful? I mean your faith in God, it stayed with you?'

'It was a difficult time, I admit. I often fell into despair.'

'Did you hate your enemy?'

Marcelin thought for a moment.

'I think because I never felt I had an enemy, it was easier not to fall into hate. Do you hate the English or the Americans?'

'I feel hate some days, but not necessarily for our enemy. Before the war I admired Britain and America. France too. I came here often after the first war, when I was a boy. My father would take me to a town near Toulouse every summer.'

Marcelin smiled.

'Maybe when the war is over you will visit again.'

'Maybe,' said Stein, though there was no conviction in his voice.

'What were their names? Your daughter and your wife?'

'My wife was called Misha and my daughter, Valda.'

'I will pray for them. And for you.'

The church door opened and several of the women murmured and backed away as Wolff strode into the vestibule accompanied by two soldiers. One of them was carrying a bundle of clothes. Wolff stood for a moment before the alter and removed his hat and crossed himself then he put his hat back on and made his way over to where Marcelin and Stein were sat talking.

'Ah Captain Stein, excellent, you are already questioning the prisoner.'

He pointed to the floor and one of the soldiers dropped the small pile of clothing he was carrying. Wolff gestured for the men to step back.

'Watch the women,' said Wolff.

Stein stood up and looked at the pile of clothes and then at Wolff.

'What's that?'

Wolff ignored the question and looked at Marcelin.

'What is your name priest?'

'My name is Father Marcelin.'

'And that is your house next door? The one adjacent to the church yard. The cottage?'

'Yes.'

'Father Marcelin, can you explain to me why you have the uniform of a British RAF officer hidden in your house?'

He bent down and lifted up a pair of light blue trousers and waved them at the old man.

'And these…' he put his hand in his pocket and came out holding four cigarette butts. They were smoked down to the filters, but two had been straightened out to reveal the brand name stamped in faded ink.

'*Embassy number one*. A British brand of cigarette. These came from two ashtrays in your house. Can you please explain how they came to be there and more urgently, why you have been lying.' He dropped the cigarette ends onto the pile of Wellum's clothes and dusted off his palms.

Stein looked at Marcelin who kept his eyes on the SS captain. Wolff leaned forward, speaking quietly.

'Father Marcelin, you have to tell me. When was the pilot here, where has he gone?' He paused and studied the priest closely. 'Or is he still hiding here in the village?'

Marcelin shook his head slowly.

'He is not here.'

'But you have seen him? And fed him and helped him?'

'Yes.'

Stein felt a cold stabbing sensation pushing against his chest. Wolff glanced at him and looked back into Marcelin's eyes like a hunter cornering his prey.

There was a long silence. Some of the women, aware of a sudden rise in tension began shifting nervously. One of the guards pointed his gun at them and whispered in German.

'Sit quietly, do not move.'

Eventually Wolff spoke again.

'You must tell me Father Marcelin. There is no other way around it. You must tell me what you know.'

Marcelin watched him from behind his spectacles.

'I will pray for you too captain.' He smiled and nodded softly. 'I will pray for you.'

'Tell me,' repeated Wolff, stepping closer to the priest. He bent forward and spoke into Marcelin's ear.

'Herr priest, you have run out of time. You must talk to me about this pilot. If you tell me you do not know where he has gone I will kill ten women, here today. But if you tell me honestly what you know I will leave.' He straightened and took a step back.

'However, if you lie to me…at all. If you tell me he has gone say, to Reims or to Amiens, and I go looking and find no trace of him then I will return here, I assure you. I will return and I will kill everyone here, in your village, and I will burn it into the ground. On that Father Marcelin, you have my word.'

Marcelin looked at Stein and then back at Wolff.

'How can you have such hate monsieur? So much hate for the world?'

'Stop,' said Wolff holding up a dismissive hand. 'Stop, priest, stop. I do this not for hate, you see. But for love.'

'For love?'

'Of course, yes,' Wolff shrugged. 'Of course for love. I love my Fuhrer deeply and I love my country and there are many things that I would do that other men might find beyond their capacity for the love I feel inside. Burning this place into the ground would not bother me in the slightest.'

He paused.

'So, what can you tell me about our English friend? Where has he gone?'

Marcelin closed his eyes and bowed his head.

'Please father. My patience wears thin.'

Stein bounced a look between them. He wanted to intervene somehow, with something, anything that he thought might pull them all out of this choking madness, but his mind simply reeled in a chasm of doubt and fear and shame. He felt horribly afraid, unlike anything he had faced on the battlefield this was worse - like an orgy of nightmares.

And he was paralysed by it.

'It is your duty Father Marcelin, whispered Wolff who had once more come in close to the priest. 'It is your duty to protect your flock. They are being hunted, it is true, and you alone can protect them. You alone can save them all. You do not owe this Englishman any loyalty or protection. You have done everything you can for him and now he is no longer your concern. You must remember that. Save your flock. Tell me where he has gone.'

Stein reached out a hand.

'Father Marcelin please, tell him. He means what he says. He will kill these women if you do not.'

Marcelin looked at Stein and held his gaze as he spoke.

'He has gone to Rouen. That is all I know.'

Stein nodded with relief. 'Thank you.'

Wolff put his finger on Marcelin's chin and turned the old man's eyes to face his own.

'You see Father, how easy that was.' He smiled.

Wolff turned to Stein.

'Hauptmann Stein, go and round up the men, have them ready to leave for Rouen in thirty minutes. If they need, they can use the ablutions in the houses. Tell them to gather food and water, bring whatever they can carry. Find out where we can get fuel for the truck.'

He turned to the group of soldiers guarding the women.

'Bauchmann, Muller.'

Two of them shouldered their weapons and crossed the church and stood in front of Wolff.

'Take the priest into the cemetery and shoot him.'

The men stood to attention and looked nervously back at the SS officer.

'Wolff, these men are Panzer Grenadiers,' said Stein. 'Not an SS firing squad. And the priest, why kill him? He's told us what he knows.'

Wolff turned to face the tank captain.

'Hauptmann Stein, if you continue to question my orders in front of the men, you and I are going to have a serious problem, understood? I will not be questioned on matters concerning the treatment of prisoners. Might I also remind you that this is an SS mission and as such these men *can* and *will* do as I have ordered them.'

Wolff turned back to the two soldiers.

'Take him.'

As they led Marcelin away the priest caught Stein's eye.

'I will pray for your family and for you.' He turned quickly to Wolff.

'And you Captain. I will pray for your soul.'

Wolff ignored him.

Stein left the church feeling desolate; his mind reeling in confusion and horror. He felt detached as though everything was happening too quickly and he was following like a child, attempting to keep up and make sense of it all. His disorientation was absolute and all consuming, and as he crossed the street and headed into the village square, he flinched as a volley of shots rang out from the churchyard.

CHAPTER FIVE
The Road to Rouen

They drove in silence.

Wellum was at the wheel, habitually scanning the sky while Brielle sat beside him, checking the mirrors and looking out over the fields as they went. As they left the town and headed south, they drove past farms and houses abandoned in haste and then on through villages where children stood on bombed and destroyed street corners under an iron grey sky and watched them.

The afternoon drew towards a pale, cold evening and they continued south for an hour before turning west and crossing the river Somme at Drueil-Les-Amiens. They rejoined the main road near Salouel.

'How far is it to Rouen?' Asked Wellum.

'From here, about one hundred and twenty kilometres.'

Wellum checked his watch. They would be there by six o'clock.

'We should stop for gas in Neufchatel, it's about an hour from here.'

'Will you buy me some cigarettes?' Asked Wellum. 'I've run out, and I seem to have forgot my wallet.'

Brielle smiled at him. 'Oui, of course.'

Wellum smiled back. 'Thank you.'

They saw nothing on the road and as dusk gathered, the atmosphere shifted. The steady thrum of the Citroen's engine and their leisurely pace drew them both in, softening the tension and relaxing their nerves. At Neufchatel-en-Bray they found a gas station and pulled off the road and parked by one of the pumps. Brielle got out and walked towards a man that came out of a kiosk. He wore overall's and boots with no laces and was wiping his hands on a rag as he hobbled towards them.

'Bonjour.'

'Bonjour madam.'

Wellum got out of the car and undid the petrol cap at the rear of the *Avent*. He leaned against the paintwork and watched Brielle walking back towards him, talking to the attendant.

'Bonjour.' Said the man as put the rag in his back pocket and took the pump handle and pushed the nozzle into the Citroen.

Wellum nodded at him and smiled. 'Bonjour.'

'Harry,' Brielle gestured to him with her head. 'Ici'

'Shouldn't we stay with the car?'

'No, it's ok. It's fine, come.'

The kiosk was small and most of the shelves were empty, but with luck they did have cigarettes. Brielle used ration tokens in exchange for the petrol then she removed a roll of bank notes from her pocket and paid the attendant for the cigarettes with those. She took two bottles of soda from an unplugged refrigerator and asked for a street atlas of Rouen. The attendant looked in a cupboard behind the till and found one, and Brielle handed him another crumpled note for the soda and the map and told him to keep the change. She handed a bottle to Wellum who was unwrapping the first box of cigarettes.

'We need to check the map and decide the best way into Rouen and also look at where we are going to meet your contact.'

It was almost dark and the sky was bruising to a blackening plum and it had turned cold. They got back into the car and Wellum started the engine and turned on the heater. He sucked on his cigarette and cracked the window open an inch and blew smoke out into the night. Brielle unfolded the map and switched on the small light above the rear view mirror. She put her finger on a road and followed it. Wellum watched her in the soft glow of the cabin light.

She was whispering to herself.

'Je pense que nous allons entrer sur cette route ici…'

She pushed her hair behind her ear with a finger and pointed at the map. She looked up at Wellum.

'What is the name of the place we are meeting your colleague?'

Wellum looked at her face. Her brown eyes were deep and dark, half caught beneath the shadow of her long black lashes and he looked at her small chin, the curve of her face.

'Harry, which street?'

Wellum looked at the map.

'We're to meet at a Brasserie called *La Petit Savoie*. It's in the old part of the city apparently, on the Rue du Montparnasse, near the cathedral.'

Brielle slid her finger, tracing a circle in the centre of the map. She mouthed the words...

'Du Montparnasse...Montparnasse.'

Wellum caught himself looking at her mouth.

'Ah, here it is.' She tapped the map. 'Just off the Rue de Tivoli.'

She looked towards the southern border of Rouen.

'I think if we go around the edges of the city to here.' She pointed at a main road running into town from the east. 'We can come in through these quieter streets and hopefully make our way unseen to the Brasserie from there.'

Wellum looked at the route. He nodded, 'alright, that sounds good.'

Brielle folded the map and put it in the glove box and Wellum finished his cigarette and dropped the filter out of the window. He put the car in gear and checked the road and pulled out and drove away.

Brielle picked up one of the bottles of soda and unscrewed the lid and took a drink. She held the bottle towards Wellum. He glanced at it as he drove.

'What flavour is it?'

She checked the label, squinting at it in the dark.

'Cherry, I think.'

Wellum took it from her and inspected it.'

Brielle watched him.

'What difference does it make?'

'What?'

'The flavour. What difference does it make? It's soda. Everybody likes soda.'

Wellum took two large mouthfuls and handed back the bottle.

'That's blackcurrant.'

She looked at the bottle again, tilting the label towards the window and the moving street lamps, beating past in a yellow, rhythmic pulse.

'Ah, oui. You're right.' She read the label aloud. '*Cassis*.' She took another drink and screwed the top back on the bottle and dropped it onto the back seat.

They drove on in silence once more. Eventually Wellum opened his window an inch and fished another cigarette from its packet. He put it in his mouth.

'Do you like being a pilot?'

Wellum thought for a moment, then lit his cigarette.

'Yes, I do.'

'Have you been in many battles?'

'Yes.'

'How many?'

'You wouldn't believe me if I told you.'

'Come on, how many?'

Wellum shrugged.

'It's hard to say really.' He pushed out a thin smile.

'Have you killed many Germans?'

'I stopped counting when I reached twenty-five.' He lied.

'Do you miss it?'

'Combat?'

'Oui, now that you take photographs.'

'Not really. I miss the comradeship of the early days, of feeling like we were the only thing standing between the

Nazis and the lives of our families and our nation's future. But I don't miss the killing or the fear or the exhaustion.'

'You were frightened often?'

'All the time. It never left me, I just learned to live with it. The constant fear that at any time, on this day or the next or the next, I might die.'

Brielle turned and looked out of the window.

'I know that feeling too. It keeps me locked away, everyday. Like my life is waiting for me somewhere,' she paused then turned to face him. '...Somewhere beyond me, that I cannot reach. Like I am hiding from the fear and from death, but that each day I become more dead than alive, living like this.'

She looked at him, though he kept his eyes on the road ahead.

'You understand that feeling, don't you?'

Wellum nodded.

'Yes, I understand how that feels.'

When they were fifteen kilometres from Rouen, Brielle suddenly sat up in her seat and peered into the car's side mirror.

'What is it?' Said Wellum, shaking himself awake from thought and checking his own mirror.

'It looks like a motorcycle.'

The single light following along behind caught them quickly, and was soon close enough that they could hear the sound of its engine. Wellum peered into his mirror again.

'It's a Wehrmacht motorcycle and sidecar, probably a patrol.'

The bike pulled alongside them and the soldier in the sidecar gestured for them to pull over.

'What's the plan?' Said Wellum keeping his eyes fixed forwards.

'There,' said Brielle, pointing a little further ahead. 'Those trees, pull over near them. We'll deal with them there.'

'Deal with them? You mean kill them?'

'Yes, it's a quiet enough road, I doubt we'll be seen or heard.'

'Shouldn't we try the identification papers first?'

Brielle had slipped her hand beneath her coat and was already discreetly cocking the MAS.

'What? And put up with a lot of pointless questions and risk getting arrested or worse?'

She looked at him. 'Besides we are at war remember, and they are the enemy, so it is our duty.'

Wellum nodded. 'Alright.'

Brielle checked the road behind was clear.

'Pull over and hand them your identity papers I'll get out and kill whichever one stays with the motorcycle, if you can manage it you kill the one that comes round to your side of the car.'

Wellum flicked on the indicator and started pulling over to the side of the road. As the car rolled to a halt and the motorcycle pulled up behind them, he took the identification papers from his pocket and threw the cloth cap onto his head.

The rider turned off the engine and climbed off the bike, his boots crunching gravel in the cold evening air as he walked towards them. He removed his gauntlets and strolled casually around to the driver's window and tapped it with a knuckle as his passenger switched on a spotlight attached to the sidecar and illuminated the scene. Wellum wound down his window and looked at the German.

'Bonjour,' said the soldier leaning forward and glancing into the vehicle. He scanned the back seat and noted the provisions.

'Puis-je vous demander ou vous allez? Where are you going please?'

'Rouen,' said Wellum flatly as Brielle opened the car door and began climbing out. The soldier in the side-car swivelled the light towards her.

'You, stand still.'

The other German beckoned to Wellum with his finger. 'Your identification papers.'

Wellum handed him the folded sheet and as the soldier opened it and turned it towards the light for inspection, Brielle swung the MAS up from the folds of her overcoat and took a step forwards and fired a deafening burst into the man in the sidecar. As she did, Wellum reached for his pistol and drew it and fired twice at the soldier stood at his door. The German crumpled soundlessly, collapsing vertically onto his haunches before rolling onto his back. A dark, puckering hole in one cheek just below another that spurted black blood from his temple. Brielle took another step forward and fired a second short burst into the sidecar. The whole incident had lasted no more than ten seconds and two soldiers lay dead beneath thin layers of gunsmoke that hung in the air like ghosts.

Wellum stepped out of the car and re-holstered his pistol. He stood for a moment and looked down at the dead German at his feet. Brielle unclipped the MAS and opened the passenger door and put it in the footwell and closed the door.

'We need to move them off the road.'

Together they lifted the rider and carried him into a small wooded area some fifteen yards from the road. They dumped him near some bushes and went back for the bike and pushed it into the trees. Brielle crouched over the bodies and began searching them.

'Here,' she handed Wellum some cigarettes and a few bloodstained bank notes and some change. 'You have these.'

Once she had searched both men, she took their weapons and headed quickly back to the car.

'Come on,' she said. 'We had better get going. Don't forget to pick up your empty cartridge cases.'

She threw the soldier's weapons into the boot of the Citroen and climbed back into the passenger seat. She checked the breach on the MAS and re-clipped it to the harness under her coat. Wellum got in and started the engine.

'Are you alright?' She said as they pulled away. Wellum looked at her and gave a small smile.

'Yes, are you?'

She looked steadily back at him.

'Oui, yes of course. Here…' she smiled and licked her thumb and rubbed his cheek.

'You have blood on your face.'

The windscreen wipers slicked back and forth, clearing the window of the pouring rain as they sat parked in a side street watching the door of the brasserie. Wellum looked at his watch.

'What time is it?' Asked Brielle.

'Just after seven.'

They sat and watched the door.

They had entered Rouen as the rain started, making their way carefully along deserted roads to the central, oldest part of the city where narrow streets, some no wider than alleyways, wound themselves into a maze of cobbled, frozen time. Buildings four and five hundred years old, made of timber and ancient stone survived in huddled groups that leaned in and over, creating a labyrinth of tunnels where people lived and drank and ate and mourned. On the outskirts of the city, destruction reigned. Collapsed buildings, burnt vehicles and shattered roads lay gouged and broken from the German occupation and months of allied bombing. Many Rouenaise had fled out into the countryside to lodge with uncles and distant cousins, but those that stayed had moved closer to the river and the cathedral, into the old town, which despite all odds was still standing.

The streets were quiet, mostly on account of the weather which now drummed on the roof of the Citroen with a fat, soothing relentlessness.

The wipers slicked across the glass.

They had talked very little since the incident with the motorcycle patrol and Wellum felt tense and disturbed. He thought about Brielle and his willingness to follow her into action. She had understood immediately the urgency of the threat and she had dealt with it decisively and seemingly without emotion. He glanced across at her. She was looking at the restaurant through the rain, and he realised that if he stood any chance of getting back to England he would need her.

She looked too small to be his saviour.

'What time are you supposed to meet the contact?'

Wellum glanced at his watch again.

'I wasn't given a specific time, just as long as it was before nine.'

'Do you think he's already in there?'

'I suppose I'd better go and see.'

He took out his revolver and checked the cylinder. Four rounds left. He put the gun back in its holster.

'I'll be back shortly.'

As he moved to get out of the car Brielle put her hand on his arm.

'Harry be careful. If it looks like trouble, get out. We can always find another way.'

He tried a reassuring smile.

'Don't worry I'll be careful. Leave the engine running and if you sense any danger out here, you go. I'll be fine.' He touched her hand. 'Thank you Brielle.'

He got out and closed the door and she watched him cross the road, putting the cap on his head as he went, and as the wipers moved across the windscreen once more, he disappeared through the restaurant door.

Inside it was warm and the lighting was low. Wellum stood in the doorway for a moment and took off his hat and brushed away the rain and put it back on his head. He unbuttoned his jacket and looked around the room. Ahead there were three steps leading down into a bar, several round tables filled the room and at one end double doors led into a dining room. Wellum could see waiters moving between tables, talking quietly to customers as they delivered their food. He walked down the steps and approached the bar. There was a group of German sailors sat in a booth against one wall smoking and talking, their arms draped over local girls in loud makeup and fishnets. A few of the other tables had couples sat round them but the atmosphere was muted and subdued.

Wellum spotted a man sitting alone at a table. He was wearing a white shirt, open at the neck and his dark hair was pushed back on his head and shone with oil. He smoked a cigarette and occasionally took his eyes from the book he was reading and tapped ash into an ashtray. He didn't look at Wellum as the pilot approached the bar and stood waiting to be served. A bartender with drooping eyelids came over and wiped down the counter with a towel. He lifted his chin,

'Oui?'

'Vodka martini, deux olives s'il vous plait.'

The man at the table turned the page of his book.

'Merci,' said Wellum as he span a crumpled note onto the bar. The barman took it and rang it into the till and passed over some change.

'De rien.'

Wellum turned and looked into the room and took a drink, it tasted bitter and strong, but the warmth against his tongue felt good. As he lowered his glass he noticed that Proust lay abandoned on the table in front of him, face down, its pages splayed out and its cracked spine announcing that it was, *in search of lost time*. The man at the table was looking blankly at him and smoking. Wellum pulled out one of the chairs.

'Attendez-vous quelqu'un? Puis-je m'asseoir?'

The man picked up his book and closed it.

'J'attends un collègue de la bibliothèque. Asseoir.'

Wellum sat down.

'Quel est votre nom?'

'Mes amis m'appellent, *Firefly*.'

Armada nodded and looked at Wellum. The sailors got up and began making their way in couples towards the door. Wellum tensed slightly and sipped his martini unconvincingly as he watched them leave. Once the door closed behind them he relaxed into his chair.

'Where did you get those clothes?'

Wellum glanced down at himself.

'A priest in a village gave them to me.'

'You look like a peasant farmer.'

'Well, I've been trying my best to blend in.' He smiled.

Armada sighed and sat back in his chair. He looked at Wellum and smoked.

'What?'

The SOE agent had a mysterious, aristocratic air about him. He was handsome in an angular, chiselled way but he looked gaunt and underfed. He glanced towards the dining room and sat forward. He put his hand close to his mouth as if to suck on his cigarette but instead hissed out a whisper.

'Why have you been sent?'

Wellum leant forward, his elbows on the table.

'What do you mean, sent? I was told you can help me.'

'Who by?'

Wellum looked confused.

'You know who by.' He said quietly. 'By London Station. The people that contacted you.'

'I know that,' hissed Armada. 'But I mean who *specifically?*'

Wellum looked back at him, unsure of how to answer. After a moment he replied.

'Why do you need to know that?'

'That's none of your business, but I insist you tell me exactly who it was that sent you here, and why.'

Wellum took another pause then lowered his voice to a hoarse whisper.

'I'm not going to discuss who or why in here, alright. I was told you were going to help me get back to England, that's all, and if it's all the same to you I think we should get on. I've had a pretty eventful forty-eight hours and I need some food and a decent cup of tea. Now, are you going to follow your orders and help me or not?'

'Just so we're clear, I don't usually take *those* sort of orders. Not from you and certainly not from the faceless bureaucrats in London.'

'So, what is it?' Said Wellum sitting back in his chair. 'You just do your own thing out here?'

'Pretty much, yes. At least I would if those interfering sods back home would leave me to get on with it.'

Armada crushed out his cigarette and considered Wellum through a squint.

'Have you got any kit?'

'Not really. Not what you could exactly could call *kit*, no.' He gestured to his outfit. 'I've got these clothes and my flying jacket, but that's outside in the car.'

'Car? What car?'

'I stole a Citroen, in Varennes.'

'Jesus Christ.'

'Don't worry, it was abandoned, I doubt anyone is looking for it.'

'Right, well it's staying where it is.'

'What if we need a car?'

'I can get access to vehicles, don't worry. The last thing we need is for it to be reported and spotted anywhere near us. Besides, if push comes to shove, you can always re-steal it cant you.'

Wellum looked less than convinced. He didn't like the idea of not having immediate access to transport.

'What did you bring with you from Varennes apart from your flying jacket and a bloody stolen car?'

'A little food, some weapons…and a girl.'

'A girl?'

'Well yes, a young woman.'

'Why on earth..?'

'She helped me. She's been with me since I arrived in Varennes and she got me access to a radio so I could contact London. She's connected to the Resistance and provided the food and weapons I mentioned.'

'Well, she's got you this far God bless her, but now she needs to fuck off back to Varennes at once.'

Wellum shook his head.

'No, she's staying.'

'What?'

'I said, she stays with me.'

'Look I'm sorry old chap, but whatever London told you about me, they gave you the wrong end of the stick. I don't do this sort of work, alright? I'm already fucking fuming about being handed this one, and now you tell me there are stolen vehicles and young women to deal with too. Are you fucking insane? I've been here for almost two years and my work is just beginning to bear fruit. London can't just expect me to drop everything and babysit you and any waif and stray that you've got tagging along just because you were bloody stupid enough to get yourself shot down.'

'Listen, Armada or whatever your name is. I think that if she goes back to Varennes she might be in danger. I think that my original contact in Lealvillers might have been compromised and the Germans may have been given information that leads them to Varennes. If that's true she can't go back there, not yet at least.'

'The Germans know you were in Lealvillers? Do you think they might be following you?'

'It's possible.'

'Oh, for fucks sake.'

'I'm sorry but that's the situation we're in alright. Now, the last time I looked we *both* fought on the same side and are *both* trying to do our bit to win this fucking war, so do me a favour and just help me get back to England as quickly as possible and you can carry on with whatever it was you were doing before I arrived.'

Wellum sat back in his chair and swallowed his drink and took out his own cigarettes and lit one. Armada watched him.

'Where did you get those?'

'What?'

'Those cigarettes, they're German.'

Wellum studied the packet in his hand before putting it back into his pocket.

'We, er we killed a couple of Wehrmacht soldiers about fifteen or so kilometres outside of the city, as we were coming here.'

Armada looked blankly back at him.

'What?'

'As we were driving here. They pulled us over and tried to question us so we killed them and hid their bodies a short distance from the road. I took their cigarettes and a little money.'

They sat looking at each other. Eventually Armada sat forward in his chair and covering one side of his mouth he whispered at Wellum.

'Alright, listen to me carefully. I have some room at the house I'm using, close to here. You and the girl can stay - *but*, you will do as you are told and keep out of sight. I'll see what I can do about getting you as far as Le Havre or better still Deauville, but from there it's on you and your *secret* London contact to get you back to England - understand? I was serious when I said I've got a job to do here and I'll be buggered if I'm going to let you and this French filly fuck it all up.'

Wellum nodded. 'Fine.'

The agent checked his watch and collected his cigarettes and his book from the table.

'You leave before me. Where's the car?'

'Just across the road, in a side street.'

'Can you see the restaurant from where it's parked?'

'Yes.'

'Alright. Go and get your things and when you see me leave, you and the girl follow along on foot. Make sure you keep a bit of a distance back so it doesn't look like we're together.'

Wellum stood up.

'And if we do pass any Germans,' Armada continued dryly. 'Do try and resist the urge to shoot them in the street.'

Outside it was still raining.

Wellum came out of the restaurant and cast a look around and walked quickly over to the car. He opened the door and got in and took off the cap and threw it onto the dashboard.

'So?' Said Brielle. 'What's he like? Will he help you?'

'He's a tad reluctant to say the least, but he said he'll hide us for a few days and then try to get me to the coast. Le Havre or some other harbour town. He said we're to leave the car and when he comes out, we're to follow him on foot. Apparently he has a house nearby.'

'You trust him?'

'Well, he's a bit prickly. But he's English and he's SOE So I suppose there's no reason to not trust him.' Wellum gestured towards the brasserie.

'There he is now. Come on, let's go.' He got out of the car and opened the back door and reached in and took out one of the bags and handed it to Brielle, then he took out the other and threw it over his shoulder and closed the door.

'Does he know about me?' Asked Brielle as they made their way across the road. Wellum glanced at her.

'I did mention you, yes.'

'What did he say?'

'He said you should go back to Varennes.'

Wellum spotted Armada about fifty yards ahead of them. He was walking casually, as if taking an evening stroll among the puddles and Wellum suddenly realised how out of place his own urgent stride must look. He tried to relax.

'Let's slow down a bit. As long as we keep him in sight we'll be alright.'

Brielle looked ahead and then instinctively checked behind them. She readjusted the bag on her shoulder with a shrug and slowed her pace.

'Do you want me to go back? To Varennes?'

'I don't know,' said Wellum. 'You said you'd help get me to Rouen and contact Armada and I'm very grateful that you have. But now you're here, I'm not sure I want you to leave just yet.'

She looked up at him as he walked beside her, his eyes never leaving the agent ahead.

'Well, then I'll stay.'

Wellum gave her a quick look and smiled thinly.

'Just until we know we can trust your new English friend.'

CHAPTER SIX
Armada

They waited for five minutes, sheltering from the weather under the awning of a shop with boarded windows. Armada had disappeared into a house on a street called Rue Etoupee, which was little more than a wide, cobbled alleyway. The rain poured noisily from its twisted ancient gutters, down onto the wet road and away, while overhead aeroplanes crawled eastwards by the hundred. Above the clouds the hypnotic sound of their engines sounded like the mournful droning of wyverns scavenging the night for souls and delivering them to hell. Wellum looked up into the blackness and listened.

A torchlight suddenly flashed in a window through the rain; a signal from Armada to approach.

They entered through a side door into a dark hallway and were ushered upstairs by Armada's voice calling to them from above.

'Up here, mind your step.'

They climbed the staircase, straight into a kitchen. Armada was taking off his coat. He hung it from a hook on the back of a door and turned to face them as they entered the room. He looked at Brielle and then at Wellum.

'Well, this is a fine pickle isn't it.' He crossed the room and picked up the kettle and filled it and put it on the stove as the two new arrivals stood awkwardly in the doorway and watched. He lit the gas with a match and shook it out and dropped it in an ashtray that was sitting on the table.

They were silent.

The sound of rain running down the guttering outside only added to the bleakness. Brielle thought the house felt cold and unwelcoming.

'I've lived here for eighteen months, or there about,' said Armada, reading their mood. 'It used to be owned by a Jewish family, but I never found out who they were.' He went to a cupboard and took out three cups and filled a teapot with leaves from a dented tea caddy. When he pulled off the lid, the sound made Wellum think of England. - Silly really.

'I have all of the downstairs rooms rigged with explosives that I can detonate from up here on a ten minute timer in case I'm discovered. Once the timers dissolve there's enough P4 to blow half the street away.' He looked at them both. 'But hopefully it'll never come to that. I'll show you how to arm it and how to detonate it, should you need to.'

The kettle began to whistle. Armada took it from the stove and poured boiling water over tea leaves. He put the lid on the teapot and carried it to the table and gestured for them to sit.

'I don't have much here,' he went on. 'And I haven't cleaned the place since I moved in. If I use a thing, I put it back where it belongs. I'd appreciate it if you'd do the same. I don't have time for housework.'

He went to a large white refrigerator and collected a bottle of milk. There was nothing else in it except for a plate, over which lay another plate mated to the first; a leftover meal yet to be eaten. He came back and poured tea through a wire strainer into each cup. He looked at Brielle as he did it.

'Do you like English tea?'

'Yes, thank you,' she said through a muted smile, then after a pause she asked. 'You said the house belonged to a jewish family. You said you never found out who they were, but do you know where they went or what happened to them?'

'Apparently, when the Germans first arrived here in Rouen in nineteen-forty, they incited several pogroms to round up any jews. The family that lived here managed to avoid detection until at least December of nineteen-forty-one, but after that they were gone. The SOE Have been using the house since January 'forty-two. I arrived in April.' He placed a cup in front of each of them and sat down.

Wellum glanced at Brielle. She was looking around the kitchen as Armada spoke.

'So these things, everything, the plates and cups and pans...everything, they all belonged to that family?'

Armada nodded.

'Yes. I live a pretty simple life. Like an ascetic some might say. I don't really own anything here, a few personal items but that's it. I find my life more manageable the less clutter I acquire.'

'What have you been doing since you arrived?' asked Wellum, knowing he probably wouldn't get an answer. He wanted to move the subject away from the vanished family.

Armada took a cigarette and offered the packet to Brielle and then to Wellum. She shook her head. Armada looked carefully at her between several strands of dark hair that had fallen forward during his walk home from *La Petit Savoie*.

'What's your name?' he asked, lighting his cigarette and ignoring Wellum's question.

'Brielle Du…'

'Brielle will do,' he interrupted her, blowing out smoke.

He looked at Wellum.

'And what about you? I can't exactly call you Firefly each time I refer to you can I?'

'My name's Harry.'

Armada nodded. 'That's better, I'll call you Harry then. It's nondescript enough.'

'And what about you?' Said Wellum lighting his own cigarette. He took a sip of tea.

'What do we call you?'

Armada looked at him.

'Who sent you Harry?'

Wellum smiled in feigned confusion and tapped his cigarette at the ashtray. He crossed his legs and looked at the agent.

'I've already told you. No one *sent* me. I was shot down, made my way to Varennes, contacted London and they told me to come here.'

Armada studied him for a minute more and then looked at Brielle.

'Harry here tells me you're connected to the Resistance.'

Brielle nodded slowly.

'In Varennes?'

'Oui. And further to the north. In a village near Miraumont.'

'Do you know any of the Resistance here in Rouen?'

She shook her head.

'No. I met some Maquis last year, that had fought near here and were living in some woods between Rouen and Amiens but I never stayed in contact with them.'

'What's the situation here with German troops?' Wellum asked.

'What do you mean?'

'I mean are there many soldiers here in the city, are we likely to be stopped on the street?'

'Luckily, there aren't many at the moment, no. There were lots at the beginning of the occupation but the allied bombing has frightened a lot of them away - little wonder. There's a naval base, south-east of the river, and there are lots of sailors there. U-boat crews too. They tend to come into the town at weekends or when their ships are being serviced and rearmed.'

'Do they behave?'

'When they're out on the town? Yes, for the most part. There's a Waffen SS camp about twenty kilometres south. When they're about the naval ratings tend to keep themselves to themselves. Or if the Gestapo are visiting, that tends to keep everyone in line.'

He looked again at Wellum's disguise.

'You'll definitely need spare clothes and I'm guessing a passable identification card. I'll get onto that first thing tomorrow.'

Armada gestured to their bags.

'What's in those?'

Brielle stood up and collected the bags and brought them to the table. She opened the first and handed it to Armada. He peered inside and began fishing out items and stacking them on the table.

'Well, this is quite the travelling pantry.'

He lifted out some tins and peered at the white labels glued to each of them.

'*Schmalzfleisch*,' he read aloud. 'And, *Truthahnbraten*?' He put them down and went dipping once more. 'German ration pack chocolate and coffee too?' He held up the small bars and packets and read the labels. 'Is everything here stolen from the German army?'

'Not everything, no.' Said Brielle.

After he'd looked over their weapons he pointed to everything now sitting on the table.

'This lot should last you for the duration of your stay. You can use the kitchen down here to prepare stuff, but I'd prefer it if you could stow your gear and eat upstairs if that's alright.' He pointed at a door that led out of the kitchen. 'I'm in these rooms here, and if it's all the same I'd prefer to keep things separate.'

'Of course,' said Wellum, with a sense of relief. 'No problem.'

'There's a bedroom upstairs and there's also a working bathroom you'll be glad to hear. If you want hot water though you'll have to boil it down here I'm afraid, though there is a small shower that I managed to get working.'

'We'll be fine,' said Wellum. He checked his watch. 'I ought to contact London and tell them I've arrived.'

Armada paused as if contemplating them for the final time.

'Right,' he said after a while. He stood up and carried the teapot over to the sink.

'We'll get on the radio and see if anyone at London Station is still awake.'

'I'll go up and take the bags,' said Brielle, putting the weapons and rations away.

'I'll be up soon.' Said Wellum, wincing at his own awkwardness, he could feel Armada looking at him.

She glanced at him and then at Armada as she shouldered the bags. She pointed at another door at the back of the kitchen. 'Is it this way?'

Armada nodded and turned away. 'Yes, there's a light switch at the top of the stairs.'

Wellum watched her go and as Brielle closed the door Armada whistled.

'I'd say you got lucky there old chap - goodness me.'

'Where's the radio?' replied Wellum, ignoring the insinuation. Armada curled out a smile.

'Through here.' He pointed to one of the doors leading out of the kitchen.

Wellum followed him through the door and into what appeared to be the family dining room. An oval table sat in the middle of the room, around which were placed four chairs. The table was entirely covered in maps and notebooks, some of which lay open alongside others that were folded and stacked in piles, surrounded by remnants of the family life that had once filled the house. Ornaments were everywhere and photographs in frames hung on the walls and stared down at them from the past and there was a sideboard on which a fine crystal decanter and glasses stood on a polished silver tray. Wellum looked at them, so out of place among the other items that were now piled up on the carpet or shoved untidily onto every available surface the room could provide. Several automatic rifles were leant against one wall, and next to the decanter on its tray was a collection of pistols, their loaded magazines lying next to to them in readiness. There was an ornate fruit bowl filled with hand grenades and what looked like more than ten boxes of army rations were stacked up against another wall. A radio sat on a table and next to that was a cot that was obviously Armada's neatly made bed. The whole room rang with gun-oil.

'This is where you initiate the explosive charges rigged on the first floor.'

Wellum walked over and looked to where Armada was pointing at a black box siting alone on the floor in one corner of the room.

'Just turn the key, and press that button.' He mimed turning the key clockwise and thumbing the raised, red disc. 'Then you've got ten minutes to get as far away as possible.

'Is there a failsafe or method of cancelling?

'No, not once you press the button.'

'Is that the only key?' Asked Wellum.

'No,' said Armada, taking the key out and putting it in his pocket. 'But this one's mine. It'll be here in position if I'm in the house but if I'm out it'll be with me. There's a spare in the safe.'

'Where's that?'

'Beneath the stairs, in a cupboard, I'll show you shortly. The code for the safe is twenty-two, fifty-five. Don't ask me why.'

Wellum pointed at the radio.

'Standard type 3, mark 2 field-radio,' said Armada, pulling out a chair and sitting down. 'I'm only authorised to burst messages though. The Germans are getting too good at tracking and pinpointing long radio transmissions so we'll have to use code and keep it brief.' He switched the radio on and tuned a dial on the front, then he put on a headset and grabbed a pencil and notepad from a drawer. He looked at Wellum.

'We're just reporting in for now yes? Telling them that you and the girl are here and awaiting further instructions.'

'Yes, fine,' said Wellum.

Armada turned and faced the radio and started keying the morse handset with quick, jabbing movements.

'I don't think we need bother telling them about your dead German patrol now do we?'

He punched out more of the message.

'Save that for your debriefing back home eh?'

Armada finished sending the report and scribbled on the notepad as London beeped out its reply. He switched off the radio and hung up the headset then turned to face Wellum.

'All sent.'

'Anything I need to know?'

Armada shook his head.

'Not at this stage, no. I suggested that if I can expedite the whole thing by using any of my local contacts they ought to agree.'

'And did they?'

'Reluctantly, yes.'

'So come on, now we're alone, what *are* you doing out here?' Said Wellum looking at the weapons, standing to attention against the wall.

Armada squinted at him.

'What do you know about S.O.E. Operations Harry? I mean, what's the talk back home?'

'Not much really. We know you're out here doing a bloody hard job, and I suppose in my naivety you might say, I imagined it was all blowing up bridges and spying on the Germans but we don't get to hear much. I expect it's all pretty hush-hush isn't it?'

'Exactly,' beamed Armada. He went to the table and began folding up the open maps and stacking them on top of the others.

'And that's the way it ought to stay, wouldn't you agree?'

'Yes, of course,' conceded Wellum. 'I was just curious, that's all.'

'To be honest, the first twelve months were pretty tedious, being out here on my own doing very little except 'blending in' as it were. I thought I was going bloody crackers at one point, but then things started moving.'

'So you're busier now?'

Armada smiled at him.

'Yes, a lot busier.' He paused for effect. 'And that's why this has all come at a pretty inconvenient time.'

'I can only apologise,' replied Wellum, dryly. 'Trust me, the sooner I can be back home and out of your hair the better.'

Armada nodded towards the door.

'What, and leave her behind? Or are you planning on hiding her in your pocket?'

Wellum shook his head.

'I really have no idea what you're talking about.'

'Right,' said Armada somewhat sceptically. 'Whatever you say…Well, I've got an early start. You'll be alright here. The Germans don't tend to do house to house searches these days and my advice would be just sit tight and twiddle your fingers until London have come up with a way to get you out of here.'

'Or until you come up with something first?'

'Yes, that too. There's a spare front door key in the kitchen, I'll give you that now.'

'Thank you. Really…I do appreciate you helping me.'

'Bloody orders.' Said Armada with a grim smile. 'Come on, let's get you that key.'

At the top of the stairs, a single lightbulb swayed back and forth on a black flex and fizzed with a weak orange glow, barely illuminating the two doors that stood facing each other across the narrow landing. A draft whistled up the staircase and the whole house seemed to moan as the wind and the rain buffeted the shutters outside. It blew up past wellum as he climbed, and it circled the landing like a ghost, disturbing the cobwebs that clung to the age-old beams and rattling the window frames on their hinges.

He could see a soft light beneath one of the doors and he knocked and waited.

Brielle opened the door and peered out. She saw it was Wellum and turned and went back into the room, allowing the door to open behind her as she went.

He followed her inside and looked around the room. There was a wardrobe and dressing table against one wall and a lamp on top of a bedside table. Brielle was sitting on the bed and looking into the open wardrobe. Wellum noticed that she was sitting on a bare mattress.

'There aren't any bedclothes,' said Brielle. She reached forward into the wardrobe and held the sleeve of one of the dresses hanging inside. She ran her fingers against the fabric.

'I thought we could use these, to sleep beneath, instead of bedsheets, but now I'm not sure.'

Wellum closed and locked the bedroom door and came and stood beside her. He looked into the wardrobe and then at the mattress. It's pale blue stripes and exposed buttons looked cold and uninviting.

'He's like a worm, living inside an apple,' said Brielle as she stroked the various dresses and shirts. 'Like a parasite, living inside a dead thing.'

Wellum looked at her.

'He's just doing his job. Like all of us.'

'I know that. I just don't trust him somehow, that's all. Happily living here inside this house, alongside these ghosts.' She wafted the clothes with a palm. 'The house...don't you think it feels haunted? Like the family are still here.' She lifted the arm of a blouse and closed her eyes and sniffed the wrist; The sweet smell of *Patou* still clinging to the fabric

'Like, they're still alive, but hidden somewhere, close by.'

Wellum wanted to touch her shoulder, but didn't. Instead, he spoke quietly,

'They might be alive, somewhere. Armada said he never knew who they were.'

Brielle stroked her face with the sleeve of the blouse, her eyes still closed.

'No, they are all dead. *Pour aux, la douleur set finie.*'

'You can't know that Brielle.'

She opened her eyes and looked at him.

'Believe me Harry, if the Germans took them, they are dead.'

'Don't say that. You can't give up hope - not yet. You're too young. There will be those that have survived, like you. And you need to be here to bring them home when all this is over. The children without parents and the widows and mothers in mourning, the fathers without daughters. Because this will all end, and you will all need each other when it does.'

'I am tired of just surviving Harry. Of having to cling to hope, blindly, day after day. You say it will end but when…when?

'I don't know.'

She turned away and closed the wardrobe door and locked it.

The rain beat on the shutters and the wind whistled outside on the landing. Up the stairs it blew, and the house moved and creaked its aching old joints.

The lamp beside the bed dimmed and dragged shadows towards them from the corners of the room then pulsed and came back. It hummed to them.

Brielle wrapped her arms around herself.

'I'm cold.'

'Come on,' said Wellum. 'Lie down.' He picked up his flying jacket and rolled it into a makeshift pillow. He put it on the mattress and Brielle lay her head on it and closed her eyes.

'Merci,' she whispered. Wellum unlocked the wardrobe and carefully covered her with dresses and blouses and skirts, all manner of colours, but muted to hues of deep purple or brown by the humming, orange lamplight.

He looked at her for a long time, then he walked around the bed and lay down and pulled an overcoat up over his legs and threw a jacket across his chest.

He listened to the rain running down the roof then through the ancient guttering that ran around the old house like bones worn on the outside, and he thought about the family who's breath had once moved the springs on this bed and who's bones had once filled the clothes lying heavily upon him now, and he wondered where they were tonight. Were they somewhere safe? Somewhere hidden, like him. Or were they dead? Their bodies being mined from some shallow scrape by the rain beating down, opening their graves to be seen and condemned.

To be mourned?

Brielle was right to despair, Wellum thought.

He looked at her and reached out and touched the back of her hand lightly with his finger, tracing over one of her small, dry knuckles, then he closed his eyes and listened to the rain and tried to sleep.

CHAPTER SEVEN

The Chateau of the Black Swan

Stein woke up with a jolt.

The truck had stopped. He peered out of the windscreen, past the idling engine through the rain. Wolff's Mercedes was parked at a checkpoint just ahead, and there was a soldier leaning forward talking to the SS officer through the rear passenger window. Stein, rubbed the corner of one eye and looked again. There was another guard standing beside a sentry box, a lantern glowing softly in its window. He had a dog tethered to a short leash, it's breath billowing up in rolling clouds and it's tongue lolling forward as it stood and watched the Mercedes.

'Where are we?' Said Stein.

The driver gestured through the glass.

'Sentry point Sir.'

They were siting on a narrow road with countless trees amassed in phalanx rows on either side.

Stein checked his watch.

'Are we near Rouen?'

When All The Birds Leap

'Yes Sir. We're actually just a few kilometres north of the city.'

The guard talking to Wolff turned and spoke to his colleague, then went around the car and lifted the barrier. He saluted smartly as the staff car rolled forward. The truck driver put the truck in gear and Stein lifted a tired salute as the guard eyed him. Stein watched in the mirror as the soldier lowered the gate, glancing at the convoy as it drove away before walking back to the guardhouse and going inside.

A few hundred yards later the road turned a gentle curve to the right and emerged into a courtyard lit with floodlights. The beams crossed and met on the front of a large chateau, gothic and austere, it's dark grey roof wore turrets crowned with battlements on either end and a spire rose from its centre reaching up towards the night, its pinnacle crowned with a flagpole running a huge red flag emblazoned with a black swastika.

There was a grand stairway leading up to a veranda where ornate doors, glazed with stained glass stood guarded by more soldiers armed with machine guns. Their iron helmets shone with the rain and rivers ran from their slick ponchos down onto their boots. They stood deathly still, like carven sentinels, silent and forbidding. Stein saw that there were more guards, similarly armed and adorned, patrolling with dogs towards the edges of the floodlit courtyard. One of the Alsatians began barking at the Mercedes and the lorry, its handler straining on its leash and talking to it as the dog pulled and urged towards them on its hind legs.

As Wolff's car rolled slowly to a stop in front of the building, a butler came down the steps carrying an umbrella. He opened Wolff's door and sheltered the officer as he emerged from the Mercedes. Wolff straightened his tunic and put on his hat and turning to face the truck, beckoned for Stein to join him.

'Captain Stein, please follow me,' said Wolff as Stein walked towards him through the rain.

'What about the men?'

'They can wait here, we won't be long.'

Stein turned and slashed his thumb across his throat at the truck driver as an indication to turn off the engine. He pointed at the truck and then at the ground.

'Wait here.'

Inside they entered a grand hallway and a warm, languid atmosphere enveloped them as the stained glass doors closed on the night and Stein felt his boots cushioned on the rich, Rococo carpet. He suddenly became self conscious and gave his chin a rub. He'd been awake and on the road for almost twenty-hours, and his stubble felt rough and coarse against his knuckle.

The butler asked them to wait, nodding with well practice cordiality as he collected their overcoats.

Wolff clicked his heels and nodded back.

'What is this place?' Asked Stein as Wolff looked at himself in a mirror, adjusting his collar and running his fingers through his hair. He still looked immaculate. He turned to face Stein.

'This Captain Stein, is *Chateau du Cygne noir,*'

'The Chateau what?'

'The *Chateau of the Black Swan.*'

'Why are we here?'

'I thought this would be a suitable place for us to stay while we search Rouen for the pilot.'

Stein looked around the exquisite hall, a marble staircase at one end climbing and dividing in two, leading off east and west towards both wings of the house. A crystal chandelier hung dramatically above their heads, lit with a hundred glittering candles that illuminated the hall with a dreamlike candescence and revealed in flickers the paintings and tapestries that were hanging from every wall.

'You've been here before?'

'I have been known to pass through, yes. The navy has a headquarters here and many of their officers use the chateau as accommodation. There are also senior SS that come and go and occasionally, agents of the Gestapo.'

'The Gestapo?'

Wolff smiled and nodded.

'Occasionally, yes. There are often operational meetings held here in the ballroom and the Fuhrer himself almost visited last year. There are barracks in the grounds where the men can billet. Do not worry Captain, we will be well looked after for the duration of our stay, and we may also find some useful contacts that might help us to track down and apprehend our quarry.'

He patted Stein on the shoulder as a deep voice barrelled from a doorway on their left.

'Ah Wolff, you scoundrel, what are you doing here uninvited eh?' The sound of Bach played upon violins drifted around the SS officer that was stood with his arms outstretched in welcome.

Wolff turned and smiled and the two men crossed the hall, meeting in the middle, each one taking the others hand in enthusiastic greeting.

'Herr Colonel,' said Wolff. 'I hope my impromptu visit has not put you to any inconvenience.'

'Not at all Haupsturmfuhrer, not at all. It is excellent to see you again.' He glanced over Wolff's shoulder at Stein. The panzer captain felt more self-conscious than ever. Wolff followed the colonel's eyes and turned and beckoned Stein forward, like a child expected to meet his new headmaster on the first day of school.

'Captain Stein, allow me to introduce the officer that has been lucky enough to find himself running this particular facility for the last two years. SS Colonel Heinz Kruger.'

'Lucky?' Laughed Kruger holding out his hand to Stein. 'Ansel, I've told you before, it has nothing to do with luck.'

'Whatever you say,' said Wolff with a grin. 'Colonel Kruger, this is Hauptmann Stein of the Tenth Panzer Division in Peronne,'

Stein looked at the face of the SS colonel. He was strikingly tall, slim and debonair but there was a hollow, almost gaunt look about the eyes, pale grey like his uniform and cold. He had a deep fencing scar running across his left cheek that pulled slightly at his lower eyelid, and his movements were surprisingly swift and elegant for such a big man. He took Stein's hand in his and shook it. His palm was warm and dry and his skin was deceptively soft.

'Colonel Kruger,' Stein clicked his heels and nodded. 'Please, forgive my appearance, it's been a long night.'

Kruger took a step back and looked Stein up and down, still smiling. After a moment he gave a slight chuckle.

'Yes, it would appear so, but never mind, come, let us sit together and we can talk.' He moved towards a door and gestured them inside before turning and addressing a butler that was standing obediently at the bottom of the stairs.

'Herr Langer, please go and find corporal Bohn and ask him to meet us in here.'

They could still hear the violins playing softly across the hall and the sound made Stein think of luxury and opulent wealth. Sitting awkwardly on a silk embroidered couch, he felt strange and detached, but he put it down to tiredness and tried to shake it off. A fire burnt hot in a wide hearth and as he sat he stared at the giant flames standing in constant moving blades and orange forks consuming the black logs piled in its heart. The heat was welcoming, but dragged him towards sleep.

'So, tell me.' Said Kruger sitting down in an armchair. 'What can I do for you gentlemen?'

Stein wanted to unbutton his tunic but didn't.

'We need some accommodation if that can be arranged,' said Wolff. 'Two officers, Captain Stein and myself. My driver, Schubert, and eleven Panzer Grenadiers that have been seconded to me, and who are currently categorised as Waffen troops.'

'How long for?' Asked Kruger.

'I'm not sure yet, at least a week, possibly longer.' said Wolff.

'Alright,' said Kruger. 'This shouldn't be too difficult to arrange. Where are the men?'

'They're outside, in a transport vehicle. Schubert is with my car.'

'Excuse me Sir,' Stein joined in. 'But, regarding my men, is there any possibility they can get some hot food tonight, and maybe a shower?' Wolff looked quickly at him, but Kruger seemed happy to oblige. The colonel checked his watch and was about to speak when there was a quick knock on the door and a young Waffen SS corporal entered the room and approached the group. He saluted smartly.

'Colonel Kruger sir, you sent for me.'

'Yes, Corporal Bhon. There are some men outside, in a truck, can you please take them down to one of the empty barrack blocks behind the east wing. I think D block is empty and has working showers. Once they're there fetch soap and towels, shaving kits and anything else they need.'

'Yes Herr Colonel.'

Kruger checked his watch again. It was getting late.

'Then go and speak to the kitchen and see if the cook can muster some hot food for them immediately. Tell him I personally sent you .'

The corporal saluted and left. Kruger turned back to Wolff.

'So, are you going to tell me what all this is about?'

'We're looking for a British pilot. A reconnaissance pilot. He was shot down north of Amiens, over some farmland, three days ago. The Luftwaffe saw him bail out and I was tasked with finding him. I contacted Captain Stein at his camp near Peronne and together we travelled with eleven of his men to apprehend the fugitive.'

'And you think he's in Rouen?'

'We do now yes. We found his aircraft at first light this morning and tracked his movements to a village called Lealvillers. After some persuasion the priest there told us that the man we are looking for travelled to Rouen at some time this afternoon.'

Stein looked at Wolff when he used the phrase, 'some persuasion,' but the SS ignored him. Stein looked back at Kruger and doubted he would care less about Wolff murdering Father Marcelin anyway.

Kruger nodded and smoked as Wolff briefed him. Eventually he looked at Stein.

'Would you like to add anything Captain?'

Stein thought for a moment.

'Not really sir, no.'

'How are your men coping with their new mission?'

'They, er, they seem quite…' he searched for the right words, his tiredness and his daylong proximity to Wolff was beginning to get the better of him. Kruger eyed him closely and waited for him to answer.

'…They seem to be growing into their task with enthusiasm sir.'

'Good,' said Kruger. 'Good.' He got up from the chair.

'Now, as wonderful as it is to see you again Ansel, I need to get back to my guests. I'll put Corporal Bhon at your disposal and my butler, Langer will see you to your rooms. If you need anything tonight - food, drink or whatever, please ask either of them. They are at your service.'

Wolff shook the colonel's hand.

'Thank you Sir. Perhaps we can have dinner tomorrow night and we can talk properly.'

Kruger nodded.

'Excellent, well, it's good to meet you Hauptmann Stein, I hope your stay will be fruitful.'

He clicked his heels and nodded.

'Gentleman, good evening.'

He turned and left. When he had gone, Stein said,

'I better go and check on the men.'

'Aren't you hungry?'

Stein was starving.

'Yes,' he said. 'I'm hungry.'

'I'll get Bohm to arrange for something to be brought to your room.'

Stein rubbed his chin.

'Thank you, could you also ask for some soap and a razor.'

'I'm sure that won't be a problem.'

Stein crossed the room, stopping by the door he turned around.

'What do we do next? About the pilot I mean.'

Wolff considered the question.

'I will arrange for you and the men to be roused at seven. After breakfast, which is always excellent here by the way, you and I will decide on the next phase of our task. I imagine a trip into Rouen would be useful, to familiarise ourselves with the city and then to make a plan of how best we can complete our objective. After that you and I will be having dinner with the colonel.'

Stein didn't relish the prospect.

'Alright. Well, I'll see you at some time after seven then.'

He turned to leave.'

'Captain Stein wait.'

Stein stopped in the doorway, half in, half out of the room. Bach floating around him from the direction of the dining room.

'Yes?'

'I just wanted to say that even though, so far I haven't really felt that you are as committed to our mission as I had hoped, the loyalty that you have shown for your men has not gone unnoticed.'

Stein waited dispassionately for him to say more.

'I will make sure it is recorded.'

Stein nodded from the doorway.

'Goodnight Haupsturmfuhrer.'

CHAPTER EIGHT
Wagner

When Wellum woke up, Brielle had gone. He reached out and felt the bare mattress next to him for traces of warmth then he checked his watch.

It was a little after nine-thirty.

As he got downstairs the smell of coffee and cigarettes met him. Armada was sitting at the kitchen table with a cigarette in the corner of his mouth. He was unscrewing the bottom of what look like a field radio.

'Morning,' said Wellum as he came into the room.

Armada glanced up from his work.

'Ah, you've risen at last. Are all you pilots such lazy bastards?' He got up and wiped his hands on a rag. 'I thought the RAF would have discouraged such indolence.' He grinned at his own joke.

'Where's Brielle?'

Armada went to the kitchen and removed the bubbling kettle from the stove and turned off the gas.

'I've no idea.'

'Have you seen her?'

'Yes, she and I were both awake three hours ago.'

Wellum checked his watch again.

'She went out?'

Armada rummaged among the contents of a cupboard and pulled out cups and a coffee can. He looked at Wellum.

'Afraid so old chap.'

He spooned coffee into a pot squinting at it with one eye closed, then took the cigarette out of his mouth and ran it under the tap.

'I tried to stop her but she's a bit headstrong that one isn't she. I almost had to wrestle her to keep her here.'

'You didn't touch her did you - I mean, you are joking?'

Armada grinned again.

'Don't worry, I'm not going to elope with her.'

'Did she say where she was going?'

Armada poured water into the coffee pot and gave it a stir. He carried it to the table along with the cups and sat back down.

'No, she didn't.'

He watched Wellum carefully for a moment then poured coffee. He handed a cup to the pilot.

'Here, sit.'

Wellum slid out a chair and sat down and gestured towards the radio.

'Is it broken?'

Armada picked up his screwdriver and began working once more.

'This? No, it's perfectly fine.'

'What are you doing with it?'

'Just a little side project.'

'What do you mean?'

Armada put his screwdriver down and looked at Wellum.

'Look, Harry. The work I do out here, it's sort of 'need to know' really, you understand?.'

'Yes of course, I was just wondering. If its just a side project I thought you might be able to tell me about it, that's all.'

Armada considered him for a moment more then sighed.

'Alright, well…' He pointed at the radio. 'Just a normal mark-2 field radio; Usually hidden inside a small suitcase.'

Wellum nodded.

'For a few weeks now, we've been using a house on the outskirts of the town as a dummy communication point. We've been sending fake radio messages from there and monitoring the German frequencies to see if they've DF'd where the messages are coming from.'

'And have they?'

'Yes. Two nights ago, we intercepted a coded message. It seems they've tracked the signal to the address we've been using and they're going to raid it at some time tonight after ten o'clock.' He put his hand on top of the radio. 'This and three others will be hidden inside the house and rigged with explosives. They'll all have anti handling switches on them so whichever one the German's inspect first will detonate.'

'Sounds marvellous'

'It'll certainly sting a bit, that's for certain. After that we'll detonate the other two remotely and open up on the house from hidden positions outside and give it a good hosing down. Kill as many of the bastards as we can and then disappear into the night. That's the plan anyway.'

'An ambush?'

Armada nodded and drank his coffee.

'That's right.'

'You said 'we', who's 'we'? The Resistance?'

'Sort of,' said Armada with a wink. 'Something like that.'

Wellum lit a cigarette and watched the agent working like a surgeon on the inside of the radio. He picked up some pliers from the table and snipped a wire, twisted one end then picked up a screwdriver and used it to prise up a bundle of cables, like entrails. He fiddled expertly with one or two before shoving them back into place with a finger.

'You said this was a side project.'

Armada glanced at him as he reached inside the wireless and attempted to get hold of something.

'Yes.'

'There's a main project?'

Armada nodded at the table, his hands still inside the radio's guts.

'Be a good chap, see that small torch? Do me a favour and shine it inside here for me.'

Wellum did as he was asked. Pointing the thin beam of light past Armada's hands into the depths of the surgery. Armada peered into the wireless, manipulating something tiny with his fingers. He pulled, and Wellum heard a snapping sound.

'Got it.'

Armada retrieved his hands and dropped a glass valve onto the table. He picked up a rag and wiped his fingers.

'There is a main project yes. A big one, but as I said earlier, it's not really one for sharing I'm afraid.' He gestured to the bits on the table in front of them.

'This is a side hustle, that's all. I like to get into these little tactical jobs as often as I can and cause as much trouble as possible. But the big picture is what I spend most of my time working on.'

'This big job, is it close to being finished or is it ongoing?'

Armada got up and took the coffee pot into the kitchen.

'You're a relentless sod aren't you?'

Wellum smiled.

'It's been said before, yes.'

'Let's just put it this way,' said the spy coming back to the table. He started collecting bits of radio and putting them into a cardboard box.

'If everything goes to plan, my work here should be wrapped up imminently and hopefully, It'll have put a sizeable spanner in the Nazis strategical plans for the rest of the war.'

'And after that, I mean once the job's complete?'

'After that I'm hoping to get back to England, at least for a while. I'll probably get re-deployed, but I'm hoping it won't be here in bloody Rouen. Too long in one place and all that.'

'You said you weren't working with the Resistance, so who are you using instead?'

Just then there was a series of knocks on the door.

Wellum startled at the sound, but Armada seemed unsurprised.

The knocks rattled again. A definite code.

Armada went to the door and peered through a spy hole. He threw back two bolts and unlocked the door, opening it a few feet as he did.

Brielle came in. She was carrying a bundle wrapped up in a bed-sheet, she also had a shopping bag made of string with a loaf of bread inside, clearly visible through the holes. She dropped the bundle on the floor as Armada closed and re-locked the door.

'Good morning,' Wellum smiled at her. She smiled back.

'Where have you been and what's this?' Asked Armada, pointing at the bundle.

Brielle reached inside her coat pocket and removed a pistol, she checked the breach and made sure the safety catch was on and put the gun on the table.

'I went to get bedsheets and some fresh bread and cheese.' She put the shopping bag on the table in front of Wellum and took off her coat.

'Is there coffee?'

Wellum pointed at the coffee pot. Brielle went to the kitchen and started opening cupboards looking for a cup.

'Where did you get these things?' Asked Armada.

Brielle came back to the table and poured herself coffee. She topped up Wellum's cup and sat down.

'My father had a business associate in Rouen, before the war. His daughter and her husband own a boulengerie on Rue Saint-Denis, they gave me the bedsheets and sold me some bread and cheese.'

She rooted in the bag.

'I got you some more cigarettes.'

She slid three packs towards Wellum.

'Thank you. Those German cigarettes kill me, though I doubt these will be any milder.'

'What are their names?' Asked Armada coming to the table and peering into the shopping.

'Who?'

The family you visited, the baker?'

'Baudman.'

'Are they Jews?'

Brielle looked at him.

'They sound Jewish,' said Armada.

'They use the name *Bernard.*'

Aramada nodded.

'I don't know them. Did they ask where you were staying?'

'No.'

Armada shook his head.

'You're sure you weren't followed back here?'

'I'm sure. I doubled back twice, then waited at the end of the street and checked. I wasn't followed.'

'Armada, she's careful.' Said Wellum. 'You can trust her.'

The spy looked at them both.

'I'm going out in a while. I'm going to get you an I.D. Card organised and some better clothes. I'll need you to come along and get a photograph, if I can organise it for later today that would be ideal, if not it'll be tomorrow first thing.'

He picked up the radio and carried it towards one of the doors leading off the kitchen.

'There are some vegetables in the pantry and some rice. If you're at a loose end, feel free to make some soup. I should be back by late afternoon.' He proffered the box of radio parts.

'Got to get these finished.' He looked at Brielle. 'Please stay here for the rest of today. Going out is risky, let's not take any unnecessary chances, alright?'

Brielle nodded and attempted a smile.

'Alright.'

The butler arrived with a silver tray. Stein sat up in bed and watched him carry it formally to a table by the window, his left arm tucked neatly behind him as he crossed the room, the coffee pot, tall and grand, glinting in the morning light. The butler put the tray down and poured the hot, black coffee into a waiting cup.

'Sugar and cream Sir?'

'No, thank you,' said Stein rubbing the sleep from his eyes. The butler nodded, 'what about breakfast Sir, have you given it any thought?'

'Just eggs and bacon if you have it.'

'Of course Sir, I'll see to it immediately.' He handed Stein his coffee.

'Thank you,' Said Stein once more. The butler re-crossed the room and opened the door and propped it ajar with his foot. He beckoned someone in the hall beyond to join him in the bedroom. A younger man, similarly dressed in a butler's uniform, pushed a gramophone on a table with wheels while the senior butler held the door open as the contraption was wheeled ceremonially inside. It was an old fashioned looking thing, a handle on one side and a large trumpet shaped horn made of polished brass.

'What's that?' Asked Stein sipping his coffee.

'Haupsturmfuhrer Wolff asked me to deliver it to your room Sir, for your spirits he said.'

He wound the handle while the young butler watched, then placed the needle precisely on the revolving shellac disc. As music crackled from the horn the older man smiled and nodded and the two men left.

Stein listened.

Wagner.

He shook his head and drank more coffee and looked out of the window over the gardens beyond. He could see his men sitting in the barracks. He could see Bothe and Gouder, sat polishing their boots, while the rest were gathered at long tables drinking coffee and smoking, two or three cleaning their weapons. He looked past them to the edges of the chateau grounds. Tall Spruce Pines planted closely together stood majestically in front of high walls, beyond which were more trees, falling away into a shallow valley and a little further still, the city of Rouen.

Stein looked at the three spires of the cathedral. The tallest of them impossibly thin and rising up to penetrate the morning mist that hung like a shroud over the streets. Palls of grey smoke rose here and there. Some signifying life and the hope of hearth and home, while others spoke of death and the still burning remains of the last air raid sent to brutalise the city. Stein could smell the smoke from here. He didn't want to go into the tangled metropolis, to see the destruction in there. He imagined how his own home must have looked the morning after it was destroyed. The smell and the charred blackness of the embers, the tattered drapes and splintered timber of the house he had built with his own hands.

He thought about Father Marcelin.

'I will pray for your family.'

He imagined his wife's fear as the bombs dropped closer and closer. He imagined her running to their daughter's room - little Valda. Gathering her up in her arms, perhaps whispering a prayer.

Perhaps.

He tried to remember the smell of his daughter's skin and the last time he had held her and sniffed her neck. His one love, the only thing that had ever really made sense.

He stared at the smoke rising in the distance, up into the flat, grey morning.

He finished his coffee and put the cup down and rubbed his eyes again. He hadn't slept well, despite the luxury of a real bed. He missed his simple cot. He looked at the men once more. Wolff had gone out and was talking to them. The SS officer waved his arms nonchalantly and some of the men laughed. He was like a conductor, plucking on them, thought Stein. Moving them this way and that with each simple wave of his hand. He observed the rapt look on their faces. It was easy to see how so many had been seduced by the Nazis. He had met more than his fair share and almost to a man he despised every one of them - Wolff was no different. He did have to admit though, their attraction was a powerful, mysterious force he had yet to fathom. Like American movie stars almost, they intoxicated those around them. It was like a mind trick, but one they themselves believed completely and without question.

Like faith.

Yes, that was close. Like a religion, it seemed all consuming and it bred a devotion unlike anything Stein could remember. Some Germans has even put their love of Naziism before the love of their children.

Valda.

He closed his eyes and felt the same crushing death inside that he had felt every day since his life had lost all its meaning. Since the telegram had arrived.

Little Valda. *His* Valda, dead beneath the rubble.

He opened his eyes and looked at the smoke, drifting over Rouen in the morning air.

He didn't blame the British, or the French or even God anymore.

He blamed the man who had taken them *all* to war. The man who had caused it, and the man that had taken him away from his child and her mother and his own parents and his friends and his life.

Adolf Hitler.

Heil!

SIEG Heil!

The Fhurer was crazy, Stein had been convinced since 'thirty-nine. He poured more coffee. He had thought it from the start, but didn't understand the nuances of Hitler's insanity until after the blitzkreig in Poland had begun.

This war is making madmen of us all.

He looked at Wolff, chatting easily with his men. *His* men. He felt a wave of jealousy.

These men were all the family he had left. He looked at their mouths open, laughing again at something Wolff had said.

'Fucking Nazi,' he whispered at the window.

'Fucking crazy Jew hating bastard.'

He stared at the SS. He watched him for a long time.

Wagner ended and the crackling of needle against shellac filled the room. A rhythmic, returning, crackle.
Again
Again
Again.
Then silence.
The sound of a peacock calling somewhere in the grounds brought him back to the room. He checked his watch automatically without taking in the time, then went to the gramophone and took the needle from the revolving black disc. He looked down the trumpet of the speaker. His face reflected in the polished brass - upside down.

Next time we're alone, out there somewhere, I should kill him and flee. Leave. Leave it all behind and start again.

He looked at the needle and the record and the gramophone and wondered how the sound was made.

A needle, running through a groove, carved in shellac…and the sound of an orchestra plays out. He couldn't connect the two ends in his mind. What happens in between?

Was it like the wars between men?

This gross, huge instrument of war and politics bearing down to an infinite point of pressure. Making people fall upon people, for nothing except the insane ambitions of one man here and another man there.

Such power.

To turn nations upon each other. To make people hate one another with just a few well chosen words.

An ideology.

A religion?

Had it always been this way?

Stein feared it had.

And that it probably always would be.

Armada unlocked the door and ushered them forward.

'Go and wait across the street for me, there's a house with a red door. Wait in front of that. When I come out, you follow on the other side of the road, a little way back. We are going to a street called Rue du Santiere. I have a contact near there where we can get you some clothes and hopefully your new identification card. If we get split up, I'll wait for you at Le Gros-Horlage, it's not far from where we're going.'

'What's that?' Asked Wellum

'It means *The Great Clock*,' Brielle explained. 'It's a sort of tourist attraction. I know where it is.'

Armada opened the door a few inches and looked discretely out onto the street.

'Alright, it's quiet, go, go on.'

Wellum led the way. As he went he checked along the road. A woman walked alone on the opposite pavement carrying a bundle of sticks over one shoulder and as he looked further, a man on a bicycle turned the corner and rode unsteadily towards them, peddling slowly.

Brielle tugged his sleeve.

'Come on, there's the house.'

Wellum looked across the cobbled street at a house similar to the one they had just left but happier somehow. Its door was painted a shining strawberry red and there was a cat sat on the doorstep cleaning itself next to an old milk bottle filled with dried flowers. The cat looked at them as they approached, closing it's eyes to slits of greeting it opened its mouth and meowed silently.

Wellum looked at the house with the red door and then looked back at Armada's dark, unwelcoming hideout. It seemed to grin at him from across the road like a squat, bone Calavera, its black windows like eyes that watched. It was their first look at the place in daylight and it looked as un-homely and forlorn on the outside as it felt on the inside.

'I bet it didn't look half as sad as that when its right family were here,' said Brielle standing at his shoulder and following his gaze.

Armada came out and twisted a key in the lock and put it in his pocket and turned and set off down the road.

Wellum and Brielle watched him walk a dozen or so paces before starting off and heading in the same direction.

It was early afternoon and the sky was a mottled silver grey and the air was cold and hard. Wellum turned up his collar and pulled the cap further down on his head. He put his hands deep into his jacket pockets, balling them to fists for warmth.

'Do you know this place?'

'Yes,' said Brielle. 'I used to visit here, when I was a child, with my parents and my sister. Travelling to Rouen was the first time I had ever been on a train.' She leaked a smile at him.

'How old were you?'

Brielle thought for a moment.

'Perhaps nine or ten.'

'And your sister?'

'She was twelve I think.'

At the end of Rue Camille Saint-Saens, Armada turned left and the three of them headed north, deeper into the old part of the city. Here the streets were immediately busier as people came and went, mingling with each other and attempting to go about their normal, daily lives. As they walked, Wellum studied the buildings. Ancient timber structures, hundreds of years old, most of which were unscathed by the bombs and the bullets of the previous three years.

'So little damage,' he said as they went on. 'We were told that Rouen was all but destroyed.'

'This is the old town. Much of it has survived this far by a miracle, they say. The rest of the city has not been so lucky.'

They weaved between street vendors, beggars and towns folk, when suddenly Wellum tensed up at the sight of two Wehrmacht soldiers leaning against a wall, talking to a group of young girls outside a coffee shop. Brielle gripped his sleeve, pulling his attention back.

'There, look.'

Armada had paused at an alley a little further ahead that appeared to run between two shops. He had turned to face them and when he caught Wellum's eye, he disappeared out of sight down the narrow passageway.

CHAPTER NINE
The Resistance

Armada knocked on the door three times in a quick, rapid rhythm, then he listened.

Wellum checked his watch and Brielle looked back towards the road.

Armada knocked again before the door opened an inch and he leaned in, speaking quietly.

'C'est moi. Que je veux voir Godfrey.'

Eyes swivelled past him from the dark and looked at Brielle and Wellum. Armada glanced at his companions then looked back at the door.

'Laisse moi, entrer.'

The eyes moved back into the shadows and the door opened a few more inches and they went in. *Another dark hallway*, thought Wellum. *More French people whispering in the shadows - at least this feels familiar.*

A short, stubby man locked the door behind them. Wellum noticed he was carrying a pistol as he walked past them towards another door and beckoned them to follow him.

'Venez, de cette façon, il est ici.'

The next room was a kitchen, at the centre of which was a large dining table. A middle aged man was sitting reading a newspaper, his glasses on the end of a slender nose and a pistol lying on the table next to an ashtray, and a cup of coffee. A woman, similar in age, her eyes worn and tired dried her hands on a tea towel while pots bubbled aromatically on the stove behind her. She dropped the towel onto the table and took a cigarette and lit it.

'Armada, it's been a while. I'm surprised you remember where we live.'

'Bonjour Irene.' He looked at the man sat at the table. 'Godfrey.'

The man closed his newspaper and drank his coffee and looked at them over his spectacles.

'Armada, please excuse my wife, she has forgotten perhaps that we are old friends.' The woman snorted dryly and sat down, tapping her cigarette at the ashtray. She crossed her legs and studied the group. 'How can we help you?' The Frenchman gestured to the empty seats on the other side of the table. As they sat, the woman spoke to the shorter man.

'Renard, faire plus de cafe.'

The man holstered his pistol and made his way through to the kitchen.

'Aren't you going to introduce us to your friends?'

Armada turned and gestured towards Wellum.

'This is Harry, he's an English pilot and this is his friend Brielle. She's from Varranes.' Everyone pushed out smiles and whispered, somewhat stilted 'bonjour's'

'And this is Godfrey and Irene Charon, they are good friends of mine, the man in the kitchen is called Renard, - also a friend.'

Godfrey relaxed back in his chair.

'So...?'

Armada lit a cigarette and passed the packet to Wellum.

'In a nutshell, Harry here needs to get back to England and London have asked me to help.'

'I thought you'd be far too busy for rescue missions,' said Irene

Armada shrugged.

'Bit of a touchy subject really.' He half smiled at Wellum.

'You are a pilot?' Said Godfrey.

'Yes,' said Wellum. I was shot down three days ago, on a reconnaissance flight.'

'What were you looking for?'

Wellum tried to look nonchalant. 'Nothing in particular. German artillery movements, things like that.'

'Where were you shot down?' Asked Irene.

'Near Varranes.'

'And how did the two of you meet?' She wafted her hand in Brielle's direction.

'A priest in Lealvillers introduced us. Brielle helped me contact London and then she helped get me to Rouen.'

Irene looked at Brielle.

'Who do you know in Varranes? Someone that can vouch for you?'

'I have lived with father Rieu at Elise-Notre-dame for the last year and a half. You could also ask Gisbert Moulain, if you know him. He will tell you who I am.'

The French couple looked at each other.

'We know Gisbert. You fought with him?'

'Yes. Many times.'

'How old are you?'

'Twenty-five.'

Irene looked at Wellum.

'How did you contact London?'

'I took him to see the Librarian.'

'Pierre?'

Brielle nodded.' Oui.'

'He needs some fake papers. Can you do it?' Said Armada.

Godfrey considered the question for a moment.

'Yes, I can do it.'

'And he needs clothes too, something less…rural.'

'I agree,' said Irene. 'I'm sure we have something that will fit.

'Thank you,' said Wellum.

Godfrey sat forward and pointed at Wellum's Jumper.

'You have blood on you. What happened?'

Wellum pulled on the collar of the jumper and looked down his nose to see if he could see anything.

'Where?'

'Near your neck, it's just a little.'

'We killed two Germans, yesterday.' Said Brielle. 'On our way here. A motorcycle patrol stopped us just outside of town.'

'That was you?'

Wellum looked bemused.

'Why?'

'We listen in to the German radio channels. They were out all night looking for those two after they failed to report in. They found their bodies this morning. It caused quite a stir you'll be pleased to hear, both within the German ranks and ours. Obviously we knew that none of our people had killed them so it was all a bit of a mystery.'

Armada looked at Brielle.

'Well it's a mystery no more.'

Brielle gave a slight shrug.

Renard came in with fresh coffee and three cups. He put the cups down and began to pour.

Godfrey turned to Armada.

'So, why haven't we seen you since summer?'

'Oh you know,' said the agent casually. He folded his hands in his lap. 'Nothing much been going on. Trying to stay quiet for a while and all that.'

Irene sucked on her cigarette and shook her head.

'You know, for a spy, you always were a terrible liar.'

'Who said I was a spy? Armada smiled wolfishly.

'What about you? Working on anything interesting?'

Godfrey held up his hand.

'We're not going to play this game.'

'What game?'

'The game where we lie to you and you lie to us and round and round we go.'

'Oh come on, you've always shared stuff with me in the past,' said Armada drinking his coffee.

'Yes but that was before we realised that there was a mole somewhere - you remember?' Said Renard, pulling out a chair and sitting down next to Irene.

The atmosphere became suddenly charged and Wellum looked at the gun sitting on the table alongside the ashtray. He looked at Irene.

'What do you mean a mole? You mean someone on our side that's really working for the Germans?'

'They're talking rubbish Harry,' said Armada with a grin.

'There's no mole.'

Godfrey eyed Armada closely.

'You're sure about that?'

Armada sat forward and smiled broader still.

'I'm certain old chap. Now give me one of those bloody awful cigarettes you Frenchie's smoke and stop talking bollocks.'

The atmosphere broke as Godfrey flipped the packet towards Armada and sat back in his chair.

'Well, someone's talking to the German's, we're convinced. They've intercepted too many operations for it just to be down to good guess work'

'Oh, come on,' said Armada. 'Even *they* have to get lucky sometimes.'

'So, why have you been working alone?'

'I haven't been alone, just not as…visible, that's all.'

They fell into an awkward silence, smoking and drinking coffee. Eventually Armada checked his watch.

'Look, if it's alright with you chaps, I'm going to leave you to it. There are a few things I need to take care of this afternoon.'

He stood up.

'Godfrey, if you let me know what I owe you for the ID card and the clothes I'll sort that out.' He turned to Brielle.

'You'll able to find your way back to the house?'

Brielle nodded. 'Oui.'

'Alright well, thank you.' He smiled at Godfrey and Irene.

'It's been good to see you both again. If there's anything you need please, let me know through the usual channels.'

He looked at the other man. 'You too Renard.'

'You'll be at the house when we've finished here?' Asked Wellum.

'That depends on the time. You've got a key anyway so if I'm not in, don't wait up, and Harry, don't worry, you're in good hands here.'

Irene rolled her eyes and stubbed out her cigarette.

'Renard, please see Armada out and lock the door.'

They went to a room on the next floor up, Irene leading the way, the stairs creaking like old bones as they climbed. On the first floor they crossed a landing and went into a bedroom, dominated by a large steamer trunk that was sitting against one wall. Irene crossed the room and flipped the lid on the trunk.

'Here, have a look though this box of clothes. Take whatever you need.' She looked at Wellum, judging his size. 'I think there are some trousers in here that will fit you and perhaps a sweater or two.'

She went to a wardrobe and reached in and took out a hanger, a grey suit dangling from its shoulders.

'Try this on.' She reached back into the wardrobe and came out with two shirts. 'If these fit I'll iron out the creases downstairs. She got on her knees and shoved her arm under the bed and retrieved a brown leather suitcase.

She placed it on the bed and unclasped it and let it fall open. 'Put everything in here.'

Wellum felt the fabric on the suit.

'Thank you.' He looked at his feet.

'We don't have shoes, sorry,' said Irene. 'Your boots, if you clean them, they will be fine.'

Wellum looked self-consciously at the faces all watching him.

'Do you want me to try them on here? Now?'

Godfrey smiled at him.

'Yes, but don't worry, I'll be in the next room setting up the camera for your photograph. Irene will wait downstairs.'

Brielle raised a finger.

'Do you have a telephone?'

'What for?'

'I want to contact father Rieu, if I may. Just to tell him we have arrived safely.'

Godfrey nodded.

'Oui, downstairs. But be quick, don't say too much.'

'Thank you,' said Brielle.

Godfrey looked back at Wellum.

'Choose your disguise Harry, when you are ready meet me in the next room along.'

The second bedroom was smaller and the curtains were drawn at the windows. In the middle of the room Godfrey was attaching a large camera to a tripod that faced a single chair, a cigarette dangling from the corner of his mouth, his glasses once more on the end of his nose. Wellum came in and closed the door.

'Please, take a seat.' Said the Frenchman.

The smell of cooking came up through the floorboards. Wellum sat down.

'Whatever it is that Irene is cooking, it smells delicious.'

Godfrey looked at him over his spectacles.

'Are you married?'

'No.'

Godfrey twisted a bulb into a flash unit and attached it to the top of the camera.

'When we are done here, we'll eat.' He smiled at the pilot.

Wellum smiled back.

'How soon will you be able to make the identification card?'

'I'll go and put the film in to develop now and I'll print the photographs later today. I should have the ID card ready by tomorrow.'

'Tomorrow when?'

'You are keen to be on your way?'

'Yes, but no…I just wondered. Will I come here to collect it?'

'Oui. Armada has never been one for house calls.'

'Why's that?'

Godfrey finished attaching the flash and removed the lens cover from the camera.

'Well, despite his show of bravado downstairs earlier. You're friend has always been a secretive sort and has become more and more suspicious of late.'

'What about?'

'About everything, and everyone. We worked quite closely together last year. He helped us set up quite a few important jobs. Fighting back, you know. Armada has been an integral part of the Resistance movement here in Rouen. He has helped us do considerable damage to the Nazi war effort. He has helped us kill many Germans.'

'So what's changed?'

'We're not sure. After the summer he seemed to retreat. He began working with a smaller group, people we've never seen before. He lost some people, we lost some people and everyone became, how do you say…paranoid? We keep probing about a spy or informer…this, mole if you like. But he won't commit, even though we know he suspects the same. When he came here with you today, it was the first time we've seen him for months. We think it's because he's working on something big but we don't know what.'

Wellum remembered the booby trapped radios, but thought it best not to mention them.

'So, is the Resistance finished in Rouen?'

'Sit still, look here.' The camera flashed and Godfrey turned a dial on the side, winding on the film.

'No. But we have had to look elsewhere for support.'

The camera flashed again.

'Have you got any jobs lined up?'

'Hold still.' The camera flashed once more and Godfrey went and opened the curtains. Wellum blinked as the sunlight shone in.

'We have one or two things planned but we need weapons.'

He crushed his cigarette in an ashtray. 'Come on let's go downstairs and eat.'

Back in the kitchen Wellum dropped the suitcase by the door. Renard was laying cutlery and bowls on the table.

'Set two more places,' said Godfrey as they came in. 'We have guests for lunch today.'

He picked up a piece of bread from a basket in the middle of the table and bit off the corner then crossed the kitchen to where Irene was ladling out bowls of stew and kissed her cheek and spoke softly in her ear. She looked at Wellum and then dipped her ladle into the pot once more.

'Please Harry,' said Godfrey collecting a wine bottle from the cupboard. 'Please, sit.'

Wellum looked out of the kitchen window onto a small yard beyond. A child's bicycle was lent against the wall.

'You have children?' He asked as Godfrey put a glass on the table and poured wine.

Irene glanced over from the kitchen.

'Yes, smiled Godfrey. Our daughter - Esmee. She is staying with relatives out in the country. Away from the city.'

'How old is she?' asked Wellum

'She's ten.'

Brielle came in. She looked drawn and grey. She sat down next to Wellum.

'Whats wrong? Did you speak to father Rieu?'

She nodded.

'Oui.' Instinctively she reached out and took the wine glass and drank the contents down in one. She wiped her mouth with the back of her hand.

'Harry, Father Marcelin is dead.'

'What, How?'

'Grillot visited Father Rieu and said that a group of SS came to Lealvillers yesterday, looking for you. They found your clothes at Marcelin's house and they shot him.'

Wellum bowed his head.

'Apparently they killed some other people in the village too.'

Irene came over to the table carrying bowls.

'Did he tell them anything?'

Brielle shrugged, 'I don't know.'

Wellum cast his hand across his eyes.

'Oh my God.'

'I doubt if Pere Marcelin would ever talk,' said Brielle. But if he did it would not have been out of weakness.'

'Did he know you were coming to Rouen?' Asked Renard.

Brielle nodded.

'Yes, but he didn't know why, or who we were meeting.'

'It doesn't matter, if they know you're in the city they'll do everything they can to find you.'

'We don't know what they know,' said Wellum,' trying to sound pragmatic. 'They might not know anything. Marcelin might not have said a word.'

Irene looked less than convinced.

'Everyone talks monsieur, it just depends where you press them.'

Wellum knew she was right.

'Well, that settles it,' he conceded. 'I need to be on my way as soon as possible.'

'Of course,' nodded Godfrey. 'Do you have a route out of France?'

'Not yet. I think Armada has some ideas, but we haven't discussed any options.'

Irene delivered more bowls of stew. She looked at Godfrey.

'Qu'en est-il d'un train? Nous pourrions parles a Matis. Il pourrait l'amener a Hornfleur?'

Godfrey nodded thoughtfully.

'Oui, perhaps.'

'What?' Said Wellum.

'I could speak to a friend of ours - Matis. He works at the railway in Rouen. The Germans now control all train movements but I think he might be able to get you onto a cargo train heading for the coast. To Hornfleur, maybe. From there the English could scoop you up at Villerville or somewhere quiet on the beach at night. Or we can see about hiring a boat, but that comes at a price and also with risks of its own.'

'When can you speak to Matis?' Asked Wellum.

'I can speak to him later today, we have a job of our own happening tonight and Matis is coming with us. I'm guessing he might be able to get you on a train in a few days from now, if one is available.'

'What is this job, tonight? Asked Brielle.

Irene sat down with her bowl and took bread from the basket. She glanced at Godfrey and then at Renard.

'Can you drive?'

'Yes,' said Brielle, 'I can drive.'

Irene began to eat, dipping the bread into her bowl.

She looked at Godfrey again, a questioning, telepathic look.

He shrugged and nodded.

'We are going to pick up some weapons tonight. You can come along if you like.'

Brielle put down her spoon and took some bread.

'Where are the weapons going to be and when are you leaving?'

'There is an abandoned quarry, around eight miles north of the city. The RAF are parachuting a canister into the quarry at eleven-thirty tonight.'

'The RAF? Who have you spoken to in England to arrange that?' Asked Wellum.

'We have a contact at the SOE in London.'

'Does Armada know?'

'No,' said Godfrey. 'As I said earlier. We are all making our own way at the moment. Just in case.'

'When are you leaving?'

'At about ten,' said Irene.

'We have a truck coming here at nine. It's being dropped off in a street nearby. We'll all travel in that. Pick up the canister with the weapons and get it back here, leave the truck where we found it and that's it.'

'Who's going on the job?' asked Wellum.

'Irene, myself, Matis and another friend called Elliot.'

'What about the person delivering the truck?'

'They'll wait at a secret location until we return. We won't even know who they are, and they won't know who is using the truck or for what purpose, the less people know, the less they can tell the Germans if they are stopped or captured. Even if they are tortured.'

Wellum winced at the thought.

'Aren't you going Renard?'

'No,' said the shorter man, standing up and heading into the kitchen with his bowl.

'Renard, is our contact man with the SOE for this job,' said Godfrey. 'He'll be here on the radio if we need to make adjustments to the plan.'

Wellum looked at Brielle. 'You want to go along?'

She nodded. 'Yes.'

Wellum looked at her. He knew he wouldn't settle if she went alone with this new group, and despite Armadas advice to stay quiet, after hearing the news about the death of Father Marcelin he was beginning to feel his own need to get back into the fight.'

'Alright,' he said looking back at Godfrey. 'I'll Come along too.'

CHAPTER TEN
The nazis at dinner

When they arrived back at the house Armada was in the kitchen.

'How did it go?'

Brielle went straight upstairs, Wellum dropped the suitcase by the table.

'Yes, it went well.'

Armada watched Brielle.

'What's wrong with her?'

'Nothing.'

Armada looked at him.

'Lovers tiff?' He poured a steaming pan into a mug.

'Want some screech?'

Wellum went into the kitchen and peered into Armada's mug.

'What's screech?'

'Hot powdered milk and brandy. I missed lunch so I'm having this.'

'No thanks,' said Wellum heading back to his suitcase. 'We got fed.'

'Ah, welcomed into the fold eh?'

'I wouldn't go that far.'

Armada came and sat down at the table. He gestured at the suitcase.

'You got some clothes?'

'Yes, a few shirts and jumpers and a suit.'

'Excellent.' He drank. 'They're good people the Charron's, very loyal, very strong.'

'But you don't fight with them anymore.'

Armada shook his head.

'Not for a while no.'

'Why?'

'Ah, it's complicated. Being out here, alone. The hardest part is trusting the people around you, and then, trusting your own mind.'

'Do you think you're becoming paranoid?'

'Is that what they said, that I've become paranoid?'

'Well, no. I'm just asking what *you* think.'

'I think I've got bloody good instincts, that's what I think.'

He sipped at his mug.

'I know something's not right in the city, i've felt it for months. I play it down but Irene and Godfrey may well be right.'

'What about?'

'About there being a mole somewhere. Somewhere close.'

'But you argued with them about that.'

'Smoke and mirrors old chap, that's all. They know I'm suspicious too.' He held up a finger. 'Suspicious, mark you…not paranoid. But it's all a game see.' He stood and went into the kitchen and came back with an ashtray. 'I find it's simpler right now to stay separate, do my own thing.'

'So you *do* work alone?'

'No. But what I do is pick my friends even more carefully than before. And I try to use the same people these days.'

'Are you still going out tonight, with your radios?'

'Yes, I'll be leaving at around nine.'

Wellum scratched his chin.

'We, er, we'll be leaving at around then too.'

'What for?'

'We're helping Godfrey and Irene with something.'

'We? You mean you and the girl?'

'Yes.'

'What?'

'What do you mean, what?'

'What do you think I mean? I mean *what* are you helping them with?'

Wellum considered lying.

'We've agreed to go and pick up some weapons with them.'

'Why?'

'Because Brielle volunteered. They needed a driver so she volunteered.'

'And you thought you'd tag along too?'

Wellum shrugged.

'Yes, I suppose you could put it like that.'

'Are you mad?'

'Why? It sounds straight forward enough. And besides, she's helped me get this far, I just wanted to…'

'Wanted to what Harry? Jesus Christ man, what were you thinking?'

'I want to help her.'

'Do you really want to help her?'

'Yes, of course.'

'Then get back to England in one piece, and do what you're best at; Flying! That's how you'll help us all. You're an asset, and an expensive asset at that. You can't be irresponsible enough to throw that away on a simple weapons drop to satisfy some silly misplaced loyalty.'

'Calm down, I'm not throwing anything away. I'm just going along to help that's all.'

'What do you think London will say?'

'They don't need to know.'

Armada frowned.

'What are you talking about?'

'I'm not going to tell them.'

'It's a mistake.'

'I'm going anyway.'

Armada pointed at him.

'Look, if you get captured I'm not coming after you, understand? I'm close to completing something far bigger than this bloody silly pick up of yours and I can't run the risk of it derailing on account of you and your love-sick adventures.'

He stood up and stormed into the kitchen.

'If you do this Harry, you're on your own.'

'Fine,' said Wellum. 'That's fine. Look I'm not trying to get in anyone's way, I just want to help Brielle. Call it gratitude if you like but I just want to be there for her and for the Charron's.'

'They don't need looking after Harry. None of them, they're stronger than you know.'

'I understand that, but I've offered to help them, so I'm going. Look, you're doing your bit, They're doing theirs and Brielle wants to be part of that, and so do I. I've felt like such a bloody burden since I got here, I just want get back into the fight however I can.'

'Alright, alright,' said Armada holding up a hand in submission. 'You're a big lad, but I meant what I said about not coming after you. I can't old chap I'm sorry. It's too much of a risk with what's around the corner for me.'

'Alright, you've said. It's not going to come to that anyway.'

'Did they say who's going on the job?'

'Someone called Elliot and another bloke called Matis, apparently the truck driver is anonymous and is dropping the vehicle close by and then waiting somewhere.'

'They don't know who's driving the truck?'

'Apparently not.'

'Mmm. What about Renard?'

'He's the contact with the SOE back in London so he'll be on the radio back at the house.'

Armada sighed.

'I don't like it.'

'I don't like any of this,' said Wellum.

'What time's the drop happening?'

'They didn't tell me,' Wellum lied.

Armada smiled.

'You're learning.'

Wellum lit a cigarette.

'Godfrey said that this chap Matis might be able to get me on a train heading to the coast. They're going to ask him about it tonight. If he can, they reckon it'll only be a day or so from now.'

'Right. That's good.'

'Hornfleur, hopefully.'

Armada nodded. 'Makes sense.' He gave a weak smile. 'Good.'

Wellum stood up.

'Right, I'm going to take a shower if that's alright. It'll be the first one since I left England.'

He picked up the suitcase and walked towards the stairs.

'Harry, wait.'

Wellum turned.

'I admire what you're doing. Really, I do. But if you get bumped tonight, I honestly can't help you - you do understand that don't you?'

'I know. You've helped me enormously already, thank you. If I don't see you before you go out, good luck with your little adventure too. I hope you mallet the lot of them.'

'Don't worry,' said Armada with a smile. 'I will.' He put out his hand. 'I'll see you for breakfast.'

Wellum took the agent's hand and shook it, 'see you in the morning.' Then he turned and headed up the stairs.

On the first floor landing, Wellum knocked on the bedroom door and waited.

'Come in,' said Brielle.

She was replacing the clothes in the wardrobe, smoothing each one on its hanger before carefully hooking it back onto the rail.

The bed was made with the linen she'd collected that morning.

'Did you tell him?'
'What about?'
She looked at him.
'About tonight.'
'Yes, I told him.'
'What did he say?'
'He said I should stay here.'

'I hate to say it, but I agree with him. You need to get back home, so you can fight in the air, that is your responsibility.'

'That's what Armada said.'

Brielle shrugged. 'So, listen to him.'

'No. I want to come, to help in any way I can.'

'Harry you don't need to do this, I don't need looking after.'

'Alright, I know what you're both saying but if I'm not fighting in the air, I need to do what I can down here. And I'm not trying to protect you, I know you don't need that, but Father Marcelin is dead, and for what? For helping me, that's what, and I can't stand that thought. I hate them Brielle, almost as much as you do and I need to fight. For me, for Marcelin and for your family and for everyone else that's suffered because of the war.' He smacked the clothes in the wardrobe with the back of his hand.

'For these people, and all the people yet to suffer the same fate. I need to do what I can and right now, this is the next job on the list and after that there will be another and another and another until all this is over. Whether it's on the ground here in France or in the air over London, or the Channel or fucking Berlin. It doesn't matter. It's all the same fight - remember?'

He sat down on the bed. She came and cradled his head and held it to her.

'Alright, I'm sorry.'

He could smell her skin and he closed his eyes and breathed her in. He took her hand and kissed it and then looked up into her eyes. He let her go, suddenly self conscious, his face filled with embarrassment.

'I'm sorry, I didn't mean to…'

'I know.' She said softly. 'I know, it's alright.'

She turned and crossed the room and picked up the suitcase.

'Go and take a shower, I'll sort these clothes out and we should eat before we go out again.'

He watched her moving around the room. She dropped the suitcase beside the wardrobe and crouched next to their supplies and began digging out rations for their evening meal. She held up two foil packets.

'Do you want beef curry or chicken?'

Wellum smiled at her.

'I'm still stuffed from Irene's stew, but if you're forcing me to eat, I'll have the chicken.'

'Here.' She threw him a towel. 'Go and get showered. Dinner will be served in ten minutes.'

'Ah Captain Stein, you join us at last.' Wolff smiled at the panzer captain stood in the doorway flanked by two butlers. Stein walked into the room.

'Good evening,' he said, glancing at the faces gathered around the dinner table illuminated by flickering candles and the amber glow of another generous hearth burning at the far end of the room.

'I'm sorry I'm late.'

'No apologies needed,' said Kruger standing and extending his hand in welcome. Stein shook the Colonel's hand and allowed himself to be guided towards an empty chair.

'Please, sit. The first course will be along at any moment.'

Stein nodded at the other guests as he sat down awkwardly. A waiter arrived at his shoulder and offered him wine.

'Yes, thank you.'

He took a drink and tried to relax.

'Captain Stein,' said Kruger, retaking his own seat and addressing the panzer captain over the candle flames. 'Please allow me to introduce our other guests.' He motioned cordially towards a woman sitting on Stein's right.

'The beautiful creature alongside you is your dining partner for this evening. Mademoiselle Colette Larue.' Stein turned and shook the woman's hand, standing up and bowing slightly as he did. The woman sipped martini, and watched him as he sat back down and straightened his jacket.

'On your left, accompanying our good Captain Wolff is Mademoiselle Elise Rose.' Stein nodded and winced a smile. He caught Wolff's eye and the SS officer raised both eyebrows at him in approval at the young courtesan's obvious beauty. Kruger went on.

'On my right we have Madame Rosalie Petit.' He kissed the back of her hand tenderly, staring into her eyes as he did. An older woman, but just as beautiful as her younger colleagues, she wore her confidence like an expensive cologne. Kruger clearly preferred experience over youth. Stein nodded politely.

'Madam.'

'And on my left is the wonderful 'Barbie Montagne,' a slightly nervous looking girl, obviously the youngest of the four, lifted her eyes briefly and managed a flickering smile before picking up her champagne glass and sipping it somewhat self consciously.

'And our final guest, I'm pleased to introduce, is detective Ebner Schenk.'

A thin man, not handsome but dark and unreadable. He nodded at Stein, but didn't offer his hand. He was the only one drinking water rather than wine and he wore a Nazi pin badge that flashed in the firelight from the lapel of his black suit. He looked more like an undertaker than a policeman.

'Captain Stein,' he said in a flat, humourless tone. 'It is good to meet you in person. Haupsturmfuhrer Wolff was just explaining to me that you had no luck tracking down your English pilot in Rouen today.'

Stein unfolded his napkin and put it across his knee,

'Unfortunately not. But it was just a sightseeing trip really, getting to know the layout of the city.'

'Detective Schenk is joining us tonight to see if the Gestapo might be able to offer any assistance in finding our man,' said Wolff.

The Gestapo? Thought Stein feeling more out of place than ever. *God help us all.*

He turned and looked at Schenk who seemed not to have moved a muscle since Stein had first come into the room, like some marionette scissored from his strings.

'Thank you detective, I'm sure with your help the hunt will be short.' He smiled thinly and took a drink of wine.

Kruger laughed.

'Well Herr Captain, if Ebner Schenk can't find him, no one will.'

The Gestapo officer paused for a moment, his gaze still fixed on Stein, then he turned and smiled at the SS officer.

'You're too kind Colonel Kruger, really.'

The door opened and a line of waiters filed in. Two carried bowls and plates and a basket of bread, while two more delivered a trolley on top of which sat a white ceramic terrine.

'Ah,' said Kruger. 'The soup, excellent.'

As the waiters delivered the first course, Colette leaned in and spoke to Stein, her deep, French accent as thick as her perfume.

'Good evening my good Captain.' She smiled as he turned to face her. He nodded politely.

'Hello, Mademoiselle Larue.' He attempted a smile of his own and took another drink.

'Colette, Herr Captain, please.'

Stein waved away the bread basket.

'Hello, *Colette*.'

She smiled again and sipped her own drink.

Kruger ordered more wine. 'Red this time, to compliment the beef,'

Stein realised it was going to be a long night.

They had spent that afternoon in the city. Starting at the outskirts and moving in. Patrolling slowly among the bombed buildings and the lingering, ever present smell of smoke.

Wolff actually accompanied the men, sitting in the cab of the truck, directing the driver while Stein sat in the back and tried to ignore the carnage. Twice an hour they would find somewhere Wolff considered worth investigating and they would disembark and go hunting like dogs on an invisible leash, harassing families and on one occasion bullying a group of young gendarme - intimidation tactics mostly, trying to get information.

'Have you seen anyone new? Who do you know in the Resistance?' Things like that. The men had risen to it, pulling people out of ruins to be questioned. Families in mourning, letting the rubble of their former lives slip through their fingers or digging through the debris looking for the body of a dead child.

'So what did you think of Rouen captain Stein? Asked Kruger, between mouthfuls of soup. He dabbed his lips with a napkin and broke bread.

Stein hovered his spoon above his steaming bowl.

'I imagine it was once very beautiful.'

Schenk slurped metronomically beside him. Stein could see him out of the corner of his eye. The rise and fall of his arm seemed strange and robotic.

'Ah, alas,' said Kruger returning to his own soup. 'When the war is over,' he said. 'I'm sure it will be beautiful once more.'

Madame Petit curled a smile towards Stein and ran a finger down Kruger's temple as he ate.

Stein nodded. 'Yes, I'm sure it will be.' He could feel Schenk peering at him as the Gestapo agent sipped his water and eyed him.

With the soup bowls empty, waiters came and poured Burgundy and cleared the table and re-laid it with fresh napkins and warm plates and meat knives that glittered sharp and cold in the firelight.

Colette put a hand on Stein's knee. She was smoking a cigarette between courses and talking to Wolff's courtesan in French. As she spoke she ran a finger along the inside of Stein's thigh, towards his groin and back down. He tried to ignore her.

Wolff spoke across the table to Schenk.

'So, as I was saying earlier. Even though we didn't really get any useful information today, we, that is Captain Stein and I, still feel that a blanket search of the city will eventually yield results.' He took a sip of wine. 'After all there can only be so many places a British pilot can go. At some point someone is bound to slip up and tell us where he is hiding.'

Schenk gave a patronising smile.

'That depends on who he's with Haupsturmfuhrer.'

'What do you mean?'

'Well, if he's fallen in with a well organised group, it may prove harder to weed him out than if say, he is simply relying on the good faith of ordinary, innocent citizens.'

The two women stopped talking and Colette tamped out her cigarette in an ashtray.

Stein reached down into his lap and gently collected her hand from his thigh and placed it back on her leg.

'You think searching the city is pointless?' He asked.

Wolff flashed him a look.

'Well, in many respects yes.' Said the Gestapo dryly.

'Well, what would you suggest we do?' Countered Wolff. It was the first time Stein had seen him ruffled, albeit only slightly.

Maybe it's the wine?

'If you are right about him arriving only yesterday I would maybe suggest waiting a day or two.'

'Waiting for what?' Asked Stein.

'Captain Stein, do you know exactly what we do in the Gestapo?'

'I think I know something of what you do, yes. But maybe not *exactly,* as you would put it.'

'What do you know?'

Stein glanced around the table. Everyone was looking at him, waiting for him to answer. He picked up his wine and tried to lighten the mood.

'Well detective, perhaps that's a conversation for a less *intimate* evening. Wouldn't you say?' He looked at Colette and feigned a smile as she ran a finger down his nose and over his lips.

Schenk watched him.

'We find the people that don't want to be found, Herr Captain. It is what we are best at. Jews, traitors, spies. We find them, and when we find them, we make them tell us where we can find more of their sort… It is what we are *best* at.'

Stein nodded.

'That's what I'd heard.'

The beef arrived. A huge steaming rib, dragged in on a carving trolley by three waiters. Vegetables did the rounds and boats of thick brown gravy were placed strategically on the table.

'Do you eat like this every night? Beamed Wolff as the provender rolled out in still more vulgar quantities. 'No wonder you're getting soft around the middle Heinz.' Elise laughed and squeezed Wolff's cheek playfully as he made the joke.

'Not every night no,' said the colonel waving the empty wine bottle at a waiter. Just four or five times a week.'

The spoils of war, thought Stein as he watched several slices of beef bleed onto his plate. He looked around at the faces, glowing pink from the wine and laughing at each others jokes. It was strange, but the only one who seemed to have any grasp on the horror of it all was the corpse-like Schenk, and Stein could only imagine what horrors that bastard had preceded over.

'How was it in Treblinka?' Asked Kruger, as if he'd read Stein's thoughts.

Schenk put down his fork and sat chewing his food. A finger resting on his top lip.

'It was a disaster.'

'Why?' Laughed Kruger. 'You didn't let any little mice slip through your fingers did you Ebnar?'

'What on earth were you doing in Treblinka, it's fucking miles away?' Asked Wolff.

'I was there trying to clean up the mess the SS left after the uprising in August.'

Wolff smiled awkwardly.

'The SS left a mess? I doubt that very much detective. The only mess we ever leave is when we leave the Jews alive.'

'Or when they escape,' replied Schenk dryly.

'What they need at Treblinka is someone like Kramer,' said Wolff pointing his knife at no one in particular.

'Isn't he still at Auschwitz?' Asked Kruger, pouring more wine.

Schenk had returned his attention to his dinner.

'Yes,' said Wolff. 'For now, but I think he wants a change. When I was at Belsen earlier this year I put in a word that they should get Kramer to take over when Haas goes back to Berlin.'

'I thought Belsen was a prisoner of war camp,' said Stein. 'Why would someone like Josef Kramer be appropriate for POW's?'

'Because my dear captain, like all of us when the need arises, Belsen is changing. As the Fuhrer takes back more land, the amount of jews we have to deal with goes up, and up and up. Most of the other camps are full and not all of the jews are useless enough to be killed straight away, so as you know we set them to work. At Belsen, they can work.'

'There are jewish prisoners there now?' Asked Stein.

'As we speak, yes, and more are being sent there every day. There is a small sub-camp nearby where some will be given special treatment and conditions and then used as currency to trade with the Americans and the British for the release of German prisoners…like coins.'

Kruger laughed inbetween mouthfuls of beef.

'Ha! They themselves have become like the money that they love so much.'

'Exactly,' agreed Wolff. 'Some will work, others will be traded and when they are no longer of use they will, quite rightly, be gassed.'

Stein looked at the blood, drying on his plate.

Kruger turned back to Schenk who was mopping up gravy with a roast potato.

'So, Ebner, how many jews got away at Treblinka and how many did you managed to catch in that net of yours?'

The agent put the potato in his mouth and chewed it thoughtfully.

'Well,' he took a sip of water. 'After the prisoners stole weapons and attacked the fences, most of them were massacred by the guards and thankfully only around two-hundred managed to escape. Of those, we killed around a hundred wherever we found them hiding, mostly in the local woods and farmland. We arrested about thirty more and the rest got away.'

'Got away? Tut, tut, tut, Ebner really?' Chided Kruger as he wiped his mouth and dropped the napkin on his plate. 'Seventy jews running wild in the polish countryside that you couldn't catch? I change my mind, Ansel,' he said turning to Wolff. 'Perhaps the Gestapo won't be able to help you track down your pilot after all.'

The women looked bored.

Stein watched the youngest, sitting next to the gestapo agent. She had a sorry countenance. Her thin birdlike neck blushed with some nervous malady and she kept her large round eyes glued to the tablecloth with only the occasional smile at a joke tugging worriedly at her face. Her wrists stuck out like polished ivory from a cream chiffon blouse, open to her breast bone. Stein looked at her skin there. Pale, and thin. Her flat chest revealed no undergarments and he stared at where her breasts should have been. Her nipples poked awkwardly at the fabric of her blouse and but for her clear, albeit wide eyed beauty, she might easily have been a boy. She sat like a mouse surrounded by cats and she nibbled her food, and sipped her Champagne.

Too frightened to speak.

Too frightened to look.

Colette lent towards his ear and whispered.

'You like little Barbie, Captain Stein?'

Stein felt himself flush. He lit a cigarette to hide behind.

'She's just a child.'

Colette glanced across at the young woman. She shrugged as she turned back.

'Maybe, but I don't think Monsieur Schenk cares, do you?'

Stein smiled politely.

'I really wouldn't know.'

Colette took the cigarette from his hand and smoked it. Stein looked at her as she pointed at Kruger and his escort. They were deep in conversation and Madam Petit was pulling gently on the colonel's ear as they talked, their faces only inches from each other.

'You prefer them older perhaps?'

He ignored the question and lit another cigarette.

'What?' Said Colette smiling at him.

'You don't think a woman should fuck to survive?'

He winced and turned towards her.

'What?'

'Oh come on Captain,' she soothed, leaning forward and looking intently at him.

She smelled good, despite her raw arrogance.

'You're not like them,' she tilted her head discreetly towards the other Germans. Stein felt the energy shift between them and it surprised him.

'You're more like us.' She put her hand on his knee once more. He ignored it.

'What do you mean?' He asked, though he knew what she meant.

She paused, just looking at his face. He suddenly wanted to kiss her, and he damned himself for it.

The waiters came and gathered up the plates. As Stein's place was cleared Colette sat back and released him from her gaze. She looked at his untouched food.

'Are you not hungry Captain?'

'My name is Max.'

'Are you not hungry…Max?'

He looked at her. She had the fireplace behind her and she appeared in that moment as if she were wreathed in flames that danced all around her and made her black hair shine like oil.

'Yes,' he said quietly. 'I'm hungry.' He looked around the table - everyone was talking. Schenk had even persuaded the childlike Barbie to say a few words. *Praying for her soul*, Stein thought.

'I'm just not *that* hungry.' He said eventually. He turned and smiled at her.

'A starving man must feed Max.' She said leaning forward again and taking his hand in hers. He looked at her skin, warm and soft, her nails, modestly manicured and clean, her fingers slender and graceful. His own felt rough and coarse and were stained with tank oil and tobacco. She lifted his hand and kissed it tenderly. Closing her eyes as she did. He felt himself sway slightly, as if he were slipping into a hypnotic trance.

'Colette…'

She opened her eyes and looked at him and his heart ached and the blood pumped through him in a dark, throbbing rhythm. Something moved inside him that had long since lain dormant and as he breathed in her warm scent, his fingers tightening around hers.

Wolff's voice broke the spell as the waiters bustled around them gathering dishes and clearing the rest of the table.

'So, after dessert can we talk over our mission with you detective? All joking aside I would very much like to hear any thoughts you might have.'

Schenk nodded in agreement, his leaden tones sounded soulless and devoid of humanity, and it seemed to Stein as if he spoke from somewhere cut off from this world.

'Of course Haupsturmfuhrer, I would be happy to help however I can.'

The waiters returned carrying a large silver platter, covered with a dome. They placed it carefully in the middle of the table and lifted the lid dramatically to reveal a gateaux so large it might have fed an entire village. The SS clapped and smiled and the women laughed. Schenk sipped his water and Colette leant in again and spoke in Stein's ear.

'I am staying here tonight. Come and visit me later - please.' She kissed him softly on the cheek and her smell overcame him once more as she breathed.

'You won't regret it Max. I promise.'

They sat in comfortable chairs by the fire, the women having since departed to separate bedrooms to prepare themselves for whatever ordeal awaited them.

The warmth of the fire and the sedation from food and drink was settling in and it was all Stein could do to stifle a yawn.

'That was a wonderful meal Heinz, please pay my compliments to your chef.' Wolff held out his glass for more brandy as a butler bowed politely and poured while another moved around the group offering cigars.

Wolff took one and sniffed it and rolled it beside his ear in the well practiced manner of those with a taste for luxury.

To Stein's surprise Schenk took one too - it was the most human thing he had done all night.

'What are these?' Asked Wolff smelling the cigar once more.

Kruger passed him a lighter.

'They're British as a matter of fact. A gift from one of Ebnar's men overseas.'

Wolff puffed grandly on the cigar as he lit it, disappearing in a cloud of aromatic smoke.

'I've always said the British have wonderful taste.' he smiled as he emerged, blinking through the fog.

Stein looked into the fire, it had been a long few days. The panzer camp back in Peronne seemed a lifetime ago. He missed the familiarity of his life there. The simplicity of routine, the closeness with his men, a quiet evening in his cabin with a book.

When the butler's had drifted away, the four of them sat and smoked for a while. Like tribal chiefs of ages past, they surrounded themselves with sweet scented smoke and drank warm cognac, their eyes narrowing to slits in the afterglow of the conquerers feast.

Eventually Kruger spoke, his voice now deep and laced with brandy and tobacco.

'So, gentlemen,' he growled. 'It's getting late and I for one have an attractive woman warming my bed. Why don't we discuss this mission of yours Ansel?'

Wolff propped his cigar in an ashtray and drained his cognac. He looked at Schenk.

'Can the Gestapo help?'

Schenk nodded.

'I think so, yes.'

'How well do you know the city?' Asked Stein.

'Personally, not really that well. But I have people here that know it intimately.'

'And who might they be?'

The Gestapo agent threw what was left of his cigar at the fire.

'We have *assets* in almost every major city in the world captain Stein.'

'You mean spies?'

'Yes, if you like. *Spies.*'

'Do you have spies in Rouen?'

Schenk nodded. 'Yes, as a matter of fact that is why I am here. One of my contacts has managed to infiltrate a group of Resistance fighters in the city. I have come to get an update on their current progress and to report back to Berlin.'

'You're their handler?'

'Broadly speaking, yes. So far, they have simply been gathering intelligence on local groups and allied sympathisers, and feeding that back to me in regular reports.'

'Are they having much of an impact?' Asked Kruger.

Schenk checked his watch.

'Well Colonel, as we speak they are coordinating a strike against an operation that one particular Resistance group has been planning for some time.'

'Tonight?' said Stein.

The agent brushed ash from his knee.

'Yes, tonight.'

'What sort of operation?'

'Forgive me for not giving you the full details Captain, but rest assured, the Resistance operation *will* fail, much to the surprise of those involved I'm sure. And I am also certain that most, if not all members of that particular group will not live to see the morning.'

'After tonight, you think this asset might be able to help us find the pilot?'

'They are well placed within the Resistance, and they are trusted.' He pondered the question for a moment more then nodded again.

'If they survive tonight then yes, I think there's a strong chance they will find him. That is, *if* your pilot has contacted the Resistance.'

He looked at Wolff.

'How did you find out he was coming to Rouen?'

'A priest told us, in the village where he first looked for help.'

'Do you trust he was telling the truth?'

Wolff glanced at Stein and then looked back at the Gestapo.

'I doubt he would lie.'

'Well, there must have been a reason for him to come here rather than any other city. I doubt very much that he selected Rouen by chance.' Schenk sipped his water. 'My guess would be that he either knows people here which seems unlikely but possible, or he managed to contact England somehow and they told him to come here to meet someone that could help him.'

'Which definitely sounds more probable,' added Kruger.

Schenk nodded.

Stein relaxed back in his chair.

'So, what happens next? Do we get to meet this person…your, asset?'

'Possibly, yes. They are due to contact me tomorrow by radio to debrief me on tonight's raid. I will speak to them about the pilot then - perhaps after that I might arrange a meeting.'

'So as you said earlier, we just wait?'

'For now, yes, I will know more tomorrow.'

'Good,' said Kruger. He turned to face Wolff who had his fingers raised in a steeple, resting on his top lip. He looked deep in thought.

'Ansel, ist gut?'

Wolff pondered on in silence for a moment more then nodded slowly.

'Ja, ja…ist gut.'

Outside in the candlelit hall, they all bid a cordial goodnight, each going off to a different corner of the chateau to indulge themselves in whichever way their remaining energy or their ardour might allow. Stein went to the front door and opened it and stood for a while on the step and took in the night air. It was fresh and cool. He watched the guards with their dogs walking along the tree line, before looking up at the sky and the stars as they flickered in and out like diamond worlds, glinting mutely at him across unimaginable distances.

He stood and he listened to the darkness.

Reaching into his pocket, he took out his cigarettes. He put one in his mouth and lit it and as he put his lighter back in his pocket he came out with a folded napkin. He opened it and read the few lines that had been written on it. It was from Colette.

Second floor.

West wing,

Third door on the right.

He folded the napkin and put it back in his pocket and he leant his shoulder against the wall and smoked and watched the guards. He stayed there for a long time, just smoking and watching and thinking.

An owl called from somewhere deep in the forest beyond the chateau walls. It was a hollow, wooden sound and it echoed along the slopes than ran down to the city. The hooting woke Stein from his rumination and as he went to go back inside the chateau, he stopped for a moment and turning his head slightly, he bent his ear to the night and the distant sound of gunfire out towards the horizon.

CHAPTER ELEVEN
The Quarry

Wellum peered through the darkness, down into the quarry from the fringes of the wood, then he looked at the quarter moon floating like a silver sickle among a thousand glittering stars, illuminating everything with a pale grey aura.

It was too light.

Brielle checked her watch as they sat and tried to soak into whatever blackness there was around them.

'How long?' asked Wellum quietly.

It had been three minutes since the RAF Lancaster had flown over them. The sound of its engines filling the air before fading into silence over the unseen horizon to the north.

She held up three fingers and Wellum lifted the binoculars and peered down into the belly of the quarry.

They were on the edge of an abandoned slate mine. An open hole some four-hundred-feet wide and around two-hundred-feet deep. It was almost circular, and was cut deep into a pine forest eight miles north of Rouen. A group of buildings huddled together away to their right on the eastern side of the pit and Wellum shifted the binoculars and looked towards them. He could just about see their pale wooden shapes squatting in the gloom, but he couldn't see Irene or Matis, though he knew they were there. He looked back down into the pit.

A red glow, reflecting off puddles seemed to pulse and throb in the darkness.

'I thought they said that damn red light could only be seen from the air.' He passed Brielle the binoculars. 'It's a good job it's buried down there,' he went on. 'If that was in a field above ground, every bloody German this side of Paris would be strolling over to have a look.'

Godfrey had driven the truck from Rouen with Brielle sitting alongside him, memorising the route as she was the back up driver for the return to the city if anything happened to Godfrey or Matis. Wellum sat in the back with Irene and the two frenchmen. Elliot was a young, good looking man from a village just outside the city. He talked about going south after the war, 'To make wine,' he had laughed, and to never work again. Irene had chided him playfully about his penchant for luxury and for his ever changing fantasies.

'Oh Elliot, mon diu. This month a wine maker, last month a diamond trader. Really?'

Wellum had smiled and offered his labours on the vineyard for free.

'See,' said Elliot to Irene. 'With Harry's help I will grow the rarest Mourvedre grapes and we we will blend them with Syrah and Grenache and we will make the finest wine the Langedouc has seen for three-hundred-years.'

Irene had rolled her eyes and blown her cheeks and smiled.

'Eh bien, lorsque tu seras un homme riche, j'espere que nous serons toujours amis.'

Matis was older and a native of Rouen. Wellum got the impression he had seen a lot of fighting. He was stoic and quiet and seemed solid and professional.

'Can you help to get me on a train?' Wellum had asked as the drove north. Matis had nodded and sat forward, accepting a cigarette from the pilot. 'I think it's possible, yes.'

He had a large moustache that moved when he spoke and he smoothed the corners habitually with his finger.

'I will find a train going west, a night train and together we'll go.'

'Together?'

Matis had nodded.

'Of course,' he patted Wellum on the knee with a heavy hand. 'Do not worry, we will get you home.' He sat back and smoked and smoothed his moustache.

A sound like a sigh and the movement of air through canvas floated towards them on a faint breeze.

'There look,' said Brielle handing Wellum the binoculars and pointing into the night ahead.

A parachute, bloated and pale drifted like an apparition before them. It was only two-hundred feet from the ground and as wellum watched, it seemed as if it was hanging motionless in the sky. He watched it dropping gracefully, its swollen, cream coloured fabric staining red from the ground light as it sank almost soundlessly to earth.

A metallic thud rang around the quarry as the canister landed and the canopy, blood red now in the light, emptied itself of air and opened like an orchid as it deflated and fell in elegant folds to its death.

Wellum checked his watch.

'Right on time.'

He looked towards the buildings on the east bank and waited for the signal. A torch flashed twice.

On then off.

On, then off.

Wellum handed Brielle the binoculars as he lifted his own torch and pointed it towards Irene's position.

'Here, look into the pit and tell me when Godfrey sends the signal to come down.'

Wellum signalled back to Irene with the torch while Brielle glassed the drop zone.

'Anything?'

'No,' said Brielle, still peering towards the red glow.

'I can see the weapons canister and the parachute lying near the light but I can't see…'

The flash made them both duck instinctively, as it illuminated the quarry in a brief and shocking instant. The explosion followed, rolling deafeningly around the pit and in the sudden brightness they saw a man running in a crouch, a weapon in his right hand, stooping and scrambling in surprise, looking for cover, splashing through puddles. As they watched, he stumbled forward and fell to the ground. The air ripped with the sound of automatic weapons and then a second grenade exploded close to the first and this time they saw many soldiers, kneeling and firing and some running. Another flash lit the night and then bursts of gunfire erupted from the east as Irene and Matis began firing down into the pit, their position suddenly illuminated from a searchlight mounted on a truck on the opposite bank of the quarry.

Wellum watched in horror as Irene, clear now in the brightness of the arc light knelt and poured fired down upon the Germans, her head suddenly snapping grotesquely to the side as she was hit with dozens of rounds and lifted and thrown backwards. Matis stepped forward to take her place and he too was cut down. Folding at the waist and collapsing, as his chest erupted in crimson, florid explosions.

'Shit, it's an ambush,' said Wellum as he got to his knees, throwing his machine gun over his shoulder by its sling.

'No, no…it can't be,' said Brielle, her voice on the edge of panic. She knelt and cocked her rifle and looked down the barrel for something to shoot at.

'Don't,' said Wellum grasping her shoulder, they'll see us, let's go, come on.'

'No, we must help them.' She cried shrugging off his hand and shouldering her weapon. She fired and reloaded and fired again. In the pit, the red light glowed, and shapes moved this way and that, shouting in German and firing sporadic, clattering volleys that rang all around and seemed to tear holes in the night. Someone was shouting in French and a weapon burst into life a hundred feet beyond the light, but then fell silent as the Germans turned and sent more grenades and a volley from a dozen guns down onto the position.

Muzzle flashes suddenly burst towards Wellum and Brielle like yellow dragon flowers, erupting angrily in ragged flames that growled in the darkness sending rounds screaming past them, destroying trees and snapping branches as the Germans shot back.

'Come on,' shouted Wellum over the noise as he fired towards the massing troops.

'It's too late, they've gone, I saw them fall, come on, we must leave.'

Brielle shot. Indiscriminate and blind, she cocked the rifle and fired, reloaded and fired, reloaded and fired again until the magazine clip sprung up past her ear with a twang. Her last shot a dead click as the hammer fell impotently against an empty chamber. She dropped the rifle and reached for her pistol, weeping bitterly as she did.

'Come on Brielle, we must go now.'

'Wait,' she cried through gritted teeth, 'No we can't...'

She fired her pistol and Wellum watched a soldier fall. He raised his own weapon and fired and knelt beside Brielle and fired again. More men fell and the red light glowed at their backs. A bullet burned past Wellum's ear, with a sudden zipping sound that made him squint and jerk his head away. He squeezed the trigger and emptied his magazine into a shape that was moving quickly towards them up the slope, but then fell and lay still.

Wellum stood up and reached down and pulled Brielle up alongside him. She fired again then holstered her weapon and followed him as he moved away, and as bullets whistled past them and the twigs and branches fell, she followed him and they turned together and ran into the forest.

They ran through the trees for ten minutes. Their lungs burning, stumbling through bracken and tripping over tree roots, falling and collecting themselves and going on. They made their way south as best they could, deep into the sweet scented forest with the thump and crack of weapons and the shouting soldiers still bellowing behind them. After a while the shooting stopped but still they ran, and now the sounds of their desperate escape and the pounding of their hearts was the loudest thing in the night.

'Stop,' said Brielle eventually. 'Wait, I need to rest.'

Wellum stopped running and crouched and listened and looked around. They were both breathing hard, and steam rose from Brielle in the moonlight as she stooped and lent on her knees gasping. She shivered and heaved in huge lung-full's of air.

'Oh god, oh god…what happened?'

'We were ambushed, ' said Wellum as he unslung his weapon and took out the magazine and tilted it towards the moon, counting the rounds.

'They seemed to come from nowhere,' said Brielle spitting into the bracken and wiping her mouth with her sleeve.

'They must have been waiting for us, said Wellum. He threw the magazine down the front of his jacket and took a new one from his pocket and fitted it and cocked the gun and reslung it over his shoulder.

'Do you know where we are?' Said Brielle.

'We ran south, so I'm guessing we're close to the small lake we passed when we arrived earlier.'

'We must also be near the truck then.'

'Maybe,' said Wellum. He took out his water bottle and unscrewed the lid and passed it to Brielle.

'But there's always the risk the Germans found it and have either booby trapped it, or are waiting to shoot or arrest anyone that returns to collect it.'

The sound of a lorry approaching along the road made them crouch.

'There, look,' said Wellum. 'Come on, this way.'

They made their way carefully a little further into the trees and hid and watched as two sets of headlights approached from the direction of the quarry.

'You were right about being close to the road,' whispered Brielle, as the trucks rumbled past on unseen tarmac just forty feet away. As they went, Wellum could see men sitting in the back of one of the lorries tending some wounded soldiers.

'Do you think that's all of them? Asked Brielle.

'Let's hope so. But we'd better stay off any roads for as long as possible, just in case.'

'Do you think they have Irene and Godfrey and the others?' She sounded desperate and horrified. She reached out her hand and attempted to stand up but Wellum pulled her back down alongside him.

'Oh God,' she sobbed. 'Are they all dead, did you see them die?'

Wellum put his hand on her shoulder, trying to calm her.

'Ssshhh, Brielle, stop. We must leave here. Do you understand, we must get back to the city, we can't linger here.'

She breathed in and exhaled slowly, calming herself.

'I'm alright,' she said, taking another deep breath. 'Oh fuck, are they dead Harry? Really?'

He didn't answer.

They went a little further, hidden in the undergrowth, always keeping the road on their left side. After a few minutes Wellum crouched against a tree, pulling Brielle down at his side, he pointed. A soldier stood with a dog on the road ahead, talking to two other Germans. As they watched a fourth man approached the group from a little further down the road and began pointing and giving orders.

'What now?' Whispered Brielle. Wellum took out his compass and checked it behind his palm. He gestured with the barrel of his weapon. 'I think if we go this way, we can box around their position and then we can begin heading south again towards the city.' He returned the compass to his pocket. Despite the cold of the night, they were both sweating from exertion and fear, and steam rose from them like silver smoke in the moonlight. 'Here,' Wellum passed Brielle the water bottle once more. 'Lets keep drinking, we're both sweating buckets.' Brielle drank and wiped her mouth and handed him the bottle.

'We should go a little further away from the road and then we can decide on the best way out of here.'

They crept forward, stepping cautiously and moving bracken and twigs to avoid any unnecessary sound. After a few minutes they stopped and Wellum checked his compass again and glanced up at the stars. Satisfied, he clicked the safety catch forward on his weapon and lay it carefully on the ground next to him.

'Alright, I think from here we're probably only about five miles from Rouen. Are you injured at all?'

Brielle shook her head. 'No, I don't think so.'

As they spoke Wellum was retying his boot laces and tucking his trousers into his socks.

'I think if we make a good push from here we can get back to the house in two hours. Once we get out of the forest and head back into the city, you'll be able to find the address won't you?'

'Yes, I think so,' said Brielle tucking in her shirt. She reloaded the pistol and put it back in the holster under her arm. She drank more water and poured some into her hand and threw it onto her face and washed her neck. She handed the canteen back to Wellum.

'Here, wash your face, you have a cut above your eye.'

Wellum touched his eyebrow with his finger tips and winced. He checked his fingers. A little blood, nothing serious.

'I must have hit a branch as we ran.'

'Let me see.'

Brielle put her hand against his cheek and turned his face gently towards the moonlight.

She came close to him her hot breath warming his mouth and nose. He closed his eyes.

'It's fine,' she whispered softly. He opened his eyes and looked at her mouth, inches from his own. He could feel the heat coming off her and the smell of her body rolled over him. She kept her hand on his face.

'It's just a scratch.'

They stared at each other in the moonlight and breathed slowly together, safe in the moment, Wellum felt reluctant to move.

'We should go now,' said Brielle.

'I know.' Said Wellum still holding her gaze.

'Come on.' He began to get up.

'Wait,' said Brielle. Her hand still at his cheek. 'Just wait, one moment more.'

Wellum relaxed and put his hand up to meet hers. He looked into her eyes, wet and dark, but shining clear in the night. They both seemed to be caught in a blueness that gathered all around them and pushed the forest away. A deep blue, burning like a halo. Eventually Wellum moved his hand and the blue flames faded and the world came back. The stars glittered above them and the night air was cold and damp once more.

'We had better get moving.' He smiled thinly. 'Wouldn't want to start freezing up.'

They headed east on a bearing that led them deeper into the woods, then after ten minutes they turned south once more and found a path that looked to be heading out towards the edges of the forest. Every fifteen minutes they stopped and checked their bearings against the compass and the stars. After an hour they could see the trees beginning to thin out and they began to perceive the faint glow of the city beyond. As they arrived at the edge of the forest they stopped and looked out of the trees. The city was about three miles away, beyond a mottled landscape of farmland and fields. They were high up and looked down over a black and grey vista, silent and still under the watchful stars. They breathed in and looked about them.

Brielle checked her watch.

David Stokes

'What time is it?' Asked Wellum.
'A little after one.'

They went on, using the hedgerows and ancient stone walls as cover and moving quicker now, they made their way in haphazard zig-zags, across fields and over fences, tacking south then east then south once more, sticking to the shadows wherever they could then running carefully whenever they had a chance.

As they went, they could hear distant gunfire and the drone of aircraft and the crump and thud of an air raid happening somewhere over the horizon. The play and counter play of death and destruction, attack and escape that forged a new link in the unbroken chain of tragedy that had been destroying peoples lives since the war had begun.

It felt as if the world had descended into Hell.

They kept off the roads, and when they arrived at the village of Chatenay on the outskirts of the city, they stayed in the darkness of the fields, drifting over them like shadows and eventually after what seemed like hours beyond count, they found their way back into the ancient, narrow streets of Rouen.

When they got back to Rue Etoupe, they stood under the awning of the boarded up shop and looked at Armada's house. It grinned at them, as was its habit, but now shrouded once more in the veil of night it's malevolence and strange hollowness seemed darker than ever.

'I can't believe we're going to have to tell him what happened,' said Brielle, shivering in the cold. 'I feel like a child.'

Wellum looked down at her; The shock and grief of the last few hours was etched into her face and she looked drawn and tired. He looked back at the house.

'Let's just get in there and warm up a bit. I think we've both earned a brandy. We can deal with Armada in the morning.'

They checked the road. It was silent and empty, then they crossed the cobbles and went to the side door and unlocked it and stepped quickly inside. Wellum turned and locked the door behind them and Brielle started up the stairs towards the kitchen. He watched her going wearily up each step, gripping the bannister and hauling herself along and suddenly he felt a wave of pain wash over him as if all of the exertions of the night poured into him in an instant. He closed his eyes and breathed deeply trying to calm himself as the fatigue and emotional exhaustion threatened to overwhelm him.

'Are you alright?' Said Brielle, stopping halfway up the stairs to wait for him.

He gathered himself.

'No,' he shook his head, then smiled. 'I'm fucking exhausted.'

Brielle smiled back.

'Let's find Armada's brandy, come on.' She turned and went on.

As they opened the door and entered the kitchen Wellum knew immediately that something wasn't right.

Maybe it was the position of the chairs in the darkness, maybe it was the faintest smell of gun smoke as they walked in, but something was definitely different.

As Brielle put her hand against the wall, searching for the light switch, a voice came out of the shadows on their right and the cocking of a pistol followed.

'Stand still. Put your hands up. Both of you.'

They froze, then both lifted their hands cautiously above their heads.

'Move forwards, slowly. Don't turn around.'

They shuffled forwards towards the dining table.

'Alright stop there.'

Someone behind them switched on a lamp.

'Turn around.'

A man, shorter than Wellum, with dark curls and a stubbled chin stood beside the door pointing a Mauser in their direction. He wore a knitted sweater and a dark blue jacket splattered with mud, and his accent was heavy with thick French undertones. His left wrist was wrapped in a rudimentary bandage that was dirty and blood stained and was held against his chest with a makeshift sling.

He gestured with the muzzle of the pistol.

'Sit down at the table, keep your hands where I can see them.'

They did as he instructed.

He watched them, his eyes moving from one the the next.

'Are you the pilot?'

Wellum didn't answer.

'Qui êtes vous? Pourquoi êtes vous ici?' Said Brielle.

He pointed the gun at her.

'Je pose les questions.'

He looked back at Wellum.

'You have a doorkey, put it on the table....slowly. Use your left hand, keep the other one where I can see it.'

Wellum reached carefully into his jacket pocket and took out the key and placed it on the table.

'Ok good, now I'll ask you once more, are you the pilot?'

His hand gripped the Mauser tighter and he moved it forward an inch pointing it at Wellum's face.

Wellum nodded. 'Yes.'

'Do you have cigarettes?'

'Yes.'

The man lowered the gun to his waist but kept it pointing towards them.

'Light one for me.'

Wellum reached into his pocket once more and came out with a crumpled packet of cigarettes. He took one and lit it and slid forward in his chair and held it out. The man stepped forward and took it and put it in his mouth and sucked hard on it. Wellum took another and lit it and sat back in his chair.

'Where's Armada?' Said Wellum eventually.

The man uncocked the pistol and took another long drag on the cigarette.

'Armada's dead.'

Brielle glanced at Wellum and then looked back at the stranger.

'My name is Yvain.'

'You're French?'

'He's not French,' said Brielle.

'Belgian,' confirmed the man.

'What happened?' Asked Wellum.

'We were out delivering some radios to an address in the west of Rouen. A gift for the Germans.'

'Yes, I know about those,' said Wellum. 'Armada showed me them yesterday.'

Yvain nodded and smoked. 'So you know how it was meant to go?'

'Roughly, yes.'

'We were to deliver the radios then stakeout the address and kill any Germans that turned up to investigate. A simple enough job.'

'Except?'

'Except, the Wehrmacht were already there when we arrived.'

'An ambush?'

'Yes.'

Brielle shuffled uncomfortably in her chair.

'We...' started the Belgian.

'Who's we?'

'Our team. Armada, myself and two others that we work with.'

Wellum nodded. 'Go on.'

'We had just arrived at the address and were setting the anti-handling switches on the radios when we heard voices outside in the street calling for us to come out and surrender.' He pulled a last lungful from the cigarette and stubbed it out in an ashtray. He smiled ruefully.

'That, er, that wasn't going to happen.'

'So you fought your way out?'

'We tried.'

'Is everyone else dead? The other members of your team?'

'Yes.'

'How come you made it out alive?' Said Brielle.

'Just lucky I guess.'

'Bullshit.'

'Look, I could have killed you both as you walked in, but I didn't did I? And if you think I'm dragging the SS behind me to capture you here, then where are they? Why aren't they here now?'

He put the pistol in a holster under his jacket and held out his palms.

'I got out through a back window and went up over the roof.'

'You saw Armada fall?' Asked Wellum.

'Yes. Initially we agreed to come out and be arrested, then we sent out grenades and machine gun fire instead. We fought them for ten minutes, shooting through the windows, killing as many as we could, then they rocketed us and the house started to burn. Armada was shot in the head. He died instantly.'

'What about the other two. Your comrades?'

'One was killed when the first rocket came in, the other, a Swiss name Macaire had both his legs badly injured by a grenade. We were the last two alive and he urged me to leave. He stayed and detonated the radios when the Germans entered the building.'

'How do you know that?' Asked Brielle.

'Because I was on a rooftop two houses away when he did it. I saw several soldiers assault the building and then it blew up. It could only have been Macaire.'

They fell silent. Eventually Wellum spoke.

'Do you know where Armada kept his brandy?'

Yvain nodded towards the kitchen then winced and held his ribs.

'In the cupboard, by the sink there.'

Wellum stood up cautiously, his hands at shoulder level.

'So, we're friends, yes?'

Yvain nodded.

'Yes, we're friends.'

Brielle didn't look convinced. She frowned towards the stranger, but Wellum went on.

'Right, well let's have a drink and then if you want, we'll have a look at your injuries.'

'I'm fine, said Yvain,' moving gingerly towards the table and sitting down.

'You don't look fine,' said Wellum from the kitchen. He collected the Korbel and three glasses. Brielle moved her chair an inch away from the Belgian.

'I fell from the roof as I ran, that's all. It's nothing really, just bruising I think.'

Wellum poured brandy and sat back down.

'Here,' he slid a glass towards Yvain. He took a drink and closed his eyes. When he opened them again he asked.

'What happened to you? Armada said you were with Irene and Godfrey tonight, something about collecting weapons or something.'

Wellum looked into his brandy.

'We got jumped too.'

'What?'

Brielle finished her drink and picked up the bottle.

'You heard him,' she said as she refilled her glass.

'We were ambushed as well.'

Yvain looked at the table and then at Wellum. He shook his head.

'Armada was right all along,' he said quietly, as if to himself.

'He suspected a mole somewhere.'

'Oui,'

'Irene and Godfrey suspected it too,' said Wellum

'We all suspect it, but never really believe it could be true. Like death. We know it can happen at any time but always, tomorrow, or the next day or the next…never today.'

'Well, now Irene is dead and Godfrey and others too,' said Brielle. 'So yes, it's real, this… this mole. They're real and they are here in Rouen somewhere and inside *your* organisation and theirs and whoever else's.' She stood up and banged her hand on the table.

'Putain de connards stupides, vous les avez putain laisses entrer. Mon dieu…idiots!'

'Hey,' Yvain shouted back at her, pointing his finger.

'Il n'y a pas de taupe dans mon équipe Vous surveillez simplement votre bouche. Ce sont mes hommes qui sont morts ce soir, pas les votres!'

Wellum stood up and held out a hand towards them both, keeping them apart.

'Stop this…stop.'

Brielle sat down breathing hard. She drank her brandy.

'This isn't going to help any of us.' Said Wellum.

Yvain and Brielle eyed each other. Wellum passed the stranger another cigarette.

'If there is a mole, do you have any idea who it might be? Any clue at all?'

Yvain shook his head and lit the cigarette.

'Not really, no.'

Wellum reached.

'Maybe the German's just got lucky.'

Brielle shook her head.

'Not twice in one night, I don't believe it.'

Wellum looked at Yvain and shrugged. The Belgian shook his head.

'No, I agree with her, not this lucky.'

They fell back into silence.

'How safe do you think this place is?' Said Wellum eventually.

'Pretty safe,' said Yvain. 'I was the only one in the group that knew Armada was living here and I think if the SS or Gestapo knew, they'd have come here and arrested or killed him weeks ago.'

'Irene and Godfrey didn't know about this place?' Asked Brielle.

'No,' said Yvain. 'Just me.'

'And what makes you so special?'

'I was sent here, to Rouen, specifically to work with Armada.'

'Sent by who?' Asked Wellum.

'The SOE in London.'

'Why did they send you?'

'I was part of the Free Belgian Forces that got out of Europe in 'thirty-nine. I joined the SOE shortly after arriving in the UK and in January of 'forty-one I was selected to join a new regiment being set up and based in Hereford.'

'The SAS?' Said Wellum.

Yvain nodded.

'Yes, I was one of the first in the fifth SAS regiment, made up only of Belgian volunteers. They garrisoned us up in Scotland for a while, near Loudon Castle, and trained us mostly in sabotage and intelligence gathering. For the rest of 'forty-one I was in and out of Belgium on SOE operations, then during Christmas of last year I was called to London and told I'd be parachuting into Rouen before the new year, to join a sleeper agent that had been working alone for the previous twelve months.'

'Armada hinted at some big jobs he was developing. You were here to help him with those?'

Yvain looked at them both. He nodded.

'Yes, well…' he paused. 'We were about to go into the planning phase for a mission Armada had been working on. Something big. My job had been to recruit a team and run some rudimentary missions to get everyone up to speed on working together.'

'The men you lost tonight?"

'Yes.'

'Did he tell you what the main mission was?'

Yvain shook his head.

'No. It was the way he worked. Keep everything under wraps until the appropriate time and then only briefing the people involved in specific tasks and timings. Like I said, after tonights job, it was the next thing on the list. Beginning the planning phase for whatever it was he had lined up.'

Wellum checked his watch. Dawn was only an hour away. He looked at Brielle, the Brandy had sedated her and she looked ready to sleep.

'We should contact London and let them know what's happened.'

Yvain agreed.

Brielle got up slowly and made for the stairs.

'I need to go to bed.' She looked at Yvain.

'Bonsoir monsieur.'

He nodded at her.

The two men watched her go, then Wellum turned back to the Belgian.

'I'm not going to tell London about where I've been tonight.'

Yvain shrugged then winced and held his ribs.

'Whatever. It's your decision.'

They went through to the radio room and Yvain sat down and switched on the wireless.

'This whole mess puts us both back at square one doesn't it.'

Wellum gave a grim smile.

'Yes, it does somewhat.'

Yvain tuned in the wireless and tapped out a morse report to his department in London and wrote down their reply. After a few minutes he got up from the chair and handed the headset to Wellum.

'Here, your turn.'

Wellum span some of the dials and tapped out his old callsign.

Lotus this is Samphire
Lotus this is Samphire
Are you reading?

The headset hissed and beeped, a pulsing, rhythmic signature Wellum recognised.

Samphire this is Lotus.

Wellum tapped the morse key.

Lotus, Armada is dead.

Silence

*Lotus, I repeat
Armada is dead
How copy?*

*Samphire
That's a good copy
Armada is dead
Over*

*Lotus, will send details as best as I can tomorrow at some time after ten-hundred hours. After that, will await further instructions.
Over.*

*Samphire, roger.
Will wait for contact tomorrow.
Over*

Samphire. Out

He dragged the headset from his head and dropped it wearily onto the table and turned off the radio.

'Well, I suppose now we just wait.'
Yvain nodded.

'Yes, I need to sleep.' He gingerly unslung his arm and looked at the bandage on his wrist.

'I'll see to this in the morning.'

Wellum got up and walked towards the door.

'I'm sorry about your team Yvain. Armada seemed like a good chap.'

The Belgian smiled thinly and shrugged.

'He was a good soldier. I never really got to know the man.'

Wellum nodded.

'Get some rest.'

Wellum stood under the shower with his head bowed and his eyes closed, the hot water flowing hard against his neck as columns of steam rose up from the bathtub and surrounded him in aromatic, soap scented clouds.

His mind played over the last few days.

He heard the sound of his stricken aircraft groaning under the strain of it's death dive as bullets broke open its side and it turned in agony towards earth, and he remembered the whistling of the wind filling his ears as he rolled clear of its burning carcass and pulled hard on his parachute's rip chord. He thought about Father Marcelin, his kind smile and his soft fingers dressing the wounds on Wellum's hand. He saw again the dead German at his feet with blood pumping from a hole, in his temple and he thought about Armada; Strange and sad somehow, alone for so long in this house full of ghosts. Then he heard the air tearing with bullets and the dull thud of grenades flashing in the night as images of Godfrey cut down in blood red puddles filled his mind and of Irene, thrown back in an eruption of crimson holes punched savagely into her breast and neck and skull. He closed his eyes and lifted his face to meet the shower, the stinging water, cleansing him, burning his skin. He rolled the soap in his palms. Fragrant and smooth, it's floral scent like a balm, soothing and comforting, he washed himself and tried to forget.

The bathroom door opened and he broke off from thought, suddenly self conscious and looked towards who was there.

It was Brielle.

Wellum half turned away and covered himself.

'I'll be finished in a minute, I'm sorry, I assumed you'd already showered.'

Brielle looked at him and shook her head.

'No, not yet, I was waiting for you.'

She closed the door and watched him, then began unbuttoning her shirt. Wellum look at where the dirt and mud on her neck stopped at her collar line, her clean, tanned skin beneath. She dropped her shirt on the floor and pulled her vest up over her head. He looked at her breasts, small and round, and as she stepped out of her heavy, army issue trousers, he held out his hand and as she took it she seemed instantly transformed. No longer a soldier, tough and determined and androgynous, but now a woman, with curved hips and smooth skin and a mouth full and soft and perfectly formed. She climbed into the shower and pressed herself against him.

'I did not want to be alone.'

He lifted her face towards him and he kissed her.

'I don't want to be alone anymore,' she whispered, her mouth opening on his and her tongue pushing softly against his lips. He held her neck and pulled her towards him as his fear fell away and he remembered how it felt to be connected to love and life. As they kissed their eyes opened, and searchingly they stared as if each one saw the other for the first time anew, and the taste of her very being filled him so completely that nothing else mattered except her purity and perfection and his complete and total surrender to it.

CHAPTER TWELVE
Colette

Part two.

It was the sound of a spoon being tapped against a coffee cup that woke Stein. He rubbed his eyes and rolled towards the light. The coffee smelled good.

'What time is it?'

Colette put the spoon on the silver tray and picked up the coffee and walked over to the bed.

'It's a little after eight.'

She handed Stein the cup.

'Did you sleep well?'

Stein took a sip of the hot coffee and put the cup on the nightstand beside the bed.

'Yes. Thank you.'

Colette smiled at him and walked back to the table. She was naked beneath a long silk dressing gown, deep purple and expensive. Her movements seemed graceful and deliberate beneath its dark folds and her skin was bone white. Stein thought she had an aristocratic air, despite herself. She sat down and looked out of the windows over the grounds and poured herself some coffee. She lifted her foot and put it on the chair and propped her chin on her knee as she stirred the cup. Stein looked at her long, smooth legs. She was taller and more elegant than he'd realised.

'It's raining,' she said, looking up at the grey sky. She turned to face him.

'Are you married Max?'

He considered not answering.

'I was, yes.'

'Was?'

He swung his legs clear of the sheets and sat on the side of the bed and dragged a finger across the stubble on his chin.

'Why are you here?' He asked tiredly.

She sipped her coffee.

'This is my room.'

'No, I mean why are you here, in the chateau?'

'I was invited to dinner.'

'Who invited you?'

She put her cup down and crossed her legs.

'We don't have to do this.'

'Do what?'

She lit a cigarette and closed the robe, folding her arm across her lap to keep it shut.

'I was invited by Rosalie.'

'Ah yes, the colonel's escort.'

'They're lovers, Max.'

'Really?'

She threw him the cigarettes and he took one out and lit it and coughed roughly and tossed the packet onto the bed next to him. He looked around the room. Clothes were scattered everywhere - his mainly, and there was an open suitcase sitting against the far wall, its contents spilling out with a makeup bag and hairbrush sitting atop the pile like decorations on a cake.

Colette watched him taking in the room. She smoked and moved her arm, allowing the robe to slide open once more.

'So, why are *you* here?' She said eventually.

'I thought I was invited.'

She nodded slowly but didn't reply.

He stood and began picking up his scattered clothes.

'I'd better be going, Wolff will be thinking I've absconded.'

She sat forward and reached out for his hand.

'Please, don't go. Not yet.'

She doused her cigarette and stood and steered him back towards the bed. Stein was surprised how easily he let himself be led.

He sat down and she lay beside him.

'Where is your wife?'

He turned and looked at her. She had green eyes that were flecked with orange sparks, sharp and bright, like coals burning inside emeralds.

Stein was deeply attracted to her.

'My wife is dead.'

Colette picked at a loose thread in the eiderdown.

'When did she die?'

Stein picked up his coffee.

'Like you said, we don't have to do this.'

She lay down, her head resting on the pillow.
'I'm sorry.'
'Really, it's fine.'
'I shouldn't have asked.'
'It's fine.'

He glanced down at her. The purple robe falling away from her pale skin once more, she lay naked beside him. He looked at her full breasts and he could still smell her perfume, lingering and mixing with the scent of them both from the night before. He wanted to fall into her again. Memories of clinging to her in the darkness came back, her taste, and the way she had taken care of him, her open mouth guiding him, allowing him to take refuge in her, like she understood exactly what he needed and why.

He suddenly felt broken and vulnerable.
'Did Kruger pay you?'
'What do you mean - *pay me*?'
Stein shook his head.
'It doesn't matter.'
'You mean did I get paid to have sex with you?'
'Did you?'
'No, I didn't'
'Really?'
She covered herself once more.
'Really.'
They sat in silence.

She reached out with her leg and rubbed his back with the ball of her foot.

He looked at her.

'I'm sorry. It's been a long time, that's all.' He paused. 'I mean since I was with anyone but Misha.'

She smiled and massaged his back with her toes.

'You said something last night at dinner that stuck with me,' he said.

'What was that?'

'You asked if I didn't think a woman should fuck to survive.'

'And?'

'I was wondering if that's what you are doing here.'

'Maybe.'

'But you're not being paid?'

She pushed him with her foot.

'My god Max, stop.'

'What? I'm just curious.'

'Don't be.'

'Why not?'

'Because I'm still pretending that all this is normal and that we aren't at war and that you and I are attracted to each other and that we met at dinner and are here because of that alone. That's why.'

'A purer version of what is.'

'I suppose.'

'And is it so far from the truth?'

'Probably further than we both fear, yes.'

He turned away and looked at his hands.

'What a nightmare.'

She nodded.

'Yes, it is.'

They listened to the rain beating against the old chateau windows, leaded and thick paned. Colette slid her legs beneath the bedsheets and pulled the eiderdown up under her chin.

'It's freezing in here. Aren't you cold?'

'No,' Stein replied, his voice far off, his mind drifting elsewhere, through memories he didn't want to share. 'I've been colder.'

He turned and spoke over his shoulder to her.

'So what is the reality then?'

Colette thought for a moment.

'Well, last night was nice.'

He turned quickly.

'Nice?'

She smiled.

'Yes. It was *very* nice.'

'And?'

She sat up and moved his dark hair away from his forehead.

'And yes, I came here because it's one way I know to survive.'

'And what about me? Why am I here?'

'Because Captain Stein, as I said last night at dinner, I don't think that you are like them and I think maybe you are here trying to survive too.'

'Meaning?'

'Meaning you are not a Nazi, despite the company you are forced to keep, and while that of course is to be applauded, it must also bring it's own pressures on you. I understand that can't be easy'

Stein narrowed his eyes.

'Am I really that transparent?'

Colette smiled.

'Don't worry you play the role very well, and I think those around you are so caught up in their ideology, they are blinded to anyone that might not completely share their…how would you say it? Their…*point of view.*'

Stein turned and lay on the bed facing her. He traced her eyebrow with his finger.

'So you slept with me only to survive?'

She shook her head and spoke softly to him.

'No Max. I came to dinner to survive and I laughed at Kruger's jokes and I smiled at Wolff and I chatted fondly to you. That's all.' She held his face. 'That's all I needed to do last night. What came after that was for me - I wanted you to be here.'

He lent forward and kissed her and the smell of her hair and her perfume and the taste of tobacco in her mouth made him feel sane again. He pulled away and looked at her and her eyes moved across his face without fear. He kissed her again.

'Tell me this isn't normal for you, this feeling. Please tell me you're not just trying to survive.' He moved back. 'You really don't need to. Please Colette, tell me that's not what this is.'

She touched a finger to his lips then kissed him softly.

'Shh, Max, it's ok. That's not what this is. I promise.'

She shook her head.

'I can feel it too.'

She held him.

'For so long, that uniform you wear has meant horror and death to me. For so long it has meant that whoever wore it could act beyond God, without fear of reprisal. That uniform meant I could be raped, or killed, right there in the street or even in my own home, at any moment. I have lost so many people, people I have loved, because of that uniform. Then I worked out that if I came close enough I could stay out of danger. If I learned what these men wanted, I could live. I know my own people hate me for it, but I have been afraid for longer than I can remember.'

He pulled her to him.

'I'm sorry Colette.'

She looked at him and touched his face and kissed him.

'You aren't like them.'

'I know.' He moved her gently away. 'But I still wear the uniform, and I still have a job to do.'

She sat back and closed her robe and shivered beneath the sheets.

She gave him a weak smile.

'I know that Max, as sad as it makes me.'

She held his hand and a heaviness filled him and they sat in the grey silence and the rain came back.

'So, what now?'

'Are you hungry?'

'I'm starving,' said Stein with a slight smile. 'I hardly ate a thing at dinner.'

'Maybe it was the company?'

He nodded.

'Maybe.'

He got up and started picking up his clothes once more. Colette lay back and watched him, her dark hair spreading across the pillow.

'Do you know how long you will be in Rouen?'

'Not really.'

'Can you tell me why you're here?'

Stein pulled on his trousers and picked up his shirt.

'We're looking for a spy. A pilot.'

'Ah yes, someone mentioned him last night. An English pilot.'

Stein nodded as he buttoned his shirt.

'That's the one.'
'Will you catch him quickly do you think?'
He sat on the bed and hauled his boots on.
'I'm not sure you and I should be discussing it.'
She laughed.
'Why? Don't you trust me?'
He stood up and collected his jacket from a chair by the window.
'I don't trust anyone Colette, don't take it personally.'
She threw back the bedsheets and lay naked once more.
'But I do take it personally. I thought we were getting along so well.'
He came and sat down beside her and ran his hand up her leg. Smooth and warm and soft like fragrant silk, the smell that came off her made him want to stay.
'How will I contact you?'
She took his hand and kissed it and placed it between her breasts on her heart. He could feel it's dull thud, pulsing faintly against his palm.
Yes… she is alive.
'You can leave a message for me at La Dolma.'
'What's that?'
'Its a cafe and bar in the city. I work there. You can tell Hector that you want me and he'll let me know.'
'But you won't give me your address?'
'Not yet Max.'
He stood up and put his jacket on and picked up his hat. She looked at the iron cross stitched to his breast pocket. He reached up and touched it instinctively then smiled and nodded and clicked his heels.

'Mademoiselle Larue, thank you for a very pleasant evening. I do hope I get chance to see you again very soon. Until then, adieu.'

She blew him a kiss.

'I hope so too Captain Stein. I really do.'

He nodded once more and put his hat on and turned and went looking for Wolff.

He found him stood in the hall at the bottom of the stairs, talking to Schenk.

'Ah, Captain Stein,' Wolff beamed as he saw the tank officer descending the stairs. He raised his eyebrows suggestively.

'I trust you had a pleasant evening.' Stein smiled thinly and gave what he hoped was a noncommittal nod. He looked at Schenk.

'Good morning detective.'

The Gestapo nodded curtly but didn't smile.

'Detective Schenk has some interesting news Captain Stein. Apparently, at first light this morning his agent contacted the Gestapo to report that his mission in thwarting a Resistance operation last night was successful. He said that several members of the Resistance unit sent out on a task were killed by the Wehrmacht.'

Stein gave another unconvincing smile and wondered what any of this had to do with him. He looked at Schenk.

'That is excellent news detective, congratulations.'

Wolff held up a finger.

'Wait, there's more. Detective Schenk was also just telling me that he has arranged to meet his agent at a restaurant in the city today for lunch and he has invited us along to join him.'

'That's very generous,' said Stein. 'Thank you.'

'Yes,' continued Wolff enthusiastically. 'It would appear that the Detective's man might inadvertently have stumbled upon someone of interest to us.'

Stein looked at Schenk, his heavily lidded eyes hadn't moved and he seemed devoid of life, stood there clutching the bannister with his clawlike hand.

'How so?'

'Hauptmann Stein, Detective Schenk's agent has made contact with our English pilot.'

When Wellum came into the kitchen Yvain was already up and cooking.

'Ah, I'm sorry if I was noisy,' said the Belgian holding up the kettle.

'Would you like some tea?'

'Yes, please,' said Wellum sitting down at the table.

Yvain gestured to the door leading upstairs.

'Is Brielle still sleeping?'

Wellum nodded.

'Yes, it was a heavy night.'

'I don't think you need to worry much about her Monsieur Wellum,' he smiled and poured water into a teapot. 'She is strong I think. Yes?'

'Oh, yes.' Wellum felt his cheeks bruising, unsure if his new housemate had the same tendency to innuendo as Armada, though for some reason he doubted if they were similar at all.

'How are you feeling?' Said Wellum

Yvain touched his ribs.

'Bit sore.' He carried the teapot over to the table and set it down gingerly. He smiled.

'I'll live.'

Wellum poured the tea.

'So, have you got any theories about what happened last night?'

The Belgian sat down at the table.

'Nothing concrete no. It's clear that someone informed the Germans about your rendezvous with the RAF and our mission, but I'm struggling to imagine who it might be.'

'Do you think they were connected?'

'It's possible, but unlikely. Armada kept all of his plans very close, especially over this last six months. The Charrons' had no idea we were going out last night so any leak at their end couldn't have included us.'

'Something got discussed on a radio perhaps? Overheard by the Germans?'

Yvain shook his head.

'No, not on our side anyway. We planned everything face to face. Irene and Godfrey might have been caught out that way though. They did have to plan their job on the wireless and I suppose someone somewhere might have overheard what they were up to.'

Wellum blew on his tea and sipped it. He put the cup down and scratched his chin.

'What about the blokes with you?'

'Macaire and Sault? No, they were both very loyal. I recruited them myself. Macaire was from Paris, an experienced Resistance fighter and Albert Sault was Austrian.'

Wellum raised an eyebrow. 'Austrian?'

'Trust me, Sault was with us all the way.'

'Could they have got lazy? Said too much to the wrong person?'

Yvain pursed his lips and shrugged.

'Of course it's possible, but I strongly doubt it.'

They sat. A fine rain blew along the Rue Etoupee and whipped at the window. The house felt hollow and cold. After a while Yvain got up and went back into the kitchen. He took a pan from a cupboard and a bag of oats from another.

'I need to eat. Are you hungry?' He gestured to the pan. 'It's just oatmeal and powdered milk I'm afraid, but I can make you some.'

Wellum nodded.

'Thanks.'

The Belgian worked at the stove, moving carefully between the hob and the sideboard. He gathered bowls and stirred the oatmeal. As he worked Wellum noticed a key sitting in the middle of the table propped against an open tin of peaches with a spoon sticking out of it.

'What's that?' He said pointing at the key.

Yvain, glanced over to the table

'What?'

'This key, it wasn't here last night.'

Yvain took the pan off the stove and came back from the kitchen.

'It's for a strongbox under Armada's bed.'

'Where did you find it?'

'The key?'

'Yes.'

'It was in a safe that only Armada and I had the combination to.'

'What's in the box under the bed, do you know?'

Yvain sat down.

'Not yet, I haven't opened it.' He glanced sideways at Wellum. 'But I think it contains the notes and plans for the mission he was working on.'

They both looked at the key, watching it expectantly as if it were about to speak or transform itself into another shape.

'So, why haven't you opened it?'

'I was waiting for you.'

'Why?'

Yvain shrugged and sat back in his chair.

'I'm not sure. Operational security I suppose. I wanted another set of allied eyes on the whole thing while I opened it.'

'This mole thing has got you really spooked hasn't it?'

'I just don't want to get accused of anything underhand that's all.'

'So, you want me to vouch for your honesty?'

'In this instance, I suppose you could say that, yes.'

Wellum picked up the key and considered it.

'Right, well let's have some of that porridge and another cup of tea and then we'll see what Armada's been cooking up shall we.'

CHAPTER THIRTEEN
Schenk meets his man

Yvain put the box on the table and turned it so the key hole at the front was facing him. The three of them looked at it.

'What if it's booby trapped?' said Brielle. Wellum glanced sideways at Yvain.

'Armada would have told me.'

'Are you sure?' Said Wellum.

Yvain placed his hand on the box as if listening. It was a small steamer trunk with a domed top that looked more like a treasure chest from a children's book than anything becoming a spy hiding out in northern France. It was old and weather worn and the two leather straps that had once been wrapped around the girth of it had long since rotted away to severed stumps.

'I guess there's only one way to find out.'

Yvain twisted the key and lifted the lid on its rusted hinges. The box lay open on the table, gaping at them, like some ancient wooden bird waiting to be fed.

They breathed a collective sigh of relief - it hadn't exploded.

Wellum peered cautiously over the rim then reached in and began removing items from inside and placing them on the table. When the box was empty he closed the lid and lifted the box and put it on the floor. They looked at the things sitting in front of them.

There were several maps of Germany, a brown manila folder, some photographs and typed out sheets of paper, all of which were stamped *Top Secret* in red ink. There was also a notebook.

Brielle picked up the black and white prints and began sifting through them. The first few were aerial photographs of what appeared to be some sort of military base or factory sitting on the edge of a forest. Large buildings and areas of hardstanding, scaffolding and smaller buildings gathered together near what looked like a long road. Brielle held the images at ams length and twisted them and tilted her head, trying to get an idea of what she was looking at. Perhaps an airfield rather than a factory. As she flipped through the pile there were several pictures of a man, tall and dark haired, wearing a black suit and small round spectacles. In one image he was surrounded by a half dozen other men, singled out with a white circle around his head, he was laughing and talking to the group, two or three of whom were wearing the black Nazi uniform of the SS. Brielle carried on through the pile of grainy images. She came to one in particular and stopped to study it more closely. It showed what appeared to be a tall, black and white machine, huge compared to the figures of the men that could be seen scurrying about at the bottom of the photograph. It had fins at its base like the shortened wings of an aircraft and it rose up to a point like a dart. Wellum glanced at the photograph Brielle was staring at and held out his hand.

'Please, can I see that.'

Brielle handed him the picture.

'What is that thing?' She asked.

Wellum studied the image carefully and then looked at the next picture. Similar, but from a different angle. He frowned and brought the photograph closer to his face. He looked at the next photograph, and then the next.

'What is it?'

'It's a missile I think.'

'A what?' said Brielle.

'A missile, a V2. A rocket.'

'What does it do?'

Wellum quickly looked at the other photographs and then dropped them on the table and opened the manila folder and dragged out its contents. There were sketches and diagrams and technical drawings and he scanned through them and then picked up the photographs again.

'What is a V2?' Asked Brielle again.

'It's a weapon,' said Yvain.

Brielle looked at him.

'What kind of weapon?'

Wellum opened one of the technical drawings that confirmed what he was looking at. A huge cutaway illustration of the rocket showing all of its constituent parts covered the plan in front of them. Wellum spread it out over the table and dropped the photographs on top of it.

Yvain picked up the pictures and began looking through them.

'The V2 is a missile,' said Wellum. 'Used to deliver an explosive warhead to a target hundreds of miles away.'

'Like a bomb?' Said Brielle looking down at the plans on the table.

'Yes, like a bomb,' confirmed Wellum. 'Except this bomb doesn't need an aircraft to carry it over the target. This bomb flies to the target on its own and arrives before anyone even knows its coming.'

'But how?'

'It's like a self propelled artillery shell, but one that doesn't need a gun or cannon to deliver it. It has a rocket engine that fires it at tremendous speed across hundreds of miles and somehow it guides itself down to a specific grid location. I'm not exactly sure how it works,' said Wellum, pointing at the drawings. 'But it looks like the Germans are pretty far along with it.'

'Who's this, do you know?' Said Yvain, holding out one of the photographs of the man in the dark suit and glasses.

Wellum shook his head.

'I've no idea.'

They opened one of the maps. It showed an isthmus of land jutting out into the sea. Wellum read the name of some of the towns that ran along its eastern edge closest to the ocean.

'Zinnowitz, Karlshagen, *Peenemunde.*' He tapped his finger on this last, strange sounding name.

'Peenemunde.' He nodded. 'It's the V2 alright.'

'What's Peenemunde? Asked Brielle.

Wellum picked up the aerial photographs.

'This is Peenemunde,' he said holding up the pictures Brielle had been studying. He dropped them onto the map.

'It's the Nazi's military research facility, based on this spur of land that juts out into the Baltic Sea.' He pointed at the northeast corner of the map. 'It's called Usedom Island. Essentially it's one large military base, where the V2 rocket and other long range weapons are being designed, built and tested.

'How do you know so much about it?' Asked Yvain. 'This all says 'top secret'.'

'I helped get these reconnaissance photographs,' said Wellum.

'You took these?' Said Brielle.

'Not these specific ones, no. But they were taken by blokes working in my department.'

'So what do you think Armada was doing in connection to all this?'

'I don't know,' said Wellum.

Yvain flipped over one of the photographs of the man in the suit and glasses. On the back someone had written.

Dr Thiel.

'We need to find out who this Thiel is, he looks like a key component in whatever this mission was about.'

Wellum collected a pile of typed sheets and started reading. They were mostly memos from London, scraps of intelligence and notes. He read one aloud dated August twenty-fifth, nineteen-forty-three.

Operation Hydra
Nominal success. So far reported casualties include;
Five-hundred technical staff and factory workers killed
Five senior engineers/scientists killed

Estimated delay to A4/V2 development and production six to eight months minimum.

'What is operation Hydra?'

'In August of this year the British bombed this facility, at Peenemunde, hoping to disrupt the V2 programme.'

'They went to destroy the factories and these V2 machines?' Said Brielle.

'No, they went to kill scientists.'

'Why the scientists?'

'Because if you cut off the Hydra's heads, the Hydra dies,' said Wellum. He picked up the photograph of the man once more and looked at it.

'Five is not many.' Said Brielle.

'Here listen to this,' Yvain was reading from Armadas notes

Positive identification of Doctor Thiel made in Amiens Radio London Station for permission to attempt contact

'And here...'

Have spoken with Dalby, he is convinced the message from Thiel is genuine. London have given permission to pursue to contact. Will meet Dalby at the usual place to begin planning phase.

'Well we know who Thiel is,' said Wellum pointing at one of the photographs. 'But who is Dalby?'

'It's a codename,' said Yvain. 'He's an SOE Operative.'

'Here in Rouen?'

'In and out, yes.'

'You know this person?' Said Brielle.

'Yes, though not all that well. He has briefed me in the past.'

'Does he know you were going to be working with Armada on this job?' Said Wellum.

Yvain shrugged, 'I'm not sure who Armada told and who he didn't.'

'Obviously we need to contact him and tell him about Armada and see what all this means. Do you know how to contact him?'

'Yes,' Yvain nodded. 'I can arrange a meeting. Armada used a drop box in the city to signal to Dalby that he wanted to meet. I'll use that.'

'When?'

Yvain checked his watch.

'I'll go now. He usually checks his drop boxes before one, and then later at around seven. Hopefully if I catch him he might meet me tonight and I can find out what's going on.'

'He might meet *us* old chap.'

Yvain looked at Wellum.

'Really, there's no need for you to come along.'

'I know,' replied the pilot, gathering up the maps and sifting through the photographs once more. 'But I'm coming along anyway.'

Yvain looked at Brielle questioningly.

'You as well?'

She nodded.

'Of course.'

The truck rolled to halt in front of la Boucherie restaurant, its wheels parked in a puddle, smashing the reflection of a neon sign into a multi coloured splash. Stein jumped down from the cab into another, deeper puddle, his boots disappearing to the ankles. He stepped up to the curb and shook his boots dry and cast a look around the grey, drizzle filled street. An old man watched him from the opposite pavement. Calm and stoic, he made no gesture towards the panzer captain, but neither did he show any sign of looking away - he simply watched. Stein stared back at him with a creeping feeling of guilt and then turned and called the men down from the truck.

'Line up here.'

Wolff got out of the Mercedes, followed by Schenk and as they approached the group of men lined up outside the restaurant Wolff glanced up at the grey clouds and gestured towards the door.

'After you Captain Stein,' he turned to the men.

'Bauchman, Ritter, come inside, the rest of you wait here.'

By the time Stein got indoors, Schenk was already talking to the Maitre'd who turned and pointed towards a corner of the dining room. Stein aimed his finger at either side of the door and the two young soldiers wordlessly took up their places.

Renard sat and sipped his wine.

Chateau Romaine 'thirty-five. He closed his eyes and savoured the cold, sharp taste. It went perfectly with the Crab-Anglaise which was excellent as usual, and he picked his teeth wth a finger nail and sucked his gums and drank his wine and wiped his mouth with a napkin.

He looked around the dining hall. The lunchtime service was busy. He didn't like it. He felt almost certain that someone in there would recognise him and it took the edge off his enjoyment of the meal.

A waiter approached as Renard tucked the napkin into his collar and returned his attention to his half-eaten plate.

'Excuse me monsieur, your lunch companions have arrived.'

Renard glanced at his watch and then looked towards the door. Schenk was annoyingly early.

He could see the Gestapo detective standing just inside the restaurant doorway talking to an SS officer who was shaking the rain from his hat. There was another German officer with them, dressed in a grey uniform and he was tall and dark and stern. As Renard watched, they appointed two soldiers as sentries at the door and following the corpse-like Schenk, began making their way across the dining hall towards his table.

Renard drank his wine and pushed his plate forward an inch and stood up and smiled and tried to look relaxed. Schenk ignored the Frenchman's outstretched hand and pulled out a chair without as much as a smile. He sat down leaving Renard standing awkwardly with his napkin still tucked into his collar like a schoolboy. As the two German officers approached, Schenk made the introductions.

'Monsieur Renard, this is Haupsturmfuhrer Wolff of the SS, and this is Hauptmann Stein.'

Renard dipped his fingers in a bowl of lemon water and dried them hastily on his napkin and extended his hand once more. Only Wolff shook it with a smile and a courteous nod.

'Bonjour Monsieur.'

They sat and Stein called over a waiter. Renard poured himself another glass of wine as Schenk spoke.

'Monsieur Renard, I have asked my colleagues to join us today so that you can brief them about the person you told me about this morning. The English pilot.'

Renard bounced a look between Wolff and Stein. He noted the lightening bolts glistening on the SS officer's collar. It was bad enough dealing with the Gestapo, now he was flirting with the SS. He drank his wine and pushed out a less than confident nod.

'Ok.'

A waiter approached. Wolff ordered coffee and when the waiter looked at Stein he nodded.

'I'll have the same'

Schenk poured himself a glass of water.

Renard watched them and then cast another anxious look around the dining room. Naturally, no one was looking their way, but he still felt hunted and exposed.

'How is the crab?' Asked Wolff congenially. Renard glanced down at his plate.

'It's good.'

'Excellent.' smiled the SS officer. There was a pause while everyone watched Renard.

'So,' said Wolff eventually. 'Detective schenk informs me that you might have had seen someone I am keen to catch up with.'

Renard nodded.

'Maybe, yes.'

Wolff gave an encouraging smile.

'So, please tell me.'

'What would you like to know?'

The SS officer sat forward in his chair.

'Why don't you just start at the beginning monsieur and tell us everything.'

Wolff dug a notebook and pen from his pocket. He placed them neatly on the table as Schenk sipped his water and sat back and crossed his legs.

'Well, the man you are talking about turned up at the Charron house, at Rue du Santiere yesterday in the afternoon, at around one o' clock.'

'The Charron's are the couple who were coordinating the local Resistance group?' Asked Wolff, scribbling in his notebook.

'Yes,' said Renard flatly.

Wolff turned to Schenk.

'And they were among those killed last night at the quarry?'

Schenk nodded. 'Yes, they were Godfrey and Irene Charron, a married couple from Rouen. They were shot while attempting to pick up weapons dropped by the RAF.' He took a slip of paper from his breast pocket. 'They were killed alongside two other members of their group.'

'Matis Greyer, and Elliot Moullie,' said Renard.

'That's right,' confirmed Schenk.

'And no other bodies have been found?'

'No, not at the quarry.'

'Alright, so this Englishman, he came to the house. Who was he with?'

'He came with a girl. She said she came from Varranes and had been part of the Resistance there.'

'The girl knew the Charron couple?' Said Stein.

'No,' Renard shook his head.

A waiter arrived and served coffee to the German officers. The group watched the waiter as he put down the cups and took away Renard's lunch plate. Renard drank his wine and rubbed his palms together anxiously. When the waiter left, Wolff stirred his coffee and looked at the Frenchman and smiled once more.

'Please, continue.'

'They came with another Englishman, someone I have only seen maybe two times before. An SOE agent called Armada.'

Wolff noted down the codename, speaking to Schenk as he wrote.

'Do we know him?'

Schenk shook his head.

'I don't recognise the name.'

'And the first Englishman, he was introduced to you as a pilot?'

'Yes.'

'Why had these people come to visit the Charron household?

'To ask for help. The pilot said he had been shot down and Armada was trying to get him back to England. They came to the house because Godfrey had photographic equipment and made fake identification papers. Armada asked if they could make the pilot an identity card and give him some clothes.'

'What was he wearing?'

'Some country clothes he'd picked up in a village near Varrannes. He looked like a farmer.'

'Yes, we know the village.' Said Wolff.

'Do you know where this Armada lives?' Asked Stein.
'No,' said Renard. 'No one does.'
Wolff looked at him and narrowed his eyes.
'You're sure?'
Renard glanced at Schenk and attempted a shrug.
'Of course i'm sure. Why would I lie?'
'Because you're a deceitful cunt that's why,' said Stein, finishing his coffee. He put his cup down and took his cigarettes out of his pocket. Wolff stopped writing and looked at him.

Renard regarded Stein. He looked at the tank captains uniform, noting the absence of SS insignia. His courage grew.

'I don't lie Captain despite what you might think of me.'

Stein looked back at him, sat there in his shabby suit with his greasy forehead shining. He despised everything the man stood for; helping the Nazis take over Europe for nothing more than personal gain.

'Don't you support the cause of the Resistance?' he asked, lighting his cigarette. He shook out the match and dropped it in an ashtray. He watched the Frenchman carefully. Wolff stirred in his seat and went to speak until Schenk raised a finger as if he wanted to hear what Renard had to say in his own defence.

'I don't support ideologies Captain, I support whoever makes the laws, whether they are French laws or German laws. I try to support the infrastructure of my country by not allowing it to dissolve into lawless chaos, and right now the German's make the laws, the German's are in charge, so naturally I support them.'

'Even against your own countrymen?'

'Monsieur, I am not interested in the bonds bestowed upon men who happen to have been born on the same piece of land. I am not a patriot in that sense. It does not matter to me if a man is French or Spanish or even a jew. If he is acting outside of the law of the land he is less a patriot than those that seek to uphold the law, even against their own brothers.'

Stein sat and smoked and watched Renard closely and though he hated to admit it, he understood at least a part of what he was saying.

'The Resistance are trying to bring the state to it's knees - I don't see how that helps the everyday French families. I only see that causing pain.'

Stein span his finger in a circle, gesturing to the table.

'So you don't do this just for money then?'

Renard sat forward.

'Captain, the Resistance believe they can push the Germans out of France but their petulant actions are no more effective than those of children throwing insults. They bring only harm. They can never bring victory.'

Schenk lowered his finger.

'So, tell me about the pilot.' Continued Wolff

Renard tore his eyes away from Stein. He sat back in his chair, remembering his place. He thought about the question.

'He was average height, average build I'd say. About six feet tall. He had slightly wavy brown hair.' He tapped two fingers on the back of his neck. 'Regulation length at the back and sides. Brown eyes, square jaw, a broad nose.'

'What about the girl?'

'She was short and slim, with close cropped dark hair. She looked Italian perhaps or Spanish. More

Mediterranean than French. Brown eyes, tanned skin. Apparently her name is Brielle.'

'And what about our English friend,' said Wolff looking up once more from his notepad.

'Did you manage to catch his name?'

Renard nodded and he flashed a look at Stein as he contemplated asking for more money. Then he smiled.

'Oui monsieur.' He poured out the last of the Romaine 'thirty-five and raised his glass in a miniature toast. 'Armada said his name was Harry.'

'How quintessentially English,' said Wolff as he wrote.

'So, you think these two, the English pilot and the girl, you think they survived the raid last night?' Said Renard.

Wolff put down his pen.

'At the moment it looks like they may have, yes. The only bodies taken out of the quarry were those of the four we have mentioned. Apparently there were other people there that have not been accounted for. Several empty cartridge cases and a discarded rifle were found and tracks leading away into the forest. There is a team of paratroopers there as we speak checking again for anyone injured or hiding, but for now it looks like this Harry got lucky and escaped…again.'

They fell into a brooding, pregnant silence. Schenk sipped his water as the sounds of the restaurant came back and Renard felt again the certainty he was being watched from somewhere in the room. After a while he spoke.

'Well obviously if I hear anything…'

'What?' Said Wolff.

'Excuse me?'

'If you hear what? Said Wolff again.

Renard looked at them, a nervous smile crawling across his face.

'If I hear, anything... About the pilot.'

'What?'

'I'll tell you.'

'When?' Said Wolf.

Renard looked at the German's cold eyes. His stare was penetrating.

'Immediately. I'll tell you immediately.'

Wolff nodded and smiled.

'Yes, good. Good.'

The SS officer stood up and put the notebook back in his pocket and lifted his hat from the table. The conversation was over.

As he stood up, Stein caught the eye of a waiter and called him over.

Renard stayed in his seat. He looked mauled by the ten minute meeting.

'Monsieur Renard it has been a pleasure,' said Wolff, putting on his hat.

'Until we meet again, I would like to thank you for your work. Detective Schenk will contact you if we need anything else, but until then if you do happen to catch wind of our English friend, please hasten to me at *Le Chateau Signet Noir,* whether it be day or night.'

'I will.'

As Wolff turned to leave, Schenk dropped an envelope next to Renard's empty wine glass, as Stein leaned in and spoke discreetly to the waiter.

'Tell me how to get to the cafe, *La Dolma.*'

When All The Birds Leap

Outside, Stein gathered the men back on the truck as Wolff gestured for Schenk to join him in the car. When the men were all onboard Stein held out his hand.

'Haupsturmfuhrer, If it's alright with you, I'm going to go into the city for a while. I'll make my own way back to the chateau a little later.'

Wolff looked at him as Schenk headed for the Mercedes.

The SS smiled.

'Of course Herr Captain, of course. Where do you plan to go? A walk by the river perhaps, or the theatre?'

'I just want some time to gather my thoughts, that's all. I feel a little…bleak. I'm sure a stroll will cure my mood.'

Wolff smiled again and put a hand on Stein's shoulder. 'I agree Hauptmann Stein. Go, relax, take in the scenery.' He gestured to a row of bombed buildings across the street.

'I'll tell the kitchen to put a plate of food in the oven for when you return.' He clapped the panzer captain jovially on the shoulder and turned and joined Schenk in the back of the car. Stein looked at the ruins of the street opposite and as the truck and the staff car pulled away he watched them go, and he thought about how he was ever going to fit back into his normal life if he ever got back to Germany.

He opened the door and went in and took off his hat and looked around the room.

Edith Piaf singing chanson from the speakers, cigarette smoke, red velvet and polished mahogany.

A large man with a black moustache stood behind the bar with a cigarette screwed into the corner of his mouth. He was wiping down the polished wooden counter with a cloth and he took the cigarette and balanced it on the edge of an ashtray as Stein approached.

'Bonjour,' said the barman without smiling.

Stein nodded and ordered whiskey.

'Bonjour.'

The man turned and picked up a glass and filled it and put the glass down on a square napkin. Stein took the drink and swirled the glass, swilling the whiskey inside, then he drank it down in one.

'Is Colette here?'

The barman picked up the cigarette and sucked on it. He nodded.

'Yes, she's here.'

Stein nudged the glass forward then took some coins for his pocket and put them on the counter. The barman refilled the glass and slid the money into his palm and rang it into the till.

Stein gestured towards a table in a corner of the room.

'I'll be sitting over there.'

He put his hat and glass on the table and sat down, then he reached into his pocket and took out his cigarettes and shrugged one out of the packet and lit it. On another table a young woman sat with a naval officer, maybe a few years younger than Stein. The couple were talking quietly together and he held her hand and kissed her fingers as they talked. The officer poured wine from an ice bucket and as she drank she smiled and touched his face like she meant it.

Stein watched them.

Like a couple in love.

So normal, so connected.

He shook his head. *What am I doing here?*

He drank the whiskey and lifted the glass, signalling the barman.

The Frenchman crossed the room, carrying a bottle and filled Stein's glass.

'Are you Hector?'

'Yes.'

'Is Colette busy?'

'She will be down shortly.'

Stein felt sick at the thought.

As the barman turned and went back, a door on the far side of the room opened and a young Luftwaffe officer came out. He stood for a moment and straightened his jacket before glancing self-consciously around the tables. He caught Stein's eye and looked away, then he went to the door and put his hat on and left.

The barman began cleaning glasses with a towel and the young woman whispered into the officer's ear and Piaf sang.

Moi, j'ai entende dire. Que l'amour fait pleurer…

After a few minutes the door on the opposite wall opened again and Colette entered the room, adjusting an earring as she came. Stein watched her. She went to the bar and took a cigarette from Hector's pack and lit it. As she did the barman spoke to her and she turned and looked at Stein.

He thought about leaving.

As he watched her she said another few words to Hector and turned and carrying the whiskey bottle and a glass with her, crossed the room towards him.

'Can I join you Captain?'
He nodded and stood up and pulled out a chair.
'Please.'
She sat and put the whiskey on the table.
'The young pilot officer that just left, was he here to see you?'
Colette poured herself a drink and turned and glanced towards the door.
He looked at her arms, her skin.
She turned back and shook her head and sipped her whiskey.
'He wasn't here with me, no.'
Stein looked over at the barman who was cleaning glasses and watching them.
'I must say, I'm surprised to see you here.'
'Really?' Said Stein.
Colette tapped the cigarette at the ashtray.
'Well, so soon, yes.'
'I wanted to see you,' said Stein. 'But now, I think maybe it was a mistake.'
'Why, because it reminds you of what I *really* am?'
'I think I just wanted to talk to someone. To you.'
'Why did you ask me about that young officer, the one that just left?'
'I'm not sure.'
'What do you fear most Max? That I fucked him or that he also wanted to talk to someone, and that ended up being me?'
Stein shook his head.
'I didn't come here to play games.'
'You don't know which is worse do you?'
Stein shrugged. He looked at her.

'Tell me,' she went on, leaning in and blowing smoke towards him. The smell mingled with her perfume and made him sway slightly. 'Have you killed anyone today?'

'What?'

She gestured to his uniform with a finger, then to his pistol, clenched at his waist in its holster.

'With that. Have you killed anyone?'

'No.'

'Not today? But what about in the past few weeks, since you've been in France?'

'You're asking me if I've killed anyone since I've been in France?'

She nodded and smoked.

'I should leave.' He stubbed out his cigarette.

She put her hand on his.

'Max until all this is over, we both have to do whatever we have to do, remember. I won't judge you…please, don't judge me.'

'I want to see you again. Properly I mean, like last night.'

She watched him.

'I could come to the chateau?'

'I'm not sure how much longer I'll be there.'

'Oh, why?'

'Just a development in my situation you could say.'

'You think you'll be leaving soon?'

'Maybe.'

They sat and watched the couple on the next table. Playing their charade, making believe it was real.

After a while Stein spoke quietly.

'My wife was killed in an air raid, last year.' He turned to face her. 'My daughter too.'

She looked at him.

'Max, I'm sorry.'

'I doubt now if I'll ever go back home to Germany, even if the Nazis win the war.'

'Will there be any safe places left?' Said Colette.

Stein gave a sort of noncomital shrug. 'Safe from what? Safe from danger, safe from our thoughts, from the consequence of our actions?'

They sat in silence once more. After a while Stein drained his glass.

'Is there anywhere here that we can be alone?' He asked.

'Yes, but I don't want to see you here.'

Stein understood why.

'I can find somewhere. Will you still be in Rouen tomorrow night?'

'I think so yes, hopefully. Just get word to the chateau, tell the Butler Langer, to only talk to me. Wherever it is, I'll be there.'

He stood up and put his hat on and squared it and dropped some money on the table.

'For the whiskey.'

She smiled up at him.

'Take care Max. Until tomorrow night at least.'

CHAPTER FOURTEEN
The Mission

They met on the cobbles of the Rue Saint-Romain as the bells of the cathedral were ringing eight o'clock. The street was little more than another of Rouen's ancient, narrow alleyways and the timber and plaster buildings that leaned in on either side were mostly old and desiccated husks with weevil-like families burrowed deep within, all miserably entombed behind the black shadow of the great cathedral, too afraid to venture out into the sunlight, waiting like small nocturnal creatures to crawl out and find food and to blink at the moon.

Under an arch set deep into the cathedral wall, Yvain found Dalby waiting and smoking and watching the sky for signs of more rain. The Englishman was tall and rough looking in the manner of a boxer or antarctic explorer of the past. He wore an Argyll fisherman's jumper and a heavy black jacket with the collar up, and he wore glasses with one dark lens that made him look like some curious, latter day pirate. He checked his watch and looked as if he was about to leave when Yvain approached him. The two men spoke quietly to each other and Dalby glanced towards Wellum and Brielle, standing across the street, waiting. He nodded in affirmation at Yvain and the Belgian turned and beckoned the couple to follow as Dalby walked briskly away along the Rue Saint-Romain in the direction of the cathedral's large front doors.

Inside the cathedral it was cool and solemn. Scattered people drifted in whispers around the nave, some sitting and praying, others lighting candles with their heads bowed in silent contemplation. Dalby moved swiftly through the echoing church with a gliding confidence, heading towards the south transept and a quiet corner of sanctuary in the Chapel of St Joan.

The group sat and Yvain introduced them.

'So, what's all this about?' Asked the agent brusquely. 'Where's Armada?'

'Armada's dead,' said Yvain.

There was a moment of silence while the Englishman processed the information.

'When?' He asked flatly.

'Last night. We were ambushed on a job delivering radios to an address on Rue St Bernard.'

Dalby shook his head. 'Fucking hell.' He looked at the Belgian.

'Who else was there?'

'Macaire and Sault. They didn't make it out either.'

'What, the whole team?'

Yvain nodded.

'How did the German's know?'

Yvain shrugged.

'Was it a passing patrol? Did they see you going in?'

'No, we were careful.' He paused, then went on. 'I think they were waiting for us.'

Dalby shook his head once more.

'Bastard spies everywhere.'

They sat in silence. After a moment the agent looked at Wellum and Brielle.

'So, you're the pilot?'

Wellum nodded.

'Yes.'

Dalby turned back to Yvain.

'I hope you haven't come here to ask me for help.'

'No, Dalby, listen.' He looked around the church and lowered his voice to a whisper. 'We know about Thiel.'

Dalby looked blankly back at him.

'What do you mean?'

Yvain nodded and held up his palms.

'We know about Thiel… it's fine, just listen. We opened Armada's strong box and found his notes and files.'

'We want to hep you compete the mission,' said Wellum.

Dalby looked at him.

'I'm not sure I know what you're talking about.'

Yvain interjected.

'Wait, I know how this must look, but I was put on the team to carry out this mission, and I'm the only one left, but that doesn't mean we shouldn't at least try.'

After a pause Dalby replied,

'It's impossible on your own.'

'Why?'

'Listen, Dalby,' said Wellum. 'I think you should at least tell us what this job entails and we can see if it's something that can still be pulled off.'

Dalby looked at Brielle.

'Vous etes membre de la Résistance.'

She looked squarely back at him.

'Oui.'

'Ou, ici a Rouen?'

She shook her head.

'Non, a Varranes.'

'We want to help in any way we can,' pressed Wellum.

Dalby looked at Yvain.

'Are you injured?'

'Not really, a few bruises, that's all.'

The spy shook his head.

'This is ridiculous.'

Dalby looked around the church and then sat back and stared up at the statue of St Joan, her arms crossed at her chest, bound in chains as the alabaster flames crept towards her knees.

Wellum pressed the agent further.

'Dalby, I know this job is important. Before he was killed Armada told me he was working on something big and if this is that mission then I think you need to consider the consequences of not continuing with it.' He paused and Dalby looked at him.

He looked at all of them.

'Alright,' he said at last. ' I don't like it, but under the circumstances I suppose there isn't any other option…' he trailed off, shaking his head as if he was questioning his own judgement and the ill twist of fate that had resulted in such a hopeless choice. He sighed, '…but I really can't emphasise enough just how important this mission is.' He paused and looked at them each in turn once more. 'Really, this isn't like booby trapped radios or Resistance skirmishes with young German conscripts.'

'I think we all understand that,' said Yvain.

Dalby looked at Wellum and Brielle. 'Alright, what do you know about the V2 programme?'

'Just start at the beginning,' said Wellum. 'Best to assume we don't know anything.'

Dalby nodded and took another look around the church. He lowered his voice and leant in.

'Since before the war, German scientists have been developing a long range rocket for military use. The V2 is the culmination of all of that development. We think roughly five or six years of testing.'

'What does this rocket do?' Asked Yvain. 'In a nutshell.'

Dalbey smiled.

'In a nutshell? The V2 is a missile capable of delivering a one-tonne warhead to a target two-hundred miles away, travelling at supersonic speed. It flies at an altitude of fifty-miles, right on the edge of space, at over three thousand miles per hour and it strikes without warning, obliterating everything and everyone within a quarter of a mile. In short, it's a devastating weapon, unlike anything the world has seen before.'

He looked at their faces. A mix of puzzlement and horror.

'Is this weapon real?' Asked Brielle quietly. 'Could there be such a thing, really?'

'Yes,' said Dalby. 'It's real enough, and just as frightening as I've described. More so in fact. Hitler is hedging his bets that the V2 will bring London to its knees within a matter of weeks.'

'How many rockets do they hope to be launching?' Asked Wellum.

'At the moment we estimate around one hundred and fifty a week at London alone.'

'What?'

Dalby nodded.

'We know he'll also be aiming at many of the English coastal towns too and obviously any landing sites used by the allies to invade France as part of a liberation attempt. There are also rumours he'll use it tactically, out in the field against troops on the ground, bridges, forward planning bases and the like. In short the V2 poses many threats, all of which will be unstoppable once the project reaches operational status.'

'It's not operational yet?' Said Brielle.

Dalby shook his head.

'Not yet, no.'

'Operation Hydra was a success then?' Said Wellum.

'Yes, and no,' said Dalby. 'As you may have heard, in August this year the RAF flew a night bombing mission to the V2 development site at a place called Peenemunde. It's an army research centre situated on Usedom Island in the north east of Germany, right up on the coast. It was a huge effort. The RAF lost forty aircraft and over two-hundred crew were killed. On the ground, five-hundred people lost their lives, most of which were the Jewish and Polish slaves forced by the Nazis to build the rockets. The aim of the raid was to kill as many scientists and technical staff as possible but unfortunately they didn't get as many as they'd hoped.'

Brielle looked at Wellum.

'Just the five men you mentioned?'

Wellum nodded.

'That's what we heard, yes.'

Dalby pursed his lips and nodded slowly.

'You're right. That's what we *heard*...unfortunately, or fortunately, depending on your point of view that's not what actually happened.'

'What do you mean?'

'After the Hydra raid, we got reports that one of the German's top propulsion scientists, Dr Walter Thiel was among those that had been killed and of course bomber command and the British government were more than happy with that as a result. Thiel has been a significant contributor to the V2 programme and apart from getting Major Dornberger or Von Braun themselves, Thiel was as high up the food chain as we could possibly have hoped.

'Thiel was important to the Nazis?'

'Yes, very important. Even though the scientist Von Braun is classed by many as the brains behind the V2 project, in reality he is more of an overseer, a project manager if you like, and it's actually scientists like Thiel and others of his caliber that have moved the development of the rocket forward so significantly.' He paused again and looked at them. 'Not to put too fine point on it, Thiel is essential to the success of the V2.'

'Surely you mean *was* essential to the plan?' Said Yvain.

'Mmm,' said Dalby cleaning his glasses on a handkerchief. 'As I said, the reports we got back said

Thiel was dead, along with his wife and children, but it would seem that wasn't entirely accurate.'

'How so?" Said Brielle.

'Misinformation I'm afraid,' said Dalby putting his spectacles back on. 'The Germans lied about the damage operation Hydra achieved and as it turns out, they lied about the casualties too. Apparently, while Thiel's family *were* killed, he was only wounded. Badly wounded, but still just wounded. We've got a rough idea on the timeline after the raid but some of the details are still a little sketchy.

Operation Hydra took place on the night of August the 17th and by August the twentieth, reports of casualties were being fed back to London by spies in Germany, and as I've said, Thiel was top of that list. On August the twenty-eighth, an anonymous source, claiming to be an unverified British agent reported that Thiel had survived the Hydra bombings and had been taken to Switzerland for life saving treatment by a doctor there, so on August the twenty-ninth after getting the go ahead from the Foreign-Office, Britain activated its spies in Switzerland for any word on the German scientist, but by the end of August it became clear that the Nazis had tricked British Intelligence into thinking that Thiel was in Switzerland, as no trace of him could be found there.

Around mid-September, we were contacted again, this time by a surgical assistant working in a hospital in Luxembourg. They reported that a high-ranking, heavily guarded German patient was being treated at the hospital there. Our interest grew when it was confirmed that the fellow was some sort of doctor or scientist. Before going silent, our contact confirmed it was Thiel and said he was due to be transported back to Germany within five days to begin a period of convalescence, but it would appear that within hours of us finding this out, Thiel somehow escaped from there alone.'

'He got away from the Germans?' Asked Wellum. Dalby nodded.

'Yes. One minute he was there and the next…he'd disappeared.'

An elderly couple moved towards them and stood for a few moments contemplating the statue of the burning Saint. After a few minutes they crossed themselves and moved quietly away.

Dalby leant forward in his chair.

'On October the fifteenth, Thiel contacted London by Morse code. We don't know how he managed it, but he said he was near Paris in a small town called Drocourt, and that he wanted to defect. He was told to wait where he was and that we would arrange for someone to make contact with him, but he said that he couldn't stay any longer and that he feared the Germans already knew where he was. Three weeks later he sent another message, this time from Amiens. He said that he had only managed to get help there by playing on his injuries and that he was desperate for someone on our side to arrange to have him picked up. It felt to him and to us that time was running out.

Armada then got word from a contact in Amiens that there was a high value German on the run there and this seemed to tally with the messages arriving in London from Thiel. Armada was given permission by one specific officer in London to attempt to make contact and together he and I have spent the last few weeks cultivating a relationship with Thiel. Yvain was selected to be part of a team sent to collect the German scientist once we could confirm Thiel was genuine and we could get to him.'

'And have you?' Said Brielle.

'Have we what?'

'Have you confirmed he's genuine?'

'Oh, he's genuine alright.'

'My god, this is huge.' Said Wellum.

'Exactly.' Said Dalby. 'It really is and it's also top secret. Even Armada's boss back at the SOE isn't aware of what we're doing. Only my directing officer and one other person at the London office knows about Thiel, and they are getting their orders directly from the top.'

'So what happens now?' Said Wellum.

'Well, in just over forty-eight hours time we are supposed to pick him in a small town about twenty-five miles southeast along the river Seine.'

'Which town? Said Yvain.

'A place called Ande.'

'Do the Nazis know he's there?'

'Maybe, but we're not certain. We know the Germans want him back, that's for sure. Himmler made it a top priority when they found out Thiel was missing. At first they thought the Allies had lifted him and smuggled him out of Europe, but when it became clear this wasn't the case, the SS feared he was on the run and trying to switch sides. If the German's do know where he is then it's a race against time as to who gets to him first. If the Nazis find him they'll almost certainly arrest him and take him back to Berlin. If we can get there before them, we are to bring him over to us; or kill him.'

Brielle looked up. 'Kill him?'

Dalby nodded.

'We can't let him go back to Peenemunde to finish his work with Von Braun. If they complete the V2 programme and it reaches its potential, it could swing the war in Hitler's favour.'

'The rocket is that powerful?'

'Not yet. They've been having problems with it - major problems. Some of which are logistical, some of which are technical, but Thiel could help solve those issues and we can't risk that happening.' The spy sat back and looked at them.

'So, he either switches sides, or we have to neutralise him. There is no other solution.'

'How has he been surviving? He's been on the run for over two months?' Said Yvain.

Dalby shook his head.

'God only knows. But he sounds close to nervous exhaustion.'

They sat in silence for a while. Eventually Yvain spoke again.

'How was the team meant to get to Ande?'

'We hadn't gone firm on a final plan. We were meant to meet up tomorrow with you and the other two members of the team; Macaire and Sault. We were going to spend the morning planning and preparing in detail, but I suppose now we will have to reconsider the whole mission feasibility on account of losing Armada and the other two.'

'Does it have to be a four man job?' Said Wellum. Brielle looked at him.

Dalby thought for a moment.

'I suppose not, but on jobs such as this we've always used four man teams in the past.'

'It's standard SAS practice.' Said Yvain. A four man patrol can provide adequate fire power for most eventualities while remaining small enough to move stealthily when needed. It also means we can have a mixed skill set on most missions. Usually a medic, a signaller, a demolitions expert and a linguist.'

'Well,' said Wellum. 'I suggest under the circumstances, when we get into the planning phase we determine what skills the four of us can bring to the table and plan around those.'

He looked at Dalby. 'I assume you'll be joining the team now? For King and country and all that.'

Brielle shook her head.

'You're not thinking of actually going on the mission yourself are you?'

Wellum thought about the question for a moment and then nodded.

'Yes, I am.'

'Why?'

Yvain spoke up.

'I have to agree Harry, now that we know what this entails, you shouldn't even be considering this. It's not your area of expertise and you really ought to be focusing on getting home.'

'Well, if what I've heard tonight is correct, this mission is pretty crucial to the war effort wouldn't you say?'

'Well yes,' said Yvain. 'But still...'

Wellum looked at Dalby .

'And I doubt if you could pull in a team that you *know* you can trust, *and* plan the job within the next forty-eight hours. Especially now the Charron's are dead and there's a possible mole in the system.'

'Godfrey and Irene are dead?' Said Dalby.

Wellum nodded. 'I'm afraid so.'

'How?'

'Last night, while Yvain and Armada were out on their job, Brielle and I joined them on a weapons drop taking place in a quarry north of the city, and like Armada's mission, we were also ambushed. Godfrey and Irene were both killed during the fighting, as well as two other members of their group.'

'Do you know who?'

'One was called Matis, the other's name was Elliot.'

'Yes, I knew them both.' The Englishman shook his head. 'What a mess.' He sat in silence and looked at the ground. Eventually he spoke to Wellum once more. 'Was Renard there too?'

'No,' said Brielle. 'He was back at the house, talking to London.'

'Well at least that's something. He might come in useful for us if we need anything specific for this job. He's very resourceful.'

'What can he get us?' Said Wellum.

'Most things,' said Dalby. 'Ammunition, vehicles.'

'Can he get us explosives?' Said Yvain.

'Probably yes.'

'Why would we need explosives? Asked Brielle.

'I'm not saying we'll need them, but I'd rather have them and not need them, than need them and not have them.'

'This is insane,' said Brielle. 'Harry, really? You're serious about this?'

'Of course I'm serious. Look, who's left if I don't go? You three? Do you really think I'm going to sit at Armada's house and watch you go off and attempt this without me.'

'I'm really not sure,' Yvain persisted.

Brielle turned to Dalby. 'Can't you just contact London and get them to parachute more people in? Postpone the job or something?'

The spy shook his head.

'No, it'd take too long to organise and as I said there are very few people in London that actually know what we're doing. Plus, there's now the added risk of there being a leak somewhere...' Wellum interrupted him.

'Look, I'm going alright.' He gestured towards the spy.

'You heard Dalby, we have forty-eight hours to get this resolved and that simply doesn't leave time to come up with an ideal solution.' He looked at Brielle. '...And out of everyone you should know how I feel. It's no different to you wanting to go to the quarry last night.'

They each looked from one to the next.

'So, what happens now?' Said Wellum eventually.

Dalby thought for a few moments more.

'Alright, that's settled then. The four of us will go.' He paused again, then went on. 'We'll meet tomorrow morning at ten o' clock to do the planning. I'll come to you, at Armada's.'

'You'll need the address.'

'I have the address,' Dalby nodded with a dry smile. Yvain squinted quizzically at the Englishman.

'I'll contact Thiel tonight,' continued the spy. 'I'll get his location and tell him to stay put. We can plan the details of the mission tomorrow knowing exactly where we're going, then I'll visit Renard if there's anything we need him to get for us. That'll give him twenty-four hours to find whatever we order and drop it off.'

'How did Thiel get his radio?' Asked Wellum.

'What?'

'You said you're contacting him still. That means he must have a radio. I just wondered how he'd got it.'

'It was parachuted into a field outside Amiens some weeks ago. The RAF dropped it along with some medicine and rations. Armada organised it. This whole thing has been his baby really, it's such a bloody shame he's not here to see it through.'

They sat digesting the conversation. A heaviness seemed to press down on them from the responsibility and the size of everything they had discussed over the preceding twenty-minutes. Eventually Dalby broke the silence as he stood and put on his hat.

'We should leave separately.' He nodded at them. 'It's been good to meet you. Stay safe, until tomorrow.' He turned away quickly and went out.

They watched him go.

'I should get on the radio and tell my commanding officer what's happened and what we intend to do.' Said Yvain.

'Why don't you wait until we have a plan laid out?' Replied Wellum. 'At least then you'll have something positive to report.'

Yvain nodded reluctantly.

'What about you two?'

Wellum checked his watch and then looked at Brielle.

'Fancy a walk back along the river?'

Brielle stood up and fastened her coat.

'Alright, come on, let's find a bar. I could do with a drink.'

They drank their vodka and put the glasses back on the bar and turned to leave. As they stepped back out into the night Wellum put his hat on.
'Are you hungry?'
Brielle shook her head.
'No,' she said with a small smile. 'Are you?'
Wellum thought about his own question.
'Not really.'
It was the first words they had spoken since leaving the cathedral some fifteen-minutes before. Yvain had gone straight back to Armada's house to do an inventory on what equipment and weapons were there, while Brielle and Wellum had wandered slowly in the direction of the river, a bleakness hanging over them as the weight of the Thiel mission sank in. They had drifted into a brasserie called *Maison Gourmande* and ordered drinks and stood at the bar unmoved by the music and the laughter and the bustle of waiters coming and going, each of them lost in their own thoughts as the vodka burned down through their emptiness and doubt.

The sky was overcast and there was no moon and the breeze that blew across the Seine was hard and cold and unwelcome. It rocked the boats that were tied to the quayside, making them rise and fall as the water ploughed roughly along, away from the ruined city towards open country and then the sea.

They walked side by side, Brielle with her arms folded at her chest, her hands drawn up inside her coat sleeves for warmth and balled into fists in the manner of a child. Wellum had his own hands deep inside his pockets, his collar pulled up around his ears. They went on. By the Rue Grand Pont bridge they turned east and headed back towards the old town and as they turned in to the Rue Jeanne d'Arc they stopped. Most of the buildings on both sides of the street had been reduced to huge piles of rubble. From the river, for more than half-a-mile, everything was destroyed and any buildings that hadn't fallen to the ground, were windowless and torn open. Smoke-stained holes lay gaping in roofs and walls and everything beyond the sightless, glassless window frames was dark and featureless black. Exposed timbers, bitten through by fire jutted here and there and seemed unnatural and obscene somehow - like twisted bones, they reeked with pain and stank of death and burning corpses and nothing good in the world.

As they continued on they looked only at their feet and they did not speak. After they had passed by Brielle looked at Wellum.

'This place, it's not far from where they burnt Joan of Arc you know.' She shook her head.

'The smell of the burning buildings, here everyday, it makes me think of her a lot.'

'Really?' Said Wellum.

Brielle nodded.

'Oui. Have you not noticed it? Since we arrived, the smell is everywhere every day.'

Wellum stopped and turned his face to the night and sniffed the air.

'You're right. I'd not noticed.'

Brielle carried on walking.

'When they burned her, she wasn't even twenty-years-old.'

'Do you believe she was sent visions from God, guiding her on a crusade to defeat the English?'

'Not really. According to your history, it was God who helped King Henry defeat the French at Agincourt only fifteen years before Joan fought for the Dauphin. I doubt even a god who loves war so much would switch sides as quickly do you?'

'You admire her nonetheless?'

'In some ways I do, yes. To be so young and so clear about needing to fight against an army that came to take what was not rightfully theirs. Yes, I admire that. Even though her faith in the honesty of powerful men speaks more to her naivety and vulnerability than perhaps is acceptable for one of God's messengers.'

'What do you mean?'

'She was betrayed at every turn; by the Dauphine, by the French and English church, by everyone. Why would God put her with people that would abandon her so quickly?'

'Do you believe in God?'

'I was raised as a Jew, but my family were not particularly pious. I was expected to believe out of tradition. But I never *really* believed and once the war started, I knew there could be no God.'

Wellum nodded.

'War does beg the question of what sort of god would allow such terrible suffering, that's for certain.'

As they walked, Wellum fought a constant urge to reach out. Neither of them had mentioned the previous night's passions, and so much had happened since then that now, as they walked along, he wasn't entirely sure if he hadn't imagined the whole thing.

'Tell me,' said Brielle as they went on. 'About your family.'

'Alright,' said Wellum. 'What do you want to know?'

'Are your parents alive?'

Wellum shook his head.

'No.'

Brielle stopped and turned and looked at him.

'I'm sorry, it doesn't matter. I shouldn't have asked.'

Wellum smiled.

'It's fine, honestly. My Mother died when I was at university.'

'How old were you?'

'I was nineteen.'

'And your father?'

'My Father...well, we think he died in the first war.'

'You don't know?'

'I'm afraid not.'

'How? I mean, why?'

'He er, he was a policeman, in London. A detective in fact. One of he best according to the stories. He met my Mother and they fell in love when she was a nurse.'

'Were they married?'

'No. He was married to his job apparently.'

Wellum took her arm and linked it through his own as they walked.

'They were on and off for months, years in fact according to my grandparents, but by the time my

Mother fell pregnant with me, my Father was being recruited by the government into a branch of the secret service. When the time came for him to make a choice between staying at home and raising a family or going off and doing his bit for Britain, he disappeared into whatever fate was awaiting him.'

'You never met him?'

'Not that I remember. He met me and loved me. Well, that's what I grew up being told anyway.'

'But he still left?'

Wellum nodded.

'Yes. The last my Mother heard was that he went to France in nineteen-fourteen. After that; nothing.'

'No one actually told you he was killed?'

'No.'

'So he might still be alive?'

Wellum pondered the question for a moment.

'I suppose, technically, yes. But if he is, he never came home, and I suppose at the end of the day, that's all that ever really mattered to my Mother. After years of hoping I think it was easier for us all to believe he'd died in a field somewhere in France.'

'You're not even curious as to the truth?'

'Not really,' said Wellum flatly. 'We went to live with my Mothers parents on their farm in the Lincolnshire fens and I had enough love from them to keep me happy and healthy. As far as I was concerned I never needed him.'

He looked at her and smiled thinly. She let go of his arm.

'What was his name?'

'Who?'

'Your father.'

Wellum looked at her.
'Why?'
'Because I want to know.'
'Yes, but why do you want to know?'
'Don't you ever think about him?'
'Occasionally, yes.'
'But you never wanted to find him?'
'Brielle, he's dead.'
'You don't know that do you? For certain. He might not be.'
'Look, I don't know what to say. He went out of our lives. It was his choice.'
'But he might have needed you.'
Wellum put a cigarette in his mouth and lit it.
'I doubt it.'
'What was his name?'
Wellum smoked and looked at her. He sighed.
'Clovis.'
'That's an unusual name.'
Wellum nodded.
'I know. Detective Sergeant Clovis Grey.'
Brielle linked his arm and they started walking again.
'Do you get your looks from him or from your mother?'
'Definitely my Mother.'
They passed a small cafe, it's lights on and the sound of music floating out. All the tables were stacked one on top of the other, as if they were about to close for the night. As they passed, Wellum and Brielle saw a woman on her own, dancing slowly in the middle of the room, her eyes closed she held out her arms as if joined by an invisible partner. She move gracefully in circles stepping lightly without even a trace of a smile.

Brielle watched her for a moment and then looked away.

'On the farm, with your grandparents, tell me about that.'

He looked down at her as they walked, but her eyes were on their feet and the cobbles in the road.

'It was only a small farm, about twenty acres or so, on the flatlands of Lincolnshire known as the Fens; Huge expanses of fertile marshland with a drying wind blowing across them in a constant moaning song, all divided by crisscrossed drainage ditches that kept the water out of the low fields.' He smiled at the memory. 'I know it sounds bleak, but it wasn't at all and the soil was rich Brielle,' He turned and faced her rolling his fingers as if remembering how it felt. 'Black peat soil so full of goodness and life that anything could grow in it.'

'Really?'

Wellum nodded.

'It's said that it takes a thousand years to make an inch of fenland soil.'

'Did you work on the farm?'

'Of course. I loved it.'

'So you're really a farmer, like John Grillot?'

She smiled.

'No, not really. I did my chores, and helped out as best I could but as I grew older I never really inherited the desire to work on the land full-time. My sights were always set on the military I'm afraid.'

'You wanted to be a fighter?'

'I'm not sure I'd put it like that, but my Grandfather, before he was a farmer, he was a soldier. For most of his life in fact. Whenever we worked together out in the fields, he would tell me stories, much to my Mother's disapproval, about where he'd been and the things he'd done. He taught me to shoot and to fish by the time I was ten. How to trap animals and then how to cook them. He taught me to read maps, how to light fires and how to collect water in the wild.'

'It sounds like a useful education for a boy. I wish I had learned these things.'

'You know them now, that's all that matters.'

'Maybe, but if I ever have a daughter, I will teach her how to survive, like that. Is your grandfather still on the farm?'

'No. He lived long enough to see me get my pilot's wings, but he never really got over the death of my Mother. He died about seven years ago.'

'One broken heart after the next.'

'Yes, I suppose you could say that.'

They walked on in silence, the moonlight occasionally seeping through gaps in the clouds and glittering off the wet cobbles in white and silver sparks. As Brielle steered them towards Rue Lecanuet, some of the buildings became more familiar and Wellum began to get a feel for where he was. He slowed their pace.

'Can I ask you something?'

She nodded.

'Oui, of course.'

They stopped walking and Wellum reached into his jacket pocket and brought out the identification card Brielle had given him in Father Rieu's house.

'Cedric Allard,' he said, holding it up. 'You said you came to Varranes together, from Miraumont.'

'Yes, and?'

'Well, I just wondered…have been wondering, if you came *together*? I mean…'

'I know what you mean,' interrupted Brielle. 'And yes, the answer is yes. Cedric was part of the Resistance in Miraumont when I arrived there and we became friends.'

'Friends?'

'Oui. Then after a time we became lovers.'

'Were you the same age?"'

'More or less.' She paused as if remembering.

'The movement in Miraumont became quite political after a while. Different people trying to take control; and the group began to fracture and split apart in December of nineteen-forty, so on Christmas Eve, Cedric and I left the town and headed south together to set up a Resistance wherever we could, in another town somewhere. We met Father Rieu through a friend of Cedric's mother and he agreed to help us. We stayed at his house. We spent Christmas there and I have been with him since then.'

'Where is Cedric now?'

Brielle looked into his eyes and a moment of reluctance seemed to hang between them.

'The following summer we met a group of Maquis that had come north from the Mediterranean, fighting their way through France. They were well organised and brave. They killed many Germans and were notorious both within the Wehrmacht and with our own people. When they first started out they were called the *Maquis du Vercors* but as they came further north they dropped that name and became the *Maquis du Mort Sacree*, or the *Order of Sacred Death*. Cedric became obsessed with them and begged for us to join them. They were heading towards Paris and he was desperate to go too.'

'You didn't want to go?'

Brielle shook her head.

'No. To be honest I was afraid. I was almost happy again, after living so long in misery...we were comfortable living with Pere Rieu, doing our bit for the struggle wherever we could, and I didn't want to take the risk. We were doing enough in Varranes, in relative safety and I told him that; I asked him not to make me choose, but he wouldn't listen. One morning he said he was going out on a raid with them and that he would be back within two weeks. I asked him not to go, but his heart was set.'

They were silent and Brielle turned and began walking slowly once more.

'Less than a week later we got word that the group had been tracked to a town called Chartres where they had taken shelter. They were attacked there by Messerschmitt's and Stuka's and an SS division from Versaille. The whole group were killed, all fifty-seven. There were no prisoners.'

'I'm sorry,' said Wellum. 'That must have been very difficult for you.'

She nodded. 'Father Rieu saved me from despair. He helped me more than anyone ever has. I owe him my life.'

They got to the Rue Etoupee and Wellum could see Armada's dark little house nestled into the shadows at the bottom of the street.

He slowed his pace once more and took out the identification papers.

'Here you should keep this.'

He held them out towards her.

'No, Harry you keep it. It might help you yet, and that is the best thing I could hope for.'

She pulled him to her and kissed him.

'I will never forget him, it's true, but I am here with you now, and that is all that matters. I will follow you on this crazy mission if that is where you are going next, even if my heart tells me we should wait here quietly and get you safely back to England.'

He kissed her. A mixture of relief and desperate need came close to overwhelming him.

'When we've got Thiel, come back with me to England.'

It was the first time he had heard her laugh.

'Really Harry, I don't think the war will end once we complete our task, or when you go back home.'

She smiled and kissed his cheek.

'There is still fighting to be done, but who knows, maybe after that, we can go and grow leeks together in the blackest soil in England.'

CHAPTER FIFTEEN
Planning

Dalby arrived at ten o'clock the next morning. He knocked on the door, but as Yvain went downstairs to let him in, he'd already come inside and was hanging up his jacket on the coat stand.

'You have a key?' Said the Belgian, stopping half way down the stairs.

'I do indeed,' confirmed Dalby. 'This is an SOE facility after all,' he reminded Yvain as he came up to join him.

In the kitchen Brielle was drinking coffee and cleaning the MAS-38 while Wellum re-read the contents of Armada's intelligence on Thiel and the V2.

'Morning,' said Dalby as he came in. He put a large tartan flask on the table alongside a small leather satchel.

'What's in the flask?' Said Wellum.

'Tea.' Said Dalby. He pointed at the satchel. 'I bought my lunch too. Force of habit I'm afraid. I can't have anything made for me. Terrified of being poisoned.'

Wellum frowned a smile.

'Really?'

'Oh yes,' said the agent, pulling out a chair. 'I'm pretty much unafraid of bullets and bombs, but the thought of getting spiked has always worried me somewhat.'

Brielle closed the breech on the MAS and fired off the action and flicked on the safety catch. She gave the weapon a quick wipe down with a rag and lent it against the wall.

'Does anyone want more coffee before we begin?' Said Yvain from the kitchen. Wellum held up his cup. 'Here please.' He turned to Dalby.

'Did you contact Thiel last night?'

'I did.'

Yvain came and poured Wellum some coffee as Brielle joined them at the table.

'Is the job still on?'

Dalby nodded. 'Yes. Thiel is ready and willing to meet us and has confirmed his wish to defect. I told him to expect a detailed plan of action sometime after eighteen-hundred-hours tonight.'

'So, he's still in Ande?'

'Yes. He's been staying in an old lighthouse, on the Ile-du-Bac. It's a small island in the middle of the Seine. Ten or fifteen summer houses and an old abandoned lighthouse. It's connected by a road bridge to Ande on the eastern shore and the town of Saint-Pierre-du-Vauvray on the western shore. It's picturesque and peaceful and far enough out of the way to not draw attention. He's been there for almost a fortnight now.'

'So, where do we start?' Said Wellum.

Dalby opened his bag and took out a notepad and put it on the table, then he lifted the lid on Armada's steamer trunk and dug out what was left inside. He glanced through the papers in front of wellum and shuffled through the photographs, selecting one or two of note and putting the rest to one side. After he'd finished he sat back down and picked up his flask and began unscrewing the lid. He poured himself a mug of tea.

'Our objective,' he began. 'Is to make contact with the German scientist; Doctor Walter Thiel. After we have successfully done that, we are to escort him back to Rouen and shelter him from Axis forces while we conceive and then prosecute a plan to transport him to England where he intends to defect to all Allied governments in opposition to the Nazi regime. Once he has defected he will contribute his scientific knowledge and expertise to the Allied war effort.'

He looked at them and drank his tea. 'Any questions?'

A brief pause.

Thiel is currently located in an abandoned lighthouse on the Ile-du-Bac on the river Seine, which is situated between the towns of Ande and Saint-Piere du Vauvray, roughly twenty-five miles to the southeast of our current location. Unless we see any reason in our planning to meet him elsewhere, and on account of our lack of local knowledge, I propose we rendezvous with him there. Are we agreed?'

Everyone nodded.

'Agreed.'

'Good.' Dalby reached for a map and unfolded it.

'This is Rouen and we are here.' He jabbed his finger at the map, then dropped it an inch and began tracing across the paper to the east.

'The river Seine runs through Rouen on roughly a northwesterly current, from Paris in the southeast and out to the sea some forty-three miles northwest of Rouen.' He tracked the shape of a snake and stopped and tapped the page. 'Here is the Ile-du-Bac.' He was pointing at an island that was shaped like a teardrop sitting in the middle of the river. 'As you can see, it connects to the towns of Ande on the eastern shore and Saint-pierre-du-Vauvray on the western shore by this bridge, simply designated as *Route Nationale* on the map. Now, having had no time to get on the ground at this location, we don't know much about the bridge's structure, but it's probably safe to assume that it's a basic beam bridge built from steel and concrete and supported along its span with concrete legs rising up from the riverbed. The lighthouse is here.' He pointed at roughly the centre of the island. 'Thiel said its reachable along this road and is surrounded by fields.'

'What's in the fields?' Said Wellum.

'I don't know. Not much I'm guessing, probably used by the locals to grow vegetables or perhaps for grazing livestock. I'm sure Thiel would have told us if they were being used for anything significant.'

'So, I suppose the first thing to decide is how we get there.' said Yvain.

'I've been giving that some thought,' said Dalby. 'And I think we should go in two teams.'

'Why?' Said Brielle.

'Because we'll be travelling at night and there's always a chance we'll be stopped and questioned on the way. If we split up, at least for the journey down there, we have twice the chance of getting one team to the target unscathed.'

'I agree,' said Yvain. 'But we should all travel back here together. That way we will stand a better chance of defending ourselves should we get into a fight.'

'The river is quiet at night, so I think maybe one pair should go by boat, the other by car.' Dalby went on.

'But that would mean getting a vehicle,' said Yvain.

'We arrived in a Citroen a couple of nights ago,' said Wellum. 'We left it in a side street near a Brasserie called *La Petit Savoie* on the Rue du Montparnasse. It's where we met Armada.'

'Two days ago? Said Dalby. 'We'll have to check but it's probably still there. Was it fuelled?'

'Yes, there would be enough to get to Ande and back,' said Brielle.

'Good,' said Dalby. 'Let's go with that option. If the car's been moved, I'll add it to the list of things we might be needing from Renard.' He made some notes.

'So, we also need a boat. I think a small, two man dinghy with an outboard motor and oars will do.'

'Can you get that?'

'Again, Renard will be able to I'm sure. If he can't I know of one or two we could steal if we had to.'

Wellum lit a cigarette and Yvain poured another round of coffee.

'Who will be in which vehicle?' He said.

'I think it's easiest if Harry and Brielle go together in the car, and you and I can go by boat.' He looked at the map, tracing lines with his finger tip.

'It's probably best to go south out of Rouen and keep to the east of the Seine all the way down to Pont-de-L'Arche. There you can cross the river and drive straight down to Saint-Pierre-du-Vauvray.' He traced more invisible lines with his fingers. 'If you drive to here and leave the car just off the road, we can take the same route back. We'll have to cross the western bridge on foot to the island, but at that time of night I'm hoping the place will be fairly deserted.'

Yvain reached over and pointed at the map.

'We can leave the boat here, underneath the bridge on the western shore. We can all rendezvous there and once we get to the island we can patrol across this field to the crossroads and the lighthouse.'

Dalby looked at Brielle and Wellum, they were both nodding in agreement. He took his pen and marked the two points on the map with a circle, then went back and marked the roads Wellum and Brielle would be using.

'We should look to RV at the bridge at twenty-one-thirty. That will gives us plenty of time to get to Thiel by twenty-two-hundred.'

'Will there be a signal? A torch light maybe?'

'No torches,' said Dalby. 'Can either of you whistle?'

Wellum nodded. 'Yes, of course.'

'That's it then. When one group spots the other, give two whistles, like a bird, nothing too obvious.'

'Like this?' Said wellum, pursing his lips together and blowing two soft notes.

'Fine,' said Dalby. 'The confirm signal will be three notes sent back.'

Wellum and Brielle nodded again.

'What do you think the travel times will be?' Wellum asked.

Dalby thought for a moment.

'We don't have time to do a practice run, but I'm guessing it'll be about an hour for both teams.'

'So we need to be ready to leave by twenty-fifteen, pushing off from here at twenty-thirty.'

Dalby nodded. He looked at Yvain.

'You'll have to check your dead letterbox at some point after eleven tomorrow. I won't risk coming back here after today unless I have to. I'll post details of the boats' location and any specific requirements at the dead drop, but wherever we'll be meeting, you should aim to be there at twenty-fifteen.'

Dalby poured himself more tea and sat back and considered the map and his scribbled notes.

'What about weapons?' Said Brielle eventually.

Dalby looked at Yvain once more.

'Did you get a list of what's here?'

The Belgian took a slip of paper from his back pocket and read aloud.

'Two Sten guns, one with a suppressor, a German MP40 submachine gun, a silenced De Lisle Carbine rifle, two Lee-Enfield 303's and three Walther PPK's, one with a suppressor.'

'Rounds for all?'

'Yes, there's also a sawn-off shotgun under Armada's cot and half a box of cartridges. I managed to find a few boxes of 7.65 for Brielle's MAS.'

'Alright good. What about grenades?'

There's a dozen Mills' pineapples in a box through there,' he gestured towards Armada bedroom. 'And I found another ten Oryx grenades lying about the place, so I put them with the others.'

'That's over twenty, so we'll take five each.' He looked around the table. 'Any preference on weapons?'

'I've got my 38,' said Brielle, so I'll just take rounds for that and one of the pistols.'

Dalby looked at Wellum.

'Harry?'

'I'll take one of the Sten's and a pistol, I think I'd like the shotgun left in the car too.'

Dalby nodded.

'Fine. Well, I've got my own MP40 and a pistol so I'll just take the grenades with me when I leave here today. Yvain, have you got anything back at your apartment?'

The Belgian shook his head.

'No I dropped my machine gun, when we got ambushed the other night. I still have my pistol and I'll take my pick from what's left here.'

It had been an intense and focused discussion. Dalby looked at his watch.

'Let's take a break and get some more coffee on the go, have you all eaten?'

Yvain took the coffee pot back into the kitchen and filled the kettle and put it on the stove.

'I'll get the ration packs from upstairs,' said Brielle. She turned to Yvain as she left.

'Yvain, as-tu faim?'

'Oui, merci. Peu importe ce que vous avez serait bien.'

Dalby reached into the depths of his satchel and came out with a fistful of corned beef sandwiches. He put one on the table and took a bite from another.

'You really think Thiel's genuine?' Said Wellum. 'I mean, you believe he's actually Walter Thiel and he's going to defect?'

As Dalby chewed he nodded.

'Yes, I do. I think it's too elaborate a trap for the Germans to come up with just to snare one or two SOE personnel sent to pick him up.'

'What if Thiel turns out to be a spy, reporting information back to Berlin about our weapons development?'

Dalby took another bite from his sandwich.

'I expect he'll be carefully monitored back in England. He'll definitely have restricted access to files and sensitive technical data for at least the duration of the war. But anyway,' he shrugged. 'That's not our concern is it? What happens after we've done our bit and brought him in is someone else's problem.'

Brielle came back into the room carrying several packets and boxes from the German ration packs.

'There are crackers and sardines and a tin of pork.' She carried them through to the kitchen as Yvain dug some spoons and forks from a drawer.

'I also found some chocolate I forgot I had.' She smiled at Wellum.

He smiled back, suddenly self conscious in Dalby's presence. He thought these SOE agents; Dalby, Yvain, Armada, were as close to military ascetics as he'd met. They were like monks, only focusing on survival and the conditions of their service, dug in behind enemy lines, dedicated to the missions they were set, without distraction.

He felt like an imposter.

Yvain came and poured Wellum fresh coffee. He put the pot on the table and sat down.

'We should discuss *actions on target*.'

Dalby nodded and dusted his hands together as he finished his corned beef.

'Well, it seems straight forward enough so far.' He stood up and leant forward on the map. The car will park here. The boat here. We'll meet here at the top of the stairs on the Il-du-Bac side of the bridge and move tactically to this crossroads.'

'What do you mean tactically?' Said Brielle as she put three plates out along with the crackers and sardines.

'Tactiquement? Il veut dire silencieusement, n'est-ce pas?'

Yvain nodded. 'Oui.'

'It means we move to here silently.'

'I'll lead off from the RV point at the top of the stairs,' said Dalby. 'Then I think it should be Brielle and Harry. Yvain, you bring up the rear.'

'Of course.'

There are some service buildings about twenty yards from the lighthouse.' He scrutinised the map again. 'They're not shown here, but Thiel said they're north of the lighthouse.' He took his pen and drew on the map. 'This will do as reference. When we get to this point. You three go firm and I'll either cross to the lighthouse and bring Thiel back to you there or take one person with me. We'll see how it pans out on the ground. After that, we'll just retrace our steps and make our way back to the car. Thiel will have to go in the boot and if it's all the same I'll drive us back to Rouen. Brielle can ride up front with me, Harry and Yvain in the back.'

They all nodded in agreement.

'What about an emergency rendezvous point?' Said Yvain.

Dalby drew on the map with his finger once more.

'This looks good.' He pointed. 'Le Jardin Marguerite, just behind the railway station. If we get split up or attacked, lets RV there. We'll call the cut-off as midnight, that's two hours after we're scheduled to meet Thiel. Any stragglers not at the emergency RV after that time will be presumed dead or captured. Anyone at the RV at midnight should then proceed back to Rouen by whatever means possible.' He paused. 'What I will add, and this has come straight from the top in London, is that if we do get compromised and it looks likely that we won't be making it back, we are to kill Thiel and leave him behind. If there is only one of us left and we are trying to get him back here and he's slow and looking likely to get himself captured as a way of staying alive, he must be killed.' He looked at each of them in turn. 'Is that clear? Thiel must not, I repeat, must *not* get back to Berlin. We either get him out and back to England or we kill him, and that includes every day that we have him until he's across the Channel.'

They all nodded once more.

Dalby checked his wrist.

'Lets synchronise our watches now, and then again at the bridge tomorrow.'

They did as he asked, each checking that the hands on their watches all pointed to exactly twelve-twenty-five. Dalby stood up and finished his tea and screwed the cup back into place on the top of the thermos flask. He began gathering his things.

'I think that just about covers everything. I'll take the grenades now and I'll leave a message for Renard to meet me later today so I can organise the boat.' He turned to

Yvain. 'Can you go and see if the Citroen is still at Rue du Montparnasse. If it's gone leave me a message.'

'What will we do if it's gone?' Asked Brielle.

'We'll have just over twenty-four hours to acquire another one.'

Dalby glanced through his notes.

'I have enough information here to mark up my own map back at my place - I'll leave this one here.' He slid the map towards Wellum then tore off a blank piece of paper and scribbled down the timings and details they had discussed.

'Read these, then reread them and memories them; both of you. Then burn them before you leave tomorrow.'

Wellum took the piece of paper and handed it to Brielle.

'We will.'

Dalby put his notebook away and fastened his satchel.

'Right, well I'll see you both on the bridge at Saint-Pierre-du-Vauvray tomorrow night.'

Wellum stood up.

'We'll be there, don't worry.'

Dalby held out his hand.

'Good luck.'

'You too.'

The spy collected his bag and made for the door, exchanging thin smiles with Brielle as Yvain saw him out.

Wellum studied the map again while Brielle collected the coffee pot and the cups and took them through to the kitchen. As she came back for the empty lunch plates Wellum looked at her.

'This could be the biggest thing either of us have ever been involved in you know.'

'Do you think if we get Thiel and stop this weapon, this V2, then maybe, hopefully the war will end sooner?'

'Well, if Thiel does go back to work for the Germans, it could prove worse for everyone, everywhere.'

'Maybe we should just kill him anyway?' Said Brielle over her shoulder as she carried the plates into the kitchen. She came back in wiping her hands on the back of her trousers.

'He is a Nazi after all.'

'His knowledge could be useful in the fight against Hitler.'

'Maybe,' said Brielle.

Yvain came back into the kitchen, putting on his jacket.

'I'm going to see if there's any sign of anyone having been near my flat. I need a change of clothes and some personal items. We can check on the Citroen first thing tomorrow.'

'You think that's sensible?' Said Wellum. 'And besides…Dalby said to check on the car today.'

'The city is too busy now. But if it makes you feel better, I'll pass by that way and see if it's still there.' He picked up his house key and put a pistol in his holster. 'Then we can collect it tomorrow early in the morning before there are too many people around.' He took in Wellum's look of concern.

'I'll be careful, trust me; If it looks like there have been German's at my place I'll stay away. I won't be more than an hour, don't worry.' He turned and went out.

Brielle filled the kettle and lit the stove.

Wellum watched her. They heard the door downstairs close and Brielle stood on her tiptoes and looked out of the window and watched Yvain turn up his collar as he crossed the street and disappeared out of view. She came away from the window and leant her back against the sink.

'Would you like more coffee?'

Wellum shook his head slowly.

'No, thank you.'

She looked at him as he sat watching her. She smiled.

'Quoi?'

'I'm feeling rather tired to be honest, planning meetings always take it out of me. I thought I'd go back to bed for an hour.'

He stood up and folded the map and looked at her.

'You going to come?'

She nodded.

'Oui.'

Her eyes flickered a smile, and Wellum saw her standing there for an instant, unburdened by the war and the death and the lingering smell of smoke and fire. He stood for a moment content simply to look at her like this, and he hoped beyond hope that soon he could take her away with him, far beyond the ruins of the city and her old life and the grief of it and together they could start again.

CHAPTER SIXTEEN
Selling secrets

They met in an abandoned railway tunnel that ran down to the docks from the Roumare Forest just west of the city. A bombing raid on the station near *Canteleu* at the beginning of nineteen-forty-two had broken and twisted the tracks into unnatural shapes a quarter of a mile away, rendering the line useless.

The tunnel roof dripped and echoed all along its length, and the whole place smelled of dead leaves and the oil filled puddles that gathered between the sleepers in shining black pools. It was another of Rouen's shattered limbs, torn off and left to rot.

Renard stood just inside the entrance to the tunnel, the unlit cigarette dangling from his lips as Dalby struck a match and lit his own cigarette before leaning forward and lighting Renard's. He dropped the match and it sizzled in a puddle at his feet.

'Any idea what happened at the quarry?'

Renard shrugged and stamped his feet and took the cigarette from his mouth.

'No. When tnone of them came back as planned it seemed obvious though. I stayed at the house until almost two, and then left. I didn't want to risk staying any longer, just in case the German's had discovered Irene and Godfrey's address.'

Dalby listened and smoked. He watched Renard closely.

'The next morning I spoke to Elliot's cousin, Michelle. She told me some people were going up to the drop site, to see if they could find anyone. Apparently, when they got up there, there were signs of a gunfight, but that was it.' He paused. 'Are they all dead?'

Dalby nodded.

'I'm sorry Renard.'

'The girl and the English pilot too?'

Dalby looked at his feet and gave a noncommittal shrug. His silence spoke volumes.

'Neither confirm, nor deny.' Renard winked and sucked on his cigarette. He smiled, flashing nicotine stained teeth.

'Fair enough.'

After a moment Dalby went on.

'I need you to get me a boat.'

Renard took the cigarette from his mouth and blew smoke up into the gloom.

'A boat? Why, what for?'

'I'm going to Ande.'

Renard laughed.

'Dalby, there's nothing in Ande, why are you lying to me?'

'I need to get there tomorrow night by twenty-one-thirty,' said Dalby, ignoring the question.

'You don't need to know the rest.

Renard spat.

'Je ne suis pas qu'un *paysan!* If I'm getting you a boat I need to know why, otherwise you're on your own. I'm not sure if you'd noticed but it's getting dangerous for me out here.'

'Alright, calm down,' said Dalby. 'I'm dropping someone off there.'

'In Ande?'

'Close by, yes.'

Renard eyed him.

'It's the pilot isn't it. I wondered if Armada would come to you for help.'

'Don't let your imagination run away with you.'

'I know..I know,' said Renard, smiling wolfishly once more. 'You're taking him to Ande - why?'

'Renard, you know the rules, now can you get me a boat or not?'

Renard nodded. 'Of course, yes.'

'It doesn't have to be large, just a small dinghy with an outboard motor but please, make sure its got petrol in it; I don't want to end up floating down the Seine with my arse hanging out.'

A sound a little further into the tunnel made them both turn and look. Three rats emerged from a deep cleft in the wall. They were large and night black and their slick, wet fur made them shine like oiled vampires. They stopped for a moment and crouched together in a huddle like a coven of witches. They looked at Dalby and Renard then they lifted their snouts and sniffed the air before turning and scampering away into the darkness.

'What time are you leaving?"

'Like I said, I need to be at Ile-Du-Bac, just across the river from Ande by twenty-one-thirty so I need to be gone by twenty-thirty at the latest.'

'You're meeting someone?'

Dalby fixed him with his eyes and changed his tone.

'Renard drop it.'

The Frenchman grinned and held up his palms in surrender.

'Alright, forget I asked.'

Dalby flicked his cigarette out towards the late afternoon drizzle.

'I'll double your usual price for large items, that's thirty-thousand Francs, but I'll pay you when I'm back, so no mishaps alright?'

Renard narrowed his eyes.

'What?'

'When I get back.'

'Half now, half when you get back.'

'Forget it I'll find someone else.' Dalby began to move towards the tunnel entrance.

'Fine, fine,' said Renard. 'Wait…It's a deal. I'll get you a boat, and you get to Ande and back *alive.*'

Dalby nodded.

'I'll do my best. Now, leave the boat at an open jetty somewhere I can see it, perhaps at Quai du Havre, there's likely to be less foot traffic there and it's pretty covert. If I see any sign of German soldiers I'll abort, so I'll need to be able to see the coast is clear and get away quickly if needs be.'

He looked at Renard.

'You can do it? No mess up's…this is important Renard. I need to know I can rely on you?'

When All The Birds Leap

The Frenchman dragged the last bit of life from his cigarette and threw it on the ground. He waved his hand dismissively.

'Yes, yes of course. Have I ever let you down before?'

Dalby nodded and checked his watch.

'Alright, good. Leave me clear instructions at my dead drop on *Rue des Requis.*'

'By the church?"

'Yes.'

'Alright.'

Dalby held out his hand.

'Thank you Renard. I'll wait to hear from you and then I'll notify you when I'm back.'

The Frenchman shook his hand.

'Good luck. Don't die, this is a lot of money you owe me.'

The agent smiled.

'I'll be in touch.' And he turned and went out into the rain and along the broken tracks that led east towards the city.

Renard watched him go. He thought about the money - enough to live the high life for quite some time. He leant back against the tunnel wall wondering how much he should demand fromWolff and the detestable Schenk for such valuable information.

The rats returned, their claws clicking on the stone sleepers like a cascade of frozen sand. Renard turned and watched them come towards him along the tunnel out of the darkness. Two of them carried dead kittens in their mouths, one silver, one red, their bulbous round heads drooping on thin necks while the largest of the three came after, dragging the lifeless body of the mother cat behind it with drops of white milk still clinging like small pearls to her swollen nipples.

He peddled north, wobbling awkwardly along streets filled with rubble and lined on either side with broken buildings that sat and festered like open wounds. People crawled like insects among the debris, rolling the wreckage aside, sifting through the mess, searching for what was left of their lives. Renard didn't pay them any heed and he felt inured against their pain and detached from the hell that many of his fellow Rouennais described as their constant, daily existence.

To Renard it felt like life had always been this way.

And was it really so bad?

The front wheel of his bicycle suddenly caught on a brick and twisted the handlebars quickly to the right, shocking him out of his musing and threatening to cast him into the gutter. He stuck his knees out in the manner of a toad and peddled on his tip toes and gripped the bicycle like it was alive, steering this way and that in an attempt to stay in the saddle. He got under control and carried on, cursing under his breath as two boys playing on the kerb pointed at him and laughed.

'Ha! regarde ce gros cochon en train de faire du vélo'

One of them threw a sod of earth.

'Rentre a la maison pour ton diner, petit cochon.'

They'd be sorry, he scowled as he went on. He would buy a car soon enough. No more bicycles for Renard. He would buy a Daimler or maybe a Mercedes of his own, or even an English Rolls Royce, and he would sit at the end of the *Boulevard des Belges* with the roof peeled back, smoking his expensive cigars and watching them as they scratched around in the dirt and the gutters like lice on dogs.

He weaved on, peddling slowly, the ever present smell of smoke suspended in the drizzle and the low clouds that painted everything below them in homologous shades of grey.

After twenty minutes he struggled to the top of Cote Sainte-Catherine and began free wheeling down the other side of the hill, out towards the edge of the city and the fields and forests beyond. Within a half mile he could see the turrets and flags of the *Chateau of the Black Swan*, standing up among the evergreens.

Two guards watched him approach along the road. As he pulled up and got off his bicycle, he took a handkerchief from his trouser pocket and wiped his face and the top of his head. One of the sentries came to meet him, his weapon slung over one shoulder, his thumbs in the belt of his trench coat. He lifted his chin at the Frenchman, gesturing towards Renard's push bike that was leaning against a bollard at the roadside.

'You can't leave that there,' said the soldier.

Renard stuffed his handkerchief into his pocket and glanced back at the bike. He stood in front of the soldier and took a breath.

'I need to see Haupsturmfuhrer Wolff immediately.' He hesitated. 'Or detective Schenk…or both of them together.' He took his handkerchief out and wiped his face once more. The German looked at him as a colleague came from the sentry box to join them.

'Wa passiert? Wer ist er?'

The first soldier held out his hand.

'You have papers?'

As Renard handed over his identification the soldier scanned them and looking back at the Frenchman spoke to the other German.

'Er mochte mit Wolff sprechen.'

'Wofur?'

The first man shrugged.

'Why do you need to see Captain Wolff?'

'I have information.'

'What sort of information?'

The other soldier leant forward and took Renard's papers and looked at them.

'Soll ich das zum Schloss hochbringen?'

'Important information,' said Renard. He eyed the guard. 'About a fugitive English pilot.'

After a pause the first soldier said,

'Alright, wait over there.' He gestured towards Renard's bicycle and the two Germans turned and walked away. The first went into the sentry box as the other climbed onto a waiting motorcycle. He started it with a kick and after tucking Renard's papers into his pocket, he pulled away along the road towards the Chateau.

Renard walked back to his bike and took a crumpled packet of cigarettes from his pocket. He dragged out the last one and put it in his mouth and patted his chest and his trousers looking for matches, the *Gitanes* dangling from his lips.

'Shit.'

After fifteen minutes the sound of a motorcycle drifted back down the road towards them. The air had begun to grow cold and Renard was sitting on the bollard next to his bicycle with his collar turned up and his unlit cigarette stuck behind one ear. The returning soldier pulled the motorbike to a stop and cut the engine and kicked down the sidestand and dismounted. He went into the sentry box. Renard could see the two guards talking and after a moment the first soldier came out and gestured for Renard to step forward. He handed the Frenchman his papers.

'You can go.' He lifted the barrier. 'Take your bike and cycle down to the Chateau; They're expecting you.'

Renard looked slightly confused.

'Does the Haupsturmfuhrer know I'm coming?'

The soldier nodded.

'Yes.' He raised the barrier.

'No car?'

'It's a five minute ride, no more than that.'

Renard wheeled his bike under the raised barrier and climbed self-consciously back onto the saddle and peddled away feeling a sudden sense of indignant anger as he went. He spat on the road as he wobbled past the sentry box, the second soldier having come out to watch him leave and grinning at him from beneath his helmet.

When he arrived at the Chateau a butler stood alongside the grand steps that led up to the front doors. Renard dismounted, sweating once more, and propped his bicycle against a statue of two cherubs, each pouring water from an ornate jug. He approached the butler.

'I'm here to see Wolff,' he said, deliberately dispensing with the SS captain's full title.

The butler nodded politely.

'Very good monsieur. The Haupsturmfuhrer is waiting for you.' He turned to go.

'Please, follow me.'

Renard took a step towards the marble staircase but the butler turned to his left and went down a path that led beneath an arbor, covered in vines.

'It's this way monsieur.'

Renard followed him. They went a short distance to a side door surrounded by red ivy and hidden completely from the main driveway. The butler turned the doorhandle and went inside and they entered a passageway lit with a single fizzing lightbulb and went through a door at the end into a room with a table and two wooden chairs.

'Please, wait here,' said the butler. He turned and went out through another door. The room was the colour of paste with no pictures on the walls, no furniture and just a single square window looking out onto a small garden beyond.

Renard sat down and drummed his fingers on the table. He looked around the featureless cell. It really wasn't what he had been expecting.

After a few minutes the door opened and Wolff came in, closely followed by Stein. The SS captain gave a broad smile and sat down opposite the Frenchman. Stein remained by the door.

'Monsieur Renard,' beamed Wolff. 'It is very good to see you again.'

Renard gave a mute nod.

'So,' said Wolff sitting forward. 'You have some information for me?'

Renard span his finger, indicating the room.

'Is this some attempt at humour?'

'What do you mean?' Said Wolff with a frown.

'This room, putting me in here, making me cycle all the way to the fucking door.'

Wolff smiled again.

'Monsieur, I'm not entirely sure why you are so upset. I was told you had information for me, so…'

'Don't play me for a fool,'

'What the fuck are you talking about?' Said Stein from the doorway.

'I'm talking about respect Captain, and the fact that you seem to think you can treat me like… like some messenger boy.' He sat back petulantly. 'I won't have it.'

'I'm sorry monsieur,' said Wolff. 'I think there might be some misunderstanding…'

'I want a drink,' interrupted Renard. 'In there.' He pointed to the door they'd come through.

Wolff pointed a thumb at the same door and raised his eyebrows.

'In there? In the Chateau?'

'Yes,' said Renard. He took the bent and sodden Gitanes from behind his ear and dropped it on the table. He looked at Stein.

'And a cigarette, I want one of your cigarettes.'

Stein looked at Wolff and the SS officer nodded. Stein stepped forward and shrugged a cigarette from a packet and held it in front of Renard who took it and put it between his lips.

'You have a light?'

Stein dropped a matchbox on the table and went back and leant on the wall once more.

Renard lit his cigarette as Wolff stood up and slid the chair back under the table.

'I apologise monsieur, and of course, you are right. We ought to sit somewhere more fitting a war hero.'

Renard winced a smile, unconvinced Wolff wasn't being sarcastic.

The SS officer went to the door.

'Let us go through to the library.'

Wolff guided Renard towards a deep armchair by the fire and put an ashtray at his elbow. He asked a butler to bring them cognac and sat down on an overstuffed couch while Stein hovered by a bookcase. When the cognac arrived Renard finished his cigarette and took a drink and relaxed.

'Better?' Said Wolff.

Renard took another sip and nodded. He turned the drink in the firelight, looking at the amber reflections jumping from the cut glass tumbler - this was more like it.

He nodded again. 'Yes, much better, thank you.'

'So, now that we are all comfortable, tell me, please, why are you here?'

Renard paused and considered them both.

'I have new information about your English pilot.'

'You've seen him?' Asked Wolff.

'No.'

'What sort of information?' Said Stein.

Renard looked at the tank commander.

'Important information Herr Captain.'

He turned back to Wolff.

'Vital information in fact.'

He waited for the Germans to speak, but save for the crackle of the open fire, the room remained silent. He took another drink the went on.

'I know where he will be tomorrow night at exactly ten o'clock.'

'What?' Said Stein joining Wolff on the couch. 'How?'

Wolff sat forward.

'Monsieur Renard, I don't think I need to tell you that if for one moment you are fucking with us, it will not go well for you.'

Renard nodded and finished his cognac.

'I know that.'

'Where did you get the information?' Said Stein handing over his cigarettes and lighting one for himself.

Renard lit his own cigarette and blew out the match and threw it at the fire.

'Before I say anymore, I want four-hundred-thousand-Reichsmark.'

'What?' Laughed Stein. 'You're insane.'

'Am I?' Renard looked at Wolff.

'Haupsturmfuhrer, I know where he'll be tomorrow.'

Wolff nodded slowly.

'I believe you.'

'And you trust me?'

'Yes, I trust you.'

'So we have a deal?'

Wolff regarded the Frenchman carefully. He sipped his drink.

'If you're information leads to the pilot's arrest. I'll pay you six-hundred-thousand-Reichsmark.'

'Wolff you can't be serious,' interjected Stein.

'What have we to lose Captain Stein?' Said Wolff with a shrug. 'If he is lying, he gets nothing. If he is telling the truth, I am willing to pay six-hundred-thousand for the head of this Englishman.'

He turned to Renard.

'So Monsieur, tell me what you know.'

Renard looked slyly back at him.

'What guarantees do I have that you'll pay me?'

Wolff smiled.

'I see this time it is you that misunderstands me monsieur, but that is understandable under the circumstances I suppose.' He took a sip of cognac and leant forward towards Renard.

'As far as I am concerned you and I, we now have a deal. You tell me what you know about this pilot and where exactly he'll be tomorrow night and I'll go and arrest him. When I get back, if my mission has been fruitful I will pay you six-hundred-thousand-Reichsmark, and you can go on your happy way.' He scratched his chin.

'Or…you can ask for some or other guarantee, which of course I am in no position to provide, or indeed, for you to uphold, at which point you can refuse to tell me what you know and I can take you outside and have you shot.'

Wolff sat back and took another mouthful of brandy as Renard let the conditions of their *deal* sink in. After a moment he spoke.

'Alright. An SOE Agent called Dalby is with him. He arranged a meeting with me this afternoon and asked me to procure him a small boat so that he might travel down the Seine tomorrow night to rendezvous with someone at the *Ile-du-Bac.*'

'Where's that?' Said Stein.

'It's an island in the river, situated near the town of Ande.'

'How far is it?'

'I'm not sure. Not far I think. An hour maybe, I've never been there.'

'You're sure this agent is taking the pilot there?'

Well, when I asked him he didn't deny it.'

'But you're not certain?'

Renard looked at Stein.

'No, but it all sounded very urgent and when I asked him directly if he was helping the pilot he didn't deny it. Also, this Dalby he works with the SOE agent Armada that was with the pilot when I first met him at the Charron's house. They are part of one group, the same group.'

He looked back at Wolff.

'I'm rarely wrong, Haupsturmfuhrer, trust me. He's delivering the pilot to someone, possibly the English or a bigger Resistance group.'

Wolff stared into the fire while Renard prattled on.

'This man you seek, I'm telling you he's moving tomorrow, he's leaving the area, leaving Rouen.'

After a while Wolff turned and looked at him.

'Very well monsieur, we will go to Ande tomorrow night and we will arrest this pilot before he has a chance to leave France.'

Renard held up a finger.

'One thing, the man I have spoken about; the SOE operative. I would appreciate it if you allowed him to escape…somehow. He owes me money.'

Stein laughed.

'Brilliant. That's brilliant.' He shook his head. 'You're such slime Renard.'

'Well he does,' snapped the Frenchman. 'And what is it to you anyway? This is my life, my livelihood. If you kill him I won't get paid.' He turned to Wolff once more. 'Plus he's an asset, he trusts me and he might have useful information in the future. So please, I'm asking you. Let him go.'

'How will we know which of these men is which?' Said Stein. 'There might be fighting. It's easy to make a mistake in the dark.'

'The spy, Dalby, he is taller than the pilot and one of the lenses in his glasses is dark. The left one.' He paused for a moment and doused his cigarette.

'Plus, I have this.'

He sat forward in his chair and reached inside his jacket pocket and took out a small photograph and handed it to Wolff.

'Who is that?' asked the SS officer looking at the picture.

'I told you the spy Armada came to visit the Charron house a few days ago looking to get an ID card made.' Renard pointed at the photograph.

'That Haupsturmfuhrer, is Harry Wellum.'

CHAPTER SEVENTEEN
Old man Lefebre

When Wellum woke up, Brielle was stood at the bottom of the bed, fastening her coat.

'Good morning,' he said squinting through one eye. 'What time is it?'

She came to the side of the bed and leant forward and kissed him.

'It's early, go back to sleep.'

Wellum sat up.

'You're going out?'

'I'm going with Yvain to collect the car. I brought you coffee.' Wellum turned and looked at the table next to the bed.

'Er, thanks. When did you arrange to go and get the car?'

'Just now. I couldn't sleep so I went down and made coffee and he was up. He suggested we go now as the streets will still be quiet.'

'I should come too.' Wellum threw back the sheets and went to get out of bed.

'No, you stay we won't be long. Yvain thought it would be better if just the two of us went as we both have the right papers.' She kissed him again and smiled. 'Keep the bed warm for when I get back.'

'You smell too nice to be a soldier.'

She mimed cocking a pistol and winked at him as she got up and went to the door.

'Vive le Résistance.'

'Bring back something nice for breakfast.'

'I'll try,' she said as she went out.

'Like warm rolls with butter,' wellum called after her. 'Or bacon and eggs…!'

He heard the door slam downstairs then lay back on the pillows and stared up at the ceiling and listened to the silence behind the silence. The house was completely still. He closed his eyes and tried to sleep.

The kettle boiled, rattling the whistle as bubbling steam seeped from the spout and filled the house with noise. Wellum turned off the gas and poured hot water into the teapot. He put a tea cosy over the pot and carried it to the kitchen table and set it down and lit a cigarette and went through into Armada's room. He stood in the doorway and smoked and looked around. Yvain had made some attempt at tidying since he'd been using the place but to Wellum it still looked like disorganised chaos. He looked at the radio and thought again if he should contact London and tell them what he was doing; He hadn't heard back from headquarters since the night of the quarry raid.

He went to the dining table and began lazily sifting through some of the maps and diagrams still lying there. He unfolded one that took in several hundred miles of Normandy, west of Rouen leading to the coast. He started thinking about getting back to England and traced a finger along the Seine, reading off the names of towns along the way;

Tancarville, Berville-sur-Mer, Pennedepie.

Small towns, quiet, isolated. All perfect locations for him to be scooped up and taken home.

It had only been a week, but he felt as if he'd been stuck in France for months. Hiding away and scurrying around for survival was not really in his nature and the need to get back flying was becoming a persistent and bothersome itch. He stubbed the cigarette in an ashtray and reconsidered making contact. As he looked at the radio he noticed the black box sitting innocently in the corner of the room. It looked insignificant and somehow out of place. Wellum went over and crouched beside it. The arming key was missing and he reached out and touched the raised red detonator button. *Where was that other key?* He lifted the box and looked at where a black wire came out of the back like a tail. He ran it through his fingers and followed it with his eyes to where it disappeared through a a hole drilled in the wall. He imagined it linking to piles of P4 and clustered stacks of dynamite in the walls and in the cellar and suddenly felt strangely vulnerable at the thought. What had Armada said? *Enough to blow half the street away…*

He winced at the thought and put the box carefully back on the floor.

By nine he heard the sound of a car pulling up outside and he glanced out of the kitchen window just in time to see the green Citroen rolling to a standstill on the kerb in front of the house. He doused his fourth cigarette under the tap and filled the kettle and lit the stove and put the kettle on it to boil. Brielle came in, unclipping the MAS from its sling as she did. She checked the breech and dropped the magazine and put the gun on the table and began taking off her coat. She smiled at Wellum.

'Good morning again.'

He took a step forward.

'Good morning.'

Yvain came into the room and hung his coat on the back of a chair. He removed his pistol from its holster and put it on the table next to the MAS.

'You got it going alright then?' Wellum pointed his thumb at the kitchen window.

Yvain shrugged.

'It was easy enough, yes.'

'And it's running alight?'

'Yes, as far as I can tell.' Yvain washed his hands at the sink.

Brielle came and kissed his cheek.

'I got us croissants.'

'Really?'

'Yes, they're still warm.' She headed for a shopping bag she'd placed on one of the chairs.

'She insisted we took a detour to collect them from a boulangerie on the other side of Rouen,' said Yvain, drying his hands.

'He exaggerates,' said Brielle blowing out her cheeks as she put the crisp, golden pastries onto a plate and got a butter knife from the draw.

'It was only a ten minute drive, and we needed to test the car was running properly anyway.'

She put the croissants and knives and a plate of butter on the table.

Wellum watched her moving between the kitchen and the table and he looked at Yvain who had sat down and opened a book and begun reading. He thought how they all looked as if they were on a vacation somehow, without a care in the world. Three friends, holidaying in Rouen, eating French pastries with coffee and reading *Honore de Balzac*. For the the first time since they had arrived, the house felt open and welcoming and the mood was light and unworried. As wellum watched Brielle make coffee he wondered how long such a reverie would last.

When they had eaten, Yvain glanced at his watch and put his book down and grabbed his jacket.

'You're going back out?' Said Wellum.

'I ought to go and see if Dalby has left me any message about where I'm supposed to meet him tonight.' He reholstered his pistol.

Wellum glanced at the widow as if checking the weather and then looked at his own watch.

It was almost ten thirty.

'How long will you be?'

Yvain smiled and looked at Brielle.

'Brielle, tu dois vraiment apprendre aux Anglaise a ne pas s'inquiéter autant.'

Wellum looked at her questioningly.

'He says I should teach you not to worry so much.'

'I'll be back in an hour,' said Yvain.

Wellum watched him go and as they heard the door downstairs close he stood up and crossed to the kitchen and checked out of the window. As he came back into the dining room Brielle looked at him.

'What are you doing?'

Wellum walked past her to a door in the opposite wall. He turned the handle and opened it.

Brielle stood up 'what's in there?'

Wellum looked inside.

'It's the cupboard under the stairs. Armada mentioned it.'

'Why, what's in it?'

Wellum took a step inside, stooping his head slightly as he went. He flicked a light switch and a bulb flickered into life and swung slightly from a short flex buried in the ceiling.

Brielle peered past him at the shelves where the debris of family life lay stacked under gathering dust; old paint pots and brushes tied together with string, a broken accordion and a moth-eaten child's teddy-bear sat looking down at them. It was a dry space of wooden floor boards and paper smells and shelves strewn with a few high cobwebs alongside one or two tins of preserved fruit.

Wellum looked at the safe, tucked in a corner beneath a stack of paper files and a desiccated pot plant. He crouched and tapped the dial with a finger.

'You know the combination?' Asked Brielle from the doorway.

Wellum span the dial lazily.

'Yes.'

'What's inside?'

Wellum put his ear close to the safe door and held the dial carefully in his fingers.

'Let's see shall we.'

He turned the dial to the left, rotating it fully, slowing as he went, then satisfied, he spun it quickly to the right, slowed again and turned it left a half turn and then right again. He leant on the handle and as it dropped with a clunk, the solid iron door swung open. Wellum peered inside then stuck his arm in up to the elbow. He came out with a small black cardboard box. He held it out towards Brielle.

'Here take this.'

She took the box and gave it a small shake trying to imagine what it contained. She looked at Wellum who had returned his attention back to the safe, searching inside it once more. When he dragged his arm free he was clutching several flat squares of cardboard. He went back in once more and came out with a bottle and several piles of bank notes all held together with rubber bands.

'What is it?'

Wellum held up the bottle and read the label.

'Well this appears to be a bottle of London Gin and a collection of vinyl records.' He scrutinised the money in the gloom of the cupboard. 'And this looks like several thousand pounds.'

He closed the safe and lifted the handle and span the combination dial then checked it was locked and stood up.

They put the collected items on the kitchen table. Wellum picked up the small box and lifted the lid. Inside there was a silver key cut like a door key.

'What's that?' Said Brielle.

'Come on I'll show you.'

They went into the dining room and Wellum led the way to the detonator sitting in the corner.

'Apparently, you put this key in there,' he pointed to the arming switch. 'Turn it to the right and then press that red button.

'And then?'

'And then you have ten minutes to get as far away as possible before the whole house goes up in smoke.'

She looked at the key and then the box.

'The whole house is rigged with explosives?'

Wellum nodded.

'Yes.'

'Do you think Yvain knows?'

'Probably, he's worked with Armada for long enough.' He held up the key. 'But Armada said there were only two keys. He had one, and this one was the spare he kept in the safe.'

'Are you going to leave it here, in the box?'

Wellum thought for a moment, then shook his head.

'No. I think we should keep it in the bedroom upstairs. In the weapons bag.'

He gave a thin smile.

'Just in case.'

They went back into the kitchen. Wellum inspected the bottle of gin while Brielle picked up the records. They ignored the money.

'Al Bowlly and Ann Shelton'

Wellum put the gin down and took the record from her. He read the cover.

'Is it good?' Said Brielle.

'You've never heard *Heartaches*?'

Brielle shook her head. 'No.'

Wellum glanced around the room.

'Armada must have had a record player.' He got up and went towards the kitchen.

'Ha, here we go.' A trolley sat inconspicuously near the refrigerator. On top was a black box, about the size of a typewriter. Wellum dragged it in from the kitchen.

'Help me move the table up against the wall.'

Brielle stood up and smiled.

'What are you doing?'

'I'm making some room. Here grab the other end, we can slide it.'

Together they moved the table aside and stacked the chairs. Wellum brought the trolley closer and unclasped the lid of the box.

'Ta-da.' He waved his hands like a magician at the record player and searched for an electric flex to plug it into the wall. He turned to Brielle.

'Pass me one of those Al Bowlly discs.'

Brielle handed him the top record. As he slid it from its cover and inspected the faint grooves cut into its surface he looked at her again and grinned. He gestured towards the kitchen.

'Quick, grab two glasses and lets have a drink of this gin.'

'Really…now?'

'Yes, wellum laughed. 'Just a small one - quick, we haven't got long before Yvain comes back and spoils our date.'

'Is that was this is? Said Brielle from the kitchen, her hands reaching inside a cupboard. 'A date?'

Wellum put the record onto the record player and lifted the arm and placed the needle onto the rotating disc. Smooth trumpets and a strummed bass emerged from the crackles.

Heartaches, heartaches...

Al Bowlly joined them in the room. They smiled at each other. Brielle handed over the glasses. She closed her eyes and listened to the music, swaying slightly to the rhythm.

'Ah, music. Its been so long since I danced.' She wrapped her arms around her waist in a self embrace and with her eyes still closed she smiled and swayed and turned on the spot.

'Il m'etait sorti de l'esprit a quel point je l'adore. Comment cela me fait me sentir vivant.'

Wellum poured two short glasses of gin and watched her. He held out a glass.

'Here.'

Brielle opened her eyes and took the glass and he offered his own in a silent toast and took a drink. The burning gin made him raise an eyebrow, then he put his glass on the table and held out his hand.

'Shall we dance?'

Brielle downed her drink and passed him her glass and raised a finger.

'Wait.'

She suddenly turned and headed towards the door that led up to their bedroom.

'Where are you going?'

'Pour me another drink said Brielle as ran up the stairs. 'I'll only be a minute.'

When All The Birds Leap

When Brielle came back down Wellum was sitting at the table listening to Roy Fox and smoking a cigarette with his legs crossed. He rocked his foot in time with the music and had a look of tranquil bliss playing across his face. Brielle stood at the bottom of the stairs and watched him for a while, then as she came into the room he woke from his daydream and he sat forward and stared at her. She was wearing a light summer dress, pale purple with small flowers of yellow and orange. It had short sleeves and an open, flowing skirt that finished above her tanned knees. She turned a circle on tip-toed bare feet.

'What do you think? Better for a date, yes?'

He stood up and took a step towards her.

'I found it in the wardrobe.'

'You look wonderful.'

She smoothed down the fabric of the dress.

'It feels so soft.'

'It suits you.'

'You don't think she'll mind if I bring it back to life for a while do you?'

'Who?'

'The girl who owned this dress.'

'No, not at all. I think she'd be happy for you to borrow it for an hour.'

He held out his hand and she took it a turned a pirouette then she fell towards him laughing and he held her and together they moved to the music. He closed his eyes and smelled her hair, and the soft sweetness of her skin made him weak with passion. He turned her face and kissed her then let her go and walked back to the record player and lifted the disc and selected another one from the pile. He took it from it's sleeve and blew the dust from its surface. He put the record on the player and dropped the needle onto it then he turned once more to face her as *Moonlight Serenade* poured from the speaker.

'Ah, I know this,' said Brielle. 'C'est tellement bon.'

He handed her another glass of gin.

'Are you trying to get me drunk monsieur?'

'I'm an officer and a gentleman mademoiselle.' He clinked his glass against hers.

'I wouldn't dream of it.'

Brielle downed the gin and put the glass on the table and took his hand and began dancing once more.

'What a pity,' she said as she lay her head against his chest as they moved. 'If I'd had much more I might have suggested having this last dance then going back to bed for an hour.'

Wellum smiled and pushed her playfully away.

'Hang on I'll get the bottle.'

By the time Yvain got back to the house it was late in the afternoon. The sun was sliding behind the cathedral and the Rue Etoupee was filling up with cold, leaden shadows. When he arrived in the kitchen he found Wellum putting the chairs back under the table which had been reinstated in the centre of the room. He came in and took off his coat and hung it on the back of a chair.

'You've been a while,' said Wellum. 'Is everything alright?'

Yvain came and joined him at the table. He sat down

'Yes, everything's fine. Where's Brielle?'

'She's upstairs. Did you see Dalby?'

'I did.'

'And?'

'He has a boat. It's being left at the Quai du Havre. I'm going to meet him at a bar near there at eight.'

Brielle came in, tucking her thick kaki shirt into her trousers. She nodded at Yvain.

'Salut.'

He smiled vaguely back at her. He looked tired.

Brielle checked her watch.

'Is anyone hungry?'

Wellum nodded.

'I'm getting there. But maybe it's a little early, we still have almost four hours before we set off'

'Does anyone want to go back over the plan?' Said Yvain.

They shook their heads.

The mood had become pensive once more. Yvain got up and went into the kitchen and began washing the plates in the sink. Wellum looked at Brielle, back in her uniform of heavy woollen trousers, boots and shirt and he noticed the return of the serious, unsmiling set of her slender jaw.

He already felt nostalgic for their afternoon alone.

Yvain clattered noisily in the cupboards as he put the clean crockery away. He muttered to himself in French. Brielle looked at her palms and then at Wellum, the Belgian seemed uneasy and out of sorts. She winced a smile then turned to Yvain.

'Ca va Yvain? Tu as l'air tendu.'

He closed the cupboard.

'Yes, yes I'm fine. I'm sorry I didn't sleep well. I think I'm just keen to get on now, that's all.'

'Oui. I know, just waiting around like this is draining.'

'Why don't we go out for dinner?' Said Wellum. 'A last supper so to speak. There must be somewhere decent close by.'

'There's a bistro two streets south,' said Yvain. *'Le Bistro Rouge et Blanc.'* I used to eat there with Armada.' He glanced at his watch. 'It doesn't open until five o' clock.'

Wellum looked at Brielle.

'Sound good?'

She shrugged. 'Yes, I'm sick of German army rations.'

Wellum turned to Yvain.

'Yes?'

'It sounds great,' he smiled. 'But I don't have an account there, and we're not exactly rolling in money are we?'

Wellum glanced at Brielle.

'We, er we actually found some money, earlier this afternoon.'

'Where? How much?'

'It was in a safe, in there.' Wellum gestured towards the cupboard under the stairs. 'Turns out to be around fifty-thousand francs.'

'What? Where is it now?'

'It's back in the cupboard said Wellum.

'In the safe?'

'No, it's just on a shelf, I hid it in an old powdered milk can. It's there if any of us need it.'

Yvain nodded slowly, then smiled.

'I suppose in that case, we're going to the Red and White Bistro for dinner after all.'

Wellum dropped his napkin on the table next to his plate and blew out his cheeks.

'Well, if that's the last meal I ever eat, I'll die a happy man.'

Brielle frowned a smile and swatted his arm with her own napkin.

'Ah, arrêté…ne did pas ca! Dont say that.'

Yvain sipped his coffee.

'Don't worry Brielle, the humour of the English fighter pilot, it takes some getting used to.'

Wellum had to agree. He grinned at her.

'He's right.'

They had been in the bistro for more than an hour, taking advantage of the peaceful atmosphere and indulging themselves fully in the deliciously comforting home cooked food. The restaurant was an intimate, family run place that had somehow stayed open throughout the turmoil of the preceding three years. The owner was and old man called Etienne Lefebre, and although he was going deaf and was half crippled with age, he insisted on being present in the kitchen for every hour the dining room was open, and had dutifully done the same for over forty years.

There were no menus, just a simple blackboard hung from a nail in the wall above the bar. It was marked up religiously by Etienne himself each morning, the chalk words scrawled in ever less decipherable hieroglyphs as the years went by, informing the patrons of the two or sometimes three dishes that were being served that day. As the war raged around them and attrition began to bite, sometimes the board would herald just a single word, floating alone on the powder streaked blackness, conspicuous in its solitary isolation; *Cassoulet* or *Bouillabaisse* if the catch had come in and occasionally simply *Croque-Monsieur*; a modest but delicious open sandwich consisting of grilled cheese and ham on bread. It didn't matter, there were always local Rouennais happy to come in and sit down for whatever it was that Lefebre was serving.

Today they had been lucky, there were two choices; *Coq au vin* and *Quiche Lorraine*, and when Wellum had ordered both, old man Lefebre had hobbled out from the kitchen on his walking stick and patted the Englishman heartily on his shoulder for minutes on end, laughing a dry cackling laugh and jabbering at him through toothless gums while waving his stick about.

Brielle checked her watch for the fourth time in ten minutes.

'We had better be heading back soon.'

Wellum smiled at her. He knew exactly how she felt. He'd experienced the same nervous anxiety dozens of times, waiting for the next mission to begin or lazing around at an airfield somewhere anticipating the clanging of a bell that heralded the order to 'scramble'.

They hadn't spoken much over their meal, choosing instead to savour the peaceful tranquility of the dining room, once more playing the part of unencumbered friends, siting idly without a care in the world, breaking bread, passing time.

Wellum wanted to hold onto the moment. He lit a cigarette to delay the meal further and he looked at Yvain.

'Do you still have family in Belgium?'

Yvain shrugged.

'I'm not sure.'

Wellum passed him the cigarettes. Yvain took one and lit it.

'Where are you from?...originally? Asked Wellum.

'My family are from Durbuy, a small city in the Ardennes. Walloon country,' said Yvain

'My father was a blacksmith, one of the busiest in Durbuy. My parents were married very young, and before I was born there were five children before me; all boys. It was a happy, normal life up until nineteen-fourteen. Before then my older brothers helped my father at work as best they could when they weren't in school, while my mother and I stayed at home, but after the war broke out when my father came home from the fighting I was eight or nine and he was different somehow.'

Wellum smoked. 'Who wouldn't have been.' He shook his head, imagining life in the trenches of Flanders and the unknown fate of his own father.

'I know,' said Yvain. 'I think compared to those that fought back then, we have it easy.'

Wellum gestured to his empty plate.

'They certainly didn't eat like this did they.'

Yvain shook his head.

'Things were never the same after the war. My father began to drink and my mother became strange and distant. Some malady of the mind according to the doctors. She began wandering in the woods and fields for days at a time. After my sister was born in nineteen-twenty-four, my mother started pronouncing that the child was a herald of woe. That she shouldn't have been born, that she was unholy...stuff like that. One night after she had been gone from the house for hours, she was brought home by the local gendarme claiming she had seen the Wild Hunt of the Ardennes flying through one of the valleys near the city.'

'The Wild Hunt of the Ardennes?' Said Brielle. 'What is that?'

Yvain gave a grim smile and blew smoke at the ceiling. He sighed, as if remembering.

'It's a Belgian folktale about a spectral gathering of ghostly huntsmen, flying at night in a terrible procession of clattering hooves and baying hounds, led by the restless soul of a fallen knight. The vision usually appears on stormy nights, and it is said that anyone who encounters it faces misfortune or death. My mother saw it is an omen of doom, that war was coming to Europe again and the this time the death would spread beyond the battlefields and the whole world would be swallowed up in its jaws.'

Brielle winced and held her elbows. She rubbed the back of her arms with her fingers.

'Your mother saw the beginning of this war?'

Yvain nodded.

'Yes. She certainly sensed something was coming - I don't know how. Of course my father and many in the city called her mad and she fell further into despair as his drinking got worse and the threat grew stronger in her mind.'

'What happened to her?'

'She begged my father to get us all out of Belgium, to save our family. But after months of trying I think she finally gave up hope. On Walpurgis night, which I think is a night very much like your Halloween Harry - when witches and spirits are meant to be active, she took my baby sister and left.'

'She left the house, the family?' Said Brielle.

'Yes, she just disappeared. One person from the town visited my father in the days after she went and said there was a rumour that my mother had gone to look for the caves of Hotton, which were said to exist a little further south in the Ardennes. Other rumours came back that she had delivered my baby sister to a local witch named Elera Vanhouven that people called *de Oude Wormvrouw*, or the Old Worm Woman, and that the baby was sacrificed to cure my mothers curse and free her of her visions. Who knows…' He sighed again. 'I left home and joined the army when I was seventeen and I haven't seen any of my family since. Then, in 'thirty-nine I got out of Belgium altogether and that was that.'

Brielle shook her head and looked at Wellum.

'It sounds like all three of us have lost our family to wars. Quel tragique gas pillage de vie et d'amour.'

Yvain nodded and winced a smile.

'Oui, c'est tragique,'

Wellum checked his watch and turned and held up a finger to ask for the bill.

'We had better be going.'

The youngest of the Lefebre daughters came and dropped the bill at Wellum's elbow and took the remaining plates away. She smiled at them as she cleared the table.

'Comment était la repas?'

The question lifted their mood.

Wellum tested his French with a compliment for the cook.

'Er, c'était sublime, s'il vous plait, remerciez le chef.'

The waitress smiled.

'Merci.' She turned and called towards the kitchen.

'Papa, papa.'

The old man's head appeared at a round window in the door. She gestured to him and he pushed the door open and hobbled towards them.

'Papa, L'Anglais a dit que ta cuisine était sublime.'

Wellum looked concerned at the use of the word English, but Brielle put her hand on his and smiled and shook her head.

'It'll be fine. I'm sure we're quite safe with Monsieur Lefebre and his family.' She stood and took her jacket from the back of the chair.

The old man hovered at Wellum's elbow, but his eyes drifted more than once to Brielle

'Monsieur, I hear you enjoyed my food, that is wonderful news, thank you.'

His pink gums shone as he smiled and he hooked his walking stick over his arm and picked up Wellum's hand and shook it warmly.

'Wherever you are going next, please, tell all those that you meet between here and Paris that they are welcome here, in the Red and White Bistro at Rouen, we will feed them well, yes? We will look after your friends. Please tell them that.'

He patted the back of Wellum's hand again then he turned and held Brielle's shoulders and he looked at her gravely and suddenly kissed her on both cheeks. He looked deep into her eyes.

'Battez-vous courageusment, fille de France. Believe in God, victory to the Resistance.' He closed one eye in a slow wink of conspiracy then reached into his pocket and pulled out a short silver chain. It had a crucifix attached to one end and on the other a tiny figure cast in silver, wearing a suit of armour and holding a lance. Its hair was cropped short like Brielle's own. He pressed the effigy lovingly to his lips then held it out to her and as she took it he wrapped his hands around hers as if in prayer and kissed her fingers.

'May the spirit of Saint Joan go with you my child.'

CHAPTER EIGHTEEN
Ande

Wellum cut the engine and the headlights and rolled the last few yards of the lane and pulled the Citroen to the side of the road. They sat in the dark and listened to the ticking of the engine. After a moment Wellum made a move to get out of the car but Brielle stopped him with a hand on his wrist.

'Wait,' she whispered. 'We should let our eyes get used to the dark for a minute.'

They sat. Wellum turned his head and cast a look through both side windows, like he was searching for enemy aircraft in the sky, peering through the darkness at unfamiliar shapes in the night. Brielle let go of his wrist and took her MAS-38 from the footwell and slowly but deliberately opened the car door and stepped out. Wellum got out and reached back into the car for the Sten-gun. They closed their doors carefully and crouched near the headlights side by side and looked ahead.

On the drive south they had spoken quietly about Father Marcelin and Father Rieu, Jean Grillot and

When All The Birds Leap

Armada and everything that had happened. Near Alizay they fell back into silence, both watching the sky towards Pont-Saint-Pierre as it lit up in the orange and white blooms of an air-raid that seemed to go on for an hour; the soft soporific light bursting in clouds, almost mesmerically peaceful yet edged somehow with terror and a constricting, groping dread.

It was a dark night with no moon and the low clouds gathering from the west threatened them with rain. Wellum pointed and came close to Brielle's ear.

'That's the bridge, the stairs down to the river are across the street.' Brielle nodded and they moved forward, staying low and keeping close to the wall that ran alongside them on the kerb.

They could hear the river moving slowly below. It rumbled on the edge of perception like a heavy leviathan, rolling beneath them in search of a tunnel through which it might find its way back to the underworld.

As they moved along, two figures emerged across the road at the top of some stairs. They were similar, crouching shapes in the dark. Wellum stopped and Brielle stopped with him. They peered into the darkness ahead and Wellum whistled two notes of signal. Almost immediately three soft whistles came back.

It was Dalby.

They crossed the road.

'Good to see you,' said Wellum as they gathered together in the shadows.

'How was the trip down? Said Dalby.

'No dramas,' said Wellum. 'You?'

'All fine for us too,' confirmed the spy.

He gestured with the muzzle of his machine gun.

'It's this way,' he whispered.

They set off in line; Dalby, Wellum, Brielle then Yvain. Keeping low and moving quietly across the bridge.

After a few minutes the concrete bollards and steel railings on their right gave way to a row of high hedges and they paused beneath a thick seam of Hawthorn and huddled together.

'This is the end of the east bridge, said Dalby quietly. 'This road crosses the Ile-Du-Bac in a straight line for a quarter of a mile then joins the southern-bridge which spans the rest of the river to Ande.'

He looked along the road.

'We have to go along this road to the crossroads ahead then turn south and go straight to the lighthouse.'

Wellum peered along the road through the gloom.

'What's that?'

They all squinted through the darkness to see what Wellum was pointing at.

Dalby reached down to a webbing pouch on his hip and unbuckled it and took out a small pair of field-binoculars and held them to his eyes. He dialled the focus wheel with his finger.

'It looks like an abandoned truck.' He passed the binoculars to Wellum.

'Yes,' confirmed the pilot. 'It's wrecked. It looks like the driver's side front wheel is stuck under the cab and the windscreen is shattered. It might have hit a mine or been strafed by an aircraft.' He passed the binoculars back to Dalby.

'It's not going anywhere in that condition.'

'I know, said the spy, peering ahead once more. 'But it's right where we need to go.' He lowered the binoculars and glanced about him. 'I don't like it.'

Brielle stepped forward and he handed her the glasses.

'It's creating a bottleneck in the road. I agree with Dalby we should box round it if we can.'

Yvain took a look, and they agreed to get into the fields as soon as possible and keep away from the broken lorry.

'I'll go ahead and see if I can find a gap or a low point in the hedge.' said Dalby. 'You three wait here and keep watch.'

Within a minute he was back.

'There's a gap under the hedge just a little further along. It's not much more than a badger scrape but we'll slide under it ok if we pass our packs through by hand.'

They found the spot and Dalby turned to them.

'Yvain, you go through first.' The Belgian shrugged off his knapsack and handed it to Dalby then got on his belly and dragged himself through. Dalby was kneeling, and as soon as Yvain had disappeared he shoved the knapsack through the gap after him.

'Brielle next.'

Once they'd got beyond the hedge, they found themselves in a field. The grass was ankle high and the ground felt soft and forgiving and the smell of wet vegetation filled the air.

Wellum checked his compass.

'If we cut through this field diagonally we'll meet the lighthouse road over there.' He gestured towards a line of trees silhouetted faintly against a paler sky beyond. The trees were tall and swayed in a breeze that blew up from the river below and the sound was like a sigh that made the cold night-air seem somehow colder still.

'Let's not go straight across, said Yvain, 'I think maybe we should keep to this hedge line and go around the outside of the field. It'll take a few minutes longer but we won't be seen as easily.'

They set off, walking in single-file, staying low and keeping the hedge on their right. After a few minutes they reached another line of hedges than ran at a right-angle to the first.

Yvain pointed ahead.

'If we follow this line it'll bring us to the bottom corner of the field, the lighthouse road will be on the other side.'

As they went on, their movements seemed to become noisier in the silent blackness that enveloped them, and they slowed their pace instinctively in an attempt to stay quiet. When they finally got to the corner of the field they stopped once more.

'Right, this is where we cut through,' said Dalby.

Wellum checked his watch, the tiny hands illuminated faintly at the end with a small dot of fluorescent paint. He could just make out the time.

'We better get on with it. It's almost ten-thirty.'

'Thiel's not going anywhere,' said Dalby, checking the hedgerow for a gap they could punch through. 'We'll be with him soon enough.'

'What's that smell?' Said Yvain.

The breeze had turned and was coming at them from the south, bringing with it a sudden foulness on the air.

'It smells like rotting corpses,' said Brielle.

Wellum raised his nose and grimaced. Dalby seemed inured.

'Well, whatever it is we need to push on.'

They found a slight gap in the hedgerow a little further along, just wide enough that they could each squirm their way through onto the road beyond. As they gathered on the other side, the clouds parted and a sickle moon glowed faintly yellow against a deep blue sky and for a moment they could see more of their surroundings. They were now crouching on a single track road with waist high hedgerows on either side running along its length. The road was deeply rutted and uneven and there were puddles here and there and tufts of grass grew on the raised sump-line that ran haphazardly down the middle of the lane. They stood up cautiously and peered over the hedges and looked about them. A few buildings stood out, farm sheds mostly and one or two low houses, but there was no livestock and no sign of any people.

'There's the lighthouse,' said Yvain.

They turned and looked south and saw it, pale and still in the moonlight, less than two-hundred-yards away. Dalby set off without another word, following the road south and staying low and close to the hedge. After seventy-yards the road ended at a gate that lead into another field that ran up a slight slope to the lighthouse. A keepers cottage and a small barn sat huddled in the dark and looked to be the last buildings on the small island. Yvain opened the gate without a sound and they filed through one by one into the field.

'What on earth is that smell?' Complained Wellum. The stench was getting worse.

'Maybe there's an abattoir nearby,' suggested Dalby. He turned to Yvain.

'Leave the gate open and wait here, keep your eyes on the road.'

The Belgian nodded and crouched beside the gate and looked back towards the way they'd come.

'Alright,' said Dalby, turning to Brielle and Wellum. 'Let's get up to those buildings.'

As they went, the ground seemed softer, like freshly ploughed soil and their boots sank up to the ankles and the thick mud clung to their soles.

At the barn they stopped and listened. They could see the stone steps of the lighthouse ahead, leading up to two doors. Dalby leant in.

'Brielle, wait here, Harry you come with me and we'll go over to the lighthouse and collect Thiel.'

Wellum nodded and looked at Brielle. She wasn't looking at him, but instead had already turned to survey the field they'd come through, her Mas-38 up in her shoulder, ready to defend their position if she needed to. He turned and went after Dalby.

They crept towards the lighthouse steps and Dalby suddenly held up his hand. He pointed at the ground then pointed to himself and then at the door. Wellum stopped.

He glanced back towards the barn and could just make out Brielle, kneeling in the shadows and he positioned himself at the foot of the steps and looked around the fields. Nothing moved, but the smell of decomposition was almost overpowering.

Something's not right here.

The spy went cautiously up the steps, the muzzle of his weapon pointing forwards. At the top he put his ear against the door and listened.

It started to rain.

When All The Birds Leap

After a moment Dalby hissed at Wellum then called him up the steps with a bending finger. He pointed at himself and then pointed at the door, pointed at Wellum then pointed to the ground. He put his palm against the door and carefully pushed it open, then he moved forward an inch but no more.

'Thiel,' he whispered into the darkness.

'Walter Thiel.'

Wellum heard the sound of movement coming from inside the lighthouse and thought he heard a voice. Dalby spoke again, this time slightly louder.

'Bist du Walter Thiel?'

The voice beyond the door spoke.

'Ja, ich bin Doktor Walter Thiel.'

'Doktor thiel, mein name ist Dalby. Bitte sagen Sie mir, was sind ihre Absichten?'

There was a slight pause, then the voice came back.

'Meine Absicht ist, zu den alliierten Streitkräften überzulaufen.'

Dalby looked at Wellum and nodded through the darkness

Thiel's intention was still to defect. Wellum sighed with relief.

Dalby lowered his weapon.

'Come with me doctor, we have a car waiting to take us back to Rouen.' He took a step outside and gestured with his hand.

'Come, we need to go now.'

As Dalby rejoined Wellum on the lighthouse steps a tall but slightly built man came to the door and peered cautiously out. He can't have been much older than Wellum but he looked older. He had a short, unkempt beard and his hair was a nest of knots and twigs and he wore a sweater of indeterminate colour with frayed wrists and holes at the elbows. He blinked at Wellum from behind round spectacles.

'This is Harry,' said Dalby. 'And we have two more of our team waiting a little further towards the road.'

Thiel took a nervous step forward.

'You, you weren't followed were you?'

'No I don't think we were,' said Dalby. He looked at Wellum.

'Harry you lead the way, straight back to Brielle and from there back to Yvain.'

'What about my radio, and my possessions?' Said Thiel, pointing a quivering finger back at the lighthouse.

'Don't worry about any of it now,' said Dalby. 'Really Doctor there's no time, please we need to go.'

Wellum took Thiel by the arm and turned and set off back towards the barn with Dalby lingering behind and covering them as they withdrew. When they got back to Brielle she studied the German closely while Thiel crouched in a puddle and stared at the ground. His thin neck looked as if the weight of his head was almost too much to bear. He bent down and dragged his fingers in the soil as they waited for Dalby to rejoin the group. Brielle watched him and he wiped the soil from his hands self-consciously when he realised he was being observed. He smiled weakly at her.

'I've missed the earth,' he explained as he patted the ground once more. 'I haven't been outside the lighthouse since the night of the massacre.'

'Massacre?' Said Brielle. 'What massacre?'

Thiel sniffed his soil stained fingers as Dalby arrived back at the barn.

'Thats enough chat,' he said curtly. 'Come on we need to get back to the car.'

Thiel wiped his hands and looked around.

'A month ago now, the SS came to Ande and they rounded up several families from the town and brought them out here and killed them and buried them in a mass grave. I only just escaped, I thought I was dead too.'

Brielle stood up and held the MAS loosely in her hand.

'Were they Jewish families?'

Thiel nodded mutely and covered his mouth as if he was about to laugh, or vomit.

'They killed Jewish families here, in this field?'

'Yes,' Thiel tittered, with a slightly unhinged laugh. He looked and sounded on the edge of insanity.

'Can't you smell them?' He put a knuckle to his lips and looked around the field like a whelp.

'I had to listen to them being shot and buried all around me. You have no idea what that was like…Begging and crying and then rotting away in my garden.'

Brielle shook her head.

'No, no…shut up.'

'Come on,' snapped Dalby. 'We don't have time for this now.'

'Yes, yes,' said Thiel, tugging at Brielle's trouser leg from where he squatted on the ground.

'We can't stay here like them, we must leave.'

Brielle shook off his hand.

'Don't touch me…'

She stood looking down at him, the rain running from her chin in rivers. She pointed the MAS at him.

'Shut up…just, shut up.'

Thiel cowered, raising his arms to protect himself.

'Stop,' said Dalby. 'That's enough. Brielle, stop this.'

She lowered her weapon and wiped away the rain on her face with the back of her hand.

Dalby turned to Wellum.

'Harry you lead off, Brielle go next.' He lifted Thiel to his feet by his armpit.

'And you, stop your jabbering, or I'll leave you here.'

As Wellum stepped out from the shadows and into the field, Brielle spoke to Dalby.

'You knew didn't you? That's why you weren't bothered about the smell. You already knew what it was.'

Dalby looked at her as he got Thiel ready to move. He nodded.

'Yes, I knew.' He gestured towards Wellum with his chin. 'Go on now, catch him up, get to Yvain.'

As they went on the rain grew harder, hammering down now in fat, cold drops that stung their faces and ears. Small puddles were forming here and there in divots and hollows and the rain splashed noisily into hundreds of tiny, glistening pools. Suddenly Thiel began squawking.

'There look, see, there and here, look, what did I tell you!'

He pointed at the ground a little to their right. A hand was sticking up out of the mud, its skin loose and hanging in strips from a withered wrist, its fingers with broken nails bent into a rigid, unmoving claw.

Brielle looked and saw it and gasped and went on. She put the back of her hand to her mouth and caught up with Wellum.

'Get me out of here,' she gasped. 'I need to get out of this place.'

Dalby shoved Thiel forward.

'Shut up and keep moving - keep your voice down.'

They got back to the gate and Brielle stumbled onto the road, coughing and sobbing.

'What is it?' Said Yvain.

Wellum came through next and went straight to Brielle.

'Shh it's ok we're out now, we're going. It's over.'

'What's going on? Said the Belgian as Dalby emerged though the rain with Thiel.

'Ah, that field, the smell,' said Dalby clumsily. 'Apparently it's a grave pit.'

Yvain looked past the agent to the field beyond.

'Really?'

Dalby nodded. 'Yes. The jews of Ande, shot by the SS and buried in there.' He gestured towards Brielle. 'It just got the better of her, but she'll be alright.'

'Horrible screams,' said Thiel, tugging at Yvain's shirt. 'Horrible.'

Yvain looked at the scientist.

'Is this our man?'

'Yes,' said Dalby. 'Looks like the last few months have taken their toll on him a bit but at least he's in one piece.'

The German smiled pathetically and took off his glasses and tried to dry them on one his frayed cuffs.

'Can we go now?' He said, anxiously pulling on Dalby's sleeve. 'I've been here too long…'

Dalby looked around them and checked the time.

'Yes we're leaving now, don't worry.' He pointed down the lane. 'A little further along and then we'll cut through the hedge and go across this field here and out the top corner onto the bridge, from there we'll be travelling by car.' He looked at Yvain. 'Go, you lead the way, take Thiel. I'll gather those two up and follow you. Stay close to the hedge.'

Yvain steered the German by the elbow and together they moved off through the downpour.

Dalby approached Wellum and Brielle.

'Are you two alright?'

'I'm fine,' said Brielle.

Wellum watched Thiel and Yvain as they found the gap in the hedge. He turned to Dalby.

'I think we're good to go.' He looked at Brielle. 'You ready?'

She nodded.

'Yes, I'm good. Come on.'

The three of them set off, following Yvain up the road, but by the time they got to the gap in the hedge the Belgian had already taken Thiel through. As they gathered on the other side of the hedgerow and looked about them it was clear the two groups had become separated.

Wellum shielded his eyes from the rain and looked across the field. 'Why didn't they wait for us here?'

Rain streaked down the lenses of Dalby's binoculars as he glassed along the hedge-line in each direction.

'It's alright they're there.' He gestured towards the southern hedge.

'There, I can just about see them.' He pointed. 'He's taken Thiel back the way we came.' He raised the binoculars again and looked diagonally across to the other corner of the field.

'But it'll be quicker if we cut across here as you suggested earlier Harry.'

'You think its safe enough?'

'We've not seen or heard anyone else since we got here, so I think it should be fine. We need to get out of here now.'

The rain beat down and as they set off the wind turned again and began beating in from the west, up off the river, blowing in gusts that whipped and drove the rain at them like razors.

When they were two-thirds of the way across the field Dalby stopped and took a knee. Wellum and Brielle joined him as the agent took out his binoculars once more and searched the gloom for where Yvain and Thiel should be.

'They're nearly at the gap under the hedge.' He put his binoculars away and buckled his webbing. 'Hopefully he'll have the sense to wait for us there before heading back to the bridge.'

They hurried on, keen to catch up with their comrades, almost as much as they wanted to get out of the worsening weather.

They arrived at the northern border of the field and found the gap they'd slid through on the way in. Yvain and Thiel weren't there.

'For fuck sake,' fumed Dalby. 'Why in the blazes didn't he wait here?'

'He must be on the bridge,' said Wellum holding out his hand for Brielle's weapon and her knapsack. She handed them over and slid underneath the hawthorn. He flung her pack through after her and then his own and lay on his front and dragged himself through onto the road.

It was as Dalby was picking up his pack and his weapon that the first scarlet tracer burned past them. It went between Wellum and Brielle in an instant, lighting them up and making them both turn away instinctively from the heat and the zipping sound that followed in its wake as the air around them suddenly burst into life. Rounds flew down the road towards them as more red tracer ricocheted off the tarmac and bullets tore the air in a hailstorm of fire aimed from the direction of the abandoned truck.

Dalby moved first.

He crouched behind a low wall and shouldered his Sten and began firing in the direction of the muzzle flashes. He turned and shouted at Wellum.

'Get to Thiel! Where's Yvain?'

Wellum winced as more rounds went by and the sound of Dalby's return fire filled the night. He looked across the road and saw Yvain crouching behind a collection of sandbags. He'd got Thiel by the collar and was holding the scientist down on the ground, keeping him out of the chaos.

Brielle stood and threw a grenade then lifted her MAS and fired towards the barrage. The grenade exploded and Wellum saw men fall, silhouetted by the roaring hot muzzle of a mounted MG-44 that screamed at them, spouting a cascade of empty cases that glinted and sparkled in the darkness.

Wellum emptied his magazine towards the Germans and saw more figures fall to their knees or backwards to the ground. He pulled the pin on a grenade and lobbed it forwards then grabbed another and threw it at two men stooping and moving towards them from the cover of the truck. He fitted another magazine and fired in three round bursts and both German soldiers fell dead.

'Where the fuck is Yvain?' Shouted Dalby as he crouched behind the wall and fitted a new clip to his weapon. He stood up and began firing once more then crouched beside Wellum again.

'They've got a mounted MG, probably a 44. If we don't move from here we're finished!'

A grenade exploded ten feet to their left and sprayed them with bits of hot shrapnel and broken tarmac. Brielle killed a soldier moving towards them carrying another light machine gun, then she ducked behind the wall and changed her magazine.

'We need to go, there are too many of them.'

Wellum stood and threw another grenade as a red tracer ripped over his head and blew several large chunks out of the wall. He ducked as powdered brick and cement dust poured over them.

Dalby called to Yvain who was peering over the sandbags towards the German position.

'Yvain, stay there!' He ducked as a bullet went past his ear, then shouted again. 'Yvain…Yvain.'

Brielle pulled him back into cover as another grenade exploded near the first.

'I'll put some fire onto that MG, you go down the road a little way and then get across to Yvain and get him firing back. If you get chance, from there see if you can get an idea of how many of them there are.' She stood and began firing once more.

Wellum glanced over at Yvain. The Belgian was looking down the road, away from the fight, Thiel was cowering at his feet with his hands over his ears.

'Why isn't he fighting?' He shouted over the noise.

Dalby ducked and fired, then turned to Wellum.

'Can you get to the car?'

'What?'

'Can you get to the car and get it started?'

'Yes, but…'

'You go. Get the engine running.' He turned to Brielle. 'You go with him.'

She stood and threw another grenade then fired three rounds from her pistol. Solid, deliberate shots. Another man crumpled on the spot and fell dead.

She crouched once more and threw another fresh magazine in the MAS as more rounds hit the ground around them.

'No, I'll go to Yvain, I'm quicker than you.' She shrugged off her pack and took two spare magazines and pushed them into her waist band.

'Wait,' said Wellum.

'No I'll be fine. Just get some fire down on that 44 to keep him off me while I get across the road.'

Dalby stood up and threw a grenade. He crouched once more.

Harry, on three, we'll empty everything at that fixed position while Brielle gets to Yvain.'

The three of them ducked together as another grenade exploded with a thud. They were getting closer.

'Once she's across you go down the line of the railings here and get to the car. If we can get Yvain in the fight we'll peel back to you in a fighting withdrawal.' He checked his magazines.

'We're running low on ammunition so let's move quickly.'

Wellum glanced across at Yvain who was dragging Thiel to his feet by the collar. The Belgian still hadn't fired a shot. He felt Dalby squeeze his shoulder as Brielle got ready to run.

'Harry. Stand by, stand by, Go!'

The two Englishmen stood as one and fired towards the fixed machine gun position which swivelled and followed Brielle as she sprinted away along the bridge. Wellum and Dalby shot everything at the MG44 which fired then spluttered then fired another short burst then stopped, its gunner collapsing forward, dead across its length with its glowing hot barrel hissing and smoking as the rain fell and blood seeped from burnt black holes in the soldiers face.

As Wellum finished firing he saw several soldiers dragging the dead man's corpse away from the machine gun and tugging furiously on the bolt to try and get the weapon cleared and back into action. He dropped back behind the wall and turned and watched as Brielle broke cover and ran out into the road towards Yvain.

Everything went quiet.

Wellum looked towards where Yvain and Thiel had been sheltering, just in time to see the Belgian dragging the scientist up by his jacket. He turned him and pushed him down the road in the direction of the car, shouting at him as the pair began to run. Brielle watched them and in her confusion suddenly slowed her pace, wondering whether to make for the cover of the sandbags or follow them off the bridge. Wellum heard her calling out but Yvain ignored her and continued to run.

'Where's he going?' Wellum heard Dalby shouting. 'What the fuck is he doing?'

Suddenly they heard voices behind them as the Germans gathered themselves. One voice ringing louder than the others as if calling to someone.

'Wolff, blieb stehe, wo gehst du hin? Wolff!'

Wellum stood and peered towards the enemy. One soldier, an SS officer, stood in front of the silenced machine gun, the rain pouring from his hat in torrents as men ran around him dragging in their fallen comrades or reloading their weapons and taking new positions for another attack. A fire had started in a pool of gasoline on the road behind them, caused by one of the grenades thrown there, and in the growing light of the flames Wellum saw more men preparing themselves to continue the fight.

The SS officer raised his pistol and closed one eye, aiming deliberately.

'Wolff, Komm sofort zurück! Du wirst dich umbringen!'

A shot rang out and Wellum saw the pistol kick in the German's hand. He turned and looked at Brielle. As the round sped past her she raised her hands instinctively and turned and made for the cover of the sandbags. Wellum heard another shot, then another and he stood and shouted as Brielle stopped and turned and raised her MAS to her shoulder, ready to fire back.

'Brielle, no, get down!'

When All The Birds Leap

The next round hit her high on the left side of her chest and punched her backwards towards the railings. Wellum froze. Brielle span then fell against the side of the bridge. She dropped her weapon as the next round hit her in the sternum, tipping her back further. She was still standing but reeling now, caught against the hand rail and the pounding German lead as two more rounds hit her in the chest.

'No, No…' Wellum heard himself, his voice edged with panic, he stood as if to run to her, but Dalby pulled him back by his sleeve.

'No wait, you'll be killed.'

The MG44 suddenly burst back into life and a hail of bullets and tracer coursed down the bridge and found their mark, hitting Brielle with a flurry of explosions that tore pieces from her shirt and her trousers. She staggered under the weight of fire and grasped at the air as she stumbled backwards, hitting the railings before tipping over and falling silently towards the river below.

Dalby lifted Wellum by his arm and pushed him forward.

'Move man, get to the car, go, run.'

Wellum stood up unsteadily, looking across the road to the section of railing where Brielle had fallen out of existence. Dalby put his hand on his back and pushed him again.

'Come on let's go.'

They began to run as the shooting started again and Dalby overtook Wellum at a sprint, stooping and weaving as he went. Bullets flew past them and with a strange, dreamlike awareness, Wellum realised he couldn't feel his legs. He ran on, watching himself as he went, he could hear the bullets and see Dalby, but couldn't feel anything. He looked at the ground and ran. Everything was fractured. His face and arms felt numb. The rain fell. The weapon in his hand felt weightless and the noise of the German guns seemed muffled and distant.

As they got towards the end of the bridge they saw the lights on the Citroen burst into life and could hear the car's engine revving wildly.

'There's Yvain,' shouted Dalby. 'Come on we're almost there.'

As they got in line with the stairs that lead down to the river, Dalby slowed his pace and began waving his arms.

Yvain was pulling away.

'Wait!' Shouted Dalby. 'Yvain, wait we're here.'

He stood waving as the Belgian pulled the Citroen over and wound down the window.

'Thank god, he's waiting,' said Dalby beckoning for Wellum to hurry. As he began to move forward once more Yvain abruptly put his hand out of the drivers window and aimed a pistol at them and fired three shots. Wellum and Dalby ducked as the car pulled away, sliding across the wet road with Yvain still firing as it went. The two men stopped and watched in disbelief as the car drove away in a screech of tyres, and bullets flew past them once more for the direction of the bridge. Wellum suddenly snapped out of his trance and he turned to Dalby, pointing towards the steps as he did.

'Quick, let's get down to the boat and get out of here.'

CHAPTER NINETEEN
The Penny drops

Wolff stood on the edge of the river, his boots submerged to the ankles. He swung the beam of a torch across the ground, looking at the scattered, chaotic footprints and the drag marks left by a boat in the mud.

He turned and looked downriver and listened as the sound of an outboard motor disappeared north. Men were walking along the bank searching, and there was a lot of noise up on the bridge as the injured and dead were seen to. A soldier at Wolff's elbow spoke to him for the darkness

'Should we try and track them by road Sir… see if we can catch them further up river?'

Wolff cast around with the torchlight and waded a little further into the shallow water at the edge of the Seine.

'No,' he said eventually, shining his torch into the darkness upstream. 'They'll be long gone by now.'

A shout broke out a little further along the bank and a young corporal came quickly towards them, slipping slightly in the mud as he did.

'Haupsturmfuhrer we've found something.'

Wolff turned towards the soldier and shone his lamp on him.

'What is it?'

'It's a body sir.'

Wolff stepped out of the water.

'Show me.' He turned to one of the other men. 'And get Captain Stein down here.'

They had found Brielle's body washed up on the northern shore, about sixty yards from where she'd fallen into the water. Stein had come down off the bridge, complaining at how many of his men were injured or dead, but when he saw the lifeless body of the young Resistance fighter he stopped talking and crouched down to look more closely at her. Wolff had the photograph of Wellum in his hand and was shining the torch between Brielle's still features and the picture. It clearly wasn't the pilot.

Stein held her chin and turned her face towards him as the rain poured down around them.

She looked so young. He looked through her pockets and found her identification papers, blood stained and now sodden with river water. He opened them carefully.

'Gabrielle Dupont, age twenty-five.' He looked at Wolff. 'From Varranes.'

Wolff shone the lamp on the papers.

'Back north near that fucking village…what was it called?.'

'Lealvillers,' said Stein, still looking at Brielle.

'She must have been helping the pilot.'

'Fuck!' Shouted Wolff suddenly. He kicked the waters edge, splashing Brielle and Stein. One or two soldiers stepped backwards out of the way.

'Fucking shit!' He fumed, storming about the bank. He shone the torch down river as if he hoped to get one last look at his escaping quarry, then he turned off the light and stared into the blackness ahead. He stood looking at the river for a long time with the sound of the rain beating rhythmically down on his hat. Eventually he turned and began walking back towards the steps that led up onto the bridge.

'Captain Stein, gather the men and let's get back to the Chateau, we can attend to the wounded there.'

'What about the girl?' Said Stein.

Wolff turned his torch back on and shone it down at the river bank. He looked at the Panzer Captain, crouching beside Brielle at the water's edge.

'Leave her there,' he said as he turned away. 'The rats of Ande can feast on her for all I care. Fucking bitch.'

Stein stood up.

'We can't just leave her here.'

Wolff turned to face him, once more silhouetted behind the torch light.

'Why not? Look at her. She's clearly a Resistance fighter.' He leaned forwards. '*The enemy* Captain Stein. Remember?' He clicked the torch off and turned and went on, followed by a line of soldiers that had been helping with the search. Stein gave a low whistle and beckoned for two of the men to join him. He waited until Wolff was half way up the steps.

'You two, wait here. When we've gone, get her body up to the village and find a church. Leave her with the priest, then commandeer a vehicle and get back to Rouen.'

One of the men spoke up.

'But sir, Haupsturmfuhrer Wolff said to leave the woman here. I heard him.'

'Well, I'm giving you different orders, alright. Now, do as I say. When you get back to the Chateau I'll make sure you get a few days off and maybe even a night on the town.'

They clicked their heels.

'Very good Captain.'

Stein looked back at Brielle.

He opened his hand that had been holding her identity papers and he looked at the small silver effigy of St Joan glittering in the moonlight and he rubbed it softly with his thumb. He put the trinket in his pocket and watched as the soldiers began dragging the lifeless body from the mud, then he turned away and climbed back up the stairs towards the road.

Dalby dropped a towel on the table in front of Wellum.

'Here dry your hair with this, hang your jacket on the back of the door.'

They were in Dalby's flat; a small, comfortable place nestled above a cobblers on the *Rue aux Ors*. The road was another narrow ally that seemed common in Rouen's old town, and was only a few hundred yards from the river. Wellum picked up the towel and unfolded it and placed it over his head, then he stood up and took of his sodden jacket and hung it on the back of the kitchen door as Dalby had instructed and came and sat back down.

Dalby filled a kettle and put it on the stove. He leant his back against a cupboard.

'Renard.'

Wellum stopped rubbing his hair and lifted a corner of the towel and looked out.

'What was that?'

'Renard,' said Dalby once more. He was staring at the flame beneath the kettle as if lost in thought. He turned to face the pilot.

'It must have been Renard that told the Germans I was going to be at the Ile-du-Bac tonight.'

Wellum considered the suggestion. 'Renard knew about the weapons drop in the quarry too.'

'Exactly.'

'So you think he's the mole?'

Dalby sighed. 'Im not entirely sure if he's *the* mole but it seems entirely likely that he's some sort of informer.'

Wellum looked at the table and thought about Brielle. He shook his head - betrayed by one of her own?

He closed his eyes and saw her again stumbling backwards, her arms up trying to fend off the bullets and the silence that broke as she hit the railings and fell forever into the darkness beyond.

Dalby took a packet of cigarettes from the side and lit one and threw the pack to Wellum.

'Are you ok?'

Wellum shrugged.

'I think so.' He went back to rubbing his hair. After a moment he put the towel on the table and asked,

'Do you know where he lives?'

'Who?'

'Renard.'

Dalby nodded.

'Yes I do. He doesn't know that though. We normally meet up out in the city somewhere. He has no idea I've got his address.'

'Yvain seemed surprised that you'd got Armadas address too.'

'I've got everybody's address dear boy.'

They sat in silence for a while, listening to the rain outside and the gas burning beneath the kettle in a constant, comforting hiss. Eventually the whistle began to blow and Dalby took the kettle from the hob and poured water over tea leaves. The warm, fragrant steam that floated up and filled the room had an instant, calming affect.

Neither of them had mentioned Yvain's betrayal.

Dalby poured the tea and delivered a mug to the pilot. They sat, each with their own thoughts for a while longer, sipping tea while the rain drove against the windows. Wellum stubbed out his cigarette and got up and went back to the teapot for more.

'Do you think Thiel will be halfway to Berlin by now?'

'Maybe,' conceded Dalby stubbing out his own cigarette. He shook his head again.

'Yvain, Yvain, Yvain…' he said quietly.

'So, what next?' Said Wellum, cutting across the agent's thoughts.

Dalby shrugged.

'I suppose I'd better contact London tonight and tell them what a cluster-fuck this has been, and then tomorrow I think I'll pay Renard a visit.' He drained his mug. 'After that, I think it's time we got you home, don't you?' He smiled thinly.

'What will you do with Renard?'

Dalby thought about the question.

'I should interrogate him really. Find out what he knows and who exactly he's working for. Then depending on how he gets on I'll probably kill him and dump him in one of the lakes outside of the city.'

Wellum winced slightly at the thought. Dalby got up and poured himself more tea.

'You won't do that here though will you?' Said Wellum looking around the little flat. 'The interrogation?'

'No, I have a few places dotted around Rouen more suitable for such unsavoury acts. A basement here, a bombed-out factory there. I'll make a few calls and get something arranged.'

'Why don't you hold off on contacting London until after you've spoken to Renard.'

'What for?'

'Well, as you said Renard is obviously talking to the Germans.'

Dalby brought his mug and sat back down at the table.

'And?'

'When you met him and asked for the boat to get you to Ande, what else did you tell him?'

'Nothing really, just that I was meeting someone and needed to be there by twenty-two hundred.'

'You didn't mention Thiel?'

'Of course not.'

'Did you mention me?'

Dalby thought.

'No, but he did.'

'What did he say?'

'He asked if you were the reason for the trip to Ande. I just ignored the question - brushed it off.'

'but he suspected you were helping me?'

'Because of my closeness with Armada, he thought it likely I guess. But what's that got to do with me contacting London?'

'If he's an agent then he's definitely got a handler, either in Berlin or...'

'You think someone back home?'

'Well, who says the mole has to be based here in Rouen?'

They fell into silence once more.

'Yvain is my real concern.' Said Dalby.

Wellum looked at the table, he still couldn't believe he had been fooled by the Belgian. The shock of seeing him drive away shooting at them was still hard to process, especially after the death of Brielle.

'All of the intelligence on Thiel has gone through me and Armada and just three people in London.' Dalby continued.

'You said Yvain came into Armada's team recently.'

'Yes, once we'd confirmed Thiel was genuine, London insisted Yvain join the group. Macair and Sault were already known to us.'

'But Yvain told me that *he* recruited them, that it was part of his job, to bring them in and train them.'

Dalby shook his head. 'That's not true. Those were my men.'

'Did Yvain know about Thiel all along?'

'It's possible. I think we should assume that everything I was feeding back to London was getting passed on to him.' He thought for a while. 'It'd have to be someone pretty high up too. Security clearance on this has been extremely tight.'

'Mmm not tight enough though.'

Dalby looked devastated.

'You think he had Armada and the others killed?' Said Wellum

Dalby nodded.

'It seems likely, yes.'

'And what about the attack tonight, at Ande?'

'No. You were there, we could all have been killed. Even Yvain and Thiel.'

'So we still suspect Renard for that?'

'Yes.' The spy rubbed his chin and then took another cigarette and lit it.

'I think we can safely say that two of the rats of Rouen have revealed themselves tonight.'

Renard woke up with a start. The rain was pouring down outside, beating the roof with a ceaseless insistence that broke and swayed as the wind blew in gusts and filled the chimney with howls and taunts like the visitation of a mourning ghost.

Beyond the rain he could hear the muffled explosions and wailing sirens of an air raid drifting through the night from the horizon; *Port Jerome* he thought or maybe the gun emplacements at *Boulleville*. He lay back and closed his eyes and pulled the warmth of the blankets back up to his chin.

The door knocked again.

He sat up and listened, straining to hear beyond the racket of the weather when another knock came, unmistakable this time. He got out of bed and crept cautiously across the bedroom. He took the revolver from its holster hanging on the back of the door and went slowly out onto the landing where he paused. He checked the gun was loaded, pulled the hammer back with his thumb, then leant his ear over the banister and listened again. The rain was coursing through the drainpipes like hollow rivers that filled the house with the sound of a relentless, rushing torrent. Renard turned and went to a window and moved the curtain aside with the barrel of the revolver and looked down onto the *Rue de Buffon*. A green Citroen was parked up on the pavement - a car he didn't recognise. The police? The Gestapo maybe?

He checked his watch. It was almost one in the morning. The front door knocked again, then a muffled voice seeped in through the letterbox.

'Renard, ouvre la porte.'

He crept slowly down the stairs, the revolver held out in front of him.

'Renard,' the voice came again, more insistent this time. 'Renard, oeuvre. C'est moi, Yvain.'

The frenchman relaxed the weapon but hesitated by the door. He put an ear to the wood then placed his eye to a spy hole and peered out.

'Renard, sil te plait, viens. Je suis en train de me tremper ici, laisse moi entrer.'

Renard looked at the carpet and touched his lip with a finger as if pondering some inner dilemma. After a moment he undid the chain and slid back the bolt and unlocked the door and opened it an inch and looked out into the rain.

Yvain stepped forward and pushed the muzzle of his own pistol against Renard's forehead. With a gasp, Renard stepped backwards, instinctively raising his hands as he went.

'Drop the gun,' said Yvain, forcing himself inside the hallway. He pushed the door closed with his foot and levelled the pistol at Renard's face. Renard opened his hand like a child allowing the revolver to drop noisily to the ground.

'Kick it towards me.'

The Frenchman searched the floor with his toes and slid the revolver across the carpet with a thrust of his pudgy foot.

'Keep your hands up and step back against the wall, then turnaround with your back to me.'

Renard did as he was instructed, shuffling slowly backwards until he felt the wall behind him, then he turned around and pressed his face against the wallpaper and closed his eyes, convinced his next breath would be his last.

'Put your hands behind your back.'

Renard crossed his hands behind him.

'What are you doing?' He asked, his voice bordering on panic. 'What's going on?'

'Shut up and stand still,' ordered the Belgian as he fastened hand cuffs to Renard's wrists.

Yvain spun him around by the shoulder.

'Sit there,' he pointed at the stairs.

Renard sat down on the third step and looked at him.

'What's all this about? He gestured over his shoulder at the manacles. 'Is this really necessary?'

Yvain collected the revolver from the hall carpet and released the hammer with his thumb and tucked the gun into the waistband of his trousers.

'Is there anyone else here?'

'What do you mean?'

'Upstairs. Girl, boy - is there anyone here?'

'No,' Renard shook his head.

'Alright, stand up and lead the way.' Yvain gestured towards the kitchen. 'Let's go in there and talk.'

Renard stood up and made his way unsteadily along the dark hallway as Yvain jabbed him in the back with his pistol.

'Remember, no sudden movements ok? I have no problem with killing you Renard, be clear about that.'

In the kitchen, Yvain ordered Renard to sit at the table, then he leant against the doorframe and looked around the room. He didn't put any lights on.

'What's going on? Said Renard once more.

Yvain regarded him from the gloom.

'I need your help.'

Renard shifted his weight in the chair and grimaced for effect as the handcuffs bit into his thick wrists.

'What with?' He winced.

'I need you to get me a car.'

Renard gestured towards the window with his chin.

'You already have a car.'

'It won't get me to where I'm going. It has three bullet holes in the radiator. It barely got me back here.'

'Back from where?'

Yvain allowed himself an unseen smile.

'From the little welcome committee you arranged for Dalby in Ande.'

'I don't know what you're talking about.'

'Of course not,' said the Belgian dryly as the rain hammered the windows. He spotted a packet of cigarettes on the side and picked them up. He shrugged a cigarette from the pack and pointed it at Renard.

'The game's up I'm afraid Renard. It's over, and I suggest you think very carefully about how you respond to my questions over the next five minutes or you might well end up on the losing side.'

Renard shook his head and tried his best to sound befuddled.

'Look Yvain, I don't know what you've been through this evening but I can assure you…'

Yvain raised a finger to silence the lies as he lit the cigarette. He shook out the match and tossed it into the sink beside him.

'Stop Renard, please. Just stop'

He sighed.

'I don't have time for this. Look, I know that you have been working both sides for some time, the Allies and the Germans.'

Renard opened his mouth and looked ready to defend himself when Yvain put the pistol on the sideboard and began taking off his sodden jacket.

'You can deny it all you want,' he said as he hung the coat on the back of the door. 'But, it would save time for us both if we just dispensed with the bullshit and moved on.' He picked up the pistol and resumed aiming it at the Frenchman.

'It would also save me the trouble of shooting you here and now and putting this meeting down to a colossal error of judgement.'

Renard didn't speak.

'I'll take that as an admission.' Said Yvain.

'So, as I was saying. I need a car.'

'How far are you going?' Said Renard quietly.

'I'm going north, over the border to Brussels and from there I'm catching a flight to Berlin.'

'Berlin? Why?'

'Because you're not the only one that has been playing both sides Renard.'

'You're a German agent?'

'In a manner of speaking, yes.'

Renard look at Yvain through squinting eyes as if he were trying to see him clearly for the first time.

'My God.'

'Quite. Now, can you get me a car or not? I'll also be needing weapons as I can't go back to my flat. Clothes and provisions for the journey, enough for two people, a field radio, water and a first aid kit - a decent one, preferably German army issue if you can manage it.'

'Provisions for two people? You want me to come to Brussels with you?'

'Heavens no. I've got someone in the car outside that I'm taking back to Germany.'

Renard glanced towards the window as the rain lashed the glass.

'Outside now?'

'Yes.'

'Who is it?'
Yvain sucked on the cigarette and looked at him.
'He's a scientist.'
'A scientist?'
'Yes. And the Germans want him back, so…' he shrugged and flicked ash towards the sink. 'I was asked to deliver him.'
'You picked him up in Ande?'
Yvain nodded.
'Surprised?'
This time it was Renard's turn to shrug.
'A little.'
'Obviously Dalby didn't tell you the real reason he wanted to go to Ande, and when we got attacked on the bridge, I guessed that you had assumed we were there with the pilot and had informed your German friends. I knew you wouldn't have sold Dalby out to the Nazis, so they can only have been there for Wellum.'
'And why is that?'
'Because Dalby pays you too much, that's why. Even you're not that stupid?'
Renard looked hurt.
'For the record they're not my friends.' He turned his face away like a moody teenager.
'You say you were attacked in Ande?' His face hidden in purple shadow. 'What happened?'
'Did you tip them off? The Germans?'
Renard turned back to face the Belgian.
'Maybe, But they were just meant to arrest the pilot.'
'Well, they didn't. We got out into the open, and were on our way back to the car with the scientist and all hell broke loose.'

'Was Dalby killed?'

Yvain finished the cigarette and dropped it in the sink where it sizzled and lay dead by the plughole. He shook his head.

'I'm not sure.'

'The pilot?'

'I didn't see. I only just got out of it alive. I think the girl helping him was killed, I saw her taking rounds as I ran, but as for the other two, I don't know. They saw me leaving in the car, but they were under heavy fire and could be dead by now.'

'Maird,' muttered Renard.

'What does it matter to you anyway?'

'Dalby still owes me money for the boat.'

'Ah, money.' Said Yvain, lowering the pistol at last.

'Listen to me Renard. If you help me get this German safely back to Berlin I guarantee you will be rewarded.'

'How much?' The Frenchman's eyes glinted in the darkness.

'Five hundred thousand Reichsmark.'

It was less than he was meant to get for Wellum but still more money than Renard had ever seen.

'And if I refuse?'

Yvain laughed.

'Renard don't be stupid, you can't refuse. Say no now and *bang*, you're dead, and if you run I will make sure the gestapo and the SS hunt you to your grave. You're a smart man, do the smart thing. If the German authorities ever found out you helped the scientist into the hands of the allies they would burn you alive.'

Renard blinked for a moment and then nodded.

'Alright, I'll help you.' He raised his wrists up the small of his back.

'Now please, take these off.'

Yvain pointed the gun once more.

'We understand each other? No tricks?'

'No tricks, I'll go out early tomorrow and find you a car, and everything else you need.'

Once freed, he rubbed his tender wrists as Yvain put the handcuffs back in his pocket.

'Who is this scientist anyway?'

'He's been working with the German army for some time, in the north, developing a new weapon.'

'What kind of weapon?' Asked Renard. He crossed the room and picked up his cigarettes.

'A missile, capable of travelling from here to London.'

Renard lit his cigarette and whistled as he blew out the match.

'Really?'

Yvain nodded. 'Really.'

Renard went to speak again but Yvain held up a hand.

'No more questions Renard, I'll tell you everything once I've had time to rest and collect my thoughts.'

The Frenchman nodded meekly. 'Very well.'

'Right, now, I'll go and get our German friend from the car, you put the kettle on and make some coffee.'

As he filled the kettle Renard peered out of the kitchen window to the street beyond. He watched Yvain disappear from sight as he moved around the house towards the parked Citroen. After a moment he came back guiding a man who's hands were held out in front of him, tied with rope at the wrists, he had a crudely fashioned bag over his head and was stumbling ahead of the Belgian who was pushing him forcefully through the rain by his arm.

Renard put the kettle on the stove and lit the gas, then he turned and using the same match touched the wick of a candle. Yvain came in with Thiel. The scientist was jabbering from beneath his hood in an inaudible stream of German. He was drenched and shivering and as Yvain turned him and sat him down roughly in a chair by the table, Renard winced as the smell of months on the run and the recent proximity to dozens of rotting corpses drifted from the Germans torn and tattered clothes.

'My god, where did you find him?' Muttered Renard.

Yvain pulled the hood from Thiel's head and the German lifted his hands and knees as if to protect himself from blows as yet undealt.

'He's been hiding in a lighthouse for weeks, but he's been on the run for months,' said Yvain.

Renard peered at the flinching, gibbering mess sitting at his dining table.

'He smells like death.'

'Yes I know. The Jews of Ande, clinging with their withered fingers to this world I'm afraid.'

'What?' Said Renard.

Yvain shook his head. 'It doesn't matter. I had to stop just outside *Igoville* and put him in the boot of the car the smell was so bad.'

Thiel looked around the kitchen with wild eyes.

'Where are we?' He begged. 'Who are you people? Where are the English men, where's Dalby?'

Renard took a cautious step towards the German, scrutinising him as one might a wild animal.

'Are you sure he's valuable? He looks half demented to me.'

'He's valuable alright - he just needs cleaning up and feeding a decent meal. He'll be fine.'

'Why don't you just hand him over to the local Wehrmacht and tell them who you are, rather than going through all the trouble of getting him back to Berlin unseen? You might get killed.'

'Because this mission is top secret, that's why. If I break cover now and hand him over to some local commander, it'll be in every English newspaper by tomorrow morning. You of all people should know that there are spies everywhere Renard. Berlin doesn't want the Allies to know he's alive, let alone on his way back to Germany. I have to get him back in secret. Those are my orders.'

Thiel looked wildly at them both and held his tied wrists towards them, his hands grasped together in prayer.

'Oh please no, don't send me back.' He fell from the chair and crawled towards Yvain on his knees. 'Please no, they'll make me work on the missile. Please no, I can't go back. Everyone I love is dead, they're dead please, no.' He began to sob and he put his face against Yvain's boot.

The Belgian lifted him roughly and pushed him back towards the chair. Thiel sat down with a thump, the tears running down his filthy cheeks, his scrawny shoulders slumped forward and moving rhythmically up and down as he sobbed.

'Bitte nicht, nein, mein Frida. Ich werde nicht zu ihnen zurückkehren, nein. Ich werd es nicht beenden, es tut mir leid, meine liebe. Es tut mir leid…'

Yvain looked down at him with emotionless eyes.

'You're going back to Berlin Walter, like it or not.'

He grabbed Thiel roughly by the chin and lifted his face to look at him. The scientist cried out in pain as the candle flame flickered and danced and cast shadows up onto the ceiling and walls.

'You stop that wailing now, understand? '

He let go of the German who brought his wrists and knees up to his chest. He rocked and sobbed quietly on the chair like a waif that had blown in on the breeze.

Yvain turned to Renard.

'Do you have a bathtub? Hot water?'

Renard nodded. 'Upstairs.'

Yvain hoisted Thiel up by his arm once more.

'You make coffee, I'm going to give him a bath, get rid of this stink. If you have any clothes that will fit him, go and get them.

Yvain stood the German up once more and turned him roughly around and shoved him towards the stairs.

Renard listened to Thiel sobbing as Yvain ran the taps and began filling the bath.

'This is all I need,' he muttered to himself as he went to fill the kettle.

But then he stopped, and with one ear bent to the rain and the other to the unfortunate scientist, he realised how he might make the whole situation play into his favour.

CHAPTER TWENTY
Stein's Plan

Part three.

Wellum looked out over the smoking chimneys of the early morning.

Just beyond the Cathedral and the ruined city he could see the grey river sliding silently by.

She is in there somewhere.

He imagined Brielle, her body being dragged by the tide, blown along through the weeds in an angelic dance with her eyes closed and a soft smile playing on her lips. He saw her tumble and twist, the light sparkling in shafts as sunbeams broke the surface and penetrated to where the shadows lurked and held, clinging to dim hollows made by boulders that had rolled down from the mountains thousands of years ago. The Seine was old and deep and held many secrets.

And now it had Brielle.

He couldn't bear the thought and he looked away, and the remembrance that he had lost her almost crushed him.

Dalby came into the kitchen at around seven and found Wellum sitting mutely at the table still staring out towards the river and he thought he could guess the pilot's mind. He busied himself boiling the kettle and collecting clean cups from a cupboard then he lifted the lid on a bread bin and took out half a white loaf and crossed the room and got butter from the pantry. He put everything on the table and when the kettle boiled he made tea.

'Have you slept?'

Wellum shook his head.

'No.'

The sound of a train rumbled along tracks in the distance, its rhythmic clattering was somehow comforting and seemed to raise Wellum from his maudlin contemplation. He looked at Dalby.

'Did you?'

The agent shook his head with a slight smile.

'No.'

Dalby poured them both some tea. He glanced at Wellum as he added milk.

'I can't stop thinking this was all my fault,' said the pilot.

'How could it be?'

'Renard sent the Germans after me - he must have, they've been hunting me since I landed in France. If I hadn't insisted on going with you to Ande, none of this would have happened. Thiel would be here with you and Brielle would still be alive.'

'You don't know that's how it would be. I might be dead. Yvain would most likely have killed me and taken Thiel anyway. At least with you and Brielle we stood more of a chance of getting him out successfully, and how were any of us to know about Renard's betrayal? As for Brielle, she had to tread her own path, and she did that right to the end.'

Wellum cast a hand across his eyes at the thought of it. He just couldn't shake off the guilt.

Dalby took a knife and began slicing the loaf.

'Come on, we need to eat.'

He buttered thick pieces of bread and dumped them on a plate in front of Wellum.

'Do you think it's safe to go back to Armada's house?'

Dalby nodded as he buttered.

'We should recce the place first. If it looks safe enough then yes. I doubt Yvain will have gone back there anyway, and as far as I'm aware he's the only one who knew where Armada lived.'

'He probably thinks we're dead.'

'Mmm, maybe,' ventured Dalby a little cautiously. 'But I doubt that he'll take the fact for granted. I suspect if he's not already left Rouen with Thiel, he'll lay very low until he does. I'll put out the word, see if we can get a whiff of him before he splits.'

'What time are you thinking of going to look for Renard?'

Dalby checked his watch.

'Around ten o'clock. I need to go and arrange a few things for when I do catch the little wretch and I'll probably have a look around his usual haunts after that.'

'You want me to come along?'

Dalby smiled.
'Not this time pal - thanks all the same.'

The driver pulled the car over and left the engine running and she took a compact from her handbag and opened it and looked at her reflection in the small, round mirror. She slid a finger over each eyebrow and looked at her teeth and ran her tongue across them then closed the compact with a snap and dropped it back in her bag. The driver was watching her through the rear view mirror.
'Turn off the engine.'
She looked at the Chateau; its turrets and battlements reminiscent of ancient castles, and the large red flags with their death black swastikas billowing menacingly in the morning breeze. She sat there just watching and listening to the flags cracking as they waved.

Stein opened his door and cast a quick look out into the corridor.
'Come in,' he said with a thin smile. 'Please.'
He stood aside and Colette entered, folding her gloves into her hand. Her smile was warmer than his.
'Good morning my good captain. I must say, I can't ever remember being called on in quite so much haste...I'm rather flattered.'
Stein ignored the comment and closed the door and locked it.
'Did anyone see you arrive?'

Colette frowned, still smiling and she shook her head.

'No, apart from the driver of course.'

Stein walked past her towards the window and a table holding coffee and pastries. He looked out over the grounds.

'Have you had breakfast?'

Colette took off her coat and draped it over the back of a chair.

'Max, it's not even eight and I've just been summoned from my bed…no I haven't had breakfast.'

He poured coffee and held out a cup.

'Here, I'm sorry.'

She took the cup and sat down at the table. She crossed her legs and relaxed back in the chair and studied him.

He looked terrible.

His trousers were filthy with dried bloodstains and mud and his braces were hanging loosely at his sides and he wore a vest with no shirt. Colette noted the empty holster lying abandoned next to his boots on the floor and the pistol sat in readiness on the bedside table.

She sipped her coffee.

'So, do you want to tell me what's going on?'

Stein poured himself a drink and came and sat down beside her at the table.

'I wanted to see you.'

She looked unconvinced, despite his obvious sincerity.

'I *needed* to see you,' he conceded after a moments silence.

She put her cup down and took his hand. She turned it over and inspected the mud and the blood stains.

'Who's blood is this?'

Stein turned his palms over and looked at them, conscious for first time of how he must look. He looked at his trousers and his bare arms.

'I'm sorry. I should have changed.'

'What's happened Max?'

Stein looked at her and shook his head slowly.

'I can't do this anymore.'

She held both of his hands in hers.

'Max, tell me. What's happened?'

He looked at her soft, full face. Her eyes sparkling like emeralds, pure and clear.

Innocent of sin.

'Last night we went to a town south of the city to arrest the English pilot.'

'Was he there?'

'I'm not sure. We ran into some Resistance types, and we fought them.' He looked at his hands again. 'They were well trained and it didn't go well for us. They killed at least eight men, and they wounded ten others.'

'My god. Were you hurt? Are you injured?'

Stein shook his head.

'No, no I'm ok.'

He got up and went to the bedside table and got his cigarettes.

'But this wasn't like any fight I've been in before.'

'Why?'

Stein passed Colette a cigarette and took one for himself.

'Because I couldn't engage the enemy. I didn't fire a shot. I couldn't, I just seemed to freeze.'

They sat silently and smoked. Eventually Stein spoke again. He was staring at the carpet, a finger pressed to his temple and his elbow resting on the arm of the chair, his voice was distant and quiet. The smoke from his cigarette rose in an unbroken column of grey.

'We only managed to kill one of their group, a young girl.' He shook his head again as if correcting his memory. 'It was Wolff actually. He stepped over the corpses of my men and he shot her.'

He sucked on the cigarette and blew out smoke as he talked.

'She fell from the bridge into the river.'

Colette just look back at him. Her face expressionless and calm.

'You were in a fight, what was he supposed to do. What were any of you to do?'

Stein shook his head.

'No,' he sighed. 'Not this time.'

'What do you mean?'

'We opened up on their group as soon as we saw them - on Wolff's orders. We could have arrested them, warned them. It didn't have to be a fight. We started it.'

He forced his palms against his eyelids and sat back in the chair and pushed his head back.

'Don't you understand? We started it, all of it…and for what? None of it is necessary, none of the fighting, the death, the mutilation…the hate. I've often thought what would my daughter Valda do were she of fighting age and if this whole situation had been reversed? She'd have fought of course she would, we all would, if the Nazis had descended on us and invaded *our* lives, we would all have done the same.'

He sat forward and looked at her.

'Two of my men that were killed last night weren't even nineteen. One boy, shot in the neck.' He held out his hands to her, showing her the bloodstains. 'He begged for me to help him. To save him.' He sucked on the cigarette and pushed his hair back from his face. 'He died Colette, there on that bridge, in the fucking rain.'

He stood up and walked in a circle on the carpet, waving his arms as he spoke.

'And the other boy, fragged by a grenade. He lost the entire top of his right shoulder, his ear and both his eyes. He bled to death, lying alone while his comrades fought on, unable to do anything…they couldn't even comfort him.'

'Max I don't know what to say.'

Stein stopped walking. 'Wolff berated anyone that showed concern for the dead or injured, he even slapped one of my men for trying to help a dying friend.'

Colette grimaced.

'Why?'

'Because he only values suffering, that's why. Because his heart is black.'

He threw his cigarette at the fireplace and sat back down heavily with his head hung low at his chest and his hands covering his face.

Colette stood and went to him and got on her knees and held his head to her heart. She soothed him.

'Shhh, shhhh, tout va bien. Je suis la, tout va bien.'

She rocked him and kissed his hair.

'Je suis la.'

Stein lifted his head and held her face and through his pain and confusion he leant forward and kissed her, and she closed her eyes and wrapped her arms around him and kissed him back, deeper and fuller. Together they stood, pulling one another closer and as his arms coiled around her shoulders they moved towards the bed and disappeared from the world into a haze where only they existed.

He sat in a cafe on the Rue Ganterie and looked out of the window onto the town square. A waitress came and stood at his elbow and he ordered two warm rolls with butter and honey and black coffee. As he spoke, she scribbled on a pad and he watched the square unceasingly without once turning to look at her. He watched each person coming and going. An old man, shuffling slowly along then another man in a pork pie hat and thin round spectacles walking briskly by as two women in long black coats, watched a group of children gathered in a corner digging greedily into a bag of roasted chestnuts.

There was a lorry parked across the street; thunder grey, it was jacked up and missing a wheel and it was surrounded by a loose flock of eight or nine German soldiers drinking bottles of milk and talking to young French women while two more worked on the kerbside mending a punctured tyre.

The waitress arrived with the rolls and coffee and Dalby thanked her with a quick smile and broke open the warm bread and buttered it and watched the square.

At at eleven o'clock, Renard came trotting clumsily around the corner from *Rue Socrate* sending a flock of pigeons clattering up into the air and almost kicking one as it flapped. It was an awkward and conspicuous entrance and Dalby shook his head at the Frenchman's lack of caution. The soldiers interrupted their conversation and looked across as the birds took flight and Renard swerved comically in an attempt to avoid being spotted. He joined the queue at a vendors cart selling gingerbread and tried to blend in. Dalby sipped his coffee and ate his rolls and watched him. The soldiers went back to their milk and their conversations and the other people in the square continued to go about their day without missing a beat.

Renard shuffled along in the queue with his hands thrust deep into his trouser pockets, continually checking this way and that, looking furtively at the soldiers then turning his head in a constant, paranoid ticking. The blue lens over Dalby's right eye glinted as he noted with a dark pleasure that Renard looked as if he knew exactly what he was;

A hunted man.

As Renard took his gingerbread and headed north out of the square, Dalby thumbed some coins onto the table and left the cafe. He followed the Frenchman along the Rue Ganterie, and he thought he could guess where he was going. Renard was on his way to visit a man called Sassoon, a local thug who can get things; weapons, vehicles, drugs, women. As untrustworthy a man as one could wish to meet in everyday, normal life.

But this is far from a *normal* life.

Renard used Sassoon to acquire whatever he needed off the black market. He used him a lot, too much in fact. But they were both greedy men and it would appear, as Dalby had often suspected of many in the Rouannais underworld; predictable.

When All The Birds Leap

As Dalby watched, he saw Renard approach a stout, tough looking man with an uncompromising air and a dark, swarthy complexion. He had a short beard and moustache and a wore a black beret. The two shook hands and as Renard spoke the other man spat and flicked a cigarette towards the gutter and gestured that Renard should follow him. The two of them disappeared down the side of a shop that Dalby knew well; a simple greengrocer above which Sassoon plied his regular trade. Dalby checked his watch and leant against a lamp post and waited and watched the alleyway.

When Renard shuffled back out into the street low clouds were scudding in from the east.

Dalby watched him check the cobbles as he fastened his jacket before putting on his cap and turning right and heading north.

The agent followed him along the pavement as the Frenchman weaved through the crowd, hurrying towards whatever self-serving errand was next on his list and after quickening his pace, finally caught up with Renard as the traitor stopped at the open door of a boulengerie to stand and breathe in the aroma of freshly baked bread.

Dalby pushed the muzzle of his pistol into Renard's ribs, griping him by the jacket as he did.

'Make a sound and you're dead.'

Renard went stiff and Dalby turned him discreetly and moved him towards the back of the shop, spinning him around next to a group of dustbins and a pile of empty flour sacks.

Renard fell back against the wall and raised his hands.

'Wait, wait. Dalby please, don't shoot.'

Dalby frisked him and took the .35 snub nosed pistol from Renard's jacket pocket and and tucked it into his own belt. He put his palm against Renard's chest and held him against the wall. He pointed the gun at his face.

'You set me up you bastard.'

'Wait, no Dalby please, wait I can explain.'

'Really? I doubt that very much.'

'I can, I can explain everything.'

'Well, you're going to get your chance. I think it's time you and I went somewhere private for a little chat.'

He grabbed Renard's collar and turned him and pushed him in the direction of the road.

'Come on, move it.'

Renard dug his heels into the ground but kept his hands raised.

'Wh, where are we going?'

'Somewhere out of the way where no one can hear you screaming that's where.'

He shoved the frenchman forward.

'If you shout out or make a fuss I'll shoot you in the street Renard, don't doubt it.'

'Dalby listen, please just listen to me.'

He turned around and faced the spy, flapping his hands urgently.

'Please wait, I have information.'

Dalby pointed the gun at Renard's nose.

'Shut up and turn around.'

'No really, I have information about last night. About Yvain and the German.'

Dalby lowered the pistol an inch. He grabbed Renard roughly by the scruff of his shirt and turned him back towards the bins. He pushed him up against the wall once more.

'What do you mean?'

Renard breathed and gasped and held his throat dramatically.

Dalby pointed his pistol at him.

'You've got ten seconds before I put you in the boot of a car and drown you in a lake somewhere. Now talk.'

'Late, last night,' Renard spluttered. 'Yvain, he turned up at my house.'

'What time?'

'After midnight.'

'Go on.'

'He said he'd been to Ande with you and the pilot to pick up a German scientist.'

'And...?' Dalby pushed his pistol towards Renard's jowls.

Renard squeezed his eyes shut.

'And he said you were attacked.'

'Yes, and that's why I'm looking for you, you sent those bastards after us didn't you?'

'Wait, wait,' squealed Renard cowering beneath his raised hands.

'Yes, I admit it. I told them, I'm sorry. But they only came for the pilot. I knew nothing about the German, I swear.'

'What else did Yvain say?'

Renard risked opening one eye.

'Please, lower your pistol Dalby and I'll tell you everything.'

Dalby lowered his weapon an inch.

'Keep it short and to the point.'

'Ok, thank you.' Breathed Renard. 'He, Yvain, he said he was taking the scientist back to Germany, via Belgium I think. Yes, by plane from Belgium… to work on a special project. Some military hardware. A bomb or something.'

'When?'

'Tonight. Once I get back with a car and some supplies. He said he doesn't want to go back to his flat.'

'I'll bet he doesn't,' said Dalby. He lowered his pistol a little further.

'What were you getting from Sassoon?'

'Weapons, rations, a medical kit. The usual.'

'And the car?'

'I have one in mind. I was going to collect that next and come back here in an hour to collect the other items from Sassoon.'

Dalby considered everything Renard had said. He lifted the pistol once more and aimed it.

'I should just kill you now you treacherous pig.' He lowered the pistol. 'But I'm not going to. You can help repair some of the damage you've done.'

Renard coward and whimpered.

'Alright, alright I will, whatever you want, I'll do it.'

'Go and get the car and then the supplies from Sassoon, then go back to your house and stall Yvain. Keep him there until at least six o'clock.'

'Alright, yes I will. Six o'clock, alright.'

'Do this and it'll go some way to paying off a huge debt you now owe me *personally*. Once I've got Thiel back, you and I will talk again, but if anything else goes wrong.' He raised his pistol once more and pushed the hard, cold muzzle against Renard's forehead.

'I'll find you, and I'll kill you.'
He lowered the gun and gestured towards the street.
'Go, but remember - keep them there 'til six.'
Renard nodded.
'I will, don't worry, I'll keep him there.'
He turned and shuffled nervously away and looked out into the street and considered running, though he knew it was pointless.
Instead he cursed his worsening luck and raised his collar against the rain and as he stepped off the kerb he shot a glance back up the alley towards the rear of the bakery but Dalby was already gone.

She watched him as he slept, running her fingers lightly through his hair and down the back of his neck. He breathed slowly and rhythmically. It was a deep and dreamless sleep.

Colette put her head on his shoulder and lay her hand on his back and closed her eyes and breathed in time with him.

After a while Stein stirred and cracked open one eye and looked at her.

'You're still here.'
She ran a finger down his cheek.
'Yes, I'm still here.'
'Thank you.'
'No need to thank me,' she smiled
He rolled onto his back and stretched.
He looked at her.
'I'm sorry about despairing.'
She shrugged.

'It's fine.'

Stein looked at his hands and his arms.

'I should get cleaned up.'

He climbed out of bed and put on a dressing gown and crossed the room. He touched his hand to the back of the coffee pot on the table.

'I'll order more coffee.'

Colette pulled the covers up under her chin and relaxed back on the pillows.

'Yes,' she said. 'Please. And now I'm hungry so maybe order some bacon too and rolls.'

Stein looked at her. Such simple requests, so mundane, yet each time he saw her, spoke to her, made love to her, he could feel himself falling further.

'Of course,'

He pulled a chord near the door, then he came and sat down beside her.

He contemplated his hands once more, still streaked with mud and blood stains.

'Are you happy Colette?'

She adjusted her position in bed, rolling onto her side.

'You mean right now, here with you?'

He turned to face her.

'No, I mean in life.'

'Of course I'm not happy Max, there's a war on.'

'But if the war wasn't happening would you be satisfied? Happy I mean, with your life?'

'I don't know.' She paused. 'I think my life would be very different.'

'Exactly.'

'Pourquoi?'

'For everyone, the war is controlling their lives. We are all being moved this way and that, threatened and brutalised, forced to do things we hate, just to survive.'

'It will end one day, it has to.'

'I'm not so sure,' he shook his head. 'But even then, if it does end, will we ever be able to smile again? To laugh? To love?'

'When the war is over, I want to get out of the city I think. I want to live in the countryside like I did when I was a girl. Keep bees perhaps, grow flowers, walk in the woods.'

She lay back and stared up at the ceiling.

'I want to forget the war ever happened.'

'How old are you?'

She picked up a cushion and swung it playfully at him.

'What sort of question is that to ask a lady? Really Max.'

'I'm thirty-four.' He said. 'How old are you?'

She looked back at him, unsmiling.

'I'm twenty-nine.'

There was a knock at the door.

Stein got up and took the half empty coffee pot from the table and went to the door and opened it a few inches. A butler stood in the hall beyond.

'You rang Captain Stein.'

Stein ordered more coffee and bacon and rolls. When the butler had left he closed the door quietly and locked it then came back and took up his place on the bed. He looked seriously at Colette, his gaze penetrating and unflinching.

'If I leave this place tonight, will you come with me?'

She sat up.

'What do you mean?'

Stein glanced at the door and lowered his voice, as if wary of unseen ears.

'Will you come with me to Switzerland?'

She lent back against the headboard.

'I'm still not sure I understand what you're asking me Max. You mean a vacation, a holiday?'

He held her hand and leant forward, speaking earnestly, his voice low and a growing intensity in his eyes.

'No, I mean if I leave the army, if I run, will you help me? Will you come with me and start again?'

'They'll kill us.'

'Only if they catch us.'

'You're serious?'

He nodded. 'Yes very serious, like I said, I can't do this anymore. I won't.'

They sat in silence.

'You really want me to come with you?'

'Absolutely.'

Colette contemplated her life. The value of each of her few friends, the lack of real love, the fear, the rejection by so many that she once held dear.

Stein squeezed her hand.

'Colette please, let's go together.'

She embraced him, her eyes closed.

'We can make a new life, together. We can forget the war?'

'Yes,' said Stein. 'I think we can.'

'But how?'

'I've been contemplating little else for days now, and I think I might have a plan that will work.'

'Go on.'

'There is a night train that leaves Rouen for Strasbourg. It's an overnight train, run by the military, but my rank would get us onboard without any questions. Once we get to Strasbourg we will find a boarding house and stay there as a married couple. From there we can catch another train that'll get us close to the Swiss border. We'll find a quiet town, near the mountains perhaps and slip through.'

'That's your plan?'

'Yes. I know it's a risk but I'm going anyway, and I think I can make it.'

Colette looked uncertainly at him.

'What time does the train leave?'

'Midnight.'

'What about money?'

'There's money here, in the Chateau, in a strong room on the third floor of the west wing next to the armoury. I don't know how much is in there but there's enough. I went yesterday with some of the men to gather weapons for last nights mission and I saw it. Thousands of French Francs, Deutschmark and some English money too I think.'

'Can you get back in there?'

'I'm an officer, I can have any of the butlers let me in there whenever I like.'

'And they won't ask why you're there?'

'No.' He looked at her eyes. The fear, the apprehension.

'Colette, trust me. We can be free from all this, if we just muster the courage.'

She breathed out, like she was letting go of a burden long carried.

'Alright,' she said at last. She smiled at him and held his face. 'I'll come with you.'

He kissed her hand.

'Good. Thank you.'

There was another knock at the door.

'Ah, my breakfast,' said Colette.

'No,' Stein shook his head. 'It's not been long enough.'

He stood up and crossed the room. Bending his ear to the door he listened.

'Who is it?'

'Captain Stein…it's Corporal Dietz.'

Stein glanced at the bed.

'Yes Dietz what is it?'

'It's Haupsturmfuhrer Wolff sir, he requests that join him immediately in the library sir.'

'Immediately?'

'Yes sir, he said it's urgent.'

'Very well Corporal, tell him that I'll be there in fifteen minutes.'

Stein listened as Dietz walked away down the hall.

'What could it be?' Said Colette.

'I don't know but i'd better get down there.'

'Should I wait here?'

'No, said Stein collecting a Clean uniform from the wardrobe. 'Get dressed. I'll have a car take you back to Rouen. Pack a bag, and meet me in front to the station tonight at eleven-thirty.'

'What should I tell Hector?'

'Do you have relatives somewhere? Someone you could say you were visiting?'

'I have a sister, near Orleans, I could tell him I was going there for a while.'

'Yes, that's perfect.'
She sat up in bed.
'Max, you will meet me won't you?'
He turned to face her.
'Trust me, I will be there.'

CHAPTER TWENTY-ONE
One deal too many

Wellum blew warm air into his balled up fist and rubbed his palms together and looked at the house. He'd been watching it for almost an hour and it looked even older than the first time he saw it.

It felt as if it was already becoming a bad memory.

He checked his watch and stepped off the curb and crossed the cobbles.

The house leered at him.

Once inside, he closed the door and locked it. He left the key in the lock and turned his head and listened. After a minute he took out his pistol and climbed the stairs and went into the kitchen and put the light on.

The house was colder and darker than ever, as if no life had stirred within it for centuries. Wellum stood in the doorway and looked around the kitchen. Half empty coffee cups sat on the table alongside a glass with traces of gin, and he looked at the gramophone still clinging to the last record they had danced to. All relics of a strangely distant past, not even a day before, but to Wellum it was like looking back into a time before memory. He couldn't picture himself being here, but he saw Brielle everywhere.

He crossed the room and went to the stairs and climbed them. At the doorway to the bedroom he hesitated with his hand towards the door handle. He knew why he was afraid to go in. He closed his eyes and breathed out slowly and pushed open the door.

The bed was unmade and the sheets seemed somehow to have been cast off in the shape of two lovers. Moulded to their bodies, hollow yet filled with the essence of life like an echo. It took him by surprise to see it, like he was looking at the ghost of some intimate act.

If there could be such a thing.

He took a few cautious steps forward and put his hand on the bed, almost expecting to feel warmth, but when his fingers brushed against the cold, dry linen he drew away instinctively as if his hand confirmed the presence of death in someone lying still and alone.

Was it all his fault?

He felt desperate.

After a while he sat down on the bed and reached forward and opened the wardrobe and looked at the clothes hanging inside. He touched the fabric of the purple dress Brielle had worn for their impromptu date, now carefully hung back in its rightful place with its family. He pulled the fabric towards him and put it to his lips. He could still smell her. Another wave of grief washed over him and he lay back, pulling the dress with him from its hanger and he curled up on the bed and pressed it to his face and wept.

When he woke up he didn't know where he was. A panic gripped him and he sat up and drew his pistol and listened. The wind outside blew along the street and circled the house and rattled the windows.

Then he remembered.

He put the pistol back in its holster and swung his legs off the bed and sat there for a moment gathering himself. The dress was in his lap and he ran his fingers across it then he got up and rehung it in the wardrobe and closed the door.

He looked around the room and spotted his bag. He began gathering up the clothes he'd been given by Irene and Godfrey, then he picked up Brielle's spare shirt and put it in the small rucksack she had brought with her. He put the remaining rations into the weapons bag and before he zipped it closed, rummaged among the empty magazines and pistols and came out holding the silver key.

Back downstairs in the kitchen he went to the cupboard beneath the stairs and took the powdered milk tin down from a shelf and opened it. He tipped the tin upside down and shook out a roll of bank notes held in an elastic band and put it into his trouser pocket. He dusted his hands on the back of his trousers then glanced at his watch, he ought really to be heading back. He took the silver key and looked at it as if mulling something over in his mind, then he went out and crossed the kitchen and entered the dining room that had been used as Armada and then Yvain's bedroom. He looked at the cot neatly made, and the few personal items Yvain had left behind. He sat on the camp bed and sifted through some of the books on the floor. One was a notebook. He dropped the others he was holding and flipped through the pages of handwritten

notes jotted neatly inside. Map coordinates, various addresses around the city and some sketched plans. Wellum looked at each page, scouring the French text for anything he recognised. Towards the back of the notebook several words began leaping out;
Thiel
Il-Du-Bac
And even *Dalby*, sat among the otherwise indecipherable French.

Wellum turned the pages back towards the beginning and looked again. At the top of some of the pages were lists of numbers and letters. Wellum ran his finger beneath the first series whispering as he read.

'3-V-522A-TOK97-Y.' He turned a few more pages and found more.

5-E-243D-ETW44-I, then three pages further on; 1-I-633C-IYX12-A. He found two more rows of code and he sat on the bed and wondered what they might mean, then he closed the book and folded it in half and put it in his inside pocket. He got up off the bed and went across the the detonation box in the corner of the room. He dragged the key from his trouser pocket and held it in his palm and looked at it, weighing it in his hand; it was almost imperceptibly light. He bent down and put the key into the detonator then went back into the kitchen. He gathered the bags and looked around and with a last glance towards the door that led upstairs to the bedroom, he turned and left.

'Where have you been?' Said Dalby.

Wellum left the bags on the floor and dropped into an armchair and rubbed his eyes wearily. He looked grim and tired, his shoulders and hair wet through with the perpetual drizzle. He sat back in the chair and sighed.

'I went to Armada's.'

'What?'

Wellum held up his hand.

'I know, I know. I was careful, don't worry. I watched the house for an hour before I went in.'

He began searching his pockets for cigarettes.

Dalby went to a window and glanced out, checking for watchers.

'For fuck sake Harry, what were you thinking man? You're sure you weren't followed?'

'It's fine, relax. No one followed me.' He paused. 'I just needed to go.'

Dalby came back and sat on the arm of a chair opposite the pilot.

'Any sign that people had been there?'

Wellum shook his head.'

'No. No one's been there.'

'You're sure?'

'Yes, I'm certain.'

Dalby looked at the bags.

'Is that all your kit?'

Wellum gave a dry laugh.

'Kit? Yeah that's it. A few begged items of clothing and some nicked weapons.'

'You know what I mean.'

Wellum dragged the roll of notes from his pocket and lobbed it to Dalby.

'Fifty-thousand Francs. Hopefully enough to get me out of here and back to England somehow.'

Dalby tossed the money back to Wellum without studying it.

'I'm not sure you'll want to go anywhere just yet. Not once you've heard my news.'

'What do you mean? Did you catch up with Renard?'

'As a matter of fact I did, yes.'

'So?'

Dalby leant forward, his one good eye glinting in the semi-dark of the late afternoon.

'Yvain and Thiel are at his house?'

'Really?'

Dalby allowed himself a smile. He nodded.

'Right now.'

Wellum pointed at the floor.

'Here in Rouen?'

'Yes. Apparently Yvain turned up there after midnight last night. He's asked Renard to get him a car and some provisions. He says he's taking Thiel into Belgium and then by plane back to Berlin.'

Wellum shook his head slowly in disbelief.

'He's taking Thiel back to the Germans?'

'It looks that way yes.'

Wellum felt as if he was going to collapse. He steadied himself as a shadow passed over him.

'The fucking traitor.'

'There's a war on old chap, don't take it personally.'

Wellum squinted at him.

'What do you mean don't take it personally? Of course I take it fucking personally.' He stood up and gestured at the bags sitting on the floor.

'Armada's dead because of that bastard and now Brielle…'

Dalby stood up and faced him.

'Harry calm down, we really need to be calm here…'

'Calm down?' Fumed Wellum.

'Yes, calm down man.' He gestured towards the chair. 'Sit down, listen to me.'

Wellum did as he was asked and Dalby sat down opposite him.

'I know you're desperately upset about Brielle and I do understand, but I think the best way for you to deal with what's happened would be for us to complete the mission.'

He paused, watching the pilot carefully as he did. Wellum breathed in slowly, settling himself. Dalby went on.

'I've told Renard to keep Yvain at his house until at least six. After that we'll go in and pay them a visit.'

Wellum checked his watch.

'That's only an hour away. What's the plan?'

'Well I'm guessing in the RAF you didn't cover 'assaulting a building', in your basic training so I'll grab a pen and paper and run through some pointers with you.'

Dalby stood up and crossed the room. Wellum sat forward and held the spy's sleeve as he walked past the chair.

'Dalby I need to be clear with you, as far as I'm concerned Renard and Yvain are both dead men, I'm not interested in bringing either of them to justice, please understand that. Don't try and stop me.' He watched for a reaction, but Dalby simply nodded and patted his wrist.

'I know that Harry, don't worry. Neither of those two traitorous bastards will live to see the morning. I promise you.'

He tapped the door with a knuckle and straightened his tunic.

'Come in.'

Stein entered the room and closed the door. Wolff was standing at a window with his hands behind his back looking out over a small garden. Stein looked towards him as he came in but then turned as he noticed Renard sitting awkwardly in an armchair by the fire, his thin hair and drooping shoulders wet with rain.

Stein addressed the SS officer.

'You wanted to see me?'

Wolff turned around.

'Yes, Captain Stein.' He looked at the tank captain from top to bottom before crossing the room and sitting in a chair opposite Renard. He gestured to the empty seat beside him.

'Please, sit down.'

Stein did as he was asked.

Wolff then turned to Renard who was perched on the edge of his chair looking nervous.

'Very well Monsieur Renard, now you may begin.'

Wolff sat back and crossed his legs.

Renard's eyes swivelled between the two Germans and he rung his hands in his lap, the air seemed thick with expectancy and the malodorous smell of the Frenchman's obvious, nervousness.

'Well,' stammered Renard. 'I have some more news that, that might be of interest to you.'

'More news?' Said Wolff dryly. 'How delicious.'

Stein glanced sideways at the SS.

After a brief pause, Renard mumbled on.

'Er, yes.'

Wolff raised his brows and rolled his hand forward impatiently.

'Go on.'

'Yes, sorry,' stammered the Frenchman. 'My apologies.' He breathed out slowly trying to gather himself.

'Last night,' he said. 'Did you manage arrest the English pilot?'

Wolff looked at Stein and smiled then he looked back at Renard.

'Monsieur, you said you had news, that is not news, that is a question.'

'Oui, I apologise,' Renard rung his hands some more. 'But, I *was* wondering about my fee.'

'Renard, get to the point, and stop fucking around.' said Stein. 'What news?'

Wolff put out a hand and shushed Stein with a smile.

'It's alright Captain Stein, please.'

He turned back to Renard.

'Monsieur, it is obvious that for some reason or another, you are clearly suffering under the weight of your conscience.'

He held his hands out like a priest.

'Please feel free to unburden yourself.'

He smiled warmly at the sweating Frenchman.

'Tell us this news, and then we can discuss last night and the information you gave us.'

'My information was good though yes? The pilot, he was in Ande, with the girl from the Resistance and the spy Dalby, like I said he would be.'

'How do you know that?' Said Stein sitting forward. 'How do you know the girl was with him?'

Renard breathed in deeply once more.

'Late last night, I got a visit from someone that was also on the bridge with you at Ande.'

'What?' Said Stein.

'It's true, please hear me out.' Said Renard urgently fearing he was running out of rope. He touched his lips, tapping them lightly with his fingers.

'But, begging your forgiveness. I must insist, this time, I wish to be paid in advance.'

'In advance of what exactly?' Said Wolff.

'The news I have, about the person visiting me, it is worth a lot I think.'

'But you just asked if the pilot was arrested, so who is this other person?'

'I want a million.'

The hair on the back of Stein's neck stood on end.

'Really?' Purred Wolff after a pause. 'Well, this information sounds very valuable indeed.'

'It is.' Renard confirmed.

'You have my interest Monsieur, but of course, I cannot agree to anything until I know exactly what it is you have to say. You must understand that.'

Renard looked at them both once more. Stein stared back at him. He hated the man more than ever.

They sat, each of them waiting for the other to speak. Eventually Renard broke.

'Very well. I will tell you what I know, the reward I will leave to you.'

Wolff smiled back at him sardonically.

'As I said, last night, I was woken by a man I have known for some time. He was, I thought, working with the British SOE agent Armada, but it would seem that I was wrong.'

'What is his name?' Said Stein.

'Yvain Bret. He's Belgian, and like I said, I thought he was working with the Allies.'

'What has made you change your mind?'

'When he came to me last night asking for my help.'

'Is he the person you are claiming was on the bridge at Ande?'

'Yes.'

'Go on, please continue,' said Wolff.

'It was after one o'clock this morning. I was woken up by the Belgian, he turned up at my house in a green car and he had brought someone with him from Ande… a German.'

Wolff sat forward.

'A German?'

'Yes,' said Renard. 'Apparently Dalby hadn't been going to Ande to hand the pilot to anyone, but instead had gone there to pick someone up. Wellum and the French girl just went along to help.'

'Who were they collecting?'

'As I said, he came to my house with a German. He said that he had orders, from the German government to take the man back to Berlin.'

'So this Yvain… sorry what was his name?'
'Bret.'
'This Yvain Bret had gone along as part of an Allied effort to pick up a German and he somehow got away and turned up at your house?'
'Yes, though he almost didn't make it off the bridge. He said the attack was quite ferocious.'
Stein looked at Wolff.
'Yes it was a little, exuberant you might say.'
Wolff slid his eyes sideways towards Stein but didn't retort.
'And now he wants what?' He asked.
'He wants me to get him a car so he can take the German north, firstly to Brussels and from there by plane to Berlin.'
'Who's the German?'
'A million.' Said Renard looking solely at Wolff.
The SS officer paused, eyeing the Frenchman. After a while he gave an almost imperceptible nod.
The room crackled with an uncomfortable, unseen energy.
'Who is at your house Monsieur?'
Renard rolled a tongue across his dry lips.
'A scientist. Someone called Thiel, Walter Thiel.'
Wolff held a hand up.
'Wait, wait.'
He looked carefully at Renard.
'You're telling me that the scientist Walter Thiel is at your house now? Here in Rouen?'
'Yes,' said Renard quietly. 'That's what I'm saying.'
'I'm a little lost,' said Stein. 'Who's Walter Thiel?'

'He's a defector,' said Wolff, still looking at Renard in quiet disbelief. 'A scientist who's loss has been gravely felt. The Fuhrer thought he was probably dead. We all did.'

'Yes but who is he, and why should we care if he's here in Rouen or not?'

'Because Dr Thiel has skills that may help us win the war, that's why.'

'Doing what exactly?'

Wolff turned to face him.

'Have you heard about the V-weapons programme Captain Stein? As an artillery man, I'd be surprised if you hadn't.'

'Only rumours. We'd heard about some secret programme to develop flying bombs, long range artillery, things like that. But I'd not heard anything about its progress for some time.' He paused and looked hard at Wolff. 'Are you telling me that this scientist, whatever his name is, is part of it?'

Wolff nodded. 'Yes, and until August that programme was making great strides.'

'What happened in August?'

'The RAF bombed the factories and test facility in the north of Germany. They destroyed much of the infrastructure but more concerning was the loss of personnel at the top of the project.'

'How many were killed?' Said Stein.

'Five hundred workers, mostly replaceable prisoners, but we also lost a handful of scientists key to the development of one of the main projects.'

'But Thiel survived? I'm sorry but I'm not sure I'm following you.'

'His family were killed, his wife and children, but he was only injured. Quite badly so I heard, but still only injured.'

Stein blanched at the memory of his own loss to British bombs, though he hid it from the room.

'So, how has he ended up here in Rouen?'

'Well, we had heard that he was taken for treatment outside of Germany and that he had escaped. There were rumours he might trying to defect and the Gestapo and elements of the SS have been hunting for him since.'

He looked at Renard.

'But it seems that he has somehow managed to contact the Allies and has been hiding in Ande, almost under our noses.'

Wolff laughed and slapped his thigh.

'Well, well, well.' He shook his head and smiled, wagging his finger at the Frenchman. 'This time Monsieur I think you have outdone yourself.' Renard wasn't entirely sure how he should take what Wolff was saying.

A compliment perhaps?

Somehow it didn't feel like that.

'So, tell me.' Wolff continued with enthusiasm. 'Are the Belgian and Dr Thiel at your house right now, as we speak?' He tugged a notebook and pencil from his jacket pocket and flipped open the pages.

Renard nodded.

'Yes, yes they are.'

'And at this moment, you are supposed to be out procuring a vehicle for them to use in their journey back to Belgium and then on to Berlin?'

'Er, yes. A car and some supplies.'

Wolff wrote in his book and curled out a smile.

'Excellent.'

'I have the car here, and I have a few items to collect later today.'

'Do you know who they are meeting in Belgium or in Berlin? Did Bret mention any names?'

'No, I'm sorry, but he didn't.'

Wolff hovered his pencil over the page.

'Are you sure?'

'Yes, I'm sure.'

'What is your address Monsieur?'

Renard looked at Stein and then back to Wolff.

'My address?'

The SS officer smiled at him and nodded.

'Oui Monsieur.'

Renard's mouth was drying and he had a growing fear, seeping down his spine. He shuffled uncomfortably in his seat.

'My reward?'

Wolff waved his pencil airily. 'Yes, don't worry, I'm getting to that.'

'I live at twenty-five *Rue de Buffon* where it crosses *rue de Glisse*, by the cinema.'

Wolff scribbled the address and closed the notepad, then placed it on the arm of the chair and folded his hands in his lap.

'Monsieur Renard, I cannot tell you how grateful I am for the information you have brought me today.' He tapped the notepad with a finger.

'Really. In fact I would go as far as saying that in this single act, you have helped the Fatherland of Germany take an important step towards victory in this terrible conflict'

Renard managed half a smile.

'Thank you.' He wiped the sweat from his brow with a handkerchief. His ordeal seemed almost at an end. 'So, you think I could to get paid now?' He glanced nervously at Stein.

Wolff steepled his fingers.

'Yes, I think it is time that got what you rightfully deserve.'

He stood up and went back to the window and looked out once more.

'Captain Stein, take the prisoner outside and shoot him.'

'Wh, what?' Said Renard waving his handkerchief. He began visibly trembling. 'Why? no.'

Stein stood.

'Wolff, you're not serious.'

Wolff swivelled on his heels and faced them both.

'It's Haupsturmfuhrer Wolff, Captain Stein and yes I am *very* serious.'

Renard slid from the chair to his knees.

'Please no I beg you, why?'

'Because I can't have you constantly coming here *demanding* such ridiculous sums of money that's why,' said Wolff dryly. 'And I doubt that after today you will have any information that might surpass what you have told me here. So you see, your work is finished Monsieur Renard and for that, on behalf of the Fuhrer himself, I thank you.' He turned back to Stein.

'Now, Captain I am giving you an order. Take the prisoner outside and shoot him.' He gestured to the window. 'Here in the garden where I can see.'

Stein knew it was pointless arguing. He knew that if he refused Wolff again he might be next for the bullet. He looked at Renard, kneeling and weeping and on the edge of madness.

'Please no,' wailed the Frenchman, ringing his hands before him in prayer.

Stein watched him, moments from the abyss. The room suddenly stank of fear; a sour, fetid stench, like shit, rising up from Renard as he crawled around wide-eyed on the carpet, sweating and shaking. Stein stepped forward and lifted him up by an elbow and marched him towards a door that led out to the garden beyond.

The square lawn was bordered with redundant flower beds, empty of blooms but instead layered with brown and yellow fallen leaves from the surrounding Birch and Beech.

Stein dragged Renard, his hands still clasped together and spun him to a stop in the centre of the small garden. As he did so, the panzer captain stumbled a little and felt as if he was teetering on the precipice of his own sanity.

This is not me...this not me.

He steadied his feet beneath him and unclipped the cover of the holster on his hip and slid the pistol out in one smooth movement.

'This is not me.'

Renard fell to his knees and squeezed his eyes closed, trembling uncontrollably, the sweat steaming off him in the cold air.

Stein cocked the pistol and stepped forward and pointed the barrel at Renard's right temple. From the corner of his eye he could see Wolff standing impassively at the window watching the execution play out. Stein turned and looked at the SS officer and the two of them seemed locked in a gaze of bitter struggle and resentment, then as Renard lifted his chin and looked at him in a last desperate plea for mercy, Stein squeezed the trigger and felt the pistol buck in his hand as the sound of the shot rang around the chateau, making all the birds leap for the safety of the sky.

CHAPTER TWENTY-TWO
Time running out

Yvain moved the curtain aside and looked out into the fading afternoon. The persistent drizzle shrouded everything and made it hard for him to see much beyond the abandoned cinema at the end of the road. The house was cold and dark. He came back into the room and contemplated lighting a fire.

'I'm hungry,' complained Thiel from the hallway. Yvain had cuffed him to the bannister of the stairs and the German had been sitting on the bottom step, complaining and gibbering all day.

Yvain sat in an armchair he'd dragged to the doorway. He pointed his pistol at the scientist.

'Be quiet.'

Thiel slid down to the floor and proffered his padlocked wrists.

'Please, just loosen these and feed me. I'm not going anywhere, you can trust me. Please, I'm starving.' He hung his head on its thin neck and whined.

Yvain half turned and looked away. His patience was stretching. He hadn't slept for over twenty-four hours and he'd been drinking coffee and smoking cigarettes continually since he'd got back from Ande. He picked up his cup and drained the last of the cold black dregs and he wondered what was keeping Renard. The Frenchman had said that he would be back by five at the latest and that was fast approaching. He got up and carried the cup into the kitchen and filled the kettle and set it down on the stove. He opened a cupboard and peered inside. A few desultory packets and some tins. He lifted out some sardines and tin of pork, then a half bag of sugar, some rice and some powdered milk. He looked at the gathered items. It was pretty much everything in Renard's larder. He took a bowl from another cupboard and opened the sardines and poured them in then dragged open a drawer and took out a spoon. He walked back into the living room and then the hall. He put the sardines on the floor and looked at Thiel. He looked emaciated and half mad, sitting at the foot of the stairs in Renard's clothes that were clearly two sizes too big for him. He crouched down and undid the handcuffs, releasing Thiel's right wrist then rebuckling him to the stairs by his left. He handed him the bowl.
'Here eat, then be quite.'
'What is it?'
'Sardines.'
'Gaahh, no. I can't eat fish,' Thiel wailed as Yvain stood and walked back to the kitchen.
'Leave it then,' said the Belgian as he went. He opened the tin of pork and shoved in a fork and started eating, then he took a saucepan and spooned in some powdered

milk and ran the pan under a tap. He added rice and then used what was left of Renard's sugar supply. He put the pan on the stove and lit a match then carried the tin of meat into the living room and sat down.

'What do you have?' Asked Thiel miserably. He was holding a quivering spoon by his cheek, trying to muster the courage to put the cold fish into his mouth.

'Pork,' said Yvain, chewing.

'Ah,' gurgled Thiel, waving his spoon about and throwing fish onto the carpet. 'The Jews of Ande will be turning in their graves.' He whined and covered his head and tittered.

Yvain remembered the rotten smell of Thiel's clothes from the night before and the stench of the Il-du-Bac. He shoved the fork into the tin and dropped it by Thiel's foot.

'Here, you can have it.'

Thiel dropped the bowl of sardines and grabbed the tin. He shoved forkfuls of pork greedily into his mouth, laughing and gurgling as he did.

'Vergiss die Juden, las sie verrotten, las sie verrotten.'

Yvain grimaced and picked up the discarded bowl of fish and began eating it with his fingers.

When he had finished, Thiel tipped the can upside down and rattled it towards his open mouth, trying to get the last of the meat.

Yvain watched him.

'Why did you run, Walter?'

Thiel peered into the can with one eye then dropped it on the floor.

'What?' He wiped his mouth with the back of Renard's sleeve.

'Why did you want to defect? Why did you run away?'

Thiel rang a finger inside his mouth searching his gums for pork. He sucked his finger then shushed Yvain.

'Shhhh. Don't ask, please don't ask me that.'

'No, come on I want to know. Why? I heard the scientists at Peenemunde were very well looked after. An important job, good money, in favour with Hitler and all that.'

Thiel stared down at the carpet, drooling slightly.

He curled his lip at the mention of the Fuhrer.

'I was never interested in making weapons.' He said at last. He looked at Yvain. 'I'm a scientist and a genius apparently.' He smiled theatrically. 'A genius.' He picked at the carpet with his thumb. 'I just wanted to build a rocket that could get to space. That's all most of us wanted to do.'

'Another Nazi that doesn't believe in the war eh?' Said Yvain.

'I was never a Nazi,' defended Thiel. 'I hated them. Taking our research and manipulating it for their own ends.' He sat back on the first step and wagged his finger, his wrist manacle clanking on the bannister as he waved his free hand about. 'General Dornberger and the others pah! Himmler, pah! what a bastard he is!' He spat on the floor.

Yvain pointed the pistol at him.

'Alright, alright, calm down.'

'Well what do you expect? Imagine, just imagine, conceiving and the creating a rocket that can fly to space. Imagine it.'

Yvain conceded.

'It does sound remarkable.'

'And it is! And what do they want to do with it? Uh? Point it at fucking London and stuff it with explosives, that's what!'

He was tugging on his manacle and rolling around, spitting and fuming in German.

'Fucking Schweine! Verschwendet! Jahre der Forschung verschwendet, Mörder!'

'Alright stop it.' Hissed Yvain. He stood up and grabbed Thiel by the scruff of his neck and dumped him back on the first step.

'Sit there, shut up.'

Thiel sobbed into his armpit.

'Shweine.'

'What difference does it make anyway? Said Yvain, lighting a cigarette and sitting back in the chair. 'There's a war on. The British or Americans would only make you do the same thing for them.'

'I'll refuse.'

'They'll jail you.'

'Ah maybe they would, but the Fuhrer will kill me if I go back.'

Yvain smoked.

'Not if you go back to work on the rocket he won't.'

Thiel shook his head.

'I can't go back. Not now they're gone.' He wiped his face with the back off his hand. 'Not now.'

Stein rolled the carbolic under the hot tap and peered at himself in the mirror. His face was reddened from the mist of blood that had engulfed him as he shot Renard. It had bloomed like a pink cloud, erupting from the corner of the

Frenchman's eye as the bullet pierced his skull above his ear, the warm moistness embracing Stein and making him blink involuntarily as Renard slumped forwards and lay dead at his feet. Stein watched Wolff until the SS officer had drawn the curtains leaving Stein alone with the corpse resting its head almost serenely on his boot.

He looked at his face in the mirror, watching his eyes move in their hollowing sockets. He looked at his square chin, covered in dark grey stubble and he saw as if for the first time the almost permanent set of his down-turned mouth; a reactionary scowl of disdain for a rotting world. A fleeting look of sadness seemed momentarily to pierce the veil and was gone. He rolled the soap between his palms and as the steam rose and fogged the mirror and his reflection disappeared and he bowed his head towards the sink and washed himself. He scrubbed his face and his neck and his hair and he poured handful after handful of the water over his head, rinsing out the blood, which drifted in circles around the bowl in fading crimson rivers, and when the water ran clear he turned off the tap and he leant on the sink and let the water run from his head in a steady, dripping baptism.

He closed his eyes and said a prayer.

He opened the drawer of the bedside table and took out the items he'd brought with him to the chateau. A copy of *Poems* by Wilfred Owen, his wedding ring and a small frameless photograph. He put the book on the table and he slid the ring halfway down his forefinger and rubbed it gently with his thumb, turning it slowly and looking at it. He took it off and put it in his pocket, then sat on the bed and picked up the photograph and looked at it. It was the first time he'd had the courage to look at it for almost nine months. It was creased in one corner and ripped here and there around the edge. He carried it everywhere; to every camp he'd been in, on every mission, but he could rarely bring himself to look at it.

Valda and Misha, sitting together on the sofa next to a Christmas tree in their house in Leonberg. Valda, no older than three, looking back at him with his own eyes.

'We are twin spirits you and I.'

He had said it to her so many times, there was a part of him that believed it was true. He stroked the photograph softly with the tip of his finger.

His world.

It all seemed so far away. Stein sat there for a long time just looking at the picture. He thought about Colette and expected to feel guilt, but he didn't.

It felt strange to realise that he had no guilt about moving on.

He knew it was time and he knew that Misha would understand that if he didn't move on soon he would die. He took the wedding ring from his pocket and looked at it again. A simple band of gold, not polished, but not dull. He kissed the warm metal and he took it and along with the photograph and the book, placed it in a bag that lay open beside him on the bed.

He got up and crossed the room and opened the wardrobe and reached in and took out some trousers and a clean shirt. He put the trousers into the bag and slid the shirt on. He was fastening the first few buttons when the there was a knock at the door.

Wolff came in without speaking and Stein closed the door behind him. The SS looked around the bedroom like he was inspecting a barracks, then he turned to Stein who was still standing near the door. He gestured to the bag on the bed.

'What are you doing here?'

Stein walked back to the bed and continued packing.

'I'm going back to my camp at Peronne, you can keep my men here if you need them.'

Wolff looked at him with emotionless eyes.

'*Your* men?'

Stein glanced sideways at the SS officer, standing smartly with his hat tucked neatly under his arm.

'My men, your men, *the* men. What difference does it make who's men they are?'

He turned his attention to the bag once more.

'Captain Stein I must say, I have found your attitude to this mission rather disappointing. When I first met you at your camp, I had hoped that you would see this opportunity as a chance to shine, a chance to make a difference to the war effort, instead of sitting in some backwater shit-hole adding little to the struggle in which we are engaged. I had hoped that you would rise to the challenge - but It would seem I was wrong.'

'I'm sorry to have disappointed you,' said Stein flatly. 'But now that the mission is over, I'm going back to my unit.'

'What makes you think that?'

Stein looked at him.

'Makes me think what?'

'What makes you think the mission is over?'

'Wolff, The pilot has gone. He's gone. Last night was our best chance of catching him and we blew it. He's probably half way to London by now.'

'You will address me as Haupsturmfuhrer, Captain Stein.'

Stein shook his head wearily.

'I'm sorry, *Haupsturmfuhrer.*'

He closed the bag and fastened it and lifted it from the bed and dropped it by the door.

'Captain Stein, I have not released you from your orders. You and I still have work to do in Rouen.'

Stein turned to face him.

'Why? You could take more men from here, officers even, young, ambitious, loyal men. I'm sure Colonel Kruger would be happy to give you whatever help you need.'

'*You* are under orders Captain and for that reason, despite whoever else might joins us, and for however long it takes, you are still this mission's second in command.'

'Do you really think you're going to find the pilot now? After that debacle on the bridge last night?'

'I admit, I am less optimistic about that than I was.'

Stein took his tunic from a hangar and put it on.

'Good, well I'm glad we could agree on something.'

'But we will continue to search the city regardless,' said Wolff.

'What?' Said Stein. 'Why?'

'Because that is our mission, that's why, and you will stay and lead your men on that mission until I release you from your duty.'

'My duty?'

Wolff stared at him.

'Captain Stein you are flirting with mutiny. You should correct your tone immediately.'

There was a seriousness about Wolff that made Stein check himself. The two of them looked at each other across the room.

After a while Stein walked to the door and bent down and picked up the bag.

'I have to go back to Peronne. I might be needed there, I haven't been in touch with the rest my men since we left. You don't need me here.'

Wolff put his cap on and straightened it. The skull on the front glittered in the growing shade of the afternoon and his grey uniform was as dark as thunder and he seemed suddenly to grow and fill the room until the skull and the thunder were all that Stein could see.

'Captain Stein I do not release you from your post and you may *not* go back to your unit. After we have completed tonight's, task, you will stay here, in Rouen where you will continue searching for the Englishman Harry Wellum, do you understand?'

Stein narrowed his eyes.

'Tonight's task?'

Wolff nodded.

'You and I are taking your remaining men into the city to collect Doctor Thiel.'

'You know that most of them are injured after last night, why not just ask Kruger for SS troops?'

'Because I'm not telling Colonel Kruger what we are doing, that's why,' said Wolff quietly.

'What are you talking about?'

'We are taking the truck and the men we brought here with us and we are going to Monsieur Renard's house where I will arrest Doctor Thiel personally. After that, you will accompany myself and the good doctor to the SS camp in Vitot, south of the city, where I will contact Berlin to tell them I have the defector in my custody. You will then return to Rouen to continue the hunt for Wellum. Once I have handed Thiel over in Berlin I will return and find you and we will go on together from there until our mission is complete.'

Stein laughed.

'You're not telling Kruger?'

'No I'm not. This part of our mission must stay top secret, which means I don't want you to talk about it with anyone; the men, Colonel Kruger or Detective Schenk. Am I clear?'

Stein Shook his head.

'You're just like Renard. You want all the glory for yourself don't you.'

In an instant Wolff pulled his pistol from its holster and took a step towards Stein.

'How dare you be so insubordinate,' he hissed.

Stein dropped the bag and instinctively held his palms out. He contemplated reaching for his own weapon but he knew he'd be dead if he did.

'I should shoot you right now,' said Wolff quietly. 'You're a disgrace to the Reich.'

'I'm not the one shooting innocent civilians am I, *Haupsturmfuhrer?* Or priests, or anyone else that happens to cross your path.'

Wolff took another step forward.

'You would be wise to ensure that you do not end up on the list of those that *cross my path*, Captain Stein.'

He held out his hand.

'Your sidearm.'

Stein reluctantly undid his holster and took out the pistol and turned it in his hand and passed it to Wolff. The SS put his own weapon away and pointed Stein's pistol back at him.

'Right, let this be an end to it. Gather the men and prepare them to leave in fifteen minutes.' He lowered the pistol and crossed the room. As he got to the door he turned and looked at Stein.

'Captain I hope that you understand the gravity of our situation. Whatever you have heard about the V2 programme you must realise that if we can get Doctor Thiel safely to Germany it will probably mean a swifter end to the fighting and I know that is what you want. Now, whether you believe it or not that is also what *I* want. But, when the fighting stops I want to be on the *winning* side. You must understand that.' He clicked his heels and nodded curtly and he went out and closed the door.

Stein looked down at the bag and then at his watch. He felt the strength drain from him as he wondered if he could get a message to Colette, telling her to wait, to stall their plans, then his hand went subconsciously to the empty holster at his hip and he thought about Wolff and the death's head insignia on his hat and the shadow of thunder and the merciless, ruthless nature of the SS and he wondered if he would ever see her again.

CHAPTER TWENTY-THREE
Revenge

The rain had stopped and the clouds were gone.

It was a good night for bombing.

The air-raid-siren began wailing as they drove the car across the *Rue de la Roquette*, heading north. They were just two streets away from Renard's house as the siren broke out and people began scurrying this way and that, looking for shelter and gathering their families to crawl away from the nightmare that was about to unfold.

Dalby had told Wellum that assaulting a house on foot was very similar to dogfighting Messerschmitts over London; it demanded maximum aggression, utilising the element of surprise and being totally ruthless with the enemy.

'We're going in there for one purpose and one purpose only; To kill Yvain and Renard and to get Thiel out.'

They were parked inconspicuously outside a line of collapsed houses that were the remnants of some previous air bombardment. Broken walls and piles of rubble and jutting, desiccated black timbers. Dalby pointed to an alley that ran between what was left of the buildings.

'Renard's house is that way. Across the road and a few houses north. When we get down to that end we'll stop and make our final preparations.'

He opened the driver's door and climbed out.

'Come on let's go.'

He unlocked the boot as people hurried by and he lifted out a small rucksack and threw it over his shoulder. He tossed another at Wellum then glanced around before removing two machine guns, handing one to the pilot and shouldering his own. He took out two more machine guns then closed the boot and walked into the alley and wellum followed him.

Dalby dropped his bag on the floor and crouched beside it and began undoing the buckles.

'We'll leave the packs and spare weapons here and collect them on the way back once we've got Thiel. We won't leave them in the car in case it gets compromised or we have to get out on foot.'

As Wellum took his own pack off and dropped it next to Dalby's he glanced at the sky. The sirens filling the air like cries from another world. No one could ever become inured to such an unearthly, sound.

'We better make this quick,' said Wellum. 'The air-aid will be starting any minute'

'Don't worry, I think they'll be going for the marina. There are U-boats in dock at the moment; Sitting ducks hopefully.'

'How do you know that?'

Dalby smiled as he put a magazine into his browning and pulled back the action.

'Because I'm the one that told the RAF the boats were there, that's how.'

They hid the bags and guns behind a pile of broken masonry and set off along the alley, going carefully with their weapons in hand and their belt kits full of spare magazines and grenades. They each wore a pistol at their hip and had pouches filled with first aid kits, and more magazines. They were only going to kill two men, but had enough ammunition to take on a small battalion.

Wellum felt grim and determined. A darkness was still upon him, and he felt some strange kinship with the black shadows of the alley as they patrolled forward with the sound of the sirens and the smell of smoke and rubble dust clinging to the air.

This was an awful, all consuming war. Reaching out with clawed fingers that penetrated all life and goodness and pierced the hearts of everyone it touched. It was unrelenting evil and Wellum felt as if his soul had finally been devoured by it. He followed Dalby through the gloom, unsure of what was coming, or how he would react when they finally confronted Yvain. Through his actions that traitor had brought death to his heart and Wellum knew that if he did nothing else for the rest of the war, he would never sleep peacefully again if he failed to deliver Yvain to the void. He gripped his machine gun tighter and bit his teeth together, setting his jaw. He had to keep the anger at bay though he felt almost overwhelmed with grief, he understood that an instant of reckless abandon could signal his own end and rob him of the vengeance he now needed. He didn't care about Thiel anymore, all he wanted now was the destruction of a traitor that had robbed him of his love.

Dalby stopped and crouched beside a wall at the end of the alley. He pointed across the abandoned street.

'That house there.'

Wellum peered through the darkness at a row of brick and timber houses.

'The one with the yellow door, that's Renard's.'

They checked their magazines and re-cocked their weapons, then felt around their belt kit making sure their spare ammunition and grenades were easily to hand.

Dalby looked at Wellum. He nodded, unsmiling and focused on the pilot's eyes.

'You ready?'

Wellum looked back with the same focused intensity.

'Ready.'

They moved off as one, crouching as they went and staying in the shadow of a low wall. As they got to Renard's, they stopped once more and listened and looked and waited. Wellum counted the beating of his heart as it thumped in his chest, drumming out a constant, beating rhythm that ached with the loss of Brielle and all the death and the fear of everyone that had fallen in this vile and vicious conflict, and as the bombs began to fall and the muffled explosions rolled towards them from the river beyond, they approached the house.

Yvain checked his watch.

'Please,' wailed Thiel from the foot of the stairs. 'Please, we must go. The bombs are coming, the bombs, listen, listen!'

He raised his shaking hands to the length of his wrist manacles as if gesturing towards the sound of the air raid sirens and the crump and thud of explosions in the distance.

'Please we must leave here now.' He slid to the floor and cowered and whimpered.

Yvain looked at him impassively.

'You've been in air raids before and survived Walter, now be quite or I'll tie you up in the garden and leave you there.'

'No, no,' cried the German as more explosions rolled towards them. 'It's time we left. The bombs are terrible, terrible.'

He hid his face in the crook of his arm and sobbed.

'Die, bomben haben sie mir genommen, mein liebe, meine Familie. Alles.'

Yvain checked his watch again. It was getting late and a doubt had begun to creep through him as to the trustworthiness of the duplicitous Renard. Paranoia picked at him, pricking him like a needle pushed into the soft skin of his palm. He shook his hand at the thought and looked at his watch once more. Maybe Thiel was right; they shouldn't wait much longer, and despite his bravado, Yvain didn't relish the thought of being crushed by allied bombs.   He crossed the room and went into the kitchen and grabbed a bag from the floor and opened it, assessing the contents. It was the bag he'd taken to Ande; two spare magazines for his Sten and one for his pistol, a compass, two grenades and a water bottle - no rations.

'What are you doing?' Called Thiel from the hall, wiping his eyes on his sleeve. 'Are we leaving?' He sniffed.

Yvain fastened the pack and slung it over his shoulder, then picked up his machine gun. He came back into the lounge digging in his pocket for the handcuff key.

'Yes, we're leaving.'

Thiel thrust his wrists towards the Belgian.

'Yes, yes, quickly unlock me, lets go, we must go now.'

Yvain put the small key into the lock and undid the cuffs, allowing Thiel to slide his arm free of the bannisters. The German sat for a moment and rubbed his wrists soothingly before Yvain snapped his fingers and reluctantly Thiel held his hands out to be locked together once more.

'Right, I'm warning you once. Any problems and I'll kill you Walter, understand? The Germans want you *alive*, but I'm also under strict orders to shoot you if you try to escape again, it makes no odds to me, I'm getting paid to bring you in dead or alive, so it's up to you.'

Thiel gave a sullen nod, and tugged at Yvain's sleeve.

'I'm not going to run, but we must go.'

The sound of the air raid siren mingled with more thudding explosions from the direction of the Seine and the drone of engines filled the sky and made the air vibrate in oppressive and terrifying waves.

As Yvain dragged Thiel to his feet and turned and pushed him towards the hall, a knock at the front door made them both stop. Yvain let go of the German's elbow and pointed his machine gun at the sound.

The knock came again. Yvain put a finger to his lips, signalling for Thiel to stay silent and he took a careful step towards the door.

A voice spoke to them from the other side of the chipped and peeling paint.

'Hello?'

Yvain shouldered his weapon.

'Hello, Renard?' The voice came again. 'Renard, c'est moi, Eric.'

Yvain lowered the Sten a few inches and looked at the door.

'Eric?'

'Oui, Eric. Er, ou est Renard?'

'Renard n'est pas ala maison. Que désirez-vous?'

'Jai une livraison de la part de Sassoon. Quelques articles que Renard a commandes.'

'Une voiture?'

'Er oui, yes, a car.'

Yvain hesitated. He lowered his weapon further.

'Where is the car?'

'In the street, nearby. I was told to deliver it here to Renard. Veuillez ouvirir la porte.'

The sirens wailed and the bombs landed on the docks. Yvain took a step forward as Thiel held out a trembling hand.

'Wait,' he whispered.

Yvain waved the German's hand away and hissed at him to be quiet.

'Shush, get back there.' He pointed to the back of the hall. 'You want to get out of here don't you? Well, this is our chance. I know this man Sassoon, don't worry.'

He took another careful step towards the door and cautiously leaned forward. He closed one eye and peered through the spy hole, out into the growing darkness of the street beyond. Immediately he stepped backwards, firing a burst from his machine gun as he did, aiming from the hip and peppering the door with bullet holes. Wood chips splintered and filled the air as Thiel screamed and dropped to the floor, covering his ears. The door lock suddenly exploded inwards sending shards of hot metal and flying fragments of doorframe into the hall making Yvain wince and turn away. He instinctively took a step to his right and dropped to one knee and he raised his machine gun to his shoulder and fired the rest of his magazine at the door. As Yvain released the empty magazine from the Sten gun and swiftly reloaded with another from his belt, the door swung violently open. Thiel flinched once more and raised his hands to cover his eyes as Yvain stumbled backwards, raising his Sten gun with one hand and firing several rounds into the ceiling. Bits of wood and plaster exploded down upon them and a glass light shade shattered into sparks and plunged the hall into darkness. Dalby came in quickly, crouching and firing at the same time while Wellum stepped through the door behind him with his own weapon on full automatic. The noise was deafening. Smoke and flames leaped from the guns, illuminating the shadows, as bullets tore into Yvain, his chest and face bursting in red gouts like ribbons of silk flung towards the fire in some ancient, arcane ritual. The Belgian stumbled and fell back and Thiel screamed in shock and fear as the firing stopped and Yvain hit the floor in a smoking, blood soaked heap. Wellum walked past Dalby over the shattered glass and broken plaster and unholstered his pistol and stood over the stricken man. Yvain looked up, past Wellum, into the distance, beyond mortal sight. His left eye was black and bulged grotesquely with a rivulet of thick blood running from the tear duct down across his cheek. Bullets had hit him in the chest, face and throat and deep black holes bled and smoked and throbbed as he coughed and spluttered his final few breaths. Wellum stared down at him and felt no pity. He raised his pistol in a steady hand and fired, released his finger from the trigger and fired again.

Then again, and again.

Each time the pistol bucked violently, Thiel flinched and lay cowering against the wall at the end of the hall. After four shots Wellum raised the gun and smelled the end of the barrel, savouring the bitter tang. The cordite smoke burned his nostrils, but it was a smell he wanted to remember.

Dalby touched his arm and spoke quietly to him.

'Harry, it's done, it's over now. We need to leave.'

Explosions rolled along the street outside. Up over the houses in waves and the ground vibrated beneath their feet.

A low moan mixed with muffled sobs drifted towards them from the far end of the hall.

'Help me,' said a weak voice. 'Please, I think I'm hit.'

'Thiel,' said Dalby as he turned and hurried towards the scientist. Wellum stepped over Yvain without looking back and followed the spy to where Thiel lay propped against the wall. He was bleeding from a gunshot wound to the shoulder and all around him the walls were peppered with holes, the wallpaper punctured with deep craters that leaked plaster dust or exposed split timbers, burnt and blackened by the bullets lodged within. It was a miracle the scientist hadn't died alongside Yvain.

Dalby sat him up and he winced and cried with pain as Wellum crouched beside them and peeled back Thiel's jacket to get a better look at the wound.

'There's no exit wound and the shoulder feels broken,' said Wellum. He opened a pouch on his belt kit and began retrieving wadding and bandages.

'We need to stop the bleeding before we move him.'

Thiel cried out in pain once more.

'No, don't leave me here. Please, take me with you.'

Dalby retrieved a morphine syrette from his own webbing and removed the small plastic cover from the needle.

'Don't worry Walter, we're not leaving you.'

He jabbed the needle through Thiel's trouser leg into his thigh and depressed the plunger and tossed the empty capsule towards a corner of the hall. Thiel ignored the pain of the needle and began moaning quietly as the morphine flooded his system and Wellum worked quickly on his shoulder wound. Dalby checked his watch.

'We need to go.'

'Almost finished here,' said Wellum. He tore off a straggling length of bandage and began tying a knot.

'Ich komme, mein liebe, geh nicht weg, ich komme, bitte bleib.' Thiel mumbled from the depths of the morphine, his head rolling listlessly on his thin neck.

'Don't go…please don't leave me again.'

Wellum tidied the dressing and pulled Thiel's blood stained shirt and jacket back into place.

'It's not perfect but it'll have to do for now, we can look at it properly when we get him back to your place.'

'Alright fine,' said Dalby, slinging his weapon over his shoulder. 'Let's try standing him up and see if he can walk.'

They both threw one of Thiel's arms around their neck and supporting his weight, stood up together, hoisting the German into a standing position.

'Walter listen to me,' said Dalby loudly. 'We need to walk now. Come on we need to get you out of here.'

They moved slowly towards the front door, but Thiel was incapable of even a single step. His head hung down on his chest and his toes dragged on the floor as the two Englishmen carried him forwards.'

'The fucking morphine's finished him off,' cursed Dalby. We can't possibly drag him all the way to the bloody car.'

They lowered him back to the carpet.

'You wait here,' said Dalby. 'I'll go and get the car and drive it round.' Another explosion in the next street blew the glass from a window in the hall. The whole house shook and dust cascaded from the ceiling and walls like powdered snow.

Wellum crouched beside Thiel coughing and wiping his eyes. The sirens wailed and the sky howled with aircraft.

'Alright go,' he shouted through the dust and smoke. 'But be quick. This air raid won't last must longer and we need to get north, away from the river and the docks as quickly as we can, we can double back once the bombers have gone.' He patted Dalby on the shoulder. 'Go on, be careful.' He coughed and spluttered again. 'I'll be ready to move as soon as you return.'

Dalby stood and crossed the hall, stepping over Yvain's body as he did. He reached the door and unslung his weapon and put in a fresh magazine and stood ready to leave. He glanced back at Wellum, kneeling beside the stricken German, then opened the door and stepped outside.

The sudden brightness of the headlights made Dalby stop and raise his arm, covering his eyes to save himself from blindness. A voice called at him from the road.

'Halt, Ne bougez pas, sinon vous serez abattu!'

Suddenly, the air raid sirens stopped and the distant drone of aircraft engines drifted westwards and away.

Dalby squinted from behind the shade of his elbow, trying to see.

'Laissez tomber votre arme…drop your weapon,' said the voice.

The spy did as instructed, lowering his Sten to the ground.

'And your pistol.'

Dalby half tuned away from the lights and unclipped his holster.

'Do it slowly, no sudden movements. Then place your webbing belt on the floor.'

Dalby closed his eyes and shrugged off the webbing and belt kit. He dropped it next to the pistol at his feet.

'Now turn around and face the door and get on your knees with your hands behind your head.'

He turned and got to his knees, thankful to be out of the lights. He opened his eyes and blinked several times, trying to reclaim some semblance of night vision. The front door was still half open and Dalby hoped Wellum had seen the lights and heard the exchange from where he sat nursing Thiel at the back of the hall.

Two soldiers grabbed him roughly, one either side and stood him to his feet while a third pushed the muzzle of a rifle against the back of his head. He was turned around on the spot and the lights of the truck went out. Several fires burned in streets a few hundred yards away and hot black clouds of smoke billowed over roof tops and blew along the road like something from a burning, choking dream. From where he stood Dalby could see almost down to the river and it looked to him as if all of the docks were ablaze.

Two German officers approached him and stood, ranked by half a dozen Wehrmacht soldiers. The shorter of the two had his pistol in his hand and wore the dark grey uniform of the SS. Dalby visibly tensed when he noted the lightening bolts at the German's throat.

The soldier stepped forward and spoke to him.

'What is your name?'

Dalby looked straight ahead.

'I'm sorry, I cannot answer that question.'

Wolff slapped him hard across the face making Dalby's ear ring immediately.

'You're English?'

'Peut-Être, peut-Être pas. Jai de l'experience,' said Dalby with a crooked smile.

The German slapped him again.

'Who's inside the house?'

'I'm sorry, I can't ans…'

Wolff put his pistol on Dalby's eyeball.

'No more games, you fucking English pig, tell me or I'll kill you now. You can't save Thiel, but you can still save yourself. The house is surrounded, so he won't be slipping out of a back window this time. You might as well tell me.'

He adjusted the pistol in his hand, tightening his grip, his finger tugging imperceptibly on the trigger. 'Now I ask you again, for the last time. I am looking for Dr Walter Thiel, is he inside?'

Dalby looked into the eyes of the SS, weighing up the price of his own sacrifice.

'Yes, he's inside.'

'Is he alone?'

Dalby shook his head.

Wolff looked at the front door, slightly ajar leading into a hallway.

'Alright go inside, stay where we can see you. Tell whoever is hiding in there to put down their weapons or we will kill everyone inside this house, including Thiel and then we will kill everyone in every house on this side of the street.'

Stein winced slightly and shuffled uncomfortably.

Dalby saw it.

He nodded again.

'Fine.'

Wolff gestured towards he door with his pistol.

'Go on, slowly, and keep your hands where I can see them.'

Dalby turned with his hands at shoulder height and moved towards the door. He pushed it open with his foot and stepped into the hall, then turned and saw Wellum stood over Thiel, aiming his machine gun from his hip towards the front door. He lowered the weapon slightly as Dalby walked into view.

The spy looked at him blankly.

'Drop your weapon Harry. The house is surrounded.'

CHAPTER TWENTY-FOUR
The chase is over

Wolff came slowly into the hall, his boots crunching on the shattered splinters of glass and the street fires reflecting like burning oil stacks on the back of his long leather overcoat. Stein followed him in, flanked by two soldiers, all aiming their weapons at Wellum. Wolff flicked the muzzle of his pistol towards the Englishman.

'Bring ihn dorthin, bring Doktor Thiel hier zurück.'

The guards shoved Dalby forwards. As they crossed the hall, Wolff looked down at Yvain lying dead in the middle of the floor. The soldiers delivered Dalby to the wall. One of them bent down and picked up Wellum's machine gun and kicked his discarded webbing to one side while the other attempted to drag Thiel from the carpet. The scientist rolled and flopped about in a semi-conscious daze.

Wolff turned and spoke to Stein.

'Go and help him.'

As Stein and the soldier hoisted Thiel up by his armpits and dragged him outside, Wolff took a few steps forward and stood in front of Yvain's corpse. He looked at Wellum, then reached into his jacket pocket and came out with the photograph Renard had given him. He studied the image, his eyes shifting from the picture to Wellum's face and back. He turned the photograph to face the pilot. Wellum didn't take his eyes from Wolff's.

'Harry Wellum, It is good to meet you at last.'

Wellum made no reaction.

The SS slid the photograph back into his pocket and smiled.

'It would appear to be *my lucky night*, as you say in England. To find you *and* Doctor Thiel at the same time and quite remarkably, at the same address…' He shook his head and searched for the right words, waving his finger as he did. '…Quite remarkable, wouldn't you say?'

He ground his boot heel against the broken glass as he looked at them.

'What is your rank?'

'Squadron Leader,' said Wellum.

'And what were you doing over France when you were shot down by the Luftwaffe?'

'I'm not going to answer that.'

Wolff smiled.

'I thought so.' He gestured to Dalby with the muzzle of his pistol. 'You and your friend think you can keep quiet forever I suppose.' He lent towards them. 'Well, we shall soon see how you cope when we question you formally Squadron Leader Wellum, you and your anonymous friend here, and then I suspect that despite your bravado you will need all of your British strength for that ordeal.'

'You were on the bridge last night,' said Wellum flatly. 'I saw you.'

Dalby shuffled and Wolff pointed the pistol at him.

'Stand still. If you move again I will shoot you.'

He turned back to Wellum and leant in once more. Wellum could smell his sweet, herbal cologne.

'Yes, I was there.'

The two men stared at each other. After a moment Wolff spoke again.

'It's the Dupont girl isn't it, that's why you're so upset. It's fine, don't worry, I can see it in your eyes. She was helping you, and now she's dead.' He nodded, feigning concern. 'Alas, these are the things that happen in such tragic times, and to one so pretty too tut tut tut. A young girl with misguided intentions meddles where she shouldn't and bump…' he shrugged. 'It is over so quickly.' He stepped back onto the broken glass once more. 'But not for you I fear… not for you.' He touched his tunic, just above his heart. 'For you I'm sure this pain will endure. And why not, why shouldn't it last?…was it love Herr Wellum, or just an unfortunate sense of loyalty that led her onto the bridge with you last night?' He waved the pistol around airily. 'Not that it matters now. She's gone and you're here so things are as they should be I suppose. After all, there was no way you could run from the SS forever, and as for the Resistance…' he smiled. 'That was never really going to save anyone was it?' He paused again and the guard shifted his weight and the crunching of broken glass beneath the German's feet was the only sound. The air between them burned and felt charged.

'You think you've already won don't you?' Said Wellum without a smile. 'You think it's already over.' He shook his head. 'But it's not.'

Wolff gestured to the pistol in his own hand

'It looks pretty conclusive from here Squadron Leader, I must say.'

'Hitler understands he can't win. You do know that don't you?' Wellum paused. 'He knows he's going to lose and he's taking you lot down with him.'

Wolff altered his grip on the pistol and the air crackled.

'You have no idea of the power of the Reich. The Fuhrer can't lose, Germany is too strong. It would need a miracle to take back Europe now.'

'I know,' said Wellum. 'I know that.'

They watched each other. Their eyes locked and penetrating but only one of them harboured a fleeting doubt.

Eventually Wolff smiled broadly and took a step back.

'...Anyway, that is enough talking for tonight. Unfortunately I must leave you now.' He turned and walked towards the front door where he stopped and looked back at them.

'But you have my word that unless the war ends within the next few days, I will return and we will talk again you and I.' He clicked his heels and nodded.

'You have my word on that.'

Stein stared up at the glowing sky and thought about Colette. He looked anxiously towards the train station to see if it had been hit, but a voice at his shoulder brought him back. It was Wolff stepping from the doorway, putting on his gloves as he came.

'It looks like our mission is almost complete after all Captain Stein.' He approached the tank commander and smiled. 'No doubt to your great relief, I'm sure.'

Stein gave a nod, but did not smile back.

'What do you mean *complete*?'

Wolff gestured over his shoulder towards the door.

'The shorter of those two. He's the pilot.'

'Wellum?'

Wolff nodded.

'Yes.'

He looked into Stein's eyes for a reaction, but there was none. He went on.

'I have a plane en route to an airfield, west of the city, near Henouville. I am going to take Doctor Thiel back to Berlin tonight.'

'You're not going to the SS camp at Vitol?'

'No,' said Wolff, I decided it would take too long and might compromise the security of my new mission. It was easy enough to arrange for a Junkers from Versailles to pick me up and hopefully get me back to Germany before the morning.' He turned and began making his way along the path towards the car. Stein followed him a little way behind.

'I'm going to take Corporal Baur with me to the airfield,' said Wolff as he walked. 'I want you to take the English prisoners back to the chateau where Baur will regroup with you and your remaining men once my flight is airborne. There are cells at the chateau, speak to Colonel Kruger and have both of the prisoners processed; you will be under the Colonel's command until I get back.' When he got to the car he turned to face the tank captain. 'I will direct a formal interrogation when I return. After that you will be dismissed.'

Stein paused but didn't reply, after a moment he turned away and began walking back towards the house.

'Captain Stein,' Wolff called after him. Stein stopped and turned as Wolff closed the door of the Mercedes and came back along the pavement to meet him.'

'Captain wait.' Wolff stopped and the two men faced each other.

'Captain,' continued Wolff. 'I would like to say that it has been a pleasure and an honour serving with you over the last few days, but regrettably I cannot.'

Stein looked unmoved. He turned to leave.

'Captain Stein wait,' said Wolff curtly. 'You will stand and hear what I have to say.'

Stein turned around once more and looked deep into Wolff's eyes while the SS officer contemplated him.

'I know you probably don't realise this, but you bring shame on them you know, when you continue to act in this manner.'

Stein narrowed his eyes.

'What did you say?'

'Your wife Misha and little Valda, you bring shame to them.'

Stein felt a numbness crawling up him. He took an awkward step backwards and his heart burned with a sudden white heat.

'Yes,' continued Wolff. 'I know their names.'

Stein shook his head slowly.

'Don't.'

'What? do you think your dear sweet little girl would be proud of her father if she could see you now? Standing here, devoid of any courage or willingness to fight for her. Do you really think she would want that? Or do you believe deep down that she deserves so little? And what about the beautiful Misha. How would she feel, knowing that your lack of love for her allowed you to find solace so quickly in the arms of a back street whore.'

Stein trembled in the darkness, but didn't bite back.

'You're pathetic,' said Wolff. 'In fact I would even go so far as to say I have never met a weaker man. The death of your wife was a mercy to her. You are a disgrace as a husband and as a father and most regrettably I have to say, as a soldier of Germany.'

He turned and walked to the car and signalled for Corporal Baur to open the door. Wolff climbed into the back seat next to Thiel, and Baur glanced nervously at Stein as he unslung his weapon and climbed into the passenger seat as the car pulled away.

Stein wanted to act, to respond, but he couldn't. Maybe Wolff was right, he had no courage left, but as he watched the lights of the Mercedes disappear into the smoke filled streets, he turned back towards the house to play a hunch he was prepared to gamble his life upon.

Stein came into the hallway.

'Go and wait outside. Get the others ready to leave.'

As the soldiers walked towards the door, Stein held out his hand.

'Ritter, your weapon.'

The young soldier hesitated for a moment, then passed the captain his MP40. Stein checked the breech and pointed the gun at Wellum and Dalby then tipped his head towards the door indicating the two German conscripts could go.

'Go on, get the men ready.'

Wellum glanced sideways at Dalby who was staring unflinchingly ahead, and realised that it might not be just him that was concerned that this German officer was about to perform an impromptu firing squad.

'Which one of you is Wellum?'

Neither man spoke.

Stein tightened his grip on the gun and pointed the barrel at each of them in turn.

'I know that one of you is called Dalby and the other is the pilot Harry Wellum, but if I'm going to help you, it would be useful if I knew which of you is which.'

'Why would you help us?' said Dalby. 'And why should we trust you anyway?'

Stein proffered the machine gun.

'You should trust me because clearly if I wanted to kill you, you'd already be dead. And as to my reasons…let's just say I don't agree with the SS's methods of interrogation and torture, which incidentally is where you two are going next.' He paused before adding. 'And I think maybe if I help you, then it will also be helping me.'

'Helping you in what way?' Asked Wellum.

'Are you Wellum?'

Wellum nodded. 'I am, yes.'

'Well, like you, I need to get away from France. Or put more precisely, I need to get away from France and the war and the Wehrmacht.'

'Why?' Said Dalby.

'Why? Frowned Stein. 'Why? Look around you.' He gestured at Yvain's corpse. 'This is madness, insanity.'

'So, you're a Nazi with a conscience?'

'I'm no Nazi.'

'Bollocks,' said Dalby flatly.

Stein looked at him.

'No, it's true. I have no loyalty to the Nazi cause and I think if Thiel ends up back in the hands of Adolf Hitler, things could get worse for everyone.' He looked at Wellum. 'I do not want Germany to win this war, and I'll do what I can to stop it now - if you'll trust me.'

'Were you on the bridge last night, in Ande?' Asked Wellum.

'Yes I was,' said Stein. 'But I played no part in the death of your companion.'

Wellum looked into Stein's eyes.

'I didn't fire a shot, on my honour I swear it, and I'm sorry for your loss. I know the pain of losing those we hold dear.'

Wellum's cautiousness lessened. After a moment Stein lowered the weapon slightly.

'You have a choice of course.'

'Go on,' said the pilot.

Stein lowered the machine gun further and uncocked the breech.

'You could kill me and take this gun and fight your way out of here, then go back on the run with Wolff and the rest of the SS and Gestapo coming after for you. But by then of course, Wolff will have successfully delivered Thiel back to the Fuhrer. Or, you can trust me and we can go after Wolff and Thiel right now together and finish your mission tonight.'

The room fell silent once more.

'Then what?'

'Then we can go our separate ways and by the time Berlin finds out what happened, hopefully you'll both be back in England and I'll be over the Swiss border.'

Wellum looked at Dalby as the sound of the truck's engine being started rolled in through the broken window. He looked back at the German.

'OK, what's your plan?'

Stein took a step back and looked out through the smashed glass onto the street beyond. The truck was sat with two wheels up on the kerb while the small group of soldiers stepped up onto the tailgate and into the back.

'Wolff has taken Thiel to an airfield somewhere near a town called Henouville, to the west of Rouen.'

'I know where that is,' said Dalby. 'It's only thirty minutes from here by road.'

'Well, unless we get there and stop him, he's going to fly from there to Germany and deliver Thiel to Hitler tonight.'

'And you want us to stop him?'

'Wasn't that your mission?'

Dalby ignored the question.

'How do you propose we get close to him?' Asked Wellum

'We'll use the truck.' Said Stein.

'And what about your men?'

'Leave that to me. All you two need to do is act like prisoners until we get to the airfield. Once we've located Wolff and Thiel we'll have another think about what the next move should be.'

Dalby and Wellum looked at each other and an acknowledgement passed unspoken between them.

'Alright, said Dalby.'

Stein nodded.

'Good.'

'What about weapons?'

'There's a weapons crate inside the truck, it contains four spare MP 40's and eight magazines, some grenades and first aid.'

'Is it locked?' Said Wellum.

'Yes, but I have a key.'

'Sounds like more than enough,'

'Let's hope so,' said Stein. He glanced at his watch. 'We better get moving. I've no idea what time the aircraft is scheduled to meet them and I'm guessing by your reckoning they'll be well on the way to the airfield.'

He held out his hand.

'I'm Max, by the way.'

They left the house with their hands raised above their heads like condemned men, walking ahead of Stein who gave them the occasional prod in the back to keep them moving.

Wellum could see flames lighting up the sky above the houses in the streets beyond and the smell of timber smoke filled the air and the sky glowed orange and the heat of the burning city rolled towards them.

As they approached the truck, Stein spoke.

'Stop here.'

He called up into the back of the lorry.

'Ritter, Goethe, come down here.' The two young soldiers jumped down and stood on the pavement looking at the English prisoners.

Stein spoke to them without taking his eyes from Wellum and Dalby.

'Go back into the house, gather all of the weapons and put them in the back of the truck.' As the men headed off, he addressed the truck once more.

'Wagner, Schneider.'

Two more men climbed from the tailgate and dropped to the pavement beside him.

'You men are to stay here, guard the house until we return.'

He gestured to Wellum and Dalby.

'You two, get in the back and keep your hands up.'

There was only one soldier left in the lorry. As the two Englishmen clambered aboard he stood up awkwardly and pointed his gun at them.

'Corporal Klaus.' Said Stein as he closed the tailgate and locked it in place.

'Guard the prisoners.'

Klaus sat down opposite Wellum and Dalby and levelled his weapon at them as they both relaxed their hands down onto their knees.

The truck rocked slightly as Stein climbed into the cab next to the driver, then they heard the door slam and the whole lorry vibrated as the engine started.

Ritter and Goethe came down the path, carrying pistols and automatic weapons and belt kit.

'Just throw them in the back' said Stein with the cab window down. He gestured with his thumb.

The men hesitated for a moment.

'Go on put them in the truck,' insisted Stein. 'Corporal Klaus is in there. Then you two stay in the house with Wagner and Schneider. Don't leave here until I get back.'

He saluted at the men, then gestured with two fingers that the driver should proceed. As the truck pulled away he leant out and spoke to the men once more.

'And you can remove those armbands, you are no longer acting SS troops. Tell the others to do the same.'

CHAPTER TWENTY-FIVE
Henouville airfield

Wolff watched the Junkers JU52 circle the airfield, its landing lights blinking red and green against the inky blackness of the sky. The plane's engines throttled down to a low drone as it skimmed the trees at the far end of the field and flew serenely passed him, touching down and rumbling away into the darkness. It throttled back up and whined as the aircraft braked and turned at the end of the runway and taxied sedately up to a group of single story buildings that were the airfield's operations room, mess hut and control centre. As the plane rolled to a halt and the pilot set the engines to idle, Wolff put his head into the Mercedes and spoke to his driver and corporal Baur then picked up his hat and put it on. The JU 52's propellers slowed and span softly and the three engines ticked and clicked in the night air and the smell of aviation fuel followed. Wolff walked towards the parked aircraft as the pilot unbuckled his seatbelts and opened the cockpit window.

'Haupsturmfuhrer Wolff?'

Wolff looked up from the concrete, holding onto his hat as he spoke.

'Yes, I'm Haupsturmfuhrer Wolff.'

'Good evening,' called down the pilot. 'I'm Oberstleutnant Goff.' He slid his flying helmet off and placed it on the instrument panel.

'I was told to meet you here but I've no idea what happens next. Are we going on somewhere else tonight?'

'Yes, to Berlin.'

'Berlin?'

'Is that a problem?'

The pilot hesitated for a moment as he made a quick mental assessment of the distance from Rouen to the German capital.

'No, not at all. I'll need to refuel though. Is there a groundcrew here?'

'Yes,' said Wolff. 'How long will the refuelling take?'

'The Luftwaffe pilot tapped a gauge on his instrument panel and took out a map.'

'I'll come down and look at a route, then I'll check the weather reports while the ground crew put the fuel onboard.' He flicked his wrist and looked at his watch.

'We should be ready to leave in about forty-five minutes.'

Wolff checked his own watch.

'Ok fine, but make sure we get airborne as soon as possible.' He waved his hand and held his overcoat closed as the pilot revved the three engines back up to speed and began taxiing the plane towards a row of fuel bowsers sitting fifty yards away.

As the truck crested the hill, Stein could see the runway lights of Henouville airfield about a mile ahead, glowing softly at the bottom of a shallow valley.

He pointed towards a layby.

'Pull the truck over there.'

As the truck bounced through the puddles and stopped, Stein opened the door and jumped down into the mud. He turned and reached back into the cab and picked up his machine gun, speaking to the driver as he did.

'Keep the engine running, wait here.'

He slammed the door closed and walked to the back of the lorry. He undid the tailgate and let it fall open.

'Klaus, come down here.'

The corporal glanced at Wellum and Dalby.

'It's fine leave them there,' assured Stein. 'Jump down.'

The young soldier did as he was ordered, shouldering his weapon and clambering off the tailgate. He stood next to the tank commander as Stein spoke to Wellum and Dalby.

'You two, come down as well.'

As the two Englishmen dropped to the ground Stein reached forward and took the corporal's machine gun and handed it to Dalby.

'Go and get the driver.'

He handed his own weapon to Wellum.

'Here, hold this.'

Klaus looked stunned, his mouth falling open he took half a step back as Stein took his revolver from him and pointed it back at the shocked soldier.'

'Stand still Corporal Klaus,' ordered the tank captain. 'Don't speak.'

'But, Hauptmann Stein wha…'

'Shut up,' said Stein curtly. He span the corporal around and jabbed the pistol against his head.

'Get on your knees, put your hands behind your back.'

Dalby came back from the cab, walking the driver ahead of him. Stein turned and aimed his pistol at the man's face.

'Next to him, on your knees.'

The driver got on his knees beside Klaus and automatically raised his hands.

'Hands behind your back,' said Stein.

He turned and gestured towards the lorry, speaking to Wellum as he did.

'In the truck, by the cab, there is a box with wrist manacles and some rags and bandages.'

They handcuffed both men and tied gags around their mouths, blindfolding each of them with the bandages, then they marched them separately about fifty yards into a small copse of trees and lay them down and tied their legs.

When they got back to the truck, Stein dug in his pocket and found a small padlock key. He jumped up into the back of the truck and went to a rectangular box, bolted to the floor and opened it and reached inside.

He piled three more machines guns and two revolvers, spare magazines for both and a half dozen stick grenades together on the seat above the box, then closed the lid and relocked it.

'Let's get these into the cab. We can divide them up when we get to the airfield.'

Wolff paced impatiently while the pilot studied his maps. He had a cup of black coffee steaming at his elbow and was chewing a corned beef sandwich, muttering to himself as he drew lines on the topography.

The two young Luftwaffe crewmen stood by awaiting orders, excited by the sudden flurry of activity that had descended on their quiet and usually uneventful little airfield while Corporal Baur stood self-consciously guarding the door, trying to look as if he knew what was going on.

Eventually the pilot dropped his pen on the map and stood up rubbing his eyes.

'Well?' Said Wolff.

'It's at least six hours,' said Goff.

'Can we do it in one flight?'

'No, we'll need to stop and refuel again. If we land in Bonn, at the base there, we can do a quick refuel that will get us all the way to Berlin. it's only four hours away and if we take-off from here by twenty-two-hundred hours we will arrive in Bonn at two in the morning. With a swift turnaround and without any hold ups we can still be in Berlin before six.

Wolff looked at the map and then at his watch.

'There's no adverse weather en route?'

'I'll contact the Wetterdeinst in Luxembourg for an update while the ground crew put the fuel on board.' He paused and looked around the room.

'Will you be travelling alone?'

'No,' said Wolff. There will be myself, and one more very important passenger. A scientist.'

'Where is he?'

'He's outside, in my car.'

Goff peered out of the window at the staff car parked a few dozen yards from the hut. He drained his coffee and called over the groundcrew with a wave of his hand. He pointed out of the window at a fuel bowser sat next to Wolff's Mercedes.

'Get that bowser down to my aircraft and put on three hundred and seventy gallons of fuel.'

'That tanker only contains three hundred litres Herr Oberstleutnant, but there is another, close to your aircraft with around seven hundred litres on board.'

'Very good, use that one then. We'll be ready to takeoff as soon as you've got the fuel on board.'

Stein pulled the truck off the road and cut the engine. They were parked beneath a small group of evergreens which stopped abruptly at a high fence, beyond which lay the airfield runway.

'There.' He pointed past the fence towards a group of low buildings. Wolff's car was clearly visible. They jumped down from the truck and Wellum closed the door quietly behind him. The three men gathered by the fence and spoke only in low voices. Wellum pointed towards an aeroplane sitting around seventy-yards beyond the main buildings. It was plugged into a fuel-bowser by a hose that attached to its left wing just behind the engine.

'Look's like they're still here.'

He looked at Dalby then at Stein.

'So, what's the plan?'

Stein studied the entire scene through binoculars.

'We have some bolt cutters in the truck. I think if we can breech the fence here and get to those buildings without being seen, we can deal with Wolff there.'

'Do you know how many ground crew, or guards are here?' Asked Dalby.

Stein shook his head. 'No, I didn't even know this place existed until an hour ago.'

'Harry, any ideas?' whispered the spy.

Wellum took the binoculars from Stein and peered through them, glassing the airfield from one side to the other.

'It looks like there are two crewmen refuelling the Junkers, but I can't see anyone else.' He handed the binoculars to Dalby.

'There might be a radio operator in the hut or a few more ground crew knocking about, but on an airfield this size and this remote I doubt if there are more than half a dozen altogether, if that.'

'Weapons?' Said Dalby as he surveyed the scene for himself.

'Not much,' said Stein. 'They're not a fighting force so I'm guessing they'll have a few personal weapons for limited protection and there's a slim chance of a small unit of men being garrisoned close by in case they are attacked by locals.'

'Right,' said Dalby as he stood up and dusted the dirt from his knees.

'Our objective is simple; We'll divide up the weapons in the truck. Two automatic rifles, a pistol, spare magazines and two grenades per man.' He pointed at the fence. 'Then we cut a hole here and we'll cross into the airfield. After that we go straight to those buildings.' He pointed towards some oil drums and what looked like discarded pallets sitting next to a tractor thirty yards from the op's building. 'We'll use that position as a start point and prepare for our attack there. I'm going to suggest that Harry then crosses to that fence line and makes his way down to the aircraft and arrests those two ground crew. Hopefully they won't be armed and we won't have to kill them. Max and I will then assault the building; kill Wolff and anyone who resists and hopefully capture Thiel alive. If we can't get him out we'll kill him too.' He looked at their faces.

'I want to deal with Wolff,' said Wellum.

'Me too,' said Stein.

Dalby looked at them both and scratched his chin.

'Alright,' he said after a pause. 'I'll see to the ground crew while you two deal with that SS bastard.'

'And after that?' Asked Stein. 'What then?'

Dalby raised the binoculars and looked back across the airfield.

'After that,' he said looking at the JU-52. 'We all need to get out of here as quickly as possible just in case there are any local troops that decide to turn up.' He lowered the binoculars and looked at Stein. 'What are your intentions?'

'I need to get back to Rouen to meet someone. I have my own plans after that.'

'You get back here and take the truck then.'

'What about us?' Said Wellum.

Dalby smiled at him and pointed towards the runway.

'We're going to steal that aeroplane and you're going to fly us back to England.'

CHAPTER TWENTY-SIX
The Effigy of St Joan

Wolff looked out of the window and sipped his coffee. Away east, he could see the orange light of the burning city just above the trees. He was eager to get back to Berlin, to stand before the Fuhrer and to offer him a prize worthy of the fight...at last. Thiel was the break he'd been waiting for, to strike a *real* blow to the allies - to make a significant contribution once more. He would deliver the scientist and then perhaps he could dine with The Fuhrer where they could discuss his inevitable promotion, maybe even a position within the SS high command. He imagined himself in the sable black of the Sturmbannfuhrer's uniform. He might even take over at the Chateau of the Black Swan for a while - or somewhere like it. He smiled at the thought. No more slogging it around like an errand boy for Himmler.

A low moaning sound brought Wolff back from his fantasy and he turned to look towards a log burner at the far end of the hut. Thiel was sitting, wrapped in a blanket in an armchair. He was finally coming round from the morphine, but had whined and moaned so much since Baur had brought him in from the car, Wolff was seriously considering drugging him back into unconsciousness.

Goff came into the hut and looked at Thiel.

'Is this the other passenger?'

'Yes,' said Wolff. '

The pilot seemed sceptical.

'This is the important scientist?'

'He might not look like much,' responded Wolff, crossing the room and putting his coffee mug on the table. 'But this man, and his colleagues in the north may well make all the difference to the war over the next few months.'

Goff gave an unconvinced nod as he began folding his maps and gathering his gloves and flying helmet.

'Right well, the ground crew have the bowser rigged and are almost finished refuelling, I've got my route planned here,' he proffered his maps as evidence. 'And the weather report is good.' He folded a map into his jacket pocket. 'Bonn are expecting us at around two a.m. So we ought to be taking off within the next ten minutes.'

'Good.' said Wolff, putting on his overcoat. 'Thank you Oberstleutnant.'

Goff glanced at Thiel once more as he turned and headed for the door.

'I'll go and do my pre-flight checks and speed up the men on the refueller. Er, do you want me to send one of them back to assist you with Doctor Thiel?'

'I don't think that will be necessary, thank you. Corporal Baur here will help me. We'll be down to you in ten minutes for boarding then, yes?'

The pilot clicked his heels and gave a smart nod. He smiled.

'Yes, I'll see you on board Haupsturmfuhrer.'

Outside, Wellum, Dalby and Stein crouched in the shadows of a small wooden hut, thirty-yards from the main operations building

They each wore belt kit, two slung automatic machine guns and pistols in holsters. As they looked ahead, they could see a fuel bowser parked towards the rear of the main building and next to that, a pile of abandoned wooden pallets and stacks of metal ammunition cases. Dalby looked though the binoculars to where the crewmen were refuelling the JU-52. He scanned the ground between them and the buildings but saw no one else. He turned to the other two.

'That crew must have almost finished refuelling that Junkers by now so I'm going to get on my toes and sort them out.' He glanced through the binoculars again and glassed the operations building.

'I can see Wolff inside talking to someone, but I can't see how many people there are in there with him.'

He handed the glasses to Wellum who raised them to his eyes.

'There are some large caliber ammunition boxes near that tractor, which means...'

He swivelled the glasses right and scanned the airfield. Around forty yards from the buildings, just on the edge of the runway, he saw what he'd suspected might be there.

'Bingo,' he said handing the binoculars to Stein. He pointed the German to where he'd been looking. A bulky, shrouded mound, covered in a tarpaulin sat surrounded by sandbags.

'Looks like a flak cannon,' said the tank captain. 'For use as an anti-aircraft weapon.' He passed the binoculars to Dalby.

'It'll be loaded then, ready for use in a raid I reckon,' said the spy. He lowered the binoculars and turned to the other two.

'Alright listen in. I'll get down to those two crewmen and get them under control. While I'm on my way, you blokes keep the binoculars on me. When I reach that second runway light you get moving. I'll surprise my two when I hear you both prosecuting the target.'

'What does that mean?' Said Stein.

'It means when we go in shooting,' said Wellum.

'If things get out of hand, we can fall back to that flak cannon and use it as a fire support base to get their heads down. Alright?'

They both nodded

'Alright.'

Dalby held out his hand to Stein.

'Just in case I don't see you again, once Wolff is dead you should go. Get back to the truck and head straight to Rouen - it's getting late.'

Stein shook his hand.

'Good luck Dalby.'

Dalby smiled at them both

'Harry, we can regroup here once we've malleted this lot, then we'll get that Junkers fired up and see what sort of pilot you are.'

He turned and checked his weapon, looked towards the south, then without another word, he moved off quickly towards the parked aeroplane.

Wellum watched him go, then turned to Stein.

'You alright?'

The tank captain took a deep breath.

'I think so yes.'

Wellum checked his weapon and then looked back at the operations building. He could see Wolff walking around inside still talking to someone. He looked at Dalby, moving quickly in a crouch, heading past the stationary tractor. The spy paused by a low wall and Wellum saw him glance back in their direction.

'Wellum, before we go.' Stein was speaking quietly, his eyes fixed on Dalby as the spy got up and started moving cautiously forward once more.

Wellum turned to face him.

'What is it?'

Stein reached into the breast pocket of his shirt.

'Here.'

He pressed his fingers into Wellum's palm, passing him something small and cool, then he moved past the pilot and crouched beside the wall and looked back towards Dalby.

Wellum opened his fingers and looked at the silver figure of Joan of Arc nestling in his hand.

'Where did you get this?'

'From your friend, the girl from the bridge.' He turned and looked at Wellum.

'I'm sorry.' He paused. 'I had them take her body to a church.'

'In Ande?'

'Yes, I couldn't leave her in the river.'

Wellum looked at the silver figure staring back at him from his palm.

'Thank you.'

Stein glanced at him once more but said nothing.

As Dalby had moved clear of the low wall and began moving past the operations building, a young man in pilot's overalls had come abruptly out of the door in front of him. Dalby instinctively crouched and swerved away towards the runway and the darkness, but Goff had seen him and called out.

'Hey, halt! Stehen sie, wer auch immer sie sind! Halt.'

He drew his pistol from its holster and fired. He saw Dalby take cover behind some oil barrels and he stepped forward and fired two more shots.

Dalby stood up with his weapon in the shoulder and fired a quick, well aimed burst, sending the German pilot sprawling backwards, then without hesitation, he turned and ran on towards the waiting aeroplane.

Hearing the sound of the pistol shots breaking the darkness, Wellum and Stein ran from the shadows and sprinted towards the operations building. They saw the burst of flame from Dalby's weapon and they saw Goff stagger then fall dead to the ground. As they ran, Wolff suddenly appeared at the window with his pistol drawn and on instinct Wellum stopped and fired towards the building.

The window erupted in an explosion of glass and wood. Wolff ducked and wellum went on, running once more to catch up with Stein.

Dalby was almost at the fuel truck when the sound of Wellum's shots tore through the night towards him. He continued to run, focused now only on getting to the aircraft and neutralising the two Germans working there. As he ran, both men came hurriedly from beneath the wing of the Junkers to investigate the sound of gun-fire. When Dalby was almost upon them, one of the men drew a pistol and aimed it, while the other took a fearful step backwards raising his hands above his head.

Dalby slowed his pace from a run to a walk and aiming from the hip, sprayed them both with what was left in his magazine, cutting them down where they stood.

He approached them cautiously, and kicked the pistol away towards the shadows behind the aircraft, then he dropped the empty magazine from his weapon, fitted a new one from his belt kit and after firing two more shots into both men, turned and made his way quickly back towards Wellum and Stein.

In the operations room all was chaos. As the window exploded inwards from Wellum's barrage, Wolff had grabbed Thiel and thrown him headlong underneath the radio table at the back of the room. The SS, took off his hat and tossed it into a corner and peeled off his coat and tunic and dropped them on the ground.

'Baur, hand me that MG-42,' he demanded pointing at a light machine gun that was lent against the far wall. He flipped over two coffee tables and crouched behind them.

'Get behind me,' he said as the panzer grenadier handed him the weapon and vaulted over the makeshift barricade.

The two of them aimed at the door, listening to the sound of firing as Dalby took care of the crewmen fifty yards away.

'What's happening?' Asked Baur, his eyes wide with fear.

'It's Wellum.' Said Wolff checking the breech of the MG-42 and unravelling a length of bullets on a belt next to him.

'What, the English pilot? How is he here?'

'Captain Stein is helping him.' Said Wolff, slamming home the mechanism on the gun and propping it against a table leg for support.

Baur looked more frightened than ever.

'Stay here,' said Wolff. 'If anyone comes through that door, kill them.'

He turned and leaving his weapon where it was, crawled towards Thiel who was cowering beneath the desk in a half-sedated stupor with his hands pressed to his ears.

'Doctor Thiel, ' said Wolff. 'Are you injured?'

Thiel gripped his bloodied shoulder with a trembling hand,

'Injured? No, no more than I was already...what the fuck is going on?' He demanded. 'Where are we?'

Wolff ignored him and moved back towards Baur as the door splintered and broke under machine gun fire from outside. Both men ducked, then Wolff knelt and took the handle of the MG-42 and the light machine gun roared into life.

Wellum and Stein took shelter behind the parked tractor as Wolff's tracer rounds coursed towards them from the operations building. The firing was intense - A long, deafening burst. Chunks of tarmac were torn up and flung all around them as they crouched and the tractor rattled and shook violently as bullets burned through its iron body; some caroming off in ricochets that whistled insanely into the night, while others buried themselves violently inside it.

When the shooting from the building ceased, Wellum stood and started firing controlled bursts towards the doors; three rounds, then four, and he could see bits of wood and plaster exploding around the doorframe. He crouched again as the '42 started pouring fire at them once more, its tracer, terrifyingly close, lighting up the night in crimson, laser-like rods.

'This is no good,' he shouted to Stein over the deafening assault. 'I can't see if our rounds are penetrating any further than the doorway.'

They stood together as the light machine gun went quiet once more, returning fire with as much accuracy as they could manage; Stein firing from the shoulder and Wellum from the hip. More brick and plaster and splintering wood exploded as the door broke off its hinges, falling gracelessly to the floor like a dead man.

They crouched again and Wellum changed his magazine.

'I think we need to get closer,' he said as a round bounced off the tractor's mudguard and screamed over their heads making them both duck.

'I agree,' said Stein, but I don't know how. That fire position is too strong, if we move from here we're dead.'

As the enemy firing paused once more, Dalby slid towards them, taking cover behind one of the tractor's bulky rear wheels. He took a grenade and pulled the pin and stood and threw it hard against a window of the operations building.

The glass broke and he ducked.

'What happened down there, with the crew?' Said Wellum as the grenade exploded inside the building with a muffled crump.

'They were armed.' Said Dalby as he checked the rounds in his magazine. 'But they're dead now.'

He stood for a moment and shouldered his weapon and emptied his magazine towards Wolff's Mercedes, then dropped back behind the tractor breathing hard, the muzzle of his MP-40 smoking grey cordite.

'That's Wolff's driver sorted too.'

The grenade came through the window and rolled to a stop beneath an armchair at one end of the operations room. As the window smashed, Baur had flinched and fired blindly towards the sound, peppering the wall with bullet holes. Wolff saw the grenade roll under the chair and instinctively ducked, pulling the young corporal to the ground next to him.

The grenade exploded, propelling the armchair into the air and across the room towards where they were barricaded. It knocked a picture from the wall and landed on top of the overturned coffee tables.

Baur cried out in shock as it hit them, dropping his weapon and covering his head with his hands.

Wolff knelt and cautiously peered over the smoking chair, through the dust and gun smoke. He shoved the armchair off the barricade and picked up the light machine gun, re-aiming it at the door. He looked at Baur.

'Get up you fool, stand ready.'

Baur got up unsteadily and retook his position next to the SS officer.

'It's no good,' said Wolff.

'What do you mean?' Asked Baur, straightening his helmet and fitting another magazine to his Stuhrmgewher.

'It's a stand off.' Said Wolff, firing a short burst towards the doors and out into the night beyond.

'We're running low on ammunition, and they are only three men so they can't be much better off.' He fired another short burst.

'We need to get out of here.'

'What?' Shouted Baur, above the deafening roar of the MG-42.

Wolff looked behind him, scanning the room for a back door they could use to exit the building.

'We need to get Thiel out to the car.'

'How?' Said Baur.

'There,' said Wolff pointing to a door at the back of the room.

Baur glanced over his shoulder but was too afraid to take his eyes from the door which was now receiving a hail of bullets once more. Both Germans ducked behind the tables as wood and chunks of masonry rained down on them. Thiel began shouting from beneath the radio table.

'Bring uns alle um, tötet alles! Wir sind sowieso alle tot!'

Wolff lent towards Baur.

'You stay here,' he shouted. 'Get as many rounds out of that door as you can. Try and hold them until I can get Thiel to the car.'

Baur looked blankly back at him.

'You want me to cover you?'

'Yes, here, get on the '42. When we go through that door, fire controlled bursts - no more than five rounds at a time, preserve what ammunition you have left corporal.'

As the soldier switched places and crouched behind the light machine gun, Wolff picked up Baur's assault rifle before resting his hand on the young man's shoulder.

'You'll get a medal for this Corporal, you're brave allegiance to the Reich will not be forgotten.'

Wolff turned and moved quickly to the back of the room, crouching as he went, the sound of the MG-42 vibrating the boards beneath his feet.

CHAPTER TWENTY-SEVEN
The end

'We need to find a way into that building,' said Wellum as another cluster of tracer rounds flew past them and away into the black distance.

Dalby peered over the wheel of the tractor, trying his best to assess the situation inside the building. After a moment he took cover once more.

'Can either of you see anything?' he called.

'I can see through the doorway but I can't see who's firing that MG.'

Wellum glanced around the side of the oil drums as more tracer shot from the door. He pulled his head back in.

'No, it's no better from here.'

Dalby made another quick assessment.

'I'm going to move forward.' He gestured ahead. 'That small outbuilding over there, I'm going for that. From there I can look to approach the door. If I can get some grenades in, it'll hopefully silence that fucking LMG.'

'We'll go together,' said Wellum.

'No,' said Dalby. 'You get over to that flak cannon and get it going. If you hose down that side of the building it might flush them towards me.' He turned to Stein. 'You stay here Max. If they come out through that door, it's down to you.'

He turned and sprinted back towards the runway, heading for what looked like another wooden shed. Wellum watched him go and then turned and made for the shrouded anti-aircraft gun.

Wolff managed to get Thiel moving. He dragged the scientist to the back of the operations room, and together they made their way clumsily towards a shattered and broken door that was riddled with bullet holes. Wolff twisted the handle and glanced outside.

'Come on,' he said grabbing Thiel by the shoulder and leading him quickly out into the thin, night air. Thiel gasped with cold and shock, the air a smacking juxtaposition to the gun smoke and plaster dust and the smell of the MG-42's glowing hot barrel.

Wolff dragged him in an arc, heading for the side of the building and the parked Mercedes and Thiel stumbled and gibbered incoherently, crying in pain as he tripped and fell and was dragged before falling once more to his knees.

Back inside the building they could hear Baur firing longer and longer bursts on the'42, then the sound of three muted explosions shook the building followed by the rattle of another machine gun before the night fell silent for the first time in what felt like hours.

Wolff hauled Thiel back to his feet, both of them panting and blowing clouds like steaming dragons into the night. They stumbled forward, managing to get alongside the Mercedes at last and Wolff opened the back door and threw Thiel headlong inside, slamming the door shut behind him, then he dragged open the driver's door and stopped and looked for a moment at Schubert lying dead across the steering wheel.

Suddenly the windscreen shattered as bullets hit the car, puncturing a diagonal row of holes in the window and smashing the rear view mirror to pieces. Wolff ducked behind the open drivers door as the firing continued, the front tyres bursting noisily, collapsing the car with a pneumatic wheeze onto its wheel rims and tearing holes in the seats.

He pointed the assault rifle and fired wildly. When the magazine was empty he dropped the weapon and he took his pistol and peered around the door and fired two more shots before moving backwards and opening the rear door and hoisting Thiel out and onto his feet.

'Run,' he said urgently pushing the scientist back towards the operations building as more bullets hit the vehicle sending sparks and bits of metal jumping into the darkness.

From where Dalby lay injured he could see Stein shooting at someone and he guessed it was Wolff going for the car. He tried to drag himself towards where he'd dropped his weapon but the screaming pain below his knee stopped him and he gripped his leg and shouted and cursed aloud. He lay still for a moment breathing heavily and looked at the stars, listening to the sound of the firing as sweat ran in streams from his brow.

As Wolff had taken Thiel and made his way out of the building, Dalby had moved forwards. He took cover behind a tool shed and watched the SS officer go out through the back door, dragging Thiel behind him. He ran from the shadows and bounded forward moving quickly, firing from the hip and he saw Baur duck behind tables, taking cover but still firing. He made it to the building and rested with his back to the wall, breathing hard. He took three grenades from his belt kit and pulled the pin on one, throwing it blindly through the broken doorway followed quickly by the other two before making a break back towards Stein as the first grenade went off.

It was the second explosion that had killed the German corporal, landing only feet from him it had exploded as he looked at it, blowing a hole in the side of his head and tearing off his left hand at the wrist. The curtains caught fire and then a chair spontaneously leapt into flames close by. As Baur fell sideways his foot stuck out awkwardly at an angle, kicking an oil lantern from a table. His body twisted as he fell dead and his hand grabbed at the trigger in a twitching reflexive action, firing one last bullet out through the door which hit Dalby in the calf of his right leg and sent him spinning to the ground.

Everything went quiet and the spy lay motionless, watching the palls of sweat rise towards the blackness above.

'Max,' he called. 'Max, what's happening.'

'Stay still,' hissed Stein from behind the oil barrels. 'Stay there, don't move.'

'Is it Wolff?'

'Yes.'

'Did you get him?'

'No, he went for the car, but he changed his mind and retreated with Thiel back towards the building.'

'Where's Wellum?' Dalby winced with pain.

'He's at the flak cannon. Are you badly hurt?'

'Mmm it's not great, but I'll live. It's my right leg, I've been shot below the knee.'

'Are you bleeding?'

Dalby craned his neck and managed to look down at his leg. His trousers were shredded and flapped about above his boots in pathetic, ragged strips and his sock was covered in blood. The wound in his calf looked black and angry and it throbbed at him.

'I think that last '42 round was probably a tracer; It's cauterised the hole.'

At the flak cannon Wellum slung his machine gun over his shoulder and grabbed the tarpaulin and dragged it to the ground. He hopped over the sandbags and stood behind the gun; cold and menacing in the darkness. Its angular shape made it look like the elongated bones of some prehistoric creature and as Wellum rotated two circular handles on either side of the beast the whole of it turned towards the right and the barrel, blacker than the night, dropped its muzzle below the glowing horizon and aimed itself at the buildings ahead.

He watched, focusing through the circular foresight fixed at its centre with a cross and he thought about Brielle. There were flames gathering at the broken window of the building and past the shattered door he could see several items of furniture were ablaze. He closed one eye and looked through the sight past the iron crucifix into the fire. The image of Saint Joan filled his mind as the flames caught the building and took hold and a faint roaring sound like a distant ocean began building in the quietness of the night. He imagined her pain and he looked down the barrel, through the cross at the shimmering heat reflecting off the concrete and making dancing shadows, long and black.

Brielle.

A sudden bitterness filled him and he almost fell into despair and he drew his sleeve across his eyes wiping away the tears. He took the handle of the mighty weapon and he looked again along its dark length like some whaling harpoon of years gone by, and he swallowed his grief and watched. As his focus shifted, Wellum could see Dalby lying on his back a few yards from the building, illuminated now by the growing fire. At first he feared the spy had been killed, but then he saw Dalby raise an arm and half turn towards the tractor. Wellum could see Stein gesturing from the shadows and though he couldn't hear their conversation, it became clear the two men were talking and he praised God that Dalby was alive.

Suddenly a movement in the corner of his eye made Wellum turn and look down the side of the burning building.

It was Wolff.

The SS officer was standing behind a fuel bowser with his pistol out, moving carefully and peering from the shadows towards the runway. A little further back Wellum could just make out the crouching figure of Thiel, collapsed on his haunches and hiding where the SS had left him. As he watched, Wolff stopped and raised his pistol, aiming down the barrel at Stein who was looking the other way, talking to the stricken Dalby.

Wellum felt as if his movements were slow, his limbs dragging against some unknown force as he turned the cannon a little further to the right. He saw Wolff aiming the pistol, preparing to kill his German colleague.

A moment of pause.

A moment of stillness.

Wellum stamped on the foot trigger and the flak cannon spewed flames and noise, recoiling violently backwards as it did, the fuel bowser detonating as cannon shells hit it smack in the middle and broke it in half, exploding inside it and igniting the fuel.

Wolff and Thiel were blown to mist in an instant.

A huge column of black smoke rose in a mushrooming cloud of gas and dirt and flames and the vaporised flesh and bones of the two dead men. High it rose, sucking everything up into a forty, fifty foot monument of soot and heat and flames. A fireball of amber and gold, rolled out across the airfield burning Dalby where he lay and making Stein duck for shelter behind the tractor. Wellum crouched and as the heat swept over him and the booming explosion disappeared towards the horizon like some visitation from hell, he waited.

Eventually he peered cautiously over the silent gun towards the flaming building which stood now without a roof, burning violently. The fuel bowser was a ragged, empty shell; crushed and distorted and bent beyond recognition and there were small puddles of petrol gathered here and there like satanic pools burning weakly on the grass and the concrete.

He looked towards Dalby. The spy had managed to sit up and was shaking his head as if he had a fly in his ear and smoke was rising for him and his skin was blackened and dry. Wellum climbed wearily down from the flak cannon and began making his way slowly forward. As he walked he saw Stein step out from behind the tractor and look towards his position. Wellum raised his hand in a weak gesture of recognition as both men waved toward the other and as he let his arm fall, Wellum felt all his strength leaving him now the fight was won and an age of tiredness seemed to descend upon him.

CHAPTER TWENTY-EIGHT
Epilogue

1.

Stein pulled the truck to the side of the road.

He could see Colette standing beneath a street light ahead and he cut the engine and sat there for a moment watching her. She was smoking a cigarette and she wore a long dark overcoat, its collar turned up against the night and she wore a hat, neat and small and adorned with a feather.

He jumped down from the truck and turned and reached into the cab and brought a bag down and set it on the pavement next to him. He straightened his tunic and picked up the bag and walked towards her.

Colette checked her watch; it was almost midnight. She threw the cigarette into a puddle and watched it sizzle and die. She contemplated leaving.

Towards the south, the city was still in turmoil, reeling with grief and fear from the air raid. Fire engines sounded their bells and the burning docks illuminated the sky, burnishing the clouds with bronze and copper underbellies. As stein approached her, a group of soldiers came from the station and passed by and each one looked at her as they went. They were burdened with equipment and every young conscript carried a rifle, slung over his shoulder. There were thirty of them and as they approached him, Stein was surprised that each man saluted, marching purposfully around him and stepping into the road to let him pass they crunched away towards a group of lorries waiting to collect them. Stein returned a somewhat self-conscious salute and as he turned back towards the station he saw Colette was watching him from beneath her halo of light. He hesitated for a moment and then continued towards her.

'Good evening Captain.' She smiled.

He dropped his bag beside hers and took her hand and kissed it.

'Only for another day or so.'

'What's that?'

'Captain.'

She took a step back and looked at him; a clean uniform, shiny boots and the bag.

'You made it back to the Chateau?'

He nodded and touched his breast pocket.

'I did and I took sixty-thousand Deutsche Marks and ten-thousand Francs.'

'Did anyone see you?'

He shook his head.

'No.'

'What about Wolff. Will he come after us?'

'Wolff's dead Colette.'

She made no sign of regret or rejoicing, but instead, raised her hand and held his cheek.

'I'm glad you didn't have time to shave.'

'Oh, I had the time,' he said, picking up his bag.

'I just decided, I want to grow a beard.'

She narrowed her eyes, unsure if he was serious.

'Really?'

'What do you think?'

She nodded.

'I suppose you can do whatever you want now, can't you?'

He smiled.

'We both can.'

The sound of shunting trains rumbled towards them from the station.

'When I heard the air raid I was worried they were going for the railway.'

Max looked south towards the bright horizon.

'Luckily for us, tonight it was the docks.'

'Do you think our luck can last?' She said.

He nodded thoughtfully, as if ruminating on the question. Then took her hand and together they went through the gates of the station towards a guard hut and on past more saluting soldiers and onto the platform beyond, and as their bags were put onboard the night train to Strasbourg, he turned to face her once more.

'Well, it's got us this far hasn't it?'

The Junkers weaved gently, tipping its wings, banking gracefully to the left before levelling out like an albatross gliding over rolling hills and black fields towards cliffs and crashing waves and then out to sea.

From the air there had been no real signs of the war. They crossed no burning cities, and the darkness hid the rest; The broken, bombed churches and the missing murdered families and the gibbet tendered corpses of rotting men - all now shrouded within a blanket of serene and silent black.

As the cliffs of northern France fell away and they flew out over the English Channel, the purple sea below them broke in lines of illuminated froth white waves moving slowly on the surface off the water, reflecting silver starlight and the pale yellow moon, quarter full and hanging low in the eastern sky.

Dalby stirred, still half stupefied by the morphine. He sat up in the co-pilots seat and rubbed his eyes then looked out of the starboard window, down towards the sea.

'Should we be this low?'

Wellum checked the altimeter and tapped it for reference.

'We're flying below radar intercept, heading towards RAF Manston.'

'In Kent?'

'Yes. I know the commanding officer there, so we should be well looked after.'

'Mmm,' said Dalby, unconvinced. 'If we can just get on the ground before we get a Spitfire up our arse.'

After taking off from Rouen they'd flown over Abbeville - high, above the clouds, then down, out over

When All The Birds Leap

the channel before they got in range of the guns at Otreau.

'How's your leg?' Asked Wellum, his face softly illuminated by the glow of the cockpit's instrument lights.

Dalby put both hands underneath his knee and adjusted the position of his bandaged limb with a wince.

'It's bloody painful,' complained the spy. 'But I'll be ok.'

Wellum dropped the aircraft another twenty feet, until they were almost skimming the surface of the water. He had the throttles on all three engines fully open and they were flying at tremendous speed; low and fast. Sea spray covered the windows and ran in narrow, wobbling streams across the glass.

'Have I been out of it long?' Said Dalby, looking out at the wave tops, clearly visible fifteen feet below them. 'What time is it?'

'It's a little before one. You went unconscious as we took off about an hour ago.'

'How far is it to Manston?'

Wellum checked his watch.

'Twenty minutes.'

'Have you spoken to anyone on the ground yet?'

Wellum looked at him.

'No, I didn't want to wake you.' He grinned.

'Do you think they'll let us land.'

'At the speed I'm going to come in I don't think there's a lot they'll be able to do to stop us.'

Dalby looked less than reassured.

'Get on the radio Harry, best not risk it eh.'

Wellum smiled again.

He reached forward and turned a dial on the panel.

'I just hope I can remember Manston's frequency, or that Spitfire up the rear might be on us sooner rather than later.'

Dalby took a spare set of headphones from a hook beneath the window and put them on. He sat back and winced again at the pain in his leg and he listened to the sound of static hissing in his ears as Wellum flew on and tuned the radio to what he hoped was a friendly frequency. Eventually the radio cleared its static and Wellum pressed a button on the control column and spoke.

'RAF Manston, this is an unscheduled approach, coming out of the southwest. Do you copy?'

The radio hissed again then after a moment a voice came back.

'Unscheduled approach out of the southwest. We do not have you on radar. Please confirm your current position and identify yourself. Over.

Wellum glanced sideways at Dalby

'Manston, I can confirm I am Squadron Leader Harry Wellum, based out of the PRU at Raf Benson. I am currently fifteen miles south west of you in a Luftwaffe Junkers JU-52, about to fly into Kent and requesting immediate emergency landing.'

'Roger that Squadron Leader Wellum. Can you confirm clearance code?'

'Manston. My clearance is; *Phoenix-Spectre-Omega-Tango-Redemption-seven-zero-three-Alpha.*'

'Wait out.'

Wellum began to throttle back the engines. He pulled back gently on the stick and the aircraft began to climb. Dalby saw cliffs ahead with white waves breaking against rocks at their base. The radio crackled once more and a new voice spoke to them.

'Wellum, it's Danford. Where the bloody hell have you been?'

'Good morning sir,' said Wellum with a smile. 'Good to hear you. It's a bit complicated I'm afraid.'

'No problem, I'll get the kettle on and you can tell us all about it.'

Wellum looked at Dalby. 'Commanding officer,' he explained. He pushed a button with his thumb.

'Thank you Wing Commander.'

'Vector one-twenty and maintain one-thousand-feet for approach. You have clearance for immediate landing on runway zero-three - The guns at Pegwell and Ramsgate know you are inbound and will hold their fire. See you on the ground… Over.'

2.

The waitress placed the teapot on the table and she put a cup down next to it and a small jug of milk next to that.

Wellum folded the newspaper and thanked her. As he poured the tea he looked out at the boats moving along the Thames and the barrage balloons; now so comfortingly familiar, floating like tethered clouds above the city while people walked happily along the south bank, chatting and smiling and going about their lives.

He drank his tea.

Dalby came in a minute or so later, leaning on a cane and walking with a pronounced limp. He smiled from the doorway as he spotted Wellum and he hung his hat and overcoat on a hatstand and made his way through the cafe towards the pilot.

Wellum stood up and shook the spy's hand.

'Morning Dalby. Thanks for coming.'

'Not at all old chap,' said Dalby. 'Hows life?'

It had only been a fortnight, but it seemed longer. Both men were cleanly shaved and Dalby wore a dark blue suit and tie.

'Why aren't you in uniform?' He asked.

'Ah, I'm still not officially back at work just yet,' said Wellum.

He was wearing slacks and a shirt with a thick pullover, and he had a brown trilby sat next to him on the table. A raincoat and umbrella were hung on the back of the chair.

'How about you? Are you working?'

Dalby ordered coffee from a waitress as she passed the table.

'I'm in no hurry to get redeployed I'll be honest. They've given me a desk at the Baker Street office. I'm overseeing a handful of agents in the field.'

The waitress delivered Dalby's coffee.

'So,' said the spy as he stirred in sugar. 'What's up? Why the call?'

Wellum lent forward and offered him a cigarette. He tried to sound casual.

'Dalby, have you been debriefed yet? Properly I mean.'

They'd both answered some rudimentary questions after they landed at RAF Manston. A military police detective even came by Wellum's flat in Knightsbridge, but the fact he'd not been called to an official de-brief was clearly bothering the pilot.

Dalby smiled and took a cigarette.

'Not yet, no. Have you?'

Wellum shook his head.

'No. But don't you think that's strange? I mean considering the seriousness of the mission?'

Dalby glanced around the cafe. He lit the cigarette with a lighter.

'Yes, it's certainly not what I'd expected.'

'Exactly,' said Wellum. 'I thought we'd have a ton of debriefs, at the SOE, the RAF and in Whitehall. I thought someone higher up would at least want some answers about Thiel. Have you spoken to anyone at the office?'

Dalby shook his head.

'No one's asked, and to be honest, I wouldn't expect them to. Most of them had no idea what I was doing in Rouen so...' he sipped his coffee.

'Haven't you been tempted to ask about debriefings though?'

Dalby looked at him carefully.

'I've been deliberately avoiding the subject if I'm honest.'

'Why?'

'Because I still have concerns.' He tapped his cigarette at the ashtray.

'About security?'

Dalby nodded.

'Yes.'

Wellum sat back in his chair, then he turned and began fishing in the pocket of his overcoat. He brought out a small notebook and put it on the table and slid it towards Dalby. He kept his hand flat on it, pinning it to the white tablecloth.

'What's that?'
Wellum looked at him.
'I want to help you find the mole.'
Dalby didn't reply.
Wellum looked down at his hand.
'Yvain messed up I think.'

He lifted his palm to reveal the book he'd found in Yvain's possessions back at Armada's house. He pinned the book to the table with his finger.

'I think Yvain left this behind by mistake. I picked it up from his stuff at Armada's when I went back there.'

Dalby reached forward and went to take the book, but Wellum kept it trapped beneath his finger.

'I need to be in on this Dalby, please. Rouen has left a mark on me old chap and I need to see it through. I want us to find whoever fucked us over.'

He moved his finger, allowing Dalby to slide the book towards himself. He picked it up and scanned the pages, stopping occasionally to read an entry here and there. He made no sign as to what he was thinking. Wellum crushed out his cigarette as Dalby looked over the top of the book at him.

'It won't be easy.'
'I know that,' said Wellum.
'There will probably be killing involved.'
Wellum nodded.
'I know.'
Dalby closed the book and handed it back to the pilot.
'Alright, we'll start tomorrow...say nine thirty at your flat?'
Wellum agreed.
'Yes, thanks Dalby.'

He put the notebook back in his overcoat pocket then took a napkin and reached inside his jacket for a pen.

'Let me give you my address.'

Dalby picked up the newspaper from the table and opened it and relaxed back in his seat and crossed his legs.

'Don't worry,' he said, winking at Wellum from above the horse racing fixtures.

'I've already got it old chap.'